PENGUIN BOOKS

The Fat Chance Guide to Dieting

Claudia Pattison is a former magazine journalist. Born on the North East coast, she now lives in the Kent countryside.

The Fat Chance
Guide to Dieting

CLAUDIA PATTISON

PENGUIN BOOKS

PENGUIN BOOKS

Published by the Penguin Group
Penguin Books Ltd, 80 Strand, London WC2R ORL, England
Penguin Group (USA) Inc., 375 Hudson Street, New York, New York 10014, USA
Penguin Group (Canada), 90 Eglinton Avenue East, Suite 700, Toronto, Ontario, Canada M4P 2Y3
(a division of Pearson Penguin Canada Inc.)
Penguin Ireland, 25 St Stephen's Green, Dublin 2, Ireland (a division of Penguin Books Ltd)
Penguin Group (Australia), 250 Camberwell Road,
Camberwell, Victoria 3124, Australia (a division of Pearson Australia Group Pty Ltd)
Penguin Books India Pvt Ltd, 11 Community Centre,
Panchsheel Park, New Delhi – 110 017, India
Penguin Group (NZ), 67 Apollo Drive, Rosedale, Auckland 0632, New Zealand
(a division of Pearson New Zealand Ltd)
Penguin Books (South Africa) (Pty) Ltd, 24 Sturdee Avenue,
Rosebank, Johannesburg 2196, South Africa

Penguin Books Ltd, Registered Offices: 80 Strand, London WC2R ORL, England

www.penguin.com

First published 2011
1

Typeset by Penguin Books Ltd
Printed in Great Britain by Clays Ltd, St Ives plc

A CIP catalogue record for this book is available from the British Library

ISBN: 978-0-141-03706-6

www.greenpenguin.co.uk

Penguin Books is committed to a sustainable
future for our business, our readers and our
planet. This book is made from paper certified
by the Forest Stewardship Council.

Acknowledgements

A huge thank you to all at Penguin, especially Mari Evans, Alice Shepherd, Helen Holman, Claire Purcell, Samantha Mackintosh and the fabulous sales team.

The Fat Chance Guide
to Dieting

Chapter One

Holly was out of breath by the time she reached the top of the stairs. For a few moments, she hovered outside the door, taking deep gulps of air as she tried to muster the courage to walk into a room full of strangers. She had a leaden feeling growing in her bowels that had nothing to do with the weather or the two Scotch eggs she'd wolfed before leaving the house. She wished she hadn't come; she wished she was at home, curled up on the sofa with her boyfriend, Rob, and a mug of hot chocolate with whipped cream and mini marshmallows.

When Holly had first arrived at the venue – a rustic gastropub in an unfamiliar part of town – she wasn't sure she'd got the right place. After performing three fruitless circuits of the lounge bar and inadvertently walking in on a private party in the dining room, she'd been on the verge of leaving when a barmaid collecting glasses had come to her rescue.

'The slimming club's upstairs,' she said, smiling.

Holly sighed with relief. 'How did you know I was looking for it?'

The barmaid's eyes flickered briefly over the bulging waistband of Holly's size sixteen jeans. 'Just a lucky guess.' She gestured to a blackboard above the fireplace on which an array of main courses – each one more delicious-sounding than the next – were handwritten in chalk. 'And, if you're feeling peckish afterwards, tonight's special is slow-roasted belly of pork with mustard mash.'

'Thanks,' Holly replied, patting her stomach. 'But I am supposed to be losing weight.'

The barmaid, who was no waif herself, made a sucking noise with her teeth. 'Seriously, love, life's too short.'

Tentatively Holly pushed open the door. Around a dozen people – most of them women – were sitting in the mismatched chairs that were grouped in the centre of the room. Another handful hovered around a long table where liquid refreshments were on offer. Above the table, a colourful banner was pinned to the wall with drawing pins. Emblazoned on it in a jaunty typeface were the words: *Fat Chance . . . because it's time to lighten up!*

Holly stood on the threshold, gripping the door handle and fighting the urge to flee to the safety of her car. Everyone else in the room, by contrast, seemed thrilled to be there. The air quivered with the sound of excited chatter, and wherever she looked women were standing in little clutches, laughing and gesticulating, obviously terribly familiar with each other. Suddenly she was aware of somebody behind her. She turned and saw an attractive woman of roughly her own age coming up the stairs. She had a heart-shaped face and lots of glossy dark hair that bounced as she moved.

'Hey there,' the woman said as she reached the top of the stairs. 'I haven't seen you here before.'

'It's my first time,' Holly replied. 'I'm feeling a bit nervous.'

The woman smiled. 'I remember how I felt on my first day at Fat Chance – like the new kid at school. But don't worry – we're a friendly bunch here.' She held out a hand. 'My name's Naomi.'

Holly took the hand, noting the long, tapered fingers and the immaculate French manicure. 'Nice to meet you; I'm Holly.'

Naomi jerked her head towards the table of refreshments. 'Fancy a coffee before Amanda gets here?'

Holly frowned. 'Who's Amanda?'

'Our esteemed leader,' Naomi replied with mock seriousness. 'She's probably in the toilets, touching up her make-up and rehearsing her lines.'

'What, like an actress you mean?'

Naomi smiled. 'She *wishes* . . .'

Just then, Holly heard someone crossing the room with footsteps that approximated those of a mother elephant looking for its young. Looking up, she saw a woman striding towards the flip chart that was positioned in front of the chairs. She was tall and slim with shoulder-length blonde hair and prominent front teeth that gave her an unfortunate equine look.

Naomi punched the air in irritation. 'Bugger, too late. Come on, let's grab a seat. Amanda hates to be kept waiting.'

Forgetting that just a few minutes earlier she'd been seriously considering doing a runner, Holly followed Naomi towards the chairs. As they slipped into the back row, Amanda cleared her throat ostentatiously, prompting a few stragglers to abandon their drinks and come scuttling towards her.

'Hello, ladies and gents,' Amanda said when everyone was seated. 'I'm delighted to see we have a new member here tonight.' She bared her teeth at Holly in a parody of a smile. 'I'm Amanda Evans, your Fat Chance leader. It's my job to teach you about healthy eating and help you lose weight so you can have the figure you've always dreamed of.' She placed her hands on her hips and thrust out one leg like a beauty queen. 'Believe it or not, I used to be just like you – fat, frumpy and fed-up – and now look at me. And it's all thanks to the Fat Chance healthy eating plan – plus a lot of hard work and dedication on my part, of course.'

She pressed her palms together, as if she were praying. 'Now, I want to give other people the benefit of my experience. I want to educate them, energize them, inspire them! You see, to me, Fat Chance isn't just a job, it's a *vocation*.' She heaved a contented sigh. 'And what could be more rewarding than dedicating oneself to the extraordinary task of transforming lives?'

Holly gave a nervous giggle, then froze in horror as Amanda's hard grey eyes locked on to hers.

'You may be laughing now – but be warned: losing weight is a serious business,' Amanda said, wagging a schoolmarmish finger. 'If you come on board with Fat Chance, I'm going to need your full commitment. Will you do that? Will you give me a hundred and ten per cent?'

'Absolutely,' Holly said, nodding hard.

'Excellent,' Amanda said. 'We'll get you on the scales later and then we'll know just how much work lies ahead of us.' Suddenly her head snapped to the side. Holly followed her gaze and saw that a woman was standing in the doorway. Despite being several stones overweight, she cut a chic figure in a black shift dress and large sunglasses. A well worn, but expensive-looking leather briefcase was hanging from the crook of her arm and her hair was cut in a sleek bob.

'Is this the slimming club?' the woman asked in a voice that was husky and well modulated.

Amanda gave a sharp nod. 'Yes,' she said, tapping her wristwatch. 'And you're three minutes and forty-eight seconds minutes late. I'll let you join us this time, but please don't make a habit of it.'

'My apologies,' the woman replied, her tone suggesting the thinnest veneer of regret imaginable.

Now everyone in the room was staring at the late-comer. Holly would have hated to feel so many pairs of eyes boring into her, but the woman didn't seem remotely bothered. After sinking elegantly into the empty seat beside Holly, she crossed one leg over the other and leaned forward slightly, chin resting on her fist, like a fashion editor at a catwalk show.

'I don't have time to do my introduction again,' Amanda said huffily, 'so do you mind if we crack on?'

'Be my guest,' the woman said, regarding her from behind the dark circles of her sunglasses like a glamorous fly.

Amanda snatched up a red marker pen and scrawled the words *WHY AM I FAT?* across the blank page of the flip chart in giant, angry capitals. 'Today, I want us all to take a long, hard look at ourselves,' she said. Her eyes flickered from person to person, cobra-style. 'You see most of us in this room are liars.' She added the word *LIARS!* to the page, then paused for a moment, letting the accusation sink in. 'You tell yourselves you've got a slow metabolism,' she hissed, 'or that you're simply too busy to prepare healthy, low-fat meals, or that you can't afford to join a gym. But these are just excuses. The reality is you're all suffering from the same affliction.' She jammed the lid back on the marker pen. 'You eat too much.'

The latecomer leaned towards Holly. 'Does she think we don't know that?'

'Apparently not,' Holly whispered back.

'And, unfortunately for you, the solution isn't simply to eat less,' Amanda went on.

'Isn't it?' the latecomer muttered.

Amanda fired her a sharp look. 'Was there something you wanted to say?'

'Not especially,' the woman replied. 'Just thinking out loud.'

Amanda's lips tightened. 'Then perhaps you could keep your thoughts to yourself. I find whispering very distracting; it ruins my concentration.'

'Sorry,' the woman said.

Amanda placed a hand on her throat. 'I've completely lost my train of thought now,' she said crossly.

Somebody in the front row raised their hand. 'You were telling us that the solution isn't simply to eat less.'

'Ah yes, thank you, Adele,' Amanda said, smiling gratefully. 'What I mean is calorie counting only ever works in the short-term. In order to keep the weight off for good, we need to pinpoint what it was that prompted us to overeat in the first place.' Her eyes

9

scanned the rows of seats before finally settling on the back row. 'Let's see what the new members have to say for themselves, shall we?' She pointed at the latecomer. 'Why don't you start by telling us your name and a little bit about yourself?'

The woman drew herself up in her chair. 'I'm Kate Pendleton,' she began confidently. 'And I'm a professor of psychology.'

Her revelation caused a little ripple of oohs and ahhs to break out around the room. Amanda, however, seemed unimpressed. She frowned at Kate. 'Do you mind taking off your sunglasses? Eye contact is vital if we're to develop a meaningful relationship.'

Kate flinched, as if a meaningful relationship with Amanda was the last thing on her wish list. Nevertheless, she acceded to the leader's request, pushing the glasses up into her hair.

'Thank you,' Amanda said with a small, triumphant smile. 'So, Kate, how long have you been unhappy with your size?'

Kate thought for a moment. 'About two years.'

'And can you recall what was happening in your life around that time?'

'Yes, I can, as a matter of fact,' Kate replied. 'My husband died.'

At this, several people clucked sympathetically.

'Oh dear, I *am* sorry,' Amanda said softly, her frosty veneer momentarily thawing. 'A widow at your age . . .

that must be tough. You can't be more than, what . . . forty?'

Kate frowned. 'Thirty-eight.'

'What happened?'

'Motorbike accident,' Kate replied.

Amanda sighed. 'How awful. Was he killed outright?'

Kate shook her head. 'He hung on for twenty-four hours, but he never regained consciousness.'

'I don't suppose you ever get over something like that, do you?'

'No,' Kate replied. 'Huw was my best friend . . . my soulmate . . . my right arm . . .' She lapsed into silence.

'No wonder you started comfort eating,' Amanda said. 'It's a perfectly normal reaction. When someone close to us passes away, we feel lonely and helpless. We're drawn to something that feels satisfying, that gives us instant gratification and fills the void. And once we get into the habit of overeating, it's very hard to stop.'

Kate smiled ruefully. 'Tell me about it.'

'Don't worry, we'll soon have you back on the straight and narrow.' Amanda's expression hardened as she turned to Holly. 'You're up next.'

Holly gulped hard. She hated speaking in front of strangers. 'I'm Holly Wood,' she began timidly.

Amanda let out a guffaw. 'I'm sorry, did you say *Hollywood*?'

Holly nodded.

Amanda clapped her hands together delightedly. 'Blimey, your parents had a sense of humour, didn't they?'

Holly sighed. She hated her name; it was an albatross she'd been wearing like a grisly pendant her whole life. 'I suppose they must,' she said glumly.

'What do you do for a living, Holly?'

'I'm PA to the creative director of an advertising agency.'

'Married? Single? Cohabiting?' Amanda said, her voice firing off the syllables like a gun emptying shells.

'I live with my boyfriend, Rob. He's an estate agent. We've been together nearly a year.'

'That's nice,' Amanda remarked insincerely. 'So what brings you to Fat Chance?' She looked Holly up and down. 'I mean, obviously you need to lose weight – quite a bit of it, by the look of you – but what finally prompted you to do something about it?'

Holly's jaw tightened. 'A man on the bus offered me his seat.'

'That was kind of him.'

Holly sighed. 'Then he asked me when the baby was due.'

'Ah,' Amanda said, stifling a smile. 'And how long have you been overweight, Holly?'

'Since I left home to go to university, twelve years

ago. I was a rubbish cook, so all I ate were takeaways and things out of tins.'

'And are you still a rubbish cook?'

'No, actually, I'm pretty good now. I'm always trying out new recipes.'

Amanda arched her eyebrows, which had been plucked into oblivion and redrawn in thin black lines. 'So why do you think you're still overeating?'

Holly shrugged. 'I guess I've just got into the habit. I've got a massive sweet tooth too, which doesn't help. I feel positively deprived if I don't have at least one bar of chocolate a day.'

'Just *one*?' Amanda said disbelievingly.

Holly looked at the floor. 'Okay, then, two. Sometimes three.'

'So what we need to do is replace those chocolate bars of yours with some new, healthy treats, so you don't feel as if you're missing out,' Amanda said.

'Is it really that simple?'

'Don't be silly. But it's a start.'

'Oh,' Holly said, disappointed. 'So what would be the next step?'

Amanda held up a hand. 'Sorry, but we're going to have to leave it there, Holly. Fat Chance isn't all about you, I'm afraid.'

Holly felt a blush rising to her cheeks. 'No, of course not.'

Amanda cleared her throat loudly and pointed to

Holly's chair, indicating that their exchange was now at an end. She took a few steps forward and smiled as she smoothed a hand down her body, from her ribcage to her pubic bone. 'I expect some of you have noticed that I'm looking especially trim this evening.'

'I did. I noticed as soon as you walked in the room,' a voice said.

Amanda turned to the speaker, a man in his early fifties. Grotesquely overweight, he wore a billowing candy-striped shirt, presumably selected in a doomed attempt to disguise his enormous girth. His black hair, flecked with silver, was thinning on top, but remained in a luxuriant thatch around the sides and back.

'Well, Tom, I can assure you that I haven't lost any weight,' Amanda chirruped. 'My svelte new figure is all down to a fabulous new development in support lingerie – the Miracle Slimming Panty.' She reached into a voluminous nylon bag that was lying at the foot of the flip chart and pulled out something flesh-coloured and elasticky. 'These are the only magic knickers with elastic micro-massage fibres,' she said, holding the undergarment aloft. 'Which means that as well as holding in all those wobbly bits, they stimulate blood circulation and cell metabolism, all without you having to lift a finger.'

'Sounds like a gold-edged invitation to a yeast infection, if you ask me,' Naomi whispered to Holly.

'They're ever so comfy too,' Amanda said. 'I hardly know I'm wearing them.'

'Can we see what they look like on?' Tom asked.

'No, you may not,' Amanda said, her tone implying a roll of the eyes.

Tom mugged at his nearest neighbour. 'Oh well, it was worth a try.'

'The Miracle Slimming Panty normally retails at eighteen pounds and nineteen pence but tonight, for one night only, I can let you have it for fifteen,' Amanda went on. And I think you'll agree that's quite a bargain. So if anybody would like to purchase a pair, let me know during your weigh-in. I have a variety of sizes and colours on offer.'

Her sales pitch over, she uncapped her marker pen and turned back to the flip chart. 'Okay, folks, tonight I'm going to explain the difference between good carbs and bad carbs . . .'

It came as a considerable relief to Holly when, some twenty minutes later, Amanda's lecture finally drew to a close.

'I hope you found today's session informative,' the leader said, beaming at her audience. 'Before you go, I'd like to give you a brief update on the Slimmer of the Year Awards.' She looked at Holly and Kate. 'For those of you who don't know, I, myself, am a former Fat Chance Slimmer of the Year. My trophy has pride of place on top of my mantelpiece at home. Whenever I'm tempted to overindulge, I look at that trophy and remember how good it felt to step on to the stage at the Margate Winter Gardens, in front of hundreds of Fat Chance members, and realize I'd beaten the lot of them.' Amanda's voice quivered with emotion. 'It was – and still is – the best day of my life. This year's awards ceremony is only ten weeks away, so we've really got to knuckle down. I don't think anyone here has got a realistic chance of winning the individual award this year.' She paused to glare at Adele. 'Not when our best hope decided to take herself off to the Dominican Republic for two weeks and undo all my hard work by taking up permanent residence at the hotel's twenty-four-hour buffet. However, if we all stick rigorously to our healthy eating plans and exercise regimes, we're still in with a shot in the Biggest Loser category.'

'*Biggest loser?*' Kate repeated. 'I'm not sure that's something I want to aspire to.'

'It's awarded to the group whose members have achieved the greatest combined weight loss over the course of the month directly preceding the awards,' Amanda explained. 'It's a wonderful honour for any Fat Chance leader and one which, despite *Herculean* effort on my part, has so far eluded me.' Amanda paused and stared at the members accusingly. 'It really would mean the world to me if we could bring home Biggest Loser this year – but, with more than forty Fat Chance groups around the country, the competition is going to be fierce.' She pursed her lips. 'A little bird tells me the Guildford crew have hired their own fitness trainer.'

'No!' Adele cried. 'Guildford can't win for the third year in a row; it's not fair.'

Amanda tossed back her blonde hair. 'Don't worry. I've got a secret weapon up my sleeve.'

Adele gasped. 'Ooh, what is it?'

'I'm not going to say just yet; I don't want you resting on your laurels. But I'd like you all to keep the weekend of the twenty-ninth and thirtieth free.'

'It sounds as if you take this competition very seriously,' Kate remarked.

'Of course I take it seriously,' Amanda snapped. 'It's my reputation that's at stake.'

'Is there a prize for the winners?' Holly asked.

Amanda rubbed her hands together. 'A cheque for a thousand pounds, to be split among the members, and an all-expenses paid weekend for two in Paris for the group leader.'

'That's not much of an incentive,' Holly said. She looked around the room. 'A thousand pounds split approximately twenty ways – that's, what . . . fifty quid each?'

Amanda's smile congealed on her face. 'We're not doing it for the money; we're doing it for the sense of achievement.'

17

'Yes, of course,' Holly said hastily. 'I just meant . . .' She heaved a sigh. 'I don't know what I meant.'

Amanda gave her a withering look. 'For the next seven days, I'd like everyone to cut out dairy,' she said. 'Which means no milk, no cheese, no butter and no yoghurt.'

A woman with pretty chestnut-coloured hair, tumbling pre-Raphaelite-style down her back, raised her hand in the air. 'What about half-fat crème fraiche?' she asked.

Amanda's eyes narrowed. 'What did I just say?'

The woman winced. 'No dairy?'

'So if you heard me the first time, why are you asking stupid questions?'

'I'm not sure we should be avoiding *all* dairy products,' Kate interjected. 'Everyone needs calcium in their diet.'

'Oh, for God's sake, Kate, I know you're a *professor*,' Amanda replied with a carefully calibrated injection of sarcasm, 'but it's only a week; it won't kill you.' She looked around the room. 'Are you with me, everyone?'

A few members muttered in agreement.

'I said, *are you with me*?' Amanda repeated, an air of menace creeping into her voice.

'Yes!' the members cried in unison.

'Good, in that case I'll see you all back here next week.'

Holly jumped up, intending to make a break for

freedom. The meeting hadn't been too awful, but all the same there were so many more exciting ways she could be spending the evening – like handwashing her underwired bras or descaling the kettle. She was half-way to the door when Amanda's voice rang out across the room.

'Holly, haven't you forgotten something?' Holly knew she should just keep going, but Amanda's tone was so stern she found herself turning and offering a simpering smile instead.

'I don't think so,' she replied.

'We need to weigh you,' Amanda said.

Holly hesitated. *Just tell her*, a voice inside her head urged. *Just tell her it's a complete waste of time because you've got no intention of coming back next week.*

'Come on, it won't take a minute.'

Holly sighed and began retracing her steps. A few moments later, she was climbing aboard a set of electronic scales.

'Twelve stone, four,' Amanda said briskly.

'How did that happen?' Holly said, scowling in disbelief at the numbers on the digital display. 'Are you sure these scales are accurate?'

'Quite sure.' Amanda wrote Holly's weight in a notebook. 'When did you last weigh yourself?'

Holly shrugged. 'About a month ago.'

'And how much did you weigh then?'

'Eleven stone thirteen.'

'And you're how tall?'

'Five foot five.'

Amanda looked at a chart. 'Hmmm,' she said. 'Technically speaking, you're not obese.'

'Great,' Holly said flatly.

'However, you *are* considerably overweight. You need to lose at least twenty pounds.'

Holly frowned. 'I really don't know if I can do this. I just don't have the willpower.'

'Nonsense,' Amanda said briskly. She reached into her bag and pulled out a glossy booklet. On the front cover a ridiculously athletic model was doing a star jump. 'This is the Fat Chance healthy eating plan. I want you to take it home and read it. All your meals are planned out, day by day. Everything's calorie-counted and extremely easy to make.' She thrust the booklet into Holly's hands. 'But I don't want you to lose too much too soon, or you'll put it back on just as quickly. Two pounds a week . . . that's all I'm asking of you.'

Holly took the booklet and stepped off the scales. 'I'll think about it,' she grudgingly replied.

Holly meant to head straight for the car park but, as she passed the refreshments table, she noticed a glass jug filled with orange squash. She was desperately thirsty. It was a warm evening and she could feel beads of perspiration trickling between her breasts. Hoping her presence would go unnoticed by the others, who were chatting in small groups while they waited for Amanda to summon them to the scales, Holly sidled up to the table and downed two plastic cups of squash in quick succession. As she turned to go, she noticed Naomi standing nearby, chatting to Kate. The next moment, Naomi caught her eye and beckoned her over. Not wanting to appear rude, Holly reluctantly went to join them.

'How was the weigh-in?' Kate asked.

'Humiliating,' Holly replied. 'I'm not warming to Amanda. She reminds me of my old headmistress at school.'

'She asks some very personal questions, doesn't she?' Kate said. 'I couldn't believe the way she was probing me about my husband's death.'

'That's nothing,' Naomi replied. 'She once asked Tom, in front of the whole group, if the fact he was morbidly obese meant he ever had problems getting an erection.'

Holly looked at her aghast. 'What did he say?'

'He told her to meet him round the back of the hall after the meeting and she could see for herself.'

Holly wrinkled her nose in distaste. 'Yuck.'

'Yeah, Tom likes to think of himself as a bit of a ladies' man. Don't let him corner you after the meetings or you'll never get away.' Naomi dispatched a withering look in Tom's direction. He was standing by the trestle table, deep in conversation with a middle-aged woman in ski pants whose enormous, quivering bottom resembled dumplings in a carrier bag. As they talked he reached behind her for a cup of squash, effectively pinning her to the table with his protuberant belly. Naomi shuddered. 'For some unfathomable reason, most of the women here seem to find him quite amusing.'

'How long have you been coming to Fat Chance?' Holly asked.

'Nearly two months. I've lost a stone already.'

'So Amanda's regime really works?' Kate asked. 'Only I've tried everything to lose weight – this is pretty much the last resort for me.'

Naomi nodded. 'The healthy eating plan's very easy to follow, and coming to the meetings really helps motivate me.'

'I don't know,' Holly said. 'I'm not convinced about this whole slimming-club thing. It all sounds terribly competitive. I'm not sure I'll be here next week.'

'Oh, can't you stick it out for a little while longer?' Kate said. 'I could really use the moral support.'

'I'll think about,' Holly replied grudgingly. She gave Kate a shy half-smile. 'I've never met a professor before. Do you teach at the university?'

Kate nodded. 'Although these days I do more research than teaching. I absolutely love my job, it's just . . .' She sighed. 'I wish I didn't feel so tired all the time. I'm hoping that if I lose some weight I'll have a bit more energy.'

'Oh, I'm sure you will,' Naomi said. 'I've noticed the difference already. I used to be flagging by eight o'clock. Now I can easily work through till midnight, if I have to.'

'*Midnight?*' Holly said in surprise. 'What is it you do?'

'Naomi smiled. 'I'm a wedding photographer.'

'That sounds like a great job,' Kate said.

'It is, although it's part of the reason I put on weight – all that wedding cake and eating at irregular hours. The fact I live on my own doesn't help. There's no one to look at me disapprovingly when I pile my plate high with pasta and some unbelievably calorific sauce.'

'You're not married, then?' Kate asked.

'Nope.'

'Boyfriend?'

Naomi shook her head. 'I don't do relationships – at least not the mutually exclusive kind.'

Kate frowned. 'I'm sorry?'

'I always pick men with . . .' Naomi grinned. 'How shall I put it . . . ? Limited availability.'

'What do you mean?' Holly asked.

Naomi smiled. 'I'm referring to married men.'

Kate gave a little gasp. 'Goodness.'

'I know lots of people wouldn't approve, but it works for me,' Naomi continued. 'It means I get the best things from a relationship – the romance, the sex, the meals in nice restaurants – without any of the domestic drudgery.'

'When you put it like that, I can see the advantages,' Kate said, nodding slowly. 'Are you seeing anyone at the moment?'

'Yeah, his name's Christopher and he's a dentist. We've only been dating for a couple of months.'

'How did you meet him?' Holly asked.

'At work.'

'At a wedding, you mean?'

Naomi nodded.

'He wasn't the groom, was he?' asked Kate.

Naomi laughed and shook her head. 'One of the ushers.'

'Do you ever feel guilty about the fact you're taking these men away from their families?' Holly asked.

Naomi made a face. 'The odd twinge every now and then, but if Christopher wasn't having an affair with me he'd be having one with someone else. And it's not as if I'm trying to break up his marriage; that's the last thing I want. Being a mistress isn't a way of getting my claws into someone else's husband – it's a lifestyle choice.'

She paused as Amanda's voice came booming across the hall. 'Naomi! Time for your weigh-in.'

'I'd better go,' Naomi said. 'I won't be long.'

'I think I'll make a move too,' Holly replied. 'I told my boyfriend I wouldn't be late.'

24

'So will we be seeing you next week?' Kate asked hopefully.

Holly shrugged. 'Maybe.' She raised a hand in farewell. 'Anyway, it was nice meeting you both, and good luck on the scales.'

'I hope she does come back,' Kate said as Holly walked away. 'She seems like such a nice girl.'

'Oh, she *will*,' Naomi said.

'How can you be so sure?'

Naomi smiled. 'She really wants to lose weight . . . more than anybody in this room. I can see it in her eyes.'

Chapter Two

When Kate arrived home, she went straight to the kitchen and selected a good Grenache from the row of bottles on the Welsh dresser. Having survived her first Fat Chance meeting, she reckoned she'd earned a drink. As she uncorked the wine, its heady aroma brought back an unexpected rush of memories: a cottage in Provence, the salt tang of the sea on her lips, Huw looking tanned and relaxed as he turned steaks on a barbecue. Smiling, Kate poured herself a generous glass, and took several large gulps. Then, despite the stern voice in her head telling her not to, she went to the fridge. Her eyes scanned the shelves until they settled on an unopened packet of salami. After only the briefest hesitation, she tore it open and began cramming slices of the spicy meat into her mouth, one after the other, barely taking time to chew each one properly before it disappeared down her throat. Only when the packet was three-quarters empty did she stop and shove it guiltily to the back of the fridge. The diet, she promised herself, would start tomorrow.

She carried her wine through to the living room and curled up in her favourite armchair – a chocolate leather recliner that had cost a small fortune, but was worth every penny. As she sipped her wine, Kate reflected on the evening's events. Despite the inauspicious start, she'd rather enjoyed her first Fat Chance meeting, especially meeting Naomi and Holly. Although she had a full and active social life, and some wonderful friends, she always relished the chance to mix with people outside her usual academic circles. Closing her eyes, Kate lay back in the recliner, enjoying the silence. She loved her home and whenever she'd been away she always looked forward to returning. As soon as she walked through the front door, a sense of calm and order would descend on her. Everything she needed was here; everything had its place.

In the first few months after Huw died, when she was almost deranged with grief, she had thought about selling up and moving somewhere smaller. The house seemed too full of memories; everything she saw and smelled and touched reminded her of Huw. His clothes were still occupying half the wardrobe, his razor sat next to the soap dish in the bathroom, his subscription to *Private Eye* had yet to be cancelled. On the desk in his office lay the Mont Blanc she'd bought for his birthday, which he'd barely had a chance to use and the laptop that had gone everywhere with him. Her friends urged her to hold off putting the house on the market while she was still in such a fragile state, and she was glad she'd taken their advice.

As the months passed and time smoothed the rough edges off her grief, Kate's feelings about the house changed. She realized she couldn't bear the thought of leaving it, of having someone else's noisy children desecrating the memory of her precious Huw. Far better that she stay here, decide which of her husband's things she wanted to keep and which she wanted to give away, and then get on with the difficult business of starting her life anew.

It hadn't always been easy. There were still times, even now, three years later, when she was filled with a terrible, choking sadness – usually at night when she lay alone in the vast French walnut sleigh bed that had been a wedding present from Huw's parents – but at least she no longer felt as if her heart had been torn from her body. If Huw's death had taught her one thing, it was that life was precious, and she was determined not to waste a minute of her own.

Marriage had not been part of Kate's life plan when she'd graduated from Oxford. Earnest and ambitious, she had scant time for romance. Her passions lay elsewhere: she wanted to make a name for herself as one of the country's foremost experts in the field of body language, to embark on a succession of groundbreaking research projects and lecture around the globe, engendering in her students the same passion she felt for the subject. The way she saw it, a husband and kids would only get in the way. She'd stuck to her guns as far as the kids were concerned, but her thoughts about marriage changed the moment she'd hooked up with Huw.

She met him at a party when she was twenty-five and a junior lecturer at a university in London. He was four years older and a rising star at the architecture firm where he worked. Drained after an afternoon of particularly combative tutorials, Kate hadn't wanted to go out on the night in question, but she'd been dragged along by her flatmate, whose boyfriend was throwing the party. She noticed Huw straight away. He was tall and dark and, even from a distance, deeply charismatic. Throughout the evening, she'd shot furtive glances at him across the room and when, just before midnight, he finally strolled over and introduced himself, a blush rose to her cheeks so quickly she felt almost faint.

In many ways, Huw was Kate's polar opposite. Witty and hugely extrovert, he liked to throw extravagant dinner parties, during which he entertained his guests with a string of humorous and frequently outlandish stories. She, meanwhile, would be watching quietly from the wings – happy to bathe in the reflected light of his glory. And whereas Kate was frequently insecure about her own abilities, Huw was utterly sure of his place in the world and his right to everything he'd been blessed with – but without ever being complacent about it. Unlike so many people, he never squandered a second of his life; every breath he took was full to bursting.

In those early days, Kate often wondered what on earth he saw in her, and yet he had this wonderful way of looking at her, which made her feel as if she were the most fascinating creature in the world. Within weeks of their first date she'd fallen for him with every fibre of her being. He made her feel happy, loved, secure – and yet at the same time he thrilled her to the core. He encouraged her to do things she didn't want to do – or at least she hadn't thought she did, until she'd tried and was safely through the ring of fire. Then, afterwards, she felt a foot taller, and so glad he'd given her that vital push. She loved him with a strength that was like a cataclysm and when, eighteen months later, he asked her to marry him, she felt her heart would burst with happiness.

Not long after their wedding, Kate got a job at another, more prestigious, university in the south of England. They moved out of their two-bedroom flat in London and into a smart townhouse in a leafy suburb. Huw didn't seem to mind the daily commute to work – how could he when it gave him the opportunity to ride his beloved Ducati, a powerful two-wheeled beast that enabled him to dodge the worst of the traffic?

Like Kate, Huw was fiercely ambitious and within four years he'd been made partner at the architecture firm. Another four years and he'd left to set up on his own. It meant much longer hours, but Kate didn't mind. She had her own interests and never felt resentful when Huw had to work late.

As the weeks and months rolled on, Kate's love for Huw continued to grow. The absence of children meant they could focus all their emotional energies on each other. They took lavish holidays, enjoyed leisurely lovemaking sessions, spent weeks planning each other's birthday celebrations. They were best friends and passionate lovers, soulmates in every sense of the word. And then, quite out of the blue, their perfect lives were ripped apart in the most brutal way imaginable.

The day of Huw's accident began innocuously enough. Kate had got up earlier than usual to do some work on a paper she was writing, and as a result she and Huw hadn't breakfasted together, like they usually did. She remembered feeling vaguely annoyed at the interruption when he stuck his head round the door of the spare bedroom, which she used as an office, and blew her a kiss.

'I'm heading off now,' he told her. 'I've got a late meeting and we'll probably go for dinner afterwards, so don't wait up.'

'Okay, see you,' she replied, without taking her eyes off the computer screen. She didn't return the kiss, much less tell him she loved him – decisions she now bitterly regretted. Without a second thought for her husband's welfare, she continued with her writing until midday, when she set off for work. At the university, she spent much of the afternoon in a longwinded departmental meeting. Afterwards, she took an hour or so responding to emails before her thoughts turned to what she might have for dinner. At six thirty, just as she was about to leave for the day, a flustered-looking colleague burst into her office without knocking.

'There are two policemen here to see you,' he said breathlessly. 'They said it's urgent.'

The officer who broke the news had only been in his mid-twenties. Kate could remember his face quite clearly. It was round and smooth with a childish innocence, which shone in his mild hazel eyes. When he told her that Huw had been critically injured after crashing his motorbike, Kate did what, up until that moment, she thought only happened in films. Her knees buckled under her and she slid to the floor.

Only when she arrived at the hospital did she understand that Huw's injuries were life-threatening. She wept when she saw his pale and motionless body rigged up to a disturbing array of machines, his beautiful thick hair shorn completely so that a brain monitor could be attached to the top of his skull. The doctors told her he was in a deep coma, following a serious head trauma. He also had four fractured vertebrae and a broken pelvis. Later, around midnight, the police gave her a bag containing Huw's torn and bloodied clothes and the platinum wedding band that had been cut from his swollen finger. They told her that, according to witnesses, he'd been going fast – well over the 40 mph speed limit – as he drove to his meeting. As he took a tight bend, he'd lost control on the rain-soaked tarmac, skidding across the road and headfirst into a tree. It was an image Kate knew would haunt her for the rest of her life.

From the outset, she was under no illusions about Huw's chances. Even if he were to regain consciousness, the doctors warned her, he might not be the same person she'd said goodbye to that morning. Fury and depression were apparently common in those who had suffered a head injury. Worse still, large chunks of his memory might have been permanently erased and there was a chance he might not even recognize her.

Huw's consultant, a dour man in his late fifties with a bone-crushing handshake, gave her regular updates on a condition that, despite being a so-called 'expert', he was frustratingly unable to clarify. It seemed there were simply too many variables to predict how – or if – Huw would recover.

During the next twenty-four hours, Kate never left her husband's side. She did everything she could think of to bring him out of the coma. She talked to him endlessly, stroked his head, kissed his cool cheek, promised him that, if he woke up, they would give up their jobs and travel the world together – something they'd often talked about doing. But then, the evening after the accident, with Kate and his parents at his bedside, Huw heaved a great sigh in his sleep and then slipped quietly away.

Nearly a hundred people turned up for the funeral. It took Kate every ounce of strength she possessed to deliver the eulogy on that dreadful day. As she stood there in the church, preparing to address all Huw's friends and family, she had closed her eyes for a brief moment. She could feel the dull throb of blood coursing through her head and the weight of all those eyes on her. When she looked up at the blurry sea of faces and thought about what she was about to do, everything seemed to be happening in slow motion, as if she were under water.

Afterwards, she couldn't bear to go to the wake that Huw's best friend, Alex, had kindly offered to host in his own home. Instead, she walked quickly down the church path. When she reached the street, she stood for a second on the pavement, holding her head. The buildings opposite were swaying alarmingly, so she sat down for a moment on someone's garden wall. The buildings jolted back into position and the blood surged to her head, and, with it, the rage. She began to walk. Her head was filled with a hot white noise that slowly diminished as she got further away. Almost imperceptibly, the sounds of the day, cars passing by, the occasional bird call, began to filter through and she slowed her pace. She was drenched in perspiration and her blouse was stuck to her back. She looked around and realized she had no idea where she was. That was what grief did to you, she discovered – made you confused, disorientated, irrational. Feeling suddenly exhausted, she called Alex on her mobile and asked him to come and get her. Later, at his house, she slipped away from the other guests and stood by the fire, drinking brandy. It was then that she finally understood, the knowledge blooming in her mind like a rapidly spreading ink stain: she was alone now and nothing would ever be the same again.

After just two weeks on compassionate leave, Kate returned to work, much to the surprise of her colleagues. She knew that if she sat at home she'd only dwell on the appalling situation in which she now found herself. It was far better to keep herself busy. Somehow, she managed to get through lectures, tutorials and meetings without losing her composure, but in the privacy of her office she often broke down, a wad of tissues pressed to her mouth, so her PA wouldn't hear her sobs through the thin partition wall.

When colleagues asked how she was coping, she simply shrugged. Just occasionally she had the urge to tell them the truth: *You want to know what it's like to lose a husband? I feel limp, helpless, verging on deranged. It's not that part of me has gone with him – because quite frankly that would be a comfort – but that whatever it was that gave me my life, my energy, my vitality has been sucked away into some deep, fathomless void.*

Is that, she wondered, what people wanted to hear? Or did they want platitudes? *It's tough, but I can see the light at the end of the tunnel. Thank you for asking.* Unsure of the protocol, she'd eventually decided that it was easier and more honest to simply shrug and say nothing.

Gradually, as the months passed, Kate started to adjust to life without Huw and, while she still thought of him every day and every hour, the serrated pain in her heart began to ease.

After a year or so, when her life had returned to some sort of normality and she'd stopped crying at the drop of a hat, she discovered that living on her own wasn't as bad as she'd feared. She was able to experience the deep contentment of settling down to watch her favourite period drama with no one else commandeering the remote control and channel flicking during the breaks. She could even, if the fancy took her as it quite often did, read until four in the morning, munching pistachio macaroons in bed with the World Service on the radio. That wasn't to say she wouldn't have given anything in the world to have Huw back, just that she was surprised how well she'd adapted to her new solo lifestyle.

Kate drained the rest of her wine and set the glass on the coffee table, resisting the temptation to return to the kitchen for another. She glanced at the clock on the DVD player: ten thirty . . . time for bed. She had a long day tomorrow, beginning with a lab meeting with her post-graduate students. Afterwards, she would host a two-hour seminar for an eminent organizational psychologist, visiting from overseas. Then, after taking the psychologist and a select group of students to a local brasserie for lunch, she would spend the rest of the afternoon closeted in her university office, working on her various research projects. In the evening, she would meet a couple of very old friends for tapas and sangria at their favourite Spanish restaurant.

As Kate moved around the room switching off table lamps, she found herself wondering how many calories there were in the restaurant's speciality dish – fresh dates filled with cream cheese, wrapped in Serrano ham and deep fried. Quite a few, no doubt. Still, she could hardly sit there nibbling lettuce leaves . . .

The diet, she told herself firmly, would start the day *after* tomorrow.

Chapter Three

Week 2
Holly 12st 2lb
Naomi 10st 11lb
Kate 13st 4lb

Naomi studied her reflection in the mirror. Considering she'd been working flat out for the past six hours, without so much as a sit down or a cup of tea, she'd didn't look too bad. She reached into her handbag and pulled out a tube of lipgloss, running its contents over her full lips until they shone. Her official duties were at an end, but there were still some *unofficial* ones she was hoping to perform.

She'd noticed him right away. Tall and broad-shouldered, he was accompanied, as husbands usually are at weddings, by his wife, an elegant brunette in LK Bennett and a rather outrageous fascinator. Pete, his name was – or at least Naomi *thought* that's what he was called – and he was the bride's second cousin. She'd caught him eyeing her up during the pre-dinner drinks as she moved around the room, taking photographs. A couple of times she'd met his gaze and they'd exchanged smiles.

Later, as Naomi approached his group, he'd drawn her to one side and, in a low voice – presumably so his wife wouldn't overhear – he'd complimented her on her dress and asked her what sort of lens she was using. They'd chatted briefly and she'd seen the way his eyes had roamed her body appreciatively.

'I'll see you later,' he said flirtatiously as they parted company.

I'll *have* you later, Naomi thought.

Naomi met most of her lovers through work. Weddings, she discovered, were the perfect hunting ground, for the men in attendance were usually tipsy, relaxed, congenial – in other words, ripe for the picking. Furthermore, the occasion often reminded them of their own wedding day, when they were young and in love and having sex more frequently than once a fortnight.

As the official recorder of events, Naomi naturally had carte blanche to approach whomever she liked. True, her targets usually had their wives in tow – but usually the women in question were too busy catching up with friends and relatives to pay much attention to what their husband was doing. And, if they did happen to see him deep in conversation with the attractive, voluptuous wedding photographer, why on earth would they be suspicious? Who, after all, would be brazen enough to pull a married man at a wedding? Naomi – that's who.

The nature of her work meant she only had a brief

window of opportunity to make her move, but she knew when a man was interested. The signs were easy to recognize: a lingering look, a preening hand smoothed over the hair, spurious enquiries about her camera equipment. And her latest quarry ticked all the boxes.

Now, as she emerged from the ladies' room, a camera bag in each hand, Naomi was keen to take their flirtation to the next level. It didn't take her long to spot him. He was standing by the bar with the best man and some of the ushers. Judging by the loose grin he was wearing, he was a little drunk. His wife, meanwhile, was nowhere to be seen.

Naomi skirted the edge of the dance floor, head bowed, not wanting to draw attention to herself. She'd said her goodbyes to the bride and groom; it wouldn't do for them to see her hanging round. When she reached the bar, she walked up to the best man and tapped him on the shoulder.

'I'm heading off now,' she told him. 'I just wanted to thank you for your help earlier, when you rounded up the guests for the formal portraits.'

'That's okay,' the best man replied. 'And thank *you* . . . I can't wait to see the pictures.'

Naomi flashed a smile around the group, deliberately letting her gaze linger a few seconds longer on Pete, or whatever his name was. 'Well, goodbye, everybody,' she said, smiling. 'Enjoy the rest of the evening.'

Pete responded immediately. 'Those camera bags look awfully heavy,' he said, reaching forward to pluck the larger of the two from her hand. 'I'll help you carry them to your car, shall I?' Naturally, Naomi didn't demur.

'I can't be too long,' Pete said, as soon as they were outside. 'My wife will wonder where I am.'

Naomi chuckled softly. 'You can always say you felt sick and needed a breath of air.'

When they reached her car – a bright yellow VW Beetle – she stowed her camera gear safely in the boot, then turned to him and pouted suggestively.

'Where shall we go?' he asked her.

She took his hand. 'I know a place.'

The wedding was a traditional affair in a country-house hotel. The ceremony had been conducted in a charming gazebo in the grounds, separated from the hotel by a line of tall conifers. Naomi knew that nobody would see them there, and, luckily, the evening was mild.

'You want to do it *here*?' Pete said in surprise, as she led him through the gazebo's flower-wreathed entrance. 'Isn't this a little . . . I don't know . . . sacrilegious?'

'I'm sure nobody will mind,' Naomi replied, pushing him down on to one of the gazebo's rose-petal-strewn seats and straddling him in one swift movement. 'In any case, it was a civil ceremony. Religion doesn't come into it.'

Before he could raise any further objections, she began kissing him, hungrily, urgently, her hands tugging at his belt buckle. Earlier on, in the Ladies', she'd taken the opportunity to remove her underwear. Now, as Pete's hand slipped obligingly up under her dress, it met with no barriers.

It had just gone eleven by the time Naomi arrived home. She hadn't eaten since lunchtime, so the first thing she did was make a mug of peppermint tea to assuage her hunger pangs. Afterwards, she returned to the living room, removed the memory card from her camera and slotted it into her laptop, eager to see the fruits of her labours. While she was waiting for the images to upload, she logged on to the internet and checked her email. There were twenty-two messages in her inbox, eighteen of them from strangersinthe-night.com, a dating website she'd recently joined, which specialized in people looking for extra-marital affairs. Given that the photo she'd posted was an old one, taken when she was three-quarters of a stone heavier, Naomi was surprised at the level of interest her profile seemed to be attracting.

She felt a delicious tingle of excitement as she opened one of the messages. At first glance, the man calling himself 'Lionheart' looked promising. His brief message revealed that he was a chartered surveyor. Married for eight years with two grown-up children from a previous relationship, he was looking for someone 'with brains as well as beauty'. At the end of the message was a link to his profile. Eagerly, Naomi clicked on it. As Lionheart's photo appeared on the screen, her heart sank. Balding and bespectacled, his expression was that of a forlorn man who had spent his entire life dragging himself from one tiny accident to another. *And*, Naomi couldn't help noticing, his eyes were too close together.

Grimacing in disappointment, she opened the next message, from a man whose pseudonym left little to the imagination. 'Cunninglinguist' was twenty-eight years old. He also had shocking grammar and a penis that was eight and a half inches long when fully erect – or so he claimed. His photograph showed him to be good-looking and heavily tattooed, with a stocky rugby player's physique. The only problem was that Naomi was looking for more than just sex. She wanted stimulating conversation, rapier wit, intimate dinners à deux in boutique hotels – and something told her Cunninglinguist was going to fall short on all those counts.

Message number three was from a private-school headmaster whose wife had refused to have sex with him since tests revealed her failure to conceive was a result of his low sperm count.

'Thanks for over-sharing,' Naomi murmured as she hit delete.

Twelve messages later and there still wasn't a single name on her shortlist. Feeling disheartened, she decided to run a bath.

As she soaked in the jasmine-scented water, her thoughts turned to her current lover Christopher. They'd met at a very upper-crust affair. The bride had worn Vera Wang and the groom was something big in futures. Christopher, in common with all the ushers, was wearing a navy silk frock coat, embossed with a rose motif. He was handsome and blonde, and when she'd asked for his help in rounding up the groom's side of the family, his eyes had moved from her face, to her breasts, to her legs as he mentally undressed her. Later at the reception, he'd approached her as she changed lenses and offered to fetch her a glass of champagne.

'No, I'm fine, thanks,' she'd told him. 'I like to keep a clear head when I'm working.'

'No problem,' he'd replied as he turned away, feeling rebuffed.

'Perhaps you could buy me a drink some other time,' Naomi said to his departing back.

He'd stopped then and smiled at her over his shoulder. 'Now there's a tempting offer.'

Once they'd met for that first illicit drink and the ground rules had been established (no unprotected sex, no phone calls to Christopher's home, no hook-ups on weekends or school holidays), the rest was easy. They saw each other as often as they could. At least once a week, Naomi came to Christopher's surgery, masquerading as a patient. He'd send his assistant off on some errand, lock the door and make love to her in his dentist's chair. These encounters were, by necessity, rather clinical, but their daring nature gave Naomi a certain frisson – and, if the reception staff wondered why there was never any charge for her treatment, they didn't ask. Most of the time, however, Christopher made the short journey to Naomi's home, having told his wife, Rosalind, he was working late. Keen to make the most of their limited time together, Naomi tried to make these evenings as romantic as possible, laying on wine, candles and a soothing massage, followed, inevitably, by bed. Christopher was never able to spend the night of course but, for a few short hours, he was all hers. Only occasionally did they venture out in public together – and then it was always to a low-key bar or restaurant. The flashier venues had to be avoided as these, Christopher had been at pains to point out, were the ones he frequented with his wife and golfing buddies.

In the beginning, Naomi was perfectly happy with the arrangement. When they were together, Christopher was charming, attentive, tactile. They had lively conversations about politics, current affairs and the people they met in the course of their respective professions. Even more impressively, Christopher was able to recall the details of these conversations days or sometimes whole *weeks* later. He was a gentle and considerate lover too, not like some of the other married men she'd been out with, who were so sex-starved they went at it like a bull at a gate.

Really, Naomi thought to herself, she had nothing to complain about. And yet, just two months into the affair, she'd found herself wanting more. Not more of Christopher's affection (he was, she knew, already spreading himself thin) – or even more of his time (she had her own friends and her own hectic social life, after all). No, what Naomi craved was glamour. She wanted to feel like a *proper* mistress, not just a bit on the side. She wanted to be admired, cherished, *indulged.*

And so, one night as they sat in a cheap trattoria with nasty plastic tablecloths, she suggested a weekend away together. To her dismay, Christopher almost choked on his tiramisu.

'Out of the question,' he said, his smooth pink skin flushing a hectic mauve. 'I couldn't possibly get away. What on earth would I tell Rosalind?'

Naomi leaned forward and twirled her hair round her finger in what she hoped was a seductive fashion. 'But don't you think it would be amazing . . . spending a whole night together?' she said breathily. 'Just think of all the things we could do.'

Christopher smiled nervously. 'Of course it would, darling.'

'So let's make it happen,' Naomi said. 'You can tell Rosalind you're going to a dental conference.'

'But I thought we had an agreement,' Christopher said, his features relaxing as he realized he had a get-out clause. 'No weekends – that's family time.'

A frown nicked Naomi's brow; this wasn't the response she'd been hoping for. 'It doesn't have to be a weekend,' she said crisply. 'In fact, midweek works better for me.'

'Hmmm,' Christopher said, raking his hands through his hair.

Over the course of the next half hour, he managed to come up with an increasingly implausible list of reasons why Naomi's plan would never work – he couldn't take time off from the surgery, he had to take his sons to cricket practice, his wife might spot the hotel's name on his credit-card statement.

As he ducked and dived, Naomi felt a growing itch of anger. Here she was, fitting around her lover's oh-so-busy schedule, making frequent purchases of expensive underwear, performing pelvic-floor exercises on a daily basis – and he wasn't prepared to spoil her, just this once.

'Fine,' she snapped eventually. 'Forget I mentioned it.'

You could have cut the atmosphere in Christopher's Porsche with a knife as he drove her home. Naomi barely said a word during the short journey and when he parked up outside her cosy, two-bedroom terrace, she didn't invite him in like she usually did. She didn't even give him a peck on the cheek.

'See you around,' she said as she slammed the car door shut and set off up the path without a backwards glance.

Once inside the house, she heard the distinctive throb of the Porsche's engine for a minute or two, as if Christopher was expecting her to reemerge and then, to her disappointment, he drove away.

Over the course of the next week, Naomi refused to take Christopher's calls. Or respond to his many texts and emails. His messages were plaintive in tone and slightly bemused, but she wasn't going to give in – not until she got what she wanted. And then, on the eighth day – success! A beautiful bouquet of open-throated lilies was delivered to her door, together with an invitation to spend two nights with Christopher at a boutique hotel in Bath the following week. As she went to fetch a vase, Naomi was smiling like the cat that got the cream.

Her good mood didn't last long, however. To start with, Christopher was two hours late picking her up. His elder son had been involved in a minor fracas in the expensive prep school he attended, and he'd had to go to the headmaster's office to pick up the offending offspring. When, finally, he did arrive at Naomi's home, he was tense and distracted, and when she asked him to turn down the air conditioning in the car, he'd sighed in irritation.

The hotel was a letdown too. Instead of the luxurious accommodation and five-star service Naomi had been expecting, they were greeted by a rickety four-poster and a rather sullen receptionist. Later, as they ate in the hotel's characterless restaurant, Christopher's mobile had gone off in his jacket pocket, earning him an evil look from the elderly man at the next table.

'Just ignore it, darling,' Naomi told him, grabbing his hand across the table.

But Christopher's other hand was already pulling the phone from his pocket. 'I'd better just see who it is,' he said, glancing at the caller ID. He grimaced apologetically. 'It's Rosalind. I'd better take it or she'll get suspicious.'

'Whatever,' Naomi sighed as Christopher got up and started walking towards the double doors that led to the lobby, the phone clamped to his ear.

'Hi, sweetheart, how are you? I'm missing you and the boys loads,' she heard him say, before he disappeared from view.

That wasn't the last they heard of Rosalind. Despite Naomi's pleas, Christopher refused to switch off his mobile – even temporarily – and his wife called another half dozen times during their stay. On the second night, Christopher even had the nerve to read his younger son a bedtime story over the phone, while

Naomi was waiting in bed in newly purchased Agent Provocateur. Even more depressingly, the weather was foul and as a result they were forced to spend much of the time mooching around the hotel, whose swimming pool and sauna were, as bad luck would have it, closed for refurbishment. Christopher, meanwhile, seemed unable to relax, as if part of his brain were occupied with the silent, ongoing calculus of guilt. Even when he smiled, his brow neglected to unknot itself, and when he made love to her it felt forced and mechanical.

On the day of departure, Christopher insisted on leaving straight after breakfast, claiming he had an important lunch meeting with his partners at the surgery – though Naomi suspected it was just an excuse. As they drove back home, she found herself thinking that she had never felt less cherished or indulged in her life.

That was two weeks ago and, while he didn't know it, Christopher had been living on borrowed time ever since. Soon, he would be dumped – but not until Naomi had lined up her next lover. Just as Christopher had his rules, so did she – and rule number one was: only get off the bus if there's a taxi waiting.

By the time Naomi emerged from her bath, she was feeling so hungry she thought she might pass out. She didn't want to spoil all her good work but surely, she reasoned, it wouldn't hurt to have a little snack. Wrapping herself in a towel, she went to the kitchen where there was a packet of tortilla chips, left over from a dinner party she'd hosted several weeks earlier, pushed to the back of the cupboard. It had been ages since she'd eaten anything quite so sinful and, as she tore open the bag, her mouth watered in anticipation. Ten chips, she told herself, that's all she was allowed. Then she'd throw the rest away.

As Naomi sat down at the breakfast bar and started to eat, she thought about Christopher's reaction when she told him their relationship was over. She imagined he'd be surprised, and quite upset too. He was, she thought, rather fond of her. Although he'd never actually said the L-word, she suspected it had been on the tip of his tongue at least twice – once when she'd just finished giving him oral sex in his car, and again when they'd gone up on to the Downs for a picnic. It had been a glorious late summer's afternoon. They'd eaten smoked salmon sandwiches (provided by Naomi) and drunk Prosecco (also provided by Naomi) and, as the rays of the setting sun painted the hills red and gold and orange, Christopher had laid his head on her lap.

'You're beautiful,' he said, looking up at her with an expression of wonderment, as if she were a rare butterfly he'd come across in a glasshouse.

'Thank you,' she replied, stroking his hair affectionately.

'I love being with you,' Christopher went on. 'I feel like it's the only time I can really relax. Life is so hectic at home.' He looked deeper into her eyes. 'If only we could see each other more often.'

'Mmmm,' Naomi said vaguely.

'I really care about you – you know that, don't you?' he added tenderly.

'Of course I do.' Sensing that a further, more profound, declaration was about to issue from Christopher's lips, Naomi rolled away from him and began packing up the picnic things. 'We'd better get going,' she said. 'It'll be dark soon.'

'Oh,' Christopher said, sounding crestfallen. 'Okay, then.'

Strange as it may sound, the last thing Naomi wanted to hear were the words 'I love you'. She didn't want a proper relationship; she was having far too much fun to be tied down to any one man. That wasn't to say she didn't have feelings for Christopher. They'd had some fun times together; it was just a shame he wasn't up to the task of maintaining a mistress. He was too busy, too self-absorbed, too damn guilty.

Sighing, Naomi looked down at the packet of tortilla chips in her hand and saw to her horror that it was nearly empty.

'Shit,' she said out loud. 'How did that happen?' Tutting in disgust at her lack of self-control, she went to the bin and thrust her fist through the swing lid. A moment later, she withdrew it and looked down at the packet in her hand. There were only half a dozen tortilla chips left. Now that she'd eaten so many, what difference was another handful going to make? Before she had a chance to talk herself out of it, she tipped her head back and emptied the salty snacks into her mouth, chewing in rapid movements to get rid of the offending evidence as quickly as possible.

Back in the living room, she went to check on the progress of her photos and saw that she had a new email in her inbox.

Claiming to be a 'retired entrepreneur', the man calling himself 'Maverick' listed his hobbies as waterskiing, polo and fine dining. Intrigued, Naomi continued scrolling down the page. Maverick had, he revealed, been married for twenty-two years to a high-flying lawyer who worked long hours. Since taking early retirement, he found himself with a lot of free time and no one to spend it with. His wife, he explained, was too wrapped up in her career to pay him much attention and he longed for a companion, someone 'intelligent' and 'sensual', who likes 'laughing in bed' and 'enjoys being pampered'. 'Please get in touch if you like what you see,' he urged her. 'I'd love to find out more about you.' Given that Maverick was, at fifty-three, more than two decades older than Naomi, she was bracing herself for disappointment as she clicked the link that would take her to his profile.

In the event, however, she was pleasantly surprised. Maverick had a strong, masculine jaw and piercing blue eyes and there was an expression of tenderness in his features that suggested he was kind to animals and telephoned his mother regularly. Yes, his hair was white as snow but, given the eloquence of his email, she was prepared to bend the rules. Naomi sat down at her desk and pushed her hair behind her ears. Then, in her clumsy two-fingered fashion, she began to type a reply.

Chapter Four

Holly's heart sank as she approached the modern apartment block where she lived with Rob. A familiar blue Mini was occupying one of the visitor spaces – badly parked as usual, with its rear wheels in a flowerbed. As she pulled in beside it, she felt a draining fatigue set in, like a suction pump to the brain. The Mini belonged to Rob's mother Diana, who attended a Scottish dancing class nearby and often popped in on her way home. Diana was perfectly pleasant and she and Holly had always got along. It was just that her interpretation of 'popping in' differed wildly from most other people's and usually meant they'd be stuck with her for the entire evening. It had been a long day and Holly had been looking forward to a nice quiet night in front of the TV.

When she opened the front door of her apartment, Holly was greeted by a waft of something warm and savoury. Diana must've cooked a meal. It couldn't have been Rob; he didn't even know where the oven gloves were kept. She stepped into the hall and looped her handbag over the coat stand. The apartment was so hot she could hardly breathe. Diana felt the cold more than most and whenever she visited Rob always whacked the heating on full blast, no matter what the time of year.

Mother and son were sitting at the table in the living room, which had been laid for three. Diana immediately rose to her feet when she saw Holly. She was a small, exquisite woman, with hair cut just so, so that it swung in precise, geometric movements. Her shoulders were fragile and narrow in her expensive cashmere sweater, her face a tiny, immaculately made-up heart. Next to her, Holly always felt like a great galumphing elephant.

'There you are!' Diana cried as she kissed Holly on the cheek, enveloping her in a cloud of asphyxiating perfume. 'Bobo and I were beginning to think you'd had an accident.'

Holly's buttocks clenched, the way they always did when Diana used Rob's childhood sobriquet. 'Sorry, there was a bit of a crisis at work,' she said, smiling apologetically. 'I had to stay late and help sort it out.'

'Had to or *chose* to?' Diana asked, frowning.

Holly shrugged. 'My boss told me to go home, but I didn't want to leave him in the lurch. Nick's only been with the firm a couple of months; he's still finding his feet.'

Diana wagged a finger. 'You work too hard, young lady.'

'She's right,' Rob said. 'You don't get paid enough to

graft such long hours and, at the end of the day, no one's going to thank you for it.'

'Actually, Nick was very grateful,' Holly said lightly.

Rob grimaced. 'Let's hope he shows his gratitude when it's time for your annual bonus.' He pointed to the steaming earthenware dish in the centre of the table. 'Mum's made dinner. We were just about to start without you.'

'Toad-in-the-hole,' Diana said. 'It was Bobo's favourite when he was a little boy. I used to make it for him every Friday night, after football practice.' She looked at her son coyly from under her eyelashes. 'Do you remember?'

'How could I forget?' Rob said as he picked up a knife and began cutting the toad-in-the-hole into quarters. 'It was the highlight of my week.'

Diana clasped her hands together. 'Oh, Bobo, you do say the sweetest things.'

'That's because I've got the *sweetest* mum,' Rob said, grinning soppily.

Holly shifted from foot to foot, not sure what part – if any – she was supposed to play in this touching family tableau. Rob was very close to Diana, and had been ever since his parents' rather messy divorce. Holly admired the ease with which mother and son were able to show their affection. However, their sentimental exchanges always left her feeling at best an outsider, at worst a voyeur.

'Hey, guess what,' Rob said, smiling at Holly. 'I had some good news at work today. Jason da Costa's leaving – and you know what that means, don't you?'

'Erm . . .' Holly mumbled. There seemed to be such a high turnover of staff at Rob's estate agency that she found it hard to keep track of who was who.

'You met him at the Christmas party . . . you know, the arrogant twat with the ridiculous goatee.'

'Bobo, please!' Diana cried.

'Honestly, Mum, the guy's a complete idiot,' Rob protested. 'I could be comfortably lobotomized and still do Jason da Costa's job better than he can.'

Diana pursed her lips primly. 'Even so, there's no need to use that kind of language.'

'No, of course not,' Rob said, looking down like a chastened, naughty child. 'Sorry, Mum.' He looked up at Holly. 'Anyway, unbelievably, da Costa's been head-hunted by another agency, which means, of course, there's going to be a vacancy at our place for a sales manager.'

'Do you think you might be in the running?' Holly asked.

Rob gave a small, sharp smile. 'I don't think – I *know*. I've been one of the firm's highest earning senior nego-tiators for the past three years. They'd be mad not to give me the promotion.'

'That's great news,' Holly said, going over and kissing him on the cheek. 'When will you know for sure?'

'Next week sometime, and when it's official I'll take my two favourite ladies out for a slap-up meal to celebrate.'

Holly felt a little flutter of disappointment. It would be so much nicer if she and Rob could go out on their own, just the two of them.

'I always knew Bobo would go far,' Diana said, her face glowing with pride. 'He's ever so ambitious. When he was a teenager, he used to fix his friends' computers to earn extra pocket money. He made a tidy sum, as I recall.'

'Oh?' Holly said, glancing at Rob. 'He never told me that.'

'That's because he's too modest for his own good. He used to collect golf balls at the local country club too and sell them back to the players. Some weekends, he'd be on that course from dawn till dusk. He always had so much energy – and still does; I don't know where he gets it from. I'm useless unless I've had my full eight hours, and his father certainly never had much get-up-and-go.' She sighed. 'Until he got up and went for good, of course. But Bobo's a real high-achiever. He was the youngest boy ever to get into his grammar school. I was dreadfully disappointed when he decided not to go to university. He just wanted to be out and earning money, you see.'

As Diana continued singing Rob's praises, Holly could feel her mind wandering. She tried to focus on what Diana was saying, but instead she began thinking of what she might wear for work tomorrow. She had a nice new pencil skirt that would look lovely with her cream ruffled blouse, but both would need ironing.

Suddenly, she realized Diana had lapsed into silence and was staring at her expectantly. 'I'm sorry,' she murmured. 'I didn't quite catch that.'

A frown nicked Diana's brow. 'I was saying that Bobo's got a real entrepreneurial spirit. I wouldn't be surprised if he didn't set up his own estate agency one day.'

Rob gave a dry cough of a laugh. 'You'd better believe it.' He patted the two placemats on either side of him. They were part of a set that Diana had given him as a housewarming present years ago. They were heavy, old-fashioned things, featuring species of British birds. Holly hated them, but Rob refused to let her buy replacements. 'Come on, you two, sit down . . . Let's eat this before it gets cold.'

Holly watched as Rob excavated a section of toad-in-the-hole and placed it on Diana's plate. She had to admit it looked delicious, the batter lying in soft golden folds, the sausages glistening plumply in their midst.

She bit her lip. 'I'm supposed to be on a diet, remember.'

Rob gave a disapproving grunt. 'Mum's gone to a lot of trouble to make this. Won't you at least try some?'

'It's fine, Holly,' Diana interjected. 'You don't have to eat it if you don't want to. I remember what I was like when I was your age, always trying to lose weight so I could look my best for Rob's father.'

'*Really?*' Holly said, staring at Diana's petite frame, unable to believe she'd carried an excess pound in her life.

'Not that it did me much good,' Diana added, rubbing one of her sparrow-like elbows. 'He ran off with a woman twice my size and half my age.' She gave a loud sniff and reached for the salt.

'It's okay, Mum, don't go upsetting yourself. It's all in the past now,' Rob said, reaching for Diana's hand and giving it a squeeze.

Holly released a breath through her nose. 'I think I'll go and change,' she said.

'Aren't you going to have *anything* to eat?' Rob asked.

'Maybe later. I'm not really hungry at the moment.'

He blinked at her with eyes that were the exact same shade of pale blue as his mother's. 'I hope you're not going to take this diet thing to extremes. I don't want you turning anorexic.'

Holly felt herself bristle. She appreciated Rob's concern, but sometimes she couldn't help feeling a little mollycoddled.

In the bedroom, she changed quickly out of her work things and into a black velour tracksuit. She knew she should go back out and join the others, but she couldn't bear to watch them tucking into that delicious toad-in-the-hole. She'd lied when she'd said she wasn't hungry; she was absolutely starving – which was hardly surprising, seeing as she'd only consumed around twelve hundred calories so far that day. Despite her initial misgivings, she'd decided to give the Fat Chance healthy eating plan her best shot – and so far it was going pretty well. Her eyes looked bigger in her face somehow and her jogging bottoms definitely felt looser round the stomach. Still, she mustn't get too excited; there was an awful long way to go.

She leaned towards the mirror and tried to see herself objectively – the way somebody else, somebody at work, say, might see her. Hair: not bad. Silky. Straight. Light brown in colour with blonde highlights that people always thought she'd had done at the hairdresser's, but which were actually natural. Face: average. Nose could do with being a bit smaller and eyes were a little too close together. Figure: obviously needed work, but her boobs were pretty good, large and firm. Rob was a breast man; she'd noticed him ogling her cleavage on their first date. They'd met at a local bar. She and her friends had been on a girls' night out and Rob had started chatting to her as she stood at the bar, waiting to be served. He was on his own, having stopped off for a pint on the way home after a particularly stressful day. Holly, who was slightly tipsy by that point in the evening, had felt sorry for him and asked if he'd like to come and sit with her and her friends. She hadn't expected him to accept, but he did, and at the end of the evening Holly had gone home with his phone number.

Things moved quite quickly after that, and five months later she'd moved into his flat. Generally speaking, she was quite happy with the arrangement. Rob was kind and thoughtful, even if he did sometimes get a bit loud and boorish when he was with his friends. He wasn't very good at housework either – or any other variety of domestic management.

Holly turned round and looked over her shoulder in the mirror to see if her bottom had got any smaller. She sometimes wondered what Rob saw in her. His lean, hard body was like a machine, never gaining weight without his express design. Not like her. The very whiff of a warm croissant and her thighs started to expand.

Sighing, she turned away from the mirror and began walking towards the door. Perhaps she would have some toad-in-the-hole after all. Just a small piece – half a sausage and no more – with plenty of green salad to fill her up. And absolutely, positively, no dessert. Or maybe just a low-fat yoghurt, with a handful of blueberries. Suddenly, she remembered Amanda's no-dairy directive. The yoghurt was definitely out –

and, come to think of it, wasn't there milk in toad-in-the-hole?

Holly groaned out loud in frustration. Who was she trying to kid? She'd attempted a ton of diets in the past and none of them had worked. Why did she think Fat Chance was going to be any easier? She may as well throw in the towel now; surely it was better to be fat and happy than slim and miserable.

She frowned at her reflection. 'Stop trying to talk yourself out of this,' she said out loud. 'You're going to lose some weight, if it bloody well kills you.'

Chapter Five

Amanda uncapped her marker pen and wrote a single word on the flip chart: *TEMPTATION!* After aggressively underlining it twice, she fixed her unflinching gaze on the rows of faces before her.

'This', she said, jerking her thumb towards the offending word, 'is your biggest enemy. It's that little voice in your head when you're having a meal out with friends. *Go on*, it whispers. *Have the double-chocolate brownie with hot fudge sauce and whipped cream. Everyone else is treating themselves – why shouldn't you?*' Amanda's voice grew louder and even more theatrical. 'It's the way your mouth starts watering when you spot the kids' leftovers as you're stacking the dishwasher. *I can't let good food go to waste*, you tell yourself, as you snaffle those leftover chips. *Think of all the starving children in Africa.*' At this point, Amanda paused and put her hand to her breast, her face contorted with ersatz emotion. 'It

67

makes your pulse race as you push your trolley up the bread aisle in the supermarket. *Eat me!* those crumpets are screaming. *Smother me in butter and gobble me up!*'

Amanda's eyes gleamed lasciviously as she surveyed her audience. 'You all know what I'm talking about . . . *don't you?*'

'Yes!' cried a woman with a long ponytail and too much blusher. 'Food talks to me all the time. Even when I'm asleep.'

In the back row, Holly stifled a snigger.

'I know it's hard, Stacey,' Amanda said soothingly. 'But, trust me, I'm going to help you wrestle those voices into submission. Now pay attention, folks, here comes the science bit.'

She took a few steps forward and folded her arms across her chest. 'Believe it or not, the key to overcoming temptation is simple. All you have to do is identify the specific factors that trigger your unhealthy eating patterns and then strengthen your mind, so that those triggers no longer overpower your resistance.' She blinked owlishly. 'I've used some big words there . . . are you all still with me?'

As she waited for a response, Kate turned to Naomi. 'What does she think this is – the special needs class?' she whispered.

Immediately, Amanda's face took on an irritable, toothachey look. 'I do wish people wouldn't talk among themselves,' she snapped.

'Sorry, Amanda,' Kate said. 'I was just wondering what you meant by *triggers?*'

Amanda allowed herself a small, smug smile. 'I'm glad you asked me that,' she said, returning to the flip chart. 'Could you come up here, Kate? I'd like to do a little exercise with you, and at the end of it you'll have the answer to your question.'

Kate, who was now wishing she'd never opened her mouth, stood up and made her way to the front of the room.

'I'd like you to start by telling me what your favourite food and drink indulgences are,' Amanda said, turning to a blank page on the flip chart. 'Indulgences being those little treats that—'

Kate raised a hand to stay her. 'It's okay. I know what they are.'

Amanda smiled tightly. 'Off you go, then.'

'Erm . . . chocolate,' Kate said. 'Green & Black's would be my first choice, but if I'm in the mood I'll eat practically anything. Last Christmas, I scoffed a whole bag of tree decorations in one go. My nephews were absolutely horrified.'

'I'll bet they were,' Amanda said as she wrote *chocolate* on the flip chart. 'What else?'

'Full-fat cappuccinos,' Kate went on. 'I've got this great coffee machine at home . . . Honestly, it's better than Starbucks.'

Amanda added *cappuccinos* to her list. 'One more, please.'

'Danish pastries,' Kate replied, smacking her lips together. 'Especially the custard-filled ones.'

'Super,' Amanda said, tossing back her hair. 'Now it's time to dig a little deeper.' She pointed to the first item on the list. 'How do you usually feel when you crave chocolate? What emotions are you experiencing?'

Kate chewed the inside of her cheek while she thought. 'I suppose it's when I'm bored or at a loose end. That's the reason I never eat it at work – because I'm always busy.'

'Good,' Amanda said, writing *boredom* in a new column, next to the word *chocolate*. 'Now I want you to do the same for the cappuccinos.'

'That's easy,' Kate said. 'I drink coffee when I'm tired and I need a quick energy boost.'

Amanda nodded, as she added *tiredness* to the list. 'And the Danish pastries?'

Kate frowned. 'That one's not quite so clear cut, but I'd say it's mainly when I'm feeling stressed. The other day, for example, I found out I was going to have move offices, to make way for the new Dean of Graduate Studies.'

'And that made you stressed?' Amanda asked.

Kate's nostrils flared. 'You're damn right it did. It's coming up to exams and I really could do without the upheaval. When I found out, the first thing I wanted to do was throw something at the wall.'

'And the second?'

70

'Bury my face in a great big fat sticky Danish – which is precisely what I did.'

Holly laughed. 'I know *that* feeling,' she said.

Several other people in the room murmured their agreement.

'So now you have the answer to your question, Kate,' Amanda continued. 'Your triggers – or at least some of them – are boredom, tiredness and stress.' She beamed. 'Congratulations, you've just taken the first step in winning the war against temptation.'

Kate smiled. 'So what's next?'

'You need to take each temptation and find a different way of dealing with the emotion that accompanies it. So next time you're feeling tired, don't fire up that fancy coffee machine of yours – go for a brisk, fifteen-minute walk instead. It'll really perk you up, as well as burning off lots of calories. And when you're stressed try going to a yoga class. It'll relax you far more than a Danish will.'

Kate sighed. 'It all sounds a bit too much like hard work to me.'

'I'm afraid that losing weight *is* hard work,' Amanda said. 'And, unless you're prepared to put in the effort, you're wasting your time and mine.'

'Oh no, I'm fully committed to this,' Kate said quickly. 'I'm just not very big on exercise, that's all.'

'In that case, let's try something else; it's based on creative visualization so I should think it would be right up your street.' Amanda began pacing up and down in front of the flip chart. 'What you have to remember is, when it comes to resisting temptation, your mind is having an almighty dingdong with your anticipated sense of physical pleasure.' She paused, waiting for her words to sink in.

'Go on,' Kate said, her interest piqued.

'Your challenge is to convince yourself that the brief reward you get from eating that Danish will be less pleasurable than the reward you get by *not* eating it.'

'And how am I supposed to achieve that?'

'Start by closing your eyes. Then try to clear your mind of any intrusive thoughts.'

Kate did as she was told. 'Okay.'

'Now I'd like you to visualize yourself tucking into that Danish pastry.'

Kate squeezed her eyes tighter.

'Imagine how good it tastes,' Amanda said. 'That creamy custard caressing your tongue, that soft, sweet pastry giving you wave after wave of pleasure as it slips down your throat – just like an orgasm, except that it's so much better than sex, isn't it, Kate?'

'Mmm,' Kate said, biting her lip as she tried not to laugh.

'Now let's take things a step further,' Amanda continued. 'Imagine the fat inside that freshly-baked Danish pastry, all twenty-five grams of it – that's one ounce for those of you who are still living in the Dark

Ages – oozing into your arteries. Think of it, Kate, great big lumps of lard clogging up those precious arteries, so that the blood has to fight to flow through them.'

Kate wrinkled her nose. 'What a revolting thought.'

'Exactly!' Amanda crowed. 'And you know the more of those pastries you eat, the narrower those arteries are going to become and the greater chance you have of suffering a heart attack or stroke.'

Kate sighed. 'Okay, I think get the message.'

'Oh, but we're not finished yet,' Amanda said gleefully. 'Next I want you to picture yourself in the changing room at Marks & Spencer.'

Kate opened one eye. 'Can't I be in Nicole Farhi?'

'You can be wherever you like,' Amanda replied. 'Now, please . . . just *concentrate*.'

Kate closed her eye and clasped her hands together penitently.

'Okay, so you're in the changing room because you've seen a lovely pleated skirt you've simply got to have.'

Kate's face revealed her horror at the prospect of a pleated skirt, but she sensibly chose not to vocalize it.

'So you get undressed and you pull on the skirt – only to discover you can't do up the zip because, thanks to all those Danish pastries, you've built up a great wobbly layer of fat round your midriff and you're a size eighteen instead of the twelve you used to be.'

Amanda began pacing up and down like a barrister in front of the dock. 'Please answer me this, Kate: was the temporary satisfactory you got from eating that Danish worth the consequences?'

Kate hung her head. 'No.'

Amanda exhaled – a long and measured breath. 'I rest my case.'

Kate opened her eyes. She suddenly felt drained. 'Is it all right if I go back to my seat now?' she said.

'Of course,' Amanda said. 'And thank you for being our guinea pig, Kate. I'm sure lots of us benefited from sharing that experience with you.' Her eyes flitted to the clock on the wall. 'Goodness, doesn't time fly when you're having fun? Before we wrap up, I'd like to give you a brief update on the Slimmer of the Year Awards. Her expression hardened. 'A little bird tells me the leader of the Guildford crew is trying to get her members to *think* themselves thin.'

'*What?*' Tom asked.

'It's true. She's training as a hypnotherapist, so she can take control of their subconscious mind.'

'Sounds like a brilliant idea,' Adele said. She stroked the roll of stomach fat that was resting on her upper thighs. 'It's my subconscious that's to blame for this.'

Naomi chuckled. 'Oh, come on, pull the other one.'

Adele gave her an earnest look. 'Honestly, it's true. I don't even know I'm putting food in my mouth half the time.' She pointed at Kate. 'She knows about psychology; she'll back me up.'

'I'm afraid hypnotherapy isn't really my field of expertise,' Kate replied. 'But the human subconscious is an incredibly powerful thing and there's a lot of evidence to show hypnotherapy can be useful in treating all kinds of conditions, including overeating.'

Adele clapped her hands together. 'So let's do it.'

'Do what?' Tom said.

'Hire a hypnotherapist.'

Amanda shook her head. 'Do you know how much that would cost?'

Adele frowned and shrugged.

'An arm, a leg and a bloody double chin, that's how much. I daresay *some* people could afford it . . .' Amanda looked pointedly at Kate. 'But I think it's going to be too expensive for most of us. No, we're just going to lose weight the old-fashioned way, by exercising a bit of willpower – it worked for me and it can work for all of you too.' She shook her hair back. 'Now, as you all know, it's a very important night. Waiting downstairs is an official from Fat Chance head office. I won't be doing the weigh-ins today, *he* will. The weights he records for each of you will form the starting point of our bid to be named Biggest Losers at the Slimmer of the Year awards. Anybody who is weighed tonight *must* be prepared to attend the awards ceremony next month, when you'll all be weighed again. If a single person fails to show, we'll automatically be disqualified.' She threw her head back haughtily. 'Anyone who doesn't wish to participate should raise their hand now.' When no one reacted, Amanda smiled. 'Wonderful, I'll pop downstairs and get him. We'll do this in alphabetical order, which means you're first up, Adele.'

As Adele plodded over to the scales with all the enthusiasm of a fattened calf en route to the abattoir, the other members made a beeline for the refreshments.

'It's a pity there's nothing stronger on offer,' Kate remarked as she helped herself to a cup of stewed tea from a giant urn. 'I could do with a stiff gin after that.'

'I'm glad it was you up there and not me,' Holly said. 'I wouldn't have been able to keep a straight face when Amanda started talking about orgasms.'

'Don't worry, you'll get your turn,' Naomi said wryly. 'Amanda always likes to put new members in the spotlight.'

'Oh no, really?' Holly groaned. 'I bet I make a complete fool of myself. Everybody's going to be laughing at me; I know they will.'

Naomi shook her head. 'No, they're not; we're a team at Fat Chance. We all support each other.'

'That's good to know,' Kate said. 'Because I, for one, am going to need all the support I can get. I'm afraid I've let temptation get the better of me rather a lot recently. Last night I ate half a tub of Ben & Jerry's. I felt quite disgusted with myself afterwards.'

'Don't be too downhearted,' Naomi said. 'It's always hard establishing a new routine.'

Kate gave a little grimace. 'Funnily enough, that's usually my forte: book club on Wednesday, shiatsu massage on Friday, a fortnightly trip to the dry cleaner's, cut and colour every four weeks . . . my life's full of routines, and that's the way I like it. But, for some reason, I find organizing my eating habits a real challenge. I rarely sit down and eat a proper meal; I'd much rather pick at things – a handful of cashews, a slice of cold quiche, a chunk of Roquefort with some really fresh crusty bread.' She sucked in her cheeks as her salivary glands went into overdrive. 'Anyway, let's not talk about food any more – it's making me hungry. What have you two been up to?'

'*I've* joined an internet dating site,' Naomi said excitedly.

'I thought you were seeing a married man,' Holly replied. 'You know, the dentist . . .'

'I *was*.' Naomi made a little moue of embarrassment. 'Actually, technically speaking, I still *am* – but not for much longer. It's just a case of finding the right moment to extricate myself.'

'I think you're doing the right thing,' Holly said. 'Dating a single guy is going to be a lot less complicated.'

'Who said anything about single guys?' Naomi replied airily. 'Strangersinthenight.com is for people looking for *extra*-marital relationships.'

Kate's eyebrows shot up. 'I didn't know websites like that existed.'

'Mmm,' Naomi said. 'Apparently it's one of the biggest growth areas in online dating.'

'It's strange to think there are so many people out there desperate to sleep with somebody other than the person they're married to,' Kate mused. 'I never so much as looked at another man when Huw was alive, but then again I never thought I'd end up having such a perfect marriage.' She smiled at the others. 'I know this sounds strange, but even though he's gone I still feel like the luckiest woman alive. To have been given such a love, to have had nine years of utter bliss, of waking up to someone who made my heart jump every time I looked at him . . . No wife could ask for more than that.'

'He sounds wonderful,' Naomi said.

'He was, and that's why he can never be replaced; I wouldn't even try.'

'So you don't think you'll ever get married again?' Holly asked.

'Absolutely not.'

'But you must get lonely sometimes.'

'Not really,' Kate replied. 'I love living by myself. I don't want some man messing up my bathroom with grubby towels and toothpaste smears and forgetting to put the loo seat down, thank you very much.'

Holly laughed. 'I can see where you're coming from.

Rob's unbelievably messy. He's the sort of bloke who leaves his underwear on the bedroom floor and waits for the pants fairy to pay a visit.'

Naomi frowned. 'But now you've moved in with him, can't he be retrained?'

Holly sighed. 'Believe me, I've tried. Unfortunately, Rob's lack of domesticity seems to be hardwired. The trouble is he's been used to his mother doing everything for him. He didn't move out of home until he was *twenty-seven*, would you believe? And even after he got his own place his mum was always popping round with frozen bricks of homemade soup and hand-knitted scarves.' She rolled her eyes. 'She even used to take away his dirty work shirts every week and bring them back the next day, all freshly washed and ironed. She'd still be doing it now if I hadn't pointed out to Rob that perhaps, at the grand old age of thirty-two, he really ought to be doing his own bloody laundry.'

'So *is* he?' Naomi asked.

Holly sighed. 'No, *I* am.'

'Oh, well,' Kate said, setting down her empty teacup on the nearest windowsill. 'I expect he does things for you too.'

Holly thought for a moment. 'Well, no, not really, but then he is very busy with work and everything.' She frowned. 'Although, come to think of it, so am I.'

'Are you two planning to tie the knot any time soon?'

Naomi asked. She gave a little wink. 'Because, if you are, I know a great wedding photographer.'

Holly smiled and shook her head. 'We've only known each other a year; we're just having fun at the moment.'

'Ah well, there's plenty of time for all that later,' Kate said. 'Why rush into marriage if you're happy just living together? Personally, I think Naomi's got the right idea.'

'You *do*?' Naomi said in surprise. 'Most of my friends are quite disapproving, especially the married ones.'

'Absolutely,' Kate replied. 'You're young and attractive – why shouldn't you go out and enjoy yourself? And it's not as if *you're* the one being unfaithful. So . . .' She leaned forward and gave Naomi a conspiratorial grin. 'Tell us more about this website. Have you met up with anyone yet?'

'I've got my first date on Friday night,' Naomi replied. 'I don't know an awful lot about him – just that his name's Toby and he's a retired entrepreneur, looking for a bit of fun while his wife's out of the country on business.'

'Children?' Kate asked.

'Two – a boy and a girl. Both grown up.' Naomi wrinkled her nose. 'The only downer is he's fifty-three, which does make him old enough to be my dad, but he scrubs up pretty well in his photos.'

'Where are you meeting him?' Holly asked.

'Denholm House,' Naomi said.

'Ooh, very swanky. Is this Toby a member?'

Naomi nodded. 'He's going to leave my name on the door.' She paused as Adele walked past, looking very pleased with herself.

'How'd it go?' Naomi asked her.

'Three and a half pounds!' Adele shrieked. 'My best week ever.'

Naomi smiled. 'I bet that's put Amanda in a good mood.'

'Actually, she didn't seem that impressed,' Adele replied. 'I don't think she's forgiven me for the Dominican Republic debacle.'

'Well, *I'm* very proud of you,' Naomi said. 'You may have blown your chances as Slimmer of the Year, but if we all pull together I reckon we've got a really good chance of winning Biggest Loser.'

'Let's hope so. It's probably one of the few things guaranteed to put a smile on Amanda's face.' Adele gave a little wave and headed off towards the refreshments table.

'You'd think Amanda could be a bit more positive about Adele's weight loss,' Kate said, frowning. 'If I was Adele, I think I'd be feeling rather demotivated right now.'

Naomi sighed. 'Yeah, Amanda can be very hard to please.'

'I wonder if it's the same in her private life,' Holly said. 'Does she have a husband . . . kids? She doesn't wear a wedding ring, I notice.'

Naomi shrugged. 'Your guess is as good as mine.' Just then, she caught a movement out of the corner of her eye. Turning her head, she saw Tom advancing towards her.

'Look out,' she said through gritted teeth. 'Casanova's on the prowl.'

A few moments later, Tom came sidling up to them.

'Good evening, ladies,' he said. 'And how are we tonight?'

'Fine, thanks,' Naomi replied in a tone designed to discourage further enquiries.

Tom turned to Kate. 'Did you enjoy the creative visualization?'

'I don't know if *enjoy*'s the right word,' she replied.

Tom's fleshy nostrils flared rhythmically. '*I* enjoyed watching you,' he said.

Kate took a step back. 'Really?'

'I often indulge in a little creative visualization in my spare time,' Tom went on. 'Though I'm not sure the details are repeatable in polite company.' He laughed, tilting back his head to show a pronounced epiglottis.

'Was there something else you wanted, Tom?' Naomi asked pointedly.

'No, no,' he said. He turned to go and then appeared to think better of it. Leaning in towards Naomi, he

82

said huskily: 'Did anyone ever tell you you're a very attractive woman?'

Naomi threw him a bored look. 'No one I wanted to hear it from, Tom.'

Scowling, her admirer sloped off towards the refreshments, his hands sunk in his pockets.

'Sorry about that,' Naomi said to the others. 'Tom can be a bit overbearing. You have to take a firm hand with him.'

'Poor thing,' Kate murmured. 'I expect he's just lonely.' She threw her head back and took a deep breath in through her nose. 'I know I said I didn't want to talk about food but can you two smell that?'

Holly stuck her nose in the air. 'Mmm, it smells amazing . . . roast rack of lamb with a garlic and rosemary crust, fondant potato and baby carrots.'

'That's a good guess,' Kate said.

'It's not a guess – it's today's special. I read the menu when I came in. These days, I have to get my kicks where I can.' Holly sighed reflectively. 'Restaurants make things so difficult for dieters. You've got no control over fat content or portion size. I've resigned myself to the fact I won't be able to eat out for the next six months at least.'

'Not necessarily,' Kate said. 'Have you heard about that new vegetarian restaurant that's just opened next door to the library? Veggie stuff's usually pretty healthy and their cocktails are supposed to be amazing.'

'We should try it,' Naomi said. 'It's ages since I had a girls' night out.'

'That's a great idea,' said Holly. 'How about one day next week – Monday?'

Kate smiled. 'You can count me in.' A moment later, Amanda's voice came ricocheting across the polished wooden floor like an assassin's bullet. 'Kate! Time for your weigh-in.'

'Wish me luck, ladies,' Kate said through gritted teeth. 'I have a feeling I'm going to need it.'

Chapter Six

It was eight twenty-nine when Holly walked into her office on the first floor of the converted warehouse that was home to Danson & Jolley. Officially, she didn't start work till nine, but she'd been coming in early ever since she was a junior secretary, fresh out of sixth-form college. Life at the advertising agency was so frenetic that she needed that quiet half-hour at the beginning of the day.

Through the glass dividing wall she could see her boss hunched over his computer screen. There were no client meetings today, so he was casually dressed in jeans and a pale blue V-neck with the sleeves pushed up to his elbows. Holly wondered how long he'd been there – hours probably, knowing him.

She switched on her computer and began unbuttoning her coat. Underneath it she was wearing a black pencil skirt, teamed with a cream blouse and black patent leather slingbacks. The other PAs at Danson & Jolley were super fashionable, with their figure-hugging dresses and killer heels, but Holly favoured a more classic look – given her generous proportions, she didn't have much choice in the matter. After sitting down at her desk, she removed a notepad from her top drawer. When she looked up again, she saw that an instant message had appeared on her computer screen.

I know you've only just walked through the door, but can you do me a massive favour?

Smiling, she typed out a reply: *Let me guess . . . coffee?*

You know me so well! Double espresso and an electric shock please. I've been up half the night working on this *&\$*@%*! Fascinations pitch. My eyelids are propped open with matchsticks.

Coming right up, Holly typed back.

Oh, and have one yourself. On me.

A moment later, another message popped up: *A coffee, that is, not an electric shock.*

Other PAs might have resented being asked to do something so menial as fetch coffee, but Holly didn't mind – it was all part of the job as far as she was concerned. She grabbed her coat and scooped up a handful of coins from the jar on her desk. As she walked towards the door, her boss looked up and mouthed the words *thank you* through the glass. He looked tired and there was a red imprint on his cheek where he'd been resting his face on his hand.

As she walked down the stairs, Holly found herself thinking how much easier life would be if everyone at Danson & Jolley were as nice as Nick Gayle. He'd joined the firm as creative director three months earlier after being poached from a rival agency. He was still only thirty-four, but already he'd made quite a name for himself in the industry – as evidenced by the clutch of awards that decorated the walls of his office.

Holly had previously spent two years working for Alasdair Swain, the deputy research director – a boorish, chain-smoking egotist who could be so oleaginous with clients you'd swear he'd been squeezed from a tube. When the head of personnel – or 'talent management', as it was known at Danson & Jolley – suggested Holly apply for the job as Nick's assistant, she'd jumped at the chance. Not only did it represent a promotion, it also meant she no longer had to endure Alasdair's annoying habits, which included clipping his fingernails while he was giving her dictation and singing 'Hooray for Holly-wood!' in an extremely loud voice every time he walked into her office.

Used to working for people she already knew, Holly had been quite anxious as she awaited Nick's arrival on his first day. She needn't have worried. Right from the start, he was charming and funny and down-to-earth, unlike so many of the other creatives Holly had worked for, whose heads were in imminent danger of disappearing up their own backsides. Best of all, Nick treated her as an equal, not just as some glorified typist like Alasdair had done.

When she reached the foot of the stairs, Holly

turned left into the achingly trendy reception area, past the huge onyx desk and the clocks on the wall that were labelled 'London', 'Paris', 'New York' and 'Wonderland'.

'Hi, Holly,' trilled Cara the receptionist, who as usual was dressed just the right side of prostitution in a tiny tartan skirt and a tight vest top, through which her black lacy bra was clearly visible. 'How's it going? Did you get up to anything fun last night?'

'Not really,' Holly replied. 'Rob and I just had a quiet one in. How about you?'

Cara grinned. 'I went clubbing with Stu and Laura from Viral Marketing – although I have to say I don't remember too much about it; we were all off our tits.'

'Sounds like fun,' Holly said lamely. Cara was only a few years younger than her, but somehow the receptionist always managed to make her feel ancient. She hooked her hair back behind her ears. 'I'm popping out for coffee. If anyone calls, put them through to my voicemail, will you?'

'Cool,' Cara said, taking out her chewing gum and flicking it in the wastepaper basket. 'That reminds me . . . I bumped into Nick last night.'

Holly frowned. 'At the nightclub?'

'No, we went to the pub first and Nick was in there with his girlfriend . . . She's stunning, isn't she?'

'Who – Melissa?' Holly said. 'I wouldn't know; I've never met her. Nick talks about her a lot, though.'

'Well, take it from me, she is,' Cara said. 'She's, like, supermodel thin and she's got this gorgeous auburn hair down to her elbows. It's probably extensions, but it still looks amazing. She seems really nice too.'

'You spoke to them, then?'

'Yeah, but only for a few minutes. Melissa was telling us she's just moved in with Nick.' Cara smiled. 'But I expect you already knew that.'

'Actually, no . . . I didn't.'

'Oh,' Cara said, sounding surprised.

Holly shrugged. 'It's not like Nick tells me *everything*.'

'I guess not.' Cara reached for a biro and began using the pointed end of the top to push back the cuticle on her index finger. 'Apparently he's got an amazing apartment. He had the guys from Viral round there once for a brainstorming session. It's got floor-to-ceiling windows overlooking the canal, and a huge roof garden with great views and a wicked outdoor sound system. It sounds as if Melissa's really landed on her feet there.'

Holly smiled tightly as she turned towards the revolving door. 'It does, doesn't it?'

Ten minutes later, she was walking back up the stairs, bearing two steaming paper cups in a carry tray. She went into Nick's office and deposited the smaller of the two on his desk.

'Thanks, Holly, you're a lifesaver,' he said, falling on the cup greedily. As he took a mouthful of espresso he peered at her through his heavy-framed black glasses, before remarking: 'I don't think I've seen that skirt before, have I?'

'No,' Holly said, feeling suddenly self-conscious. 'I only bought it at the weekend.'

Nick took another gulp of espresso. 'It really suits you. You should wear that style more often.'

'Thanks,' Holly said, bending down to throw the lid of her coffee cup in the bin, so Nick wouldn't see her cheeks ripening. As she straightened up, she noticed an image on his computer. It showed a couple standing on a balcony overlooking a spectacular harbour. Above them, a barrage of fireworks illuminated the night sky. 'Is that the Fascinations ad?' she asked.

'Yeah, what do you think of it?' Nick asked, clicking his mouse. A moment later, the ad filled the screen.

Holly was silent for a few moments while she studied the picture. The man in the photograph was square-jawed and handsome. He was wearing an expensive-looking suit and round his neck a bow tie lay casually unknotted. His companion was equally arresting in a long backless dress and diamond earrings. Her eyes were large and improbably blue, her skin so smooth and perfect it had clearly been Photoshopped to within an inch of its life. Her heart-shaped face was wreathed in smiles as she accepted a box of Fascinations cocoa-dusted truffles from her paramour. The caption at the bottom of the ad read simply: *Fascinations – give the gift of love.*

'It's a beautiful picture,' Holly began.

'But?' Nick said, sensing the hesitation in her voice.

'I don't believe it.'

'What do you mean?'

Holly snorted. 'Look at that girl. I bet she exists on a diet of cabbage leaves and dust. The minute that bloke's back's turned, she'd chuck those chocolates in the bin.'

Nick rubbed his chin. 'Yeah, I can see what you're saying.'

'I hate the way posh chocolate ads always use skinny model types,' Holly said, glaring at the screen. 'It's like they're saying: *If you're bigger than a size eight, forget it, love. Treat yourself to a king-size Snickers instead.*'

Nick frowned. 'So what sort of woman would you rather see?'

'A *real* woman – one with a bit of meat on her bones,' Holly replied. 'And I want to see her actually *enjoying* the chocolate.' She gave Nick a sideways look. 'Did you know that sixty-five per cent of women prefer chocolate to sex?'

Nick chuckled. 'Who told you that?'

'I read it in a magazine,' Holly replied. 'And maybe you could capitalize on that research by doing something really provocative with the Fascinations pitch.'

'Like what?'

Holly took a sip of her skinny latte. 'I don't know. Maybe the woman in the photo could be really pigging out. She could have chocolate all round her mouth and her eyes could be half-closed in ecstasy, almost like she was, you know . . .' She blushed in anticipation of what she was about to say. 'Having sex.'

Nick nodded slowly, as if he were thinking. 'What about the bloke? What would he be doing?'

'He could be standing in the background, looking pissed off because his girlfriend's more interested in the chocolate than she is in him.'

Nick drummed his fingers on the table. 'I like it.'

'It was just a suggestion,' Holly said with a mild shrug. 'You're the expert.'

Nick smiled. 'It's always good to get a fresh perspective. Thanks for your input – and thanks for the coffee too.' He drained the remainder of his espresso. 'Now, if you'll excuse me, I'd better crack on.'

'Sure thing,' Holly said, picking up the empty cardboard cup. 'If you need anything else, just shout.'

As she walked towards the door, she could see Nick's face behind her, reflected in the glass wall. He hadn't turned back to his computer screen; he was watching her. Then she saw that Cara was on the other side of the glass, bent over a photocopier. Her miniscule skirt had ridden up to reveal an expanse of firm, creamy thigh. Holly rolled her eyes. That was why Nick was staring ahead: he was checking out Cara.

Either that, she thought, *or he can't believe the size of your big fat arse.*

Holly spent the rest of the morning dealing with emails and typing up the minutes from a big meeting that Nick had chaired the day before. By lunchtime she was ravenous but, rather than heading to the deli for a slice of pepperoni pizza or a tuna melt like she usually did, she turned instead to a Tupperware box she'd brought from home. As she opened the lid, her heart sank: the chickpea and rocket salad that was part of her Fat Chance healthy eating plan now seemed even more unappetizing than it had done when she'd prepared it that morning.

As she ate her salad, which didn't taste quite as bad as it looked, Holly began flicking through a glossy magazine she'd bought on the way to work. Cara was having a twenty-fifth birthday party the following week and she'd invited the entire office. All the other girls would be dressed up to the nines and Holly wanted to look her best. She'd been hoping the magazine would provide her with some inspiration but, as she turned the pages, she found that she couldn't identify with the willowy, perfectly made-up models in the photographs. Just like the Fascinations ad, the magazine seemed to be peddling a dream. What if your hair wasn't soft and silky? she thought to herself. What if your waist-to-hip ratio wasn't a perfect nought point seven? What if your facial features weren't entirely symmetrical? Did that make you less desirable . . . less of a woman?

Holly had just turned to a double-page lingerie spread – modelled, naturally, by a series of impossibly long-limbed, pert-bottomed creatures – when her office door burst open. It was Nick, back from a meeting with the production department.

'Sorry to interrupt your lunch,' he said, walking over to her. 'I was just wondering if you'd had a chance to type up those minutes from yesterday.'

'Here you go,' Holly said, picking up a manila folder from her out-tray and handing it to him. 'If you want to give these the once-over, I'll take in any corrections and email the final draft to all the attendees this afternoon.'

'Thanks,' Nick said. 'I should've known you'd be one step ahead of me.' Frowning, he pointed to the Tupperware box. 'What's that?'

'Chickpea and rocket salad.'

'Sounds very healthy.'

'I'm on a diet,' Holly said with a grimace.

'You don't need to lose weight.'

Holly gave a wry smile. 'It's okay, you don't have to be polite.'

Nick looked mildly affronted. 'I'm not being polite. I think you've got a lovely figure.'

'Oh,' Holly said, momentarily taken aback. 'Thanks.'

Nick's gaze wandered to the magazine lying open on her desk. 'What's this?' he said, smiling as he read the headline. '*Luscious lingerie for sexy support from dawn till dusk.*' He winked at Holly. 'It looks as if somebody's boyfriend's in for a treat.'

For the third time that day, Holly felt a blush unfurling across her face. 'Yeah, in his dreams,' she muttered. 'Have you seen how much this stuff costs?'

Nick picked up the framed photo of Holly and Rob that sat on the corner of her desk. It had been taken in Morocco, on the last night of their first holiday together. They'd had a wonderful evening, and as a passing waiter took their picture Holly had drunkenly rested her head on Rob's shoulder.

'How long have you two been together?' Nick asked casually.

'Nearly a year.'

Nick put the photo down and sat on the corner of Holly's desk. She could feel the heat emanating from his thigh where it almost touched her hand. 'And was it love at first sight?'

'I wouldn't say that,' she said.

'But you think he's the one . . . You must do, otherwise you wouldn't be living together – right?'

Holly squirmed in her seat. Although she and Nick got on brilliantly, they'd never talked about intimate things, like relationships.

'I guess,' she said, not sure if she really meant it. 'What about you and Melissa? It sounds as if you two are getting pretty serious. A little bird told me you'd moved in together.'

Nick looked faintly embarrassed. 'And which little bird's that?'

'Cara. She said she bumped into you two last night.'

'Ah, yes.' He ran a hand through his thick, dark hair. 'It's only a temporary arrangement. The contract on Mel's rented house was coming up for renewal. The landlord told her she'd be able to stay on but, at the last minute, he decided to put the place up for sale instead.'

'That's annoying,' Holly said.

'Yeah, Mel was gutted because it's a lovely house. She started looking around for another place but, at such short notice, she couldn't find anything suitable in her price range.'

'So the knight in shining armour stepped in.'

'Well, yes, in a manner of speaking,' Nick said. 'I told Mel she could stay with me for a couple of months until she found somewhere.'

'So how are you finding it? Living together, I mean.'

'It's okay.'

'Just *okay*?'

Nick picked up a handful of paperclips from Holly's desk tidy and began absent-mindedly linking them together. 'Mel and I have only been seeing each other a few months. I didn't realize she was quite so fiery. She gets worked up about small things; it's almost as if she enjoys arguing. Me . . .' He lifted his eyes to Holly's. 'I'm the complete opposite. I hate confrontation. The sound of a raised voice is enough to put me on edge.'

Holly smiled. 'I'm the same. I remember one time Rob and I had this massive argument about his mother. Afterwards, I felt physically sick.'

'What's the matter? Don't you get on with her?'

'Oh no, we get on fine. In fact, Diana's been very sweet to me. I just wish she and Rob weren't so close.' Holly winced. 'I know that sounds awful, but she dotes on him as if he were a five-year-old, not a grown man. And he's just as bad, always wanting to include her in everything we do.'

'Was that what the argument was about?'

'Kind of. I knew Rob had been planning to take me away for the weekend as a birthday present. I had no idea where we were going, just that it was a spa hotel, some place in the country. Then, a couple of days before we were due to set off, Rob casually announced Diana was coming with us.'

Nick gave a bemused shake of the head. 'What sort of bloke wants to take his mother away on a romantic weekend with his girlfriend?'

'A rather insensitive one,' Holly replied. 'I don't often lose my temper, but I did on that occasion. I used every swear word I could think of, then I stormed off to our bedroom, barricaded the door with a chair and refused to come out.'

'What was Rob's response?'

'He stood on the other side of the door, apologizing over and over again. He said he'd only invited

Diana because he thought she deserved a bit of pampering and, seeing as how she and I got on so well, he didn't think I'd mind if he killed two birds with one stone.' She shook her head. 'Unbelievable.'

'So did you relent in the end?'

Holly nodded. 'I did consider telling Rob to go off and have a jolly time with his mum on his own, but I didn't want Diana to feel bad about ruining my birthday.' She sighed. 'It wasn't too awful in the end, although having Diana in an adjoining room was a bit of a passion killer.'

Nick laughed. 'I can imagine.' Just then, his mobile started ringing. He pulled it out of his pocket and squinted at the caller ID. 'It's Mel,' he said. 'I'd better take it.' He slid off the desk and began walking towards the door.

'Hi, gorgeous,' Holly heard him say into the phone as he exited her office. 'Are you having a nice day?'

She turned her head, hoping to catch more of the conversation, but the next moment she heard the door of Nick's office slamming shut. She turned back to her half-eaten salad with a sigh, but when she picked up her fork she realized she'd lost her appetite. She looked at Nick through the glass partition. He was leaning back in his chair, looking happy and relaxed as he laughed into the phone.

A moment later, Cara came bursting into her office,

carrying a plate of biscuits. 'These are left over from the production meeting,' she said, lowering the plate so it was level with Holly's nose. 'Want one?'

Holly breathed in, inhaling the rich aroma of butter and chocolate. 'I'd love to, but I can't. I've just joined a slimming club.'

'Good for you,' Cara said. 'How much are you hoping to lose?'

'A stone and a half.' Holly sighed. 'But even then I'll still be twice the size of you.'

'Oh, don't be so silly.' Cara tilted her head to one side. 'I don't know why you're always putting yourself down, Holly. There's nothing wrong with being curvy – and you're ever so pretty.'

Holly brushed some fluff from her skirt. 'Am I?'

'Yeah, you've got beautiful skin and your hair's gorgeous, especially when it catches the light and you can see all the different colours in it.'

'Thanks,' Holly said, smiling. 'It's nice of you to say so.'

Cara held out the plate of biscuits again. 'Sure I can't tempt you?'

Holly shook her head. As Cara bounced out of the room, she closed her eyes and sighed. Why did dieting have to be so revoltingly, stomach-rumblingly, mouth-wateringly hard?

Not far away, in the function suite of a three-star hotel, Naomi was also facing temptation. Sitting cross-legged on the floor opposite her was the groom's little brother. He was young, early twenties at most, with a slender body and stunning features – a perfect valentine of a mouth and mesmerizing storm-coloured eyes.

'I can't,' Naomi said, looking at the piece of sugar-rose-encrusted wedding cake he was holding in the palm of his hand.

'Why not?' he asked.

'I haven't got much of a sweet tooth,' she lied, loath to admit she was on a diet.

'Go on.' He playfully jabbed her nose with the cake.

'Why don't *you* have some?' she said, grabbing the cake and smearing it over his mouth. Laughing, he took her in a bear hug and pulled her on top of him, pressing his cake-covered lips against hers. Naomi responded enthusiastically. He wasn't her usual type, but he was funny and good-looking and, most important of all, he was up for it. She gasped as his hand slipped between her legs.

'We can't do it here,' she murmured.

'Why not?' he replied. 'No one's going to come back in here, and, even if they do, they won't see us.'

Naomi thought for a moment. She had to admit he had a point. They were sitting – or rather lying – under the top table, hidden from view by the floor-length cream linen tablecloth. Above them the half-eaten wedding cake lay abandoned. The wedding guests too were long gone, having decamped to the hotel bar following a rather unimaginative buffet lunch. She pulled away from him and reached into her camera bag, where she always kept a stash of condoms.

'What are you doing?' he asked.

'Just getting these,' she said, holding aloft a foil-wrapped packet.

Grinning, he started to unbutton his suit trousers.

Holly's earlier good mood had evaporated by the time she got home from work. She'd had to stand up for half the train journey and, when she did manage to get a seat, it was next to a haemorrhoid-faced business-man with an irritating cough and a mobile phone that wouldn't stop ringing.

When she pushed open the front door, she found the flat was empty. She glanced at her watch – six forty-five. Rob's last viewing was at six; he should be home any minute. Holly went to the bedroom and swapped her work clothes for jeans and a baggy sweatshirt. A pile of Rob's clean washing was lying in a pile on top of the wooden blanket box at the foot of the bed. She'd taken it out of the tumble dryer two days ago and asked him to put it away – an instruction that appeared to have gone in one ear and straight out the other one. Sighing, Holly bent down and began separating underwear from shirts, matching socks with their mates as she went. It was a task Diana would no doubt have relished, but not one Holly found much joy in, try as she might.

Afterwards, she hung Rob's shirts in the wardrobe and carried his underwear over to the chest of drawers, thrusting his boxer shorts into the top drawer, not bothering to stack them neatly, one on top of the other, the way she knew Diana would have done. Opening Rob's sock drawer, she found it full to overflowing. Sighing, she swiped some of the socks to the side to make room for the newcomers. As she did, her knuckles brushed against something hard. Looking down, she saw that one of the pairs of balled-up socks had a strange bulge, as if something were hidden inside. Without a second thought, Holly pulled the socks apart to reveal a small square box, covered in burgundy velvet. She realized with a tender jolt of surprise that it was a ring box. Her heart began thumping madly. It couldn't possibly be . . . *could* it? After a few seconds' hesitation, she flipped the hinged lid. What she saw made her cheeks grow hot: a large square-cut sapphire, flanked by two diamonds, set on a slim gold band. It was large and rather showy, not the sort of thing she would have chosen herself, but it looked as if it had cost a month's wages – at least. For a vertiginous moment everything seemed to hang in the air, as if she were standing over an abyss. She became aware of a peculiar ticking sound in her left ear. Its breathless knocking seemed to come from somewhere outside her, as if someone were tapping at the window. She was just wondering whether she ought to sit down when she heard the sound of a key turning in the front door. Quickly, she closed the box and returned it to its hiding place, rearranging the other socks so Rob wouldn't notice anything was amiss.

'Holly! Where are you?' Rob sounded tired and slightly tetchy.

'In the bedroom,' she called back, closing the drawer with her hip.

A second later Rob came stalking into the room with a face like thunder.

'What's up?' she asked.

'I didn't get the promotion,' he said, hurling his briefcase against the wardrobe door.

'You're kidding,' she said, going over to him.

'No one did. The bastards are going to advertise externally.'

Holly put her arms round his neck. 'I'm so sorry, darling. I know how much you wanted that job.'

'They said I wasn't ready for the responsibility.' Rob's fists clenched at his sides. 'Fucking idiots. They've just made the biggest mistake of their lives. I'm seriously thinking about handing in my resignation tomorrow.'

Holly drew away from him. 'Are you sure that's a good idea?' she said gently. 'I know you're feeling angry right now, but I don't think you should rush into anything. Why don't you look around and see what other jobs are out there before doing something you might regret?'

Rob released an exasperated breath, and for a

moment she thought he was going to fire back some angry retort but then, all at once, his anger seemed to dissipate. 'Yeah, you're probably right,' he said. He pulled her back towards him and held her tight. 'What would I do without you, eh?'

Holly thought of the ring nestling in the drawer. *And what would I do without you?* a little voice in her head asked.

Chapter Seven

Naomi couldn't help feeling nervous as she pushed open the anonymous black door. This was only the second blind date she'd ever been on. The first, when she was a student at sixth-form college, had been a mortifying experience. The evening had begun with pizza, eaten from a box in her date's purple Punto. As they tried to ignore the steamy-windowed vehicle next to them, and the other cars, circling in a predatory fashion, indicator lights flashing manically, it slowly dawned on them that they were eating stuffed crusts in a dogging car park. Worse still, they were an hour late for the film they were supposed to be seeing, as Naomi's date – who spent most of the evening talking about the ex-girlfriend he so obviously hadn't got over – had misread the cinema times.

Still, Naomi told herself as the door closed smoothly behind her, tonight's blind date represented a marked improvement – at least if his choice of venue was anything to go by.

In the course of her career, Naomi had seen some spectacular interiors, and Denholm House was up there with the best of them. Decorated in a sumptuous neoclassical style, its grand entrance hall managed to be welcoming and terrifying all at the same time. The walls were lined with saffron silk, which created a warm atmosphere and complemented the twinkling lead crystal chandeliers above, while the polished marble floor and glass display cases, filled with eighteenth-century objets d'art, put her in mind of an overpriced, look-but-don't-touch antique shop.

As she passed an ormolu wall mirror, Naomi paused to check her appearance. Normally, she would've dressed more casually for a first date, but Denholm House demanded more of an effort. At the same time, she didn't want to look as if she'd tried *too* hard; that way, she might come across as desperate. After trying on – and rejecting – half a dozen outfits, she finally settled on a silk jersey wrap dress, teamed with knee-high boots. But now, as she studied her reflection, she found herself wishing she'd worn something a little less clingy.

She heard a discreet cough and when she looked over her shoulder, she saw a uniformed concierge hovering behind a small reception desk. 'Can I help you, madam?' he asked, his hooded eyes looking her over, as if he were assessing her suitability for admittance to such an exclusive establishment.

'Yes,' she said, walking towards him. 'I'm meeting a friend in the bar. My name should be on the guest list – Naomi Corrigan.'

The concierge glanced at a ledger on his desk. When he looked up again, his snooty expression had been replaced by a Cheshire-cat grin. 'Welcome to Denholm House, Ms Corrigan!' he exclaimed, as if he were greeting a long-lost friend. 'May I take your coat?'

Bemused by the concierge's sudden change in demeanour, Naomi handed over the fur-trimmed gilet she was carrying on her arm.

'Mr Pennington-Smith is waiting for you in the bar,' the concierge told her as he reached for a coat hanger.

'He is?' Naomi said, frowning. She had deliberately arrived fifteen minutes earlier than the agreed time. That way, she reasoned, when her date arrived he would find her looking utterly at home in her surroundings, legs elegantly crossed as she sipped what would doubtless be an outrageously expensive cocktail.

'Yes, he arrived some time ago. The bar's just down the corridor, first door on the right.' The concierge offered a glutinous smile. 'I do hope you enjoy your evening with us.'

'So do I,' Naomi murmured as she set off down the corridor.

The atmosphere in the bar was quite different to that in the imposing entrance hall. Low ceilinged and cosy, the room had a faintly spiced odour of cloves and nutmeg mixed with the heavy scent of roses. There were no ceiling lights; instead oversized table lamps cast rhomboids of soft light across the walls, which were lined with ink-and-wash architectural drawings. Naomi paused on the threshold and looked around. The place was only half full – the men in brogues and blazers, the women in heels and flirty dresses. Most people were in groups of twos and threes; she could only see one single man and he was a well-fed thirty-something, drinking whisky at the bar. As she made her way towards a vacant table, she noticed a man sitting alone in a shadowy corner. She couldn't make out his features but, as she took a seat on a low leather sofa, he stood up and walked over to her.

'Good evening,' he said, in a voice that was rich and deep like burnished mahogany. 'Would you happen to be Naomi by any chance?'

She smiled, recognizing the high forehead and piercing blue eyes from his photographs. 'Yes,' she said. 'Which means you must be Toby.'

'I am indeed.' He bent down to kiss her on the cheek and she caught the scent of a powerful, but not unpleasant, aftershave.

'I'm sorry I didn't come over straight away,' he said. 'Only I wasn't sure it was you. You look much slimmer than your photo.'

Naomi smiled. 'Yes, I have lost a bit of weight.'

'Pity,' he murmured.

Before Naomi could work out what he meant, he was gesturing to the leather-bound menu on the table. 'What would you like to drink? The cocktails here are fantastic. I can recommend the watermelon martini.'

'Sounds lovely.'

Toby looked over his shoulder. A moment later, a waiter came hurrying towards him. 'Good evening, Mr Pennington-Smith,' he said as he drew level. 'What can I get you?'

'Two watermelon martinis, thanks, Rick,' Toby replied. 'And have you got any of those nice olives . . . the ones stuffed with pimento? I couldn't see them on the menu.'

'I'll find some for you, Mr Pennington-Smith,' the waiter said, backing away as if he were talking to royalty.

Toby turned back to Naomi. 'May I?' he said, gesturing to the sofa.

Wonderful: old-school manners too, Naomi thought to herself. 'Of course,' she said, moving her handbag to make room for him.

As he made himself comfortable, she took the opportunity to check him out. While he wasn't classically handsome, she found herself admiring his broad shoulders and the unobtrusive strength of his chin. He was very well groomed too: his skin was smooth and tanned, and his dark suit, worn with a crisp white shirt, open at the neck, was clearly designer.

'Did you find your way here okay?' he asked her.

'Yes, thanks. I've walked past this place loads of

times, but never actually been inside.' She stroked her collarbone languidly. 'It's a beautiful building. Have you been a member long?'

'Actually, I'm one of the co-founders,' he said casually.

Naomi's mouth dropped open. No wonder the concierge had been falling over himself as soon as he realized whose guest she was. 'Wow,' she said. 'I'm impressed.'

Toby swiped a hand in front of his face, as if to play down the achievement. 'I take a back seat these days, so I don't have much to do with the day-to-day running of the club.'

'Was that your full-time job, then – before you retired?'

Toby shook his head. 'Denholm House is just a little hobby of mine. My main business was property developing. I got in early – before every Tom, Dick and Harry jumped on the bandwagon – made a killing, then got out while the going was still good. I've been retired for five years now.'

'Even more impressive.'

Toby smiled. 'You sound like a pretty shrewd businesswoman yourself. The wedding-photography business must be very competitive. I imagine you'd have to be good to make a decent living.'

'You do,' Naomi said. 'People often think any idiot with a digital camera and the vaguest idea about aperture settings can take wedding photos, but there are so many skills you need to do the job well – and I'm not just talking about the technical stuff either.'

'I guess you have to be fairly sociable.'

Naomi nodded. 'Having a sense of humour helps too – as does shedloads of patience. But the biggest trick of all is knowing when to give direction and when to fall back and let events unfold naturally – and that's something nobody can teach you. It only comes through experience.'

'How long have you been doing it?'

'Nearly ten years. I studied photography at art school, then I worked as an assistant to a fashion photographer for a while.'

'That sounds very glamorous. What made you change direction?'

'I decided that I wanted to work with people.' Seeing his confused look, she grinned. 'I mean *real* people, as opposed to mannequins.'

'And is there much opportunity to be creative?'

'Yes, I wouldn't do it otherwise,' Naomi replied. 'It's true that wedding photography is full of clichés. I'm sure you know the sort of thing – brideless wedding gowns hanging in doorways; lines of ushers walking towards the camera; *Reservoir Dogs*-style, close-ups of gap-toothed bridesmaids – but most of my stuff is reportage, which means I can be as creative as I like.'

'So you're more of a photojournalist, then?'

'I wouldn't go that far.'

Toby smoothed a hand over his closely cropped hair. 'I think you're being too modest. I'd certainly be interested to see some of your work.'

'Would you?'

'Of course,' he said, looking at her intently. 'Because by studying your pictures, I'd get to find out more about *you*.'

'That's an interesting hypothesis,' she replied, meeting his gaze head on. 'What do you want to know?'

His eyes grew larger. 'Everything.'

There was a break in the conversation as the waiter arrived with their drinks and a selection of exotic-looking nibbles, including the requested olives.

'Mmm, that's good,' Naomi said, taking a sip of ice-cold martini.

'It is, isn't it? Our head bartender's a genius. We poached him from one of the top clubs in Manhattan.'

Naomi took another sip, sighing in pleasure as the vodka announced its presence in her brain. 'So what do you do with all your free time?' she asked him.

'I like to keep fit.'

Naomi's eyes flitted over his body. 'I can see that.'

'I'm learning to fly too.'

'You're quite the action man, aren't you?'

Toby smiled. 'I like gentler pursuits too . . . reading, walking, playing chess.'

'Well, it certainly sounds as if you're making the most of your retirement.'

'Yes, but there's still something missing. I have a very low boredom threshold, you see; I need constant stimulation – and with my wife away on business so much . . .' He let the sentence trail.

'You're looking for a playmate.'

'In a manner of speaking – yes.'

'Have you had affairs before?'

'Yes.'

'How many?'

He shrugged. 'Ten. Maybe fifteen. I don't know exactly.'

Naomi coughed into her martini. 'That's a lot of affairs.'

'Are you shocked?'

'A little. Does your wife know?'

'We haven't discussed it directly, but Felicity's no fool. She's aware of my dalliances, I'm sure of it.'

'Doesn't she mind?'

'Put it this way: she has her fair share of adventures when she's abroad.'

'I see,' Naomi said. 'It sounds like the perfect arrangement.'

'It works for us.' He leaned towards her, propped his chin on his palm and gazed directly into her face. 'I like the fact you're not afraid to ask questions,' he said. 'I don't care for women who pussyfoot around.'

'I need to know what I'm getting into, that's all.'

'Very sensible,' he replied. 'I'll tell you something else too, just so you have all the information you need before you decide whether or not you'd like to meet up again.'

'I'm listening.'

'I love my wife and I have no intention of leaving her. It's just that I have needs she's unable to fulfil.' He gave a slow, lizard-like blink. 'Does that make me sound terribly hard and unfeeling?'

'A bit,' Naomi replied. 'But it's not a deal-breaker.'

Toby's mouth twitched at the corners. 'I'm very pleased to hear it.' He selected an olive and dropped it into his mouth. 'Have you met up with many people from the website?'

'Actually, you're the first.'

He broke into a full-on smile, showing teeth that were as white and symmetrical as bathroom tiles. 'I'm honoured.'

For the next hour and a half, conversation flowed easily and, as the evening wore on, Naomi began to find Toby more and more attractive. He was everything she looked for in a potential lover: intelligent, well presented, interesting and *interested*. So when she saw him glance at his watch she felt a prick of disappointment.

'What is it?' she asked. 'Is your wife expecting you home?'

'Not at all, she's in Brussels, on business.' Toby leaned closer. 'Actually, I was wondering if you'd let me buy you dinner. There's a wonderful restaurant upstairs. I don't have a reservation, but I'm sure they'll be able to accommodate us.'

Naomi smiled. 'I'd love to.'

Upstairs, the restaurant was heaving but, after a few quiet words with the maître d', they were ushered to a table for two beside the stunning Palladian-style fireplace.

'What's it like to be so powerful?' Naomi asked playfully, as the maître d' went to fetch the wine list.

Toby chuckled. 'It's only at the club I get special treatment. Outside of this place I'm just Joe Average.'

'Aren't you worried that someone you know might see us together?' Naomi asked, looking around the packed dining room.

'Not really. In any case, this is a very discreet establishment. I doubt anyone's going to go telling tales.' He reached across the table and casually placed his hand on top of hers. 'You know, I really enjoyed reading your emails, Naomi. They were so lively and funny. I could see right away you had such a zest for life.'

'And now that you've met me?'

'You've exceeded my expectations. Ten-fold.'

'Wonderful,' Naomi purred, thrilled that she'd made such a good impression.

A waiter arrived with the wine list. Toby's hand

remained on Naomi's. 'We'll have a bottle of Krug,' he said. 'We're celebrating.'

'Are we?' Naomi said, as the waiter slid smoothly away.

'Yes, we're celebrating my good fortune in meeting you,' Toby said, giving her hand a little squeeze as he withdrew his.

'But you've only known me for two hours. How do you know tonight isn't going to turn into a complete disaster?'

'I don't, but I have a good feeling. I'm a very instinctual person; I know when something is meant to be.' His face grew suddenly earnest. 'I want you to know that I'm not just looking for a roll in the hay. If I start seeing someone, I need to feel that special connection . . . that meeting of minds, as well as bodies.' He gave a rueful smile. 'It's proved rather elusive so far.'

Another waiter came to take their food order, and then the first waiter returned with champagne.

'Let's make a toast,' Toby said when both their glasses were full.

'To what?'

'To getting to know each other better.'

Naomi chinked her glass against his. 'I'll drink to that.'

'And my first question is,' Toby took a sip of champagne and set his glass down on the table, 'what on earth is a gorgeous, intelligent woman like you doing on a site like strangersinthenight? Surely you'd rather have a proper relationship rather than a part-time affair with a married man?'

'It's simple really: I want intimacy, but not commitment,' Naomi replied. 'When I'm with a man, I want to be the one and only focus of his attention. When I'm not with him, I want to be free to live my own life without someone looking over my shoulder telling me what I should and shouldn't be doing.'

He looked at her curiously. 'Do you really mean that?'

'Yes. Why wouldn't I?'

'It's just that, in my experience, most women who start off by saying they don't want commitment soon change their tune. As soon as they get comfortable in a relationship, they start to make all sorts of demands.' He shook his head. 'The fallout can be very messy.'

Naomi's eyes locked on his. 'I'm sorry you've had bad experiences with mistresses in the past, but I can tell you categorically that I'm not that sort of woman.'

'Mmm,' Toby said thoughtfully. 'So, what would you say are the three most vital components of a successful affair?'

'What is this – a job interview?' Naomi said wryly.

'Yes, in a manner of speaking, I suppose it is.'

'Okay, then, let's see . . .' Naomi tapped her chin with a forefinger. 'Sexual compatibility – that's essential – otherwise, why bother? Mutual respect – that's important too. As for number three ... Oh, that would have to be absolute discretion of course.'

Toby nodded, as if to indicate that her responses had met with his approval. 'What about children?'

'What about them?'

'Do you want them?'

'Yes, one day, but I figure I've got a few years left for all that stuff. Right now, I just want some no-strings fun.'

'Are you involved with anyone at the moment?'

'No.' It was Naomi's first deliberate lie of the evening.

'It's just that I'm looking for a one-on-one relation-ship.'

'But you're married,' Naomi pointed out. 'How can it be one-on-one?'

'You know what I mean,' he said, slightly brusque. 'Is that something you think you could agree to?'

Naomi stroked her throat languorously. She could see he was impatient for her answer and she enjoyed keeping him in suspense. 'I think so,' she said at length.

'Excellent!'

They fell silent as the waiter arrived with their starters.

'I hope you enjoy the food,' Toby said, as he ground black pepper on to his asparagus. 'Our chef won a Michelin star at his previous establishment. We're hoping he'll do the same at Denholm House.'

'I'm sure I shall, if this soup's anything to go by,'

Naomi said, smacking her lips. She reached towards the bread basket. 'Do you ever feel bad about cheating on your wife?'

Toby shook his head.

'Not even a little bit?'

'No – and that's the honest truth. In my opinion, affairs can actually enhance a marriage.'

'How do you work that out?'

'They help one refocus pent-up sexual and emotional hunger.' He dabbed the corners of his mouth with a napkin. 'In any case, I'm not convinced that trying to maintain a sexual bond with one person forever is entirely natural. In the rest of the animal kingdom, monogamy is the exception, not the rule.'

'I'm not sure I agree,' Naomi said. 'If and when I ever get married, I intend to be completely faithful. But I'm glad you don't feel guilty; it will certainly make my life a lot easier.' She checked herself, not wanting to appear too keen. 'If, that is, we decide to move forward with this.'

'Oh, Naomi,' he said, stroking her forearm. 'I can see that you and I are going to get along famously.'

Over the main course, the conversation turned to lighter matters – like their favourite books and films, and other typical first-date fodder. Before long, they had finished the champagne and moved on to a very good Chablis. After surreptitiously checking the wine's price, Naomi mentally added 'generous' to Toby's growing list of attributes. By the time their plates were being cleared away she felt replete, relaxed and rather light-headed.

'Can I tempt you to pudding?' Toby asked, as the waiter proffered the dessert menu.

Naomi's hand went to her stomach. 'I shouldn't really.'

'Oh, go on,' Toby urged. 'The pastry chef is a personal friend of mine. He'll be offended if we don't order something.'

Naomi studied the menu. 'The baked lemon cheesecake does sound delicious,' she conceded.

'Good, that's settled. One cheesecake and a black coffee, please,' Toby told the hovering waiter.

Naomi looked at him in dismay. 'Aren't you having anything?'

'Sorry, I have to watch my cholesterol levels,' he replied. 'In any case, *my* enjoyment will come from watching you eat.'

'Talk about cheap thrills,' Naomi said, smiling.

Toby lifted the Chablis from the cooler and topped up her glass. 'When you get to my age, my dear, you take your pleasure wherever you can.'

When the cheesecake arrived, Naomi felt a stab of guilt. It was weeks since she'd allowed any refined sugar to touch her palate and now she was about to undo all her hard work in one fell swoop. Still, she wasn't about to let a good dessert go to waste. As she dug her spoon into the cheesecake, she could feel her heart racing. Slowly, she lifted the spoon to her mouth. The next moment, her tastebuds were overwhelmed by a glorious citrus sweetness. She glanced at Toby and saw that his face was lit up, like a little boy on Christmas morning.

'How is it?' he asked eagerly.

'That,' Naomi said, as she licked biscuit crumbs off her spoon, 'is the best cheesecake I have ever tasted. Are you sure you don't want to try some?'

'No, really, I'm fine.' He leaned forward across the table. 'I love a woman who enjoys her food,' he said in a low, seductive voice. 'Go on, have some more.'

Naomi didn't need further encouragement. She cut some more cheesecake and raised the spoon halfway to her lips. Then, realizing it was an indecently large mouthful – the sort of size she'd have if she was eating alone – she hesitated.

Toby caught his breath. 'Don't stop,' he said.

Not wanting to disappoint him, Naomi opened her mouth wide and inserted the spoon. As she ate, she could feel her cheeks puffing out like a hamster.

'Describe the taste to me,' Toby said, staring at her fixedly.

'Mmm,' Naomi said. 'It's really rich and creamy and the lemon's wonderfully sharp. I'm getting a hint of spice too . . . I think it's ginger.' She rolled her eyes. 'My slimming-club leader would kill me if she could see me now.'

Toby looked at her askance. 'You want to lose *more* weight?'

'Another ten pounds at least,' Naomi said, putting down her spoon. 'In my twenties I could eat anything I liked and not put on an ounce, but as soon as I hit thirty my metabolic rate changed almost overnight. I've tried every diet under the sun, but I've never been able to stick at them. Fat Chance is different, though; it really seems to be working.'

Toby put his hand over hers. 'Believe me when I tell you that you don't need to lose any more weight, Naomi. That's what I liked about your photo on the website – your beautiful feminine curves.' He picked up his cup of coffee. 'You really are an exceptional woman – in every way.'

Naomi was flattered. She was used to receiving compliments from men, but none had ever been quite as effusive as this one.

'I can't bear skinny women,' Toby went on, in a tone that was almost aggressive. 'I don't care what the magazines say – no man wants to go to bed with a bag of bones.'

'Don't worry, I'm not going to get carried away,' Naomi told him. 'I just want to get down to a size twelve.'

Toby shook his head firmly. 'Size twelve is far too small.'

'Are you serious?' Naomi said, pushing the half-eaten cheesecake to one side.

'Absolutely. I know I'm in the minority here, but I just happen to find fuller figures attractive. They're so much more sensual.'

'So where would you draw the line? How big is too big?'

Toby shrugged. 'I'm not sure that I *would* draw a line. So long as a woman carries herself with confidence – like you do – she can be any size.'

'I see,' Naomi said thoughtfully. 'Just out of interest, what size is your wife?'

Toby sighed. 'An eight – more's the pity. She was a sixteen when we got married and an absolute knockout, but in her early forties she went through some sort of midlife crisis. She lost a ton of weight on one of those silly milkshake diets and started doing exercise classes four times a week. I was hoping it was just a phase, but she's been like that for years now. I've told her a hundred times that I prefer her the way she used to be, but she won't listen.'

'Surely that's her choice, though, isn't it?'

'Of course it is, but as her husband I'm entitled to my opinion.'

'Is that why you started having affairs – because you don't find your wife sexually attractive any more?'

Toby paused with his wine glass halfway to his mouth. 'I love my wife . . .' he began.

'You've already said that – and I believed you the first time.'

Toby grimaced. 'Sorry. The answer to your question is yes. I can't help it; I adore curvaceous women.' His hands traced the outline of a female form in the air. 'Their softness, their yielding flesh, their generosity. I love to watch women eating. I find it very . . .' He paused and licked his lips like a cartoon wolf. 'Arousing.'

Naomi felt a tremor of excitement. She'd never met a man like this before. Even Christopher, who professed to love her rounded hips and belly, had gently suggested she might benefit from joining a gym.

Toby gave her a long, appraising look. 'Have you had a nice time tonight, Naomi?'

She smiled. 'I've had a wonderful time.'

'Then would you like to do it again? I know I would.'

She paused, just long enough for a flicker of concern to register on Toby's craggy features. 'Yes, that would be lovely.'

Toby ran a finger round the rim of his glass. 'Perhaps we could go somewhere a little more private next time. I know a nice hotel with a good restaurant a few miles from here. We don't have to stay the night, of course, but I could book a room – just in case.'

Naomi twirled her hair round her index finger flirtatiously. 'Why don't you do that?'

'Perfect.' Toby picked up his dessertspoon and nodded towards the cheesecake. 'Do you mind if I . . . ?'

'Be my guest,' Naomi replied, pushing the plate towards him.

She thought he was going to finish off the cheese-cake himself, but instead he loaded his spoon and held it out to her. 'We can't have this delicious dessert going to waste,' he said with a wink.

Naomi sighed. 'I can see you're going to be a very bad influence on me.'

Toby smiled as she wrapped her lips round the spoon. 'I do hope so.'

For Holly, the evening had also been somewhat eventful. When she got home from work the flat was strangely silent. The estate agency closed early on a Friday and she'd been expecting to find Rob sitting in front of the TV, feet on the coffee table, tie lying twisted in a question mark on the floor beside him.

'Hello?' she called out from the hallway as she took her coat off. There was no reply. She went into the living room, frowning as something crunched beneath her left shoe. When she flicked the light switch and saw what it was, she gasped. A dried pink rose petal. The carpet was covered with them. Holly bent down and picked one up, wondering what on earth was going on. As she turned it over in her hand, Rob's head popped up from behind the sofa, making her jump. 'Shit,' she said, the rose petal fluttering to the floor as she stood up. 'What on earth are you doing there?'

Rob grinned. 'I wanted to surprise you,' he replied, shuffling towards her on his knees like a pantomime dwarf. He was wearing his work clothes – pinstriped trousers and a pale blue shirt that Diana had bought him for his birthday – and clutching a large and rather forlorn-looking teddy bear, the sort of thing you might win at the fair. Holly's mouth filled with the metal tang of adrenalin and her heart began to race. Suddenly she knew what this was.

Rob stopped shuffling. 'I love you, Holly,' he said, looking up at her with big, earnest eyes. 'I loved you from the first moment I saw you.'

Holly smiled nervously. 'How could you love me when you didn't even know me?'

His eyebrows clenched, as if he were annoyed at this deviation from the script. 'I just did,' he said shortly. He thrust the teddy bear into her trembling hands. 'This is for you,' he said.

Holly stared at the beast, bemused. Then she noticed the red ribbon tied round its neck. Hanging from the ribbon was the sapphire-and-diamond ring she'd found in Rob's sock drawer. She mimed shock. 'Goodness, what's this?' she said in a high, glassy voice.

'*Iwantustobetogetherforever*,' Rob said, the hurried words falling over themselves like dominoes in a line. He pressed his palms together. 'Will you marry me?'

Holly looked at him. A long silence revolved between them. She drew in a breath and let it out again slowly. She tried to speak, but the words didn't seem to want to come out. 'I'm flattered,' she floundered. 'But . . .'

'But what?' Rob said impatiently.

A rush began to well up behind Holly's face like an approaching sneeze. Her eyes burned, her mouth pulled taut, her forehead creased. 'Do I have to give you my answer now?'

Rob slumped back on to his heels. 'You don't want to marry me.' The words sounded like an accusation.

'I didn't say that. I just need some time to think about it, that's all.'

Rob gave a short, mirthless laugh. 'Fine,' he said. 'But don't think I'll wait around forever.'

Chapter Eight

Week 4
Holly 11st 10lb
Naomi 10st 8lb
Kate 13st 1lb

Kate frowned at the menu. 'Which of these is the least fattening?' she asked. 'Wholewheat spaghetti carbonara with tofu, or sweet potato and cashew nut curry?'

'The curry I should think,' Holly replied. 'That pasta sauce will be loaded with calories.'

'Personally, I think you'd be better off with the carbonara,' Naomi said. 'Did you know that a single tablespoon of cashews contains five grams of fat?'

'Bloody hell,' Kate muttered. She continued studying the menu. 'Maybe I should play it safe and go for the lentil moussaka.'

'I fancied that too,' Holly said, 'but then I realized it's probably going to be covered in cheese.' She sighed. 'Maybe we could ask them to hold the cheese.'

Kate tapped her menu. 'It comes with garlic bread.'

'Mmm, my favourite,' Holly replied.

'Mine too,' Kate said wistfully. 'But aren't unrefined

carbs the work of the devil – at least according to the gospel of Saint Amanda?'

'Shit,' Holly said. Her gaze drifted towards the selection of condiments that was sitting on a terracotta plate in the centre of the table. 'According to this magazine I was reading the other day, lots of supermodels stay thin by sipping vinegar before meals. Apparently it acts as an appetite suppressant.'

'Really?' Kate said, eyeing up a bottle of oak-aged balsamic vinegar. 'I might give that a try.'

Naomi grinned. 'So, apart from vinegar, what's everyone drinking?'

'I think I'll stick to spirits,' Holly said. 'A vodka and tonic is only fifty calories. An average-sized glass of wine, on the other hand, is more than a hundred.'

'It's not, is it?' Kate said, mentally totting up all the glasses of wine she'd drunk over the past week.

'Ladies, *please*,' Naomi said, banging the table with the palm of her hand. 'We've come here to enjoy ourselves. Can't we forget our diets, just for one night?'

Ten minutes later, a waitress was delivering a jug of pear mojito to their table, together with a shared starter of nachos, smothered in guacamole and cheese.

'It was a great idea to meet up like this,' Kate said. 'I don't often get a chance to socialize with non-academics.' She picked up the jug and began dispensing mojito. 'I've got some fantastic friends at the university, but when a group of us get together the conversation can be a little dry. It's like that joke: how many academics does it take to change a lightbulb? One to climb the ladder and ten to theorize about why the lightbulb needed changing in the first place.'

Naomi laughed. 'I'm sure Holly and I can provide you with some *light* relief.'

'Was your husband an academic?' Holly asked.

'No, he was an architect, and a very talented one too.' Kate took a sip of mojito, half closing her eyes in pleasure as the cold sweet liquid hit the back of her throat. 'We often talked about buying a plot of land and building our own house. Huw had already planned the whole thing out in his head. He knew the exact dimensions of every room and what sort of underfloor heating we would have. He was even planning to build me a state-of-the-art office in a separate outbuilding, linked to the main house by an intercom.'

Holly smiled. 'He sounds very thoughtful.'

'Oh, he was – and very romantic too. He'd always plan something special for our wedding anniversary. The year he died, he took me to a fabulous boutique hotel in Edinburgh. We did lots of walking and talking and eating; it was heaven.' Kate paused. 'I'm making him sound like Mr Perfect, but don't get me wrong – Huw had his faults. He could be arrogant and over-critical at times, and even though he was a very sociable person he sometimes found the company of other people – even me – stifling. At weekends and evenings, he often used to take himself off for long rides on his motorbike. Sometimes he'd be gone for hours.'

'Didn't you resent being left on your own?'

Kate shook her head. 'I like my own space too. That's part of the reason our marriage was so successful: we respected each other's need for independence.'

'I can't imagine how it must have felt to lose him,' Naomi said. 'And so suddenly too.'

'It's certainly not an experience I'd care to repeat.' Kate stroked the rim of her glass, casting her mind back to that dreadful, savage time. 'It's funny, but when Huw died my overwhelming emotion wasn't sadness or regret; it was outrage. I remember waking up the morning after Huw's death feeling absolutely furious that the world had kept turning and the sun had come up as if nothing had happened. But the world does keep turning and, while the pain never really goes away, I've found ways of incorporating it into who I am.' Suddenly her throat thickened with remembered emotion. Oh, how she had loved him. His confidence and strength, the smell of his skin, his beautiful almond eyes – a legacy from his Indonesian great-grandmother. It was a torrent of love, of rightness and recognition. Two souls who were meant to be together.

Just then, the waitress arrived with their main courses, interrupting Kate's ruminations.

'Mmm, this curry smells divine,' she said, bending

her face low over the plate and inhaling deeply. 'I'm going to savour every last gram of fat in these cashew nuts.' She turned her head towards Naomi. 'I've been dying to ask . . . how did your date go the other night?'

'Much better than I expected,' Naomi said as she cut into her aubergine and ricotta roulade. 'I was worried the whole thing would feel a bit sleazy, but Toby was the perfect gentleman: charming, polite, sophisticated – generous too. He insisted on paying for an extremely expensive dinner, as well as my taxi ride home.'

'Was he good-looking?' Holly asked.

'I didn't think so at first, but the more we talked, the more attractive I found him.' Naomi's eyes sparkled as she remembered how Toby had kissed her passionately outside the club before hailing a taxi for her. 'He's very well connected too. He's only one of the founding members of Denholm House. The staff treated us like royalty.'

'He almost sounds too good to be true,' Holly observed.

'I know – and get this: he actually prefers plus-sized women to average-sized ones. He says he finds them more . . . now what was the word he used? Ah yes.' She gave a little giggle. '*Sensual.*'

'Now that *is* a rarity,' Kate said. 'Huw much preferred slender women; in fact, he could be quite disparaging about friends of mine who'd "let themselves go", as he put it.' She paused with a forkful of curry halfway to her mouth. 'He'd be horrified to see how much weight I've put on.'

'Rob's the same,' Holly replied. 'He says he likes me the way I am. But sometimes, when we're sitting in front of the TV and I'm halfway through a packet of biscuits, I catch him looking at me with a strange expression on his face.'

'What sort of expression?' Naomi asked.

Holly thought for a moment. 'Pity mainly. With a dash of disgust.'

'So you think that, secretly, he'd prefer it if you were slimmer?'

Holly nodded. 'But he'd never come out and say it; he wouldn't want to hurt my feelings.' She tore off a hunk of garlic bread. 'So have you arranged another date with Toby?'

Naomi nodded. 'He and his wife are going to New York to visit their son next week, but we've arranged to meet the week after – and this time he's booked a hotel room.'

'Goodness!' Kate exclaimed. 'Things *are* moving quickly.'

'In my experience, it's always better to cut straight to the chase,' Naomi replied. 'We need to find out whether or not we're sexually compatible, otherwise there's no point in pursuing a relationship.'

'And where will Toby's wife be when you two are giving each other marks out of ten?' Holly asked.

'Away on business – and you don't have to feel sorry for her; she has affairs too.'

'But if they're both at it, why do they bother staying married?'

Naomi shrugged. 'Because they love each other, I guess.'

'It all sounds horribly complicated,' Holly said.

'Maybe for them, but not for me,' Naomi responded breezily. 'All I'm doing is having fun.'

Kate gave her a sideways look. 'There's something I've been wanting to ask you about these married men of yours. I hope you won't be offended.'

'Of course not,' Naomi replied. 'Ask me anything you like.'

'I'm interested to know . . . on your dates, does etiquette demand that the man always pays?'

'Generally speaking, yes,' Naomi replied. 'And if he's smart he'll pay in cash to avoid any incriminating evidence popping up on his credit-card statement.'

'Do they ever buy you presents?' Holly asked.

'Sometimes.'

'Expensive ones?'

'Mostly it's just flowers and lingerie, although I did get a pair of diamond earrings once.'

'And what do you give them in return?' Kate asked.

'Apart from sex, you mean?' Naomi said, dabbing the corners of her mouth with a napkin.

Kate gave a little cough of embarrassment. 'Yes, apart from that.'

'Well, first of all I make sure I'm always looking nice for them. That's an important part of being a mistress. The men I date don't want to see me slobbing around in a pair of tracksuit bottoms with unwashed hair and no make-up; they get all that at home. I listen to them too – and I mean *really* listen. Even if they're boring me to tears, I smile and frown and nod in all the right places. And if they're stressing over something – whether it's work or their kids playing up or their nagging wife – I try to take their mind off it by pouring them a drink or giving them a shoulder rub. Basically, I'm their fantasy woman – the one who makes them feel important and gives them the unconditional affection they don't get at home.'

'Sounds like a lot of hard work to me,' Holly said.

Naomi shrugged. 'The benefits are worth it as far as I'm concerned. In any case, a good mistress *has* to work hard to keep her man: she's dispensable after all; a wife, on the other hand isn't so easy – or so cheap – to get rid of.'

'What happened to that other man you were seeing?' Kate asked. 'The dentist.'

'I finished with him the day after my date with Toby. I told him it wasn't working out. I didn't see the need to rub his nose in it by saying I'd met someone else.'

'How did he take it?'

Naomi frowned, recalling Christopher's reaction during their final brief encounter, which had taken place in a café round the corner from his surgery. 'He seemed more relieved than anything, which I must admit I found rather hurtful. We've been having sex twice a week for the past two and a half months. You'd think he'd be a tiny bit upset, wouldn't you?'

Kate shrugged. 'Perhaps he was just glad he wasn't going to have to lie to his wife any more.'

'Oh, Christopher's an expert when it comes to deception,' Naomi said. 'He's had several mistresses before me and his wife's never suspected a thing. She doesn't know about his offshore bank account either.'

'What does he need one of those for?' Holly asked.

'It's a safety net. Every month he secretly stashes ten per cent of his salary away. That way, if his wife ever does find out about his affairs and divorces him, she won't be able to lay claim to the cash in any settlement.'

Holly tutted. 'How sneaky is that?'

'Tell me something,' Kate said, peering at Naomi over the top of her glasses. 'Have you ever been in love? I mean truly, madly, crazily in love. The kind of love where your body leaps and your molecules scream and your legs turn to jelly every time you see him.'

Naomi thought for a moment. 'There was a guy I was seeing at art college who had that effect on me, but no one since then.'

'Would you like to settle down with someone eventually?'

'Sure, but not yet.' Naomi's eyes sparkled. 'Not when I'm having so much fun.'

Kate turned to Holly. 'What about you and Rob? I take it you're in for the long haul.'

'Actually . . .' Holly paused and rubbed her lower lip. 'Rob has asked me to marry him.'

'Oh my God, how exciting!' Naomi squealed. 'Why didn't you tell us straight away?'

Kate raised her glass. 'Congratulations, Holly, that's wonderful news.'

Holly looked down at the yellow gingham tablecloth. 'I haven't said yes yet.'

'Oh.' Kate lowered her glass. 'Do I take it you weren't expecting Rob to propose?'

'Yes and no,' Holly replied with a heavy sigh. 'A couple of days ago, I found an engagement ring hidden in Rob's sock drawer. I was shocked. We've never discussed marriage; I thought we were happy the way we were. I didn't tell him I'd found it and then last night I came home from work to find the living room floor in our flat covered in dried rose petals.'

'How romantic,' Naomi murmured.

Holly covered her eyes with her hand. 'I know this is going to sound awful, but instead of being overjoyed that I was about to be proposed to, all I could think about was what a horrible mess those rose petals were making of the carpet.'

'And how did you feel when he actually popped the question?' Kate asked.

'Flattered. Excited. Slightly panicky.' Holly sighed. 'It's very confusing. I love Rob, but we've only been together a year. I don't know if I'm ready to get engaged just yet.'

'So what did you say?' Naomi asked.

'That I needed some time to think about it.'

Naomi winced. 'That must have knocked the wind out of his sails.'

'When I saw how disappointed he was, I felt awful.' Holly sighed again. 'I don't know what's wrong with me. Rob's a great guy and I know he won't wait around forever. Why didn't I just say yes?'

'I think you're being very sensible,' Kate said. 'Marriage is a huge commitment – the biggest one you're ever likely to make. It's important that you think very carefully about whether or not Rob's the right man for you.'

'When Huw proposed, did you say yes straight away?' Holly asked.

Kate nodded. 'You couldn't get me up that aisle quick enough. And the funny thing is I'd never thought of myself as the marrying kind – with me it was always career first, relationships second, but when something's right you just know.'

Holly set her fork down on the side of her plate.

'My main concern is that Rob and I have such different views on family life. He's very old fashioned. I'm sure he'd be quite happy if I got pregnant, gave up work and became a full-time housewife, just like his mum did when she got married.'

'And that isn't what you want?' Naomi asked.

'I'd like to have kids one day, but not for a long time. And I'd never give up my job; I love it too much.' She bit her lip. 'There's something else too — or rather some*one* else . . . this guy at work.' She blushed. 'He's my boss.'

Naomi's eyes grew round. 'You're having an affair?'

'God no,' Holly said quickly. 'It's nothing like that; Nick and I are friends, that's all. But I really like him. He's clever and funny and he asks my opinion about things. He makes me feel, I don't know, special I suppose.'

'Do you fancy him?'

'I think he's very attractive,' Holly said, reaching for another piece of garlic bread.

Naomi grinned. 'I'll take that as a yes, then.'

'I'm not saying I want to go out with him or anything,' Holly protested. 'In any case, he's got a girlfriend.'

'So what *are* you saying?' Kate asked.

'Just that if I was really ready to commit to Rob, I shouldn't even be looking at other blokes, should I?'

'There's no harm in looking,' Naomi said. 'And if a

few idle fantasies help the working day go faster then why ever not? I do it all the time. A few weeks ago I was at a big wedding down on the south coast. The bride wasn't on speaking terms with her father, so her granddad gave her away. He must have been at least seventy, but he was still a good-looking bloke. As I watched him walk her down the aisle, I found myself wondering what it would be like to have sex with somebody that old.'

Holly giggled. 'I hope you didn't find out.'

'Of course I didn't.' Naomi cocked her head and looked off into the distance, as if she were thinking. 'As I recall, on that occasion I ended up shagging the groom's second cousin.'

'I used to have a crush on our window cleaner,' Kate offered. 'He had lovely full lips and strawberry blond hair that curled over the collar of his shirt. Whenever he came round, I used to imagine what it would be like to run my fingers through it. But it was just a daydream; I never once contemplated being unfaithful to Huw.' She smiled at Holly. 'Naomi's right – there's nothing wrong with fantasizing about other people. It's only if you feel the need to act on those fantasies that you need to be concerned.'

Naomi picked up the jug of mojito and refilled their glasses. 'Has Rob given you a deadline for your answer?'

'No, but I said I'd let him know by the weekend. I

don't think it's fair to keep him dangling any longer than that.'

'Well, whatever you tell him, I have every faith you'll make the right decision,' Kate said. She pushed her empty plate to the side and gave a contented sigh. 'That was delicious. I could eat it all over again.'

'There's always pudding,' Naomi said.

Holly looked longingly at the next table, where a woman was feasting on something moist and chocolatey. 'Do you think we ought to? What if Amanda finds out?'

'She's not *going* to find out,' Kate replied. 'It can be our little secret. After all, what's the point in being naughty, unless we're going to be *really* naughty?'

Chapter Nine

'Happy birthday, Cara!' Holly called out as she walked up to the reception at Danson & Jolley. 'This is for you,' she said, sliding a cardboard box across the desk. 'Just don't let me anywhere near them, okay? I went out with some of the girls from my slimming club on Monday night and ate about a week's worth of calories in the space of two hours.'

Cara broke into a smile as she lifted the lid of the box to reveal half a dozen brightly iced cupcakes. 'Aw, thanks, Holly, that's really sweet of you. You are coming to the party tonight, aren't you?'

'Of course,' Holly replied. 'I've bought a new dress especially.'

'Great, we're heading over to the bar at six-ish,' Cara said. 'Is Rob going to meet you there?'

Holly shook her head. 'He's not coming. He's, uh, got to work late.'

'That's a shame.' Cara cast a quick look from left to right to make sure she couldn't be overheard. 'Speaking of working late, I think Nick slept in the office last night.'

Holly frowned sceptically. 'Why would he do that?'

Cara shrugged. 'All I know is, when the cleaners came in at six thirty this morning, they found him fast asleep on the sofa in the first-floor boardroom.'

'In that case,' Holly said, turning round and heading back towards the revolving door, 'he'll be needing coffee.'

Ten minutes later, she was walking through the open door of Nick's office. He was sitting at his desk, going through some paperwork. His hair was all rumpled and he was still wearing yesterday's shirt.

'There you go,' she said, placing a double espresso and a blueberry muffin on the corner of his desk. 'Our eyes and ears on reception tells me you've been here all night, so I'm guessing you haven't had breakfast.'

Nick fell greedily on the coffee. 'Thanks, Holly, that's very thoughtful of you.'

'Did you really sleep in the first-floor boardroom?'

Nick nodded sheepishly.

'But why?' Holly asked him. 'Everyone at Danson & Jolley already thinks you're a genius. You don't need to prove yourself by working through the night.'

Nick stroked the dark shadow of stubble at his throat. 'Actually, I wasn't working; I was hiding.'

Holly frowned. 'Hiding from who?'

'Melissa. We had a big row last night. Things got pretty heated and I ended up walking out. I didn't mean to stay here the whole night, but I couldn't face going back to the apartment.'

'What were you arguing about?' Holly smiled tentatively. 'You can tell me to mind my own business if you like.'

'No, it's okay,' he said, sighing. 'Mel's decided she wants a breast enlargement. I told her it was a stupid idea and that her breasts were fine the way they were.'

'Sounds like a perfectly reasonable comment to me.'

'That's what I thought, but unfortunately Mel didn't see it that way. She accused me of being unsupportive. She claimed that not only had several of her friends had boob jobs, but that their boyfriends had coughed up the cash for them – the implication being that I should offer to do the same. I told her she must be mad if she thought I was going to pay her to mutilate her body – and that's when she lost it.' He shuddered. 'I've never seen Mel lose her temper like that before. She was almost unrecognizable; it was quite scary.'

'What did she do?'

'First, she called me every name under the sun, then she proceeded to smash a very expensive Heals dinner service, piece by piece, against the wall.'

Holly winced. 'Ouch.'

'The worst thing was, in the middle of it all, I had a flashback to when I was a kid.' He drew his hand across his face. 'My mum and dad had what you might call a fiery relationship. They used to have these big screaming matches that frequently involved a bit of ornament smashing or saucepan throwing. My sister and I would run upstairs and hide under my parents' bed. Sometimes, we'd stay there for hours, too frightened to come out in case we went downstairs and discovered our parents had killed each other.'

Holly felt a rush of tenderness. 'My parents had a pretty rocky marriage too, but luckily I didn't have to put up with the arguments for too long – when I was eight, they got divorced.'

Nick grimaced. 'Mine celebrated their ruby wedding anniversary last year.'

'So what are you going to do – about Mel, I mean?'

'I'll give her a call later on, see if she's calmed down.'

Holly felt a jangle of concern. 'You are still going to Cara's party, aren't you?'

'Course I am,' Nick replied. He smiled such a warm and sexy smile that Holly felt a wave of colour come into her face. 'And Cara's not the only one who's going to be celebrating.'

'Why, what's happened?'

'I heard this morning . . . we won the Fascinations contract. The client thought our concept for the press campaign was really innovative.'

'That's great news,' Holly said, smiling. 'Congratulations.'

'I don't know why you're congratulating *me* when it was your idea.'

Holly stared at him in surprise. 'You actually ran

with it, then? The fuller-figured model pigging out, while her boyfriend looks bored in the background?'

Nick nodded. 'We made a few tweaks, but nothing substantial.'

'Wow,' Holly said. 'I was only thinking out loud. I didn't imagine for one minute you'd take me seriously.'

'It was a brilliant idea – of course I took it seriously,' Nick said. 'Everyone else on the team loved it too – and I made sure they all knew it was *your* idea.' He leaned back in his chair and cradled his head in his hands. 'Tonight, I'm going to buy you a large drink to say thank you. In fact, I'm going to buy you several large drinks.'

Holly felt a hot glow of pleasure. 'You don't have to do that.'

'I know, but I'm going to anyway.'

'Great, I look forward to it.' Holly shuffled from foot to foot, not knowing what to say. 'Right, then, I'd better get back to my desk.'

'Oh, can you book a meeting room for me for midday on Wednesday? Get some sandwiches and stuff in too, will you? We're doing the brainstorm for that women's magazine launch.'

Holly frowned. 'I thought the brainstorm was last week.'

'It was, but now the client's changed the brief. They've decided they don't want a straightforward press ad after all. They want an in-store campaign.'

'Oh?' Holly said, her interested piqued. 'Like posters, you mean, or some sort of giveaway?'

'Yeah, only I think we're going to have to be a bit edgier than that. The problem is there are so many women's magazines out there – we need to find a way of making this one really stand out from the crowd.'

'Do you know anything about the launch edition?'

'They're calling it the *Naked* issue – they've persuaded half a dozen female celebrities to pose in the nude and talk about their feelings about their bodies. It's a great idea, but what we need is some way of advertising that to potential customers as soon as they walk into the shop.' He picked up his cooling cup of espresso and downed it in a single gulp. 'Mmm, thanks for that; it was just what I needed.'

'IM me if you fancy another one,' Holly said, turning towards the door.

'What would I do without you?' Nick replied.

Holly felt a twist in her heart, remembering how Rob had said the exact same thing just a few days earlier.

The rest of the morning passed quickly. Holly responded to the usual slew of emails, confirmed Nick's availability for various meetings and made travel arrangements for his forthcoming trip to Danson & Jolley's Amsterdam office. And all the time, Rob's proposal was at the back of her mind, chafing at her conscience like a stone in her shoe. She still couldn't make up her mind. One moment, the thought of losing him filled her with a dark and breathless panic. An hour or so later, the panic seemed far away, a small irretrievable flutter in the distance. She remembered how giddy and out of control she'd felt in the early days, like a bee drunk on pollen. And how that early infatuation had quickly developed into something more meaningful. Rob would be a good husband – she had no doubt of that. He would love and protect her, and comfort her in her hour of need, and do all those other things husbands were supposed to do. And yet there was something bothering the far corners of her mind, something casting a shadow.

Suddenly, Holly was aware of someone standing next to her. She looked up and saw that it was Nick.

'Penny for them,' he said.

'Sorry,' she replied. 'I was miles away.'

'I'm off to meet that photographer now,' he said, buttoning up his jacket. 'Where did you book us in for lunch again?'

'Le Bouchon, the new French place on the river.'

'Perfect. We're going to check out a couple of locations together afterwards, so I'll be out for the rest of the afternoon. You can get me on my mobile if you need me.'

'I guess I'll see you at the party, then.'

Nick smiled. 'You can count on it.'

*

As soon as he'd gone, Holly left her office and went to the stationery cupboard down the hallway, where she helped herself to an A3 sketchpad. She'd been planning to spend her lunch hour looking for some pretty earrings to go with the new dress she'd bought for the party, but now she'd thought of a much more productive way to spend it.

The office was deserted by the time Holly finally switched off her computer. She could have finished nearly two hours ago and joined the gaggle of women who'd converged in the ladies' toilets, chattering excitedly as they wriggled into party dresses and sprayed clouds of perfume into the air. Instead, she'd returned to the project she'd begun at lunchtime. It wasn't finished, not by a long shot, but she'd got the bare bones of it.

In the toilets, she changed into the dress she'd bought – a silver beaded tunic dress that covered all her lumps and bumps – and a pair of black satin pumps. Afterwards, she touched up her make-up and pulled her hair out of its ponytail before curling it softly with cordless tongs.

Down on reception, the night security guard was sitting in Cara's seat, squinting at the tiny TV that was positioned on the desk in front of him.

'Night, Tony,' Holly called out as she walked past him.

He did a double take. 'Holly, is that really you?'

Holly rolled her eyes. 'Ha, ha, very funny.'

'No, really,' the security guard protested. 'You look beautiful, really you do.'

'Well, thank you, Tony,' Holly said, smiling. 'And have a good evening.'

'You too,' he replied, his eyes tracking her as she exited through the side door.

The bar Cara had hired for the party was less than ten minutes' walk away. Low ceilinged and dimly lit, it was furnished in a fashionable retro style. Holly spotted Cara right away. She was wearing a pink satin baby doll dress that contained less fabric than some of Holly's underwear and she was holding court in the middle of the room, in the midst of a group of male account managers. The men were of varying ages and levels of seniority, but all appeared to be hanging on the receptionist's every word. Holly hovered on the sidelines for a few moments, marvelling at Cara's self-assurance, derived, no doubt, from the knowledge that she was one of the most attractive – and certainly the thinnest – woman in the room.

Just then, Cara flailed one of her long, tanned, gooseflesh-free arms in Holly's direction. 'There you are!' she cried tipsily. 'We were wondering where you were.' She grabbed Holly's hand, drawing her into the centre of the group. 'I love that dress,' she said. 'It really suits you.' She sighed stagily. 'You've got fabulous tits, you know; I wish I had tits like yours.' She turned to the men. 'Hasn't Holly got great tits?'

Holly felt her face warming as a dozen pairs of eyes swivelled towards her bust. Before anybody had a chance to comment on the veracity or otherwise of Cara's observation, she pointed to the half-empty glass in her friend's hand. 'Can I get the birthday girl a drink?' she asked.

'No, I'm okay, thanks. We've got a bottle of champagne here. Do you want some?'

Holly shook her head. 'I'm sticking to vodka tonight.' She turned sideways and squeezed through the gap between two of the account managers. 'I'm off to get a drink. See you in a bit, everyone.'

Holly went over to the bar and stood there for several minutes, waiting to be served. Suddenly, she felt a tap on her shoulder. She turned round and saw that it was Nick. He was wearing jeans and a black shirt, open at the neck.

He smiled at her, his eyes crinkling attractively at the corners. 'Have you just got here?'

'Yeah, I was finishing up some stuff in the office,' she said, aware that she sounded slightly breathless.

Nick half turned towards the bar. 'Now let me get that drink I promised you.'

'Oh, um, thanks. I'll have a vodka and slimline tonic, please.'

Unlike Holly, Nick managed to attract the barman's attention straight away.

'You look very nice, by the way,' he said, as he handed her the drink.

'Thanks,' she said, trying not to blush.

'So,' he said, taking a pull from his bottle of beer. 'Is Rob coming along later?'

'No, they've got a training evening at the estate agency where he works.' It was the second time Holly had lied about Rob's whereabouts. In reality, her boy-friend was at home, no doubt enjoying a takeaway curry as he watched one of the American legal dramas he was addicted to. She'd told him Cara's birthday bash was going to be a low-key affair, just a few drinks with the girls from the office, knowing he wouldn't expect to be included in the invitation. She wasn't sure why she'd lied; all she knew was that she didn't want him there.

'That's a shame,' Rob said. He pointed to the cardboard tube she was carrying under her arm. 'What's that – a present for Cara?'

'No, actually, it's an idea I had for that women's magazine launch. I've sketched it out for you, and don't worry – I did it in my own time. That's why I'm late.'

Nick gave a little laugh of surprise. 'Can I see it?'

As Holly reached for the cardboard tube, he took her by the crook of the elbow. 'Hang on, let's go some-where a bit quieter, shall we?' He led her over to a vacant table and pushed aside a couple of empty beer bottles. 'Right, let's see what you've got.'

Holly was feeling nervous as she removed a roll of paper from the tube. She desperately didn't want to look stupid in front of Nick. Her idea for the Fascinations pitch might have been a total fluke. At the end of the day, she was only a glorified secretary after all. 'It's still a work in progress,' she said, 'but I think you'll be able to get the gist from my drawing.'

She unrolled her sketch and spread it out on the beer-splattered table, frowning as little Rorschach blotches of damp began appearing all over it. 'Okay, the problem is that the magazine's *Naked* issue is in danger of getting lost on the shelf,' she began, trying to sound confident. 'The solution is to take the consumer by the hand as soon as she enters the newsagent or supermarket and bring her directly to the magazine.'

'And how are we going to do that?' Nick asked. She looked up at him and saw he was smiling – whether in amusement or encouragement, she couldn't be sure.

'By creating the illusion that a woman has stripped off in the store,' she replied.

Nick's eyes widened. 'Now that would really grab people's attention.'

Holly turned the paper over. 'What I'm proposing is that we create a series of floor decals, each one depicting a different item of clothing.' She pointed to the sketch she'd done. 'As you can see from my drawing, the clothing trail would begin at the entrance to the store with, say, a scarf.' Her finger moved to the next item of clothing she'd drawn. 'Then we'd have a pair of gloves, followed by a coat, jumper, skirt and so on, all leading towards the magazine stand. The very last items of clothing would be a bra and knickers and at the end of the trail, when the customer is standing right in front of the magazines, we could print some kind of call to action on the floor, to help the consumer link the clothing trail to the magazine and put a smile on their face.' She threw a hand in the air. 'I don't know, maybe something like: *Don't be shy. Get Naked.*' She paused and gave him a sidelong glance. 'What do you think?'

Nick didn't respond right away. For a few moments, he just stared at her drawing intently. Then all at once he broke into a smile. 'Holly, I think it's brilliant.'

Holly felt a tingle on the back of her neck. 'Do you mean it?'

'Holly, I wouldn't say it if I didn't mean it.' He studied the drawing again. 'Seriously, if I had a vacancy on my creative team, I'd hire you tomorrow.'

Holly looked at Nick. Nick looked right back at her. For a moment, the air between them seemed to tremble like an electrical current. Then Liam Flanagan from digital marketing came barging in.

'Hey, Nick, Melissa's here,' he said, clapping Nick on the back. 'I've just seen her checking her coat in.'

'Ah,' Nick said, turning towards the entrance. 'Thanks, Liam.'

Holly cast a quick, curious glance at her boss. 'You two have made up, then?'

'Yeah, I went home to change my clothes before I came out tonight. Mel was there, full of apologies. Our row's all water under the bridge now.'

'That's good,' Holly said, forcing a smile.

'Yeah.' Nick stood on tiptoes and began waving over the top of Holly's head. 'I'll introduce you if you like.'

Looking over, Holly saw a tall redhead in skinny jeans and a gold chainmail top approaching. She was, as Cara had said, stunning. All at once, Holly felt fat and dowdy in her new dress. 'Actually, I'm bursting for the loo,' she said quickly. 'Maybe I'll come over and say hi later.' She snatched her drawing off the table and began walking away before Nick had a chance to respond.

Inside the vast white marquee, Naomi was growing impatient. She'd finished taking pictures half an hour earlier, but still she lingered, waiting for the right moment. Then, just as she was thinking about cutting her losses and leaving, she spotted her opportunity. The vicar – who, aside from conducting the service, was a friend of the bride's family – was finally alone. Naomi had chatted on the phone with him a couple of times before the wedding to discuss logistics. He'd been exceedingly friendly and helpful, and when they'd met in the flesh for the first time, just a few hours earlier, she'd been surprised at how attractive he was for a man in his mid-forties. She looked to see if he was wearing a wedding ring; he wasn't. She'd checked out his ring finger right away – it was bare. When he arrived at the reception, he was still wearing his dog collar, but he'd swapped his white and gold surplice for jeans and a rather debonair black velvet jacket. During breaks in shooting, Naomi had been observing him closely, noting that a glass of red wine was never far from his hand. Also, that his gaze had frequently strayed to the trio of barely-out-of-their-teens bridesmaids, who'd spent most of the evening writhing on the dance floor, mere feet away from where he was sitting. From Naomi's perspective, all the signs were good. Without further hesitation, she scooped up her camera bags and went over to his table, sliding into the seat that had just been vacated by the groom's elderly aunt.

'Hi, Vicar, are you having a good time?' she said, shrugging off her cardigan so that his view of her cleavage was unrestricted.

'I'm having a lovely time, thank you, Naomi,' he said, his grey eyes twinkling. 'How about you – did you get all the pictures you wanted?'

'Pretty much.' She fanned her face with her hand. 'It's very warm in here, isn't it?'

'It is a little,' he replied.

Naomi picked up a half-empty glass of champagne that lay abandoned on the table and took a slug. 'Oh well, I guess I'd better get going,' she said, sighing stagily. 'Back to my cold, empty bed.'

He looked at her. 'I can't believe a stunning young lady like you is single.'

Naomi shrugged. ''Fraid so and, I must admit, I do feel lonely sometimes, especially after a wedding.' She tilted her head on one side. 'Do *you* ever get lonely, Vicar?'

'Occasionally,' he said, smiling. 'But God is never too far away.'

'And what about your *physical* needs?' Naomi asked.

The vicar ran a finger along the inside of his dog collar. 'I'm not sure I know what you mean.'

'Oh, Vicar, I think you do. I saw the way you were looking at those bridesmaids earlier.' Naomi leaned in closer. 'I bet you were imagining what it would be like to run your hands over their firm young bodies, weren't you?'

The vicar looked at her, horrified. 'I was thinking no such thing.'

Naomi reached under the table and placed her hand on his thigh.

'We all have urges; it's nothing to be ashamed of.' She began inching her hand upwards. 'And at the moment, my urge is very strong.'

The vicar coughed. 'What are you suggesting?'

'That two lonely souls offer each other a little comfort, that's all.'

The vicar sighed softly as Naomi's hand reached his crotch. 'I'm not sure that would be appropriate behaviour for a man in my position.'

Naomi withdrew her hand abruptly. 'Of course; I understand. But if you change your mind I'll be in the car park for at least another five minutes, packing away my gear. You can't miss my car – it's a bright yellow Beetle.' With that, she picked up her camera bags and strode towards the marquee's entrance without so much as a backwards glance.

Naomi was slamming the boot of her car shut when she heard the crunch of gravel behind her. Turning round, she saw the vicar moving towards her at speed, head bowed, hands shoved deep into his pockets.

'Vicar!' she said, acting more surprised than she was.

The vicar cast a furtive look around. The car park was deserted; none of the other guests would be leaving any time soon. Suddenly he placed his hand on Naomi's left breast. 'You dirty girl,' he said hoarsely, teasing her nipple beneath the thin fabric of her dress. 'Trying to lure a man of the cloth into temptation. Don't you know that lust is a sin? I should make you do penance.'

Naomi laughed softly as she grabbed the back of the vicar's neck and pulled his face into her cleavage. 'I could say a hundred Our Fathers, if you like,' she murmured. 'Or you could take off my tiny pink G-string with your teeth and spank my bottom until it turns red.'

The vicar gave a low, primitive grunt. 'Get in the car,' he said. 'The vicarage is less than a mile away.'

It was just before midnight when Holly's taxi pulled up outside the apartment. She hadn't had anything to eat since a mid-afternoon snack of carrot sticks, and the six vodka and tonics she'd drunk had gone straight to her head.

Rob was in bed, snoring softly. Asleep he looked much younger than his thirty-two years, now that the frown lines had been stripped from his expression. Holly undressed in the dark, too tired and too drunk to take off her make-up. Rob moaned in his sleep as she slipped under the duvet. She pressed her naked body close to his and began planting little kisses on his neck and shoulders.

'That's nice,' he said, his voice doughy with sleep.

'The answer's yes,' she whispered.

'Mmm?' Rob mumbled.

Holly pressed her lips closer to his ear. 'Yes, Rob McIntyre, I will marry you.'

Chapter Ten

Week 5
Holly 11st 10lb
Naomi 10st 9lb
Kate 13st 2lb

Holly sank down into her chair and stared at the floor, hoping to escape Amanda's attention. Just a few moments earlier, the Fat Chance leader had asked for two volunteers to join her at the front of the room. With only one taker so far, her gaze was now hovering on the back row.

Suddenly, Amanda clapped her hands together. 'Holly!' she exclaimed with a feigned quiver of delight. 'You'd be perfect for this role play.'

Holly sighed. 'Do I have to?'

'No, of course you don't *have* to,' Amanda replied, 'but if you're not going to participate fully in the meetings, there's really no point in you being here.'

Kate, who could feel Holly's embarrassment undulating in silent waves towards her, raised her hand in the air. 'I don't mind doing it,' she said.

'Thank you, Kate, but I think I'd prefer Holly for

this one.' Amanda gave a hard little smile. 'Well, Holly, what's it to be? Are you brave enough to face your demons?'

'Oh, all right, then,' Holly said, her face taking on an expression of stoic anguish, like a six-year-old squaring up to the task of eating her greens. She made her way to the front of the room, where Tom, the other volunteer, was standing beside the flip chart. He rubbed his hands together as she approached, as if she were a succulent kebab he was looking forward to tucking into. Holly took up position beside him and waited for further instructions to be communicated. But the group leader's attention was now fixed on Stacey, who was rummaging noisily in her handbag. Amanda gave a small cough into her fist, but it failed to have the desired effect. Instead, she watched in horror as Stacey tore open a bag of liquorice comfits and tipped her head back to receive the rattling sweets into her gaping mouth.

The pointed toe of Amanda's right shoe beat out a furious tattoo on the floor. 'Stacey, what on earth do you think you're doing? You know I don't tolerate eating during meetings.'

'But these are only a hundred and fifty calories,' Stacey replied, her smile acting on her face like a pebble thrown into a lake. Flesh rippled; jowls wobbled; chins multiplied.

'I think you're missing the point, dear. It's not about

the calories. Chewing is very distracting – for me and for the people sitting around you.' Amanda imitated the sound of Stacey's grinding jaw. '*Mnyum, mnyum, mnyum.* See? Horrible, isn't it?'

'But I'm hungry,' Stacey protested. 'I haven't eaten for two hours and that was only a few oatcakes with cottage cheese.' She grimaced guiltily. 'Oh, and half a cold pizza that was left over from the kids' tea last night.'

Amanda pressed her tongue into the side of her cheek and stared off into the middle distance. 'It's up to you if you want to stuff your face with sweets, Stacey, but, if you must *masticate* with such enthusiasm, kindly do it outside.'

Her choice of verb brought a schoolboy smirk to Tom's face. Amanda frowned at him. *Grow up,* her expression said.

'But it's chilly outside,' Stacey said, probing with her index finger at a little piece of liquorice that had become stuck in one of her molars. 'Can't I just finish them off here? There are only a few left.'

Tom made an impatient noise. 'Look, Stacey, just put the sweets away, okay? Amanda's time is precious. She's got better things to do than stand here arguing the toss with you,' he said, in what was clearly a thinly veiled attempt to get back into Amanda's good books.

'She gets paid for it, doesn't she?' Stacey said sulkily. 'I know she makes out she's some sort of Mother flaming Theresa, doing this out of the goodness of her heart, but we all know that's not true.'

'Stacey!' Tom cried. 'That's a horrible thing to say. Apologize to Amanda right now.'

Amanda raised her palms in a peace-making gesture. 'No, Stacey is quite right,' she said with an odd cast in her voice. 'I do get paid an amount just above minimum wage to stand in this pokey little room on a Tuesday night and try and put you lot on the path to healthy eating and a new life, free from high blood pressure, low self-esteem and shocking indigestion.' Her expression grew rigid. 'What I *don't* get paid for is all the hours of overtime I put in – reading up on the latest obesity research and testing new low-fat recipes with ingredients I've bought with my own money, hunting out revolutionary products to help you lose weight or make you look slimmer.' She thrust out her chin imperiously. 'Several of you have come up to me personally and thanked me for introducing you to the Miracle Slimming Panty.'

Stacey made a noise like a rooting pig. 'Yeah, and I bet you got a healthy cut of the sale price, didn't you? What are you on – fifteen per cent? *Twenty?*'

Amanda shot Stacey a look of pure venom. '*And*,' she said, acting as if she hadn't heard the accusation, 'I certainly don't get paid to be abused by the people I'm doing my utmost to help.' She looked her attacker up and down, as if silently auditing her flaws: her elephantine thighs, the flapping skin on the underside of her arms, the large hairy mole just above her left eyebrow. Then she jabbed a finger towards the door. 'I'd like you to leave, Stacey. You're not welcome at Fat Chance any more.'

'Fine,' Stacey said, rising heavily to her feet. 'It's crap here anyway. I've been coming for six months and I've still only lost half a stone.'

'That's because you eat like a fucking horse.'

A few people gasped in shock as the uncharacteristic expletive issued from Amanda's lips.

'Yeah, well, at least I don't look like one,' Stacey retorted, as she began gathering up her things.

Amanda shook her fist in the air. 'Get out!' she shouted. 'Get out, before I throw you out.'

Stacey lumbered to her feet. 'You haven't heard the last of this. I'm going to make an official complaint to head office.'

'Go ahead,' Amanda snapped. 'If I'm called to give an account of myself – which I very much doubt – I shall say that you broke the rules and I was forced to penalize you accordingly.'

Tom folded his arms across his chest. 'And if you need a witness, Amanda, I want you to know that I'm here for you – day or night.'

Amanda smiled at him. 'Thank you, Tom.'

For a moment, Stacey seemed lost for words. Then she picked up her handbag and stared around the room at her fellow Fat Chance members. When nobody met her eye, she kicked her chair away. 'Right, then,' she said. 'Sod the lot of you.'

Holly felt quite sick as she watched Stacey waddle towards the door. Amanda was scary enough when she was in a good mood, but now that she was quite clearly in a foul one there was no telling what humiliations she might inflict on her unwilling volunteer.

Amanda waited until the door had banged shut before she spoke. 'I'm so sorry you had to witness that appalling scene,' she said, holding the back of her hand to her forehead like a Victorian heroine with the vapours. 'Now, where were we? Ah yes, the role play.' She clasped her hands together and began pacing up and down. 'So I'm sure you'll all agree that one of the hardest times to resist food is at social gatherings – especially when everyone around you is eating. In these situations, it's easy to cave in to pressure; I've done it myself, although, admittedly, not for a very long time.' Amanda paused and absent-mindedly touched her jaw, her stomach, her hips, as if reassuring herself of her own slimness. 'Today, I'd like to show you how to abstain from eating without causing offence, even when you're faced with the most persistent of hosts.' She bent down and picked up a small metal tray that was lying behind the flip chart. 'Here you are, Tom, you're going to need this.' As she handed over the tray, Amanda looked Tom up and down with the dissatisfied expression of an artist assessing her own defective handiwork. 'Have you put on weight?' she said accusingly.

Tom's hand rose defensively to his florid neck. 'Erm, yeah, I think I might have put on a couple of pounds. I had my cousin and his new girlfriend to stay at the weekend, you see.'

Amanda raised her eyebrows in mock surprise. 'What did you do – cover them in barbecue sauce and spit-roast them?'

Tom grinned. 'Not quite – although my cousin's girlfriend is pretty tasty.'

'Please tell me you didn't have one of your blow-outs,' Amanda said, pressing her palms together as if she were praying.

'I'm afraid I did,' Tom admitted. 'I don't know what came over me. I just lost all self-control.'

Amanda sighed. 'I think you'd better tell us exactly what happened.'

'We went to an Indian restaurant on Saturday night,' Tom began. 'I had no intention of over-indulging. I'd decided what I was going to have before we'd even got there.'

'Which was?' Amanda asked.

'Vegetable balti, plain boiled rice and some sparkling mineral water. I'd even promised myself I wasn't going to touch the after-dinner mint.'

'So what went wrong?'

Tom's eyes flickered from side to side as if he were reliving the evening in question. 'I made the mistake of looking at the menu and once I saw all the delicious things on it my willpower went straight out the window. Before I knew what I was doing I was ordering chicken vindaloo and peshwari naan and aloo ghobi and two portions of rice – one pilau, one saffron – as well as a bhaji platter to start.'

Amanda's hand went to her mouth as if she were about to gag or vomit. 'Did you eat all of it?'

'Yes, every last mouthful . . . and I had four pints of lager.'

'Oh, Tom!' Amanda cried in disgust.

'Mind you, I paid the price for it later,' Tom said, rubbing a hand across his ample belly. 'I had shocking wind all night. Seriously, I kept waking myself up – it was that bad.'

'Too much information, thank you, Tom,' Amanda snapped.

Tom smacked his brow with his hand. 'I feel so ashamed of myself.'

'You should do. You've ruined all those weeks of hard work with half an hour of sheer gluttony.' Amanda's brow corrugated. 'I can't tell you how disappointed I am.'

Tom looked at her with his heavy-lidded, slow-blinking eyes. 'It won't happen again,' he said. 'I promise.'

'It better hadn't,' Amanda said menacingly. 'Or you'll have me to answer to.' She took a couple of steps back and surveyed her volunteers. 'So, here's the scenario. You two are at a party . . . let's say a housewarming for the sake of argument. Tom, you're the host.' She gestured to the tray. 'Imagine this is laden with delicious canapés that you've spent hours preparing.'

'But I can't cook to save my life,' Tom said. 'I'm not even sure I know what a canapé is.'

'I said *imagine*, didn't I?' Amanda replied, in a tone that indicated her patience was wearing thin. 'Holly's one of your guests and in a moment you're going to approach her and offer her something to eat. Remember, you've spent a lot of time making these canapés and you're keen to impress Holly with your culinary abilities because you've fancied her for ages. I want you to do everything in your power to convince her to try one.' She turned to her second volunteer. 'The problem is Holly's on a diet and she can see that these canapés are packed with high-calorie ingredients, so the challenge for her is to refuse them in the politest way she can. So, are you both ready?'

'I am,' said Holly, who was just desperate for the whole thing to be over.

Tom, apparently, was also ready because all at once he started shimmying towards her, his man boobs jiggling grotesquely as he wove his way between imaginary guests with the tray held aloft in one hand.

He thrust the tray under Holly's nose. 'Hello, love, fancy a nibble?' he said, with a wolfish smile.

'No, thank you,' Holly replied through gritted teeth. 'I'm watching my weight.'

'But I've been at it all night.' Tom winked broadly. 'God knows how I've found the time to make these canapés as well.'

Holly suppressed a shudder. 'They look delicious, but I mustn't, really.'

Tom stared at her breasts. 'I don't know why you're worried about losing weight. You look gorgeous tonight; that dress really brings out the blue in your eyes.' He moved closer, treating her to a blast of his sour breath. 'How are you anyway? It's been ages.'

'Fine, thank you,' she said tightly.

'Are you seeing anyone at the moment?' Tom asked.

Holly frowned. 'I've got a boyfriend, Tom, you know that.'

'It's role play, remember,' he stage-whispered. 'Just go with the flow.'

Holly sighed. 'Okay, then . . . no, I'm not seeing any-one. Is that what you want me to say?'

'Good,' he replied as he reached out and brushed a stray strand of hair away from her forehead with one of his sausagey fingers. 'In that case, perhaps you and I could have dinner one evening next week. You could come to my house.' His bottom lip convulsed. 'If you're really good, you could even stay the night.'

Holly looked away, repelled by the vampiric excitement in his voice. 'Is this really necessary?' she asked Amanda. 'Only I don't see what it's got to do with losing weight.'

Amanda shook her head. 'I'm sorry, Holly. Tom often gets carried away during role play.'

'I was only trying to set the scene,' Tom said in a wounded voice.

'Fair enough, but we haven't got all night,' Amanda told him. 'Let's get back to the canapés, okay?'

Over the course of the next five minutes, Tom tried a variety of tactics – including charm, bribery and, finally, begging – as he tried to weaken Holly's resolve. She found it surprisingly easy to rebuff him but eventually, keen to bring the role play to an end, she gave in.

'Oh, go on, then,' she said to Tom, who by this stage was on his knees in front of her. 'I don't suppose one little bruschetta will hurt.'

'Oh, Holly!' Amanda exclaimed. 'You were doing so well up to then.'

Holly shrugged. 'Yeah, well, I'm afraid Tom was just too persuasive.' She shifted from foot to foot, painfully conscious of the dark flowers of perspiration blooming at the armholes of her T-shirt. 'Can I sit down now?'

'In a *minute*,' Amanda said, as if Holly were a child demanding ice cream. 'Now that you've demonstrated to everyone just how hard it is to refuse an offer of food, I need to tell you what I would've done in those circumstances. She looked around smugly, as if she were about to reveal next week's winning lottery numbers. 'Rather than engaging in a pointless and time-consuming battle of wills with my host, I would have helped myself to one of the canapés – nothing deep-fried, mind – taken a bite and told my host how delicious it was. Then, the minute he had moved on to the next guest. I would've wrapped the rest of the canapé in a tissue and discreetly slipped it into my handbag or pocket, before disposing of it at the earliest possible opportunity. No embarrassment, no fuss, no offence.' She flashed an insincere smile at Holly. 'See how easy it is when you know how.'

Holly knew she was supposed to smile and nod and say thank you, Amanda, for that *fascinating* tip, before beetling back to her seat, flushed with excitement at the prospect of a shiny new weapon in her weight-loss armoury. But, instead, she stayed right where she was. 'That technique would never work for me,' she said, folding her arms across her chest.

'What are you talking about?' Amanda said, in a voice heavy with weary exasperation.

'I couldn't take one bite of something, then throw it away,' Holly explained. 'Once I'd tasted it, I'd have to eat the whole thing.'

Amanda's eyes narrowed. 'Are you *trying* to be awkward?'

'No,' Holly said indignantly. 'I'm just being honest. It's the same when I'm at home. I can't just eat one biscuit – I have to eat the whole packet. I've tried all sorts of things to stop myself. Once, I even threw half a chocolate cake in the bin to stop myself finishing it off.'

'Did it work?'

Holly shook her head. 'Half an hour later, I was slipping on a rubber glove and fishing it out.'

Amanda looked horrified. 'Did you eat it?'

'Of course I did.'

Naomi gave a grunt of recognition from the back row. 'I've done the same thing,' she said. 'More times than I care to remember.'

'Me too,' admitted a shiny-faced woman sitting a few feet away. 'Last week I ate a fondant fancy covered in tea leaves.'

Amanda shook her head in benign reproof. 'The depths you people will sink to never ceases to amaze me,' she said. 'But don't worry. I have a technique that will help you. It's very simple, but surprisingly effective.' She bent down and rummaged in her handbag for a few moments, before finally pulling out an elastic hair bobble. 'Hold out your hand, Holly,' she said.

'Why?' Holly said warily. 'What are you going to do to me?'

Amanda's lips twitched in displeasure. 'I wish you wouldn't keep questioning me, Holly. You should know by now that I would never do anything that wasn't in your best interests.'

'Sorry,' Holly mumbled. She held out her hand and watched, mystified, as Amanda slipped the hair bobble over her fingers and on to her wrist.

'Okay, Holly, next time you feel the urge to go foraging in the dustbin for food, I want you to do this.' Amanda took hold of the pink plastic daisy on the bobble and pulled it hard, so that the elastic snapped painfully against the soft underside of Holly's wrist.

'Ouch!' Holly said, pulling her hand away sharply. 'How on earth is that supposed to help me?'

'It's a kind of aversion therapy. Behavioural therapists use it all the time,' Amanda said loftily. 'Think of it as a milder form of an electric shock.'

Frowning, Holly tore the elastic off her wrist and held it out to Amanda.

'Keep it, I think you need it more than I do,' Amanda said. 'Thank you, Holly, you can sit down now.' Her eyes glittered dangerously. 'Now, everyone, I have some very exciting news. You may remember that a little while ago I asked you to keep the weekend after next free, so I could unleash my secret weapon for helping us to victory at the Slimmer of the Year Awards.'

'Ooh yes,' Adele said. 'I've been dying to know what it is.'

'I'm taking you all off to a boot camp,' Amanda said with a cruel smile. 'It's run by a good friend of mine, a former Royal Marine. He's designed a special programme of activities, just for us – and, be warned, he takes no prisoners.'

Kate buried her face in her hands. 'Please tell me she's joking,' she muttered.

'She looks deadly serious to me,' Naomi replied under her breath.

'Joe's going to put you all through an intensive two-day exercise and diet programme,' Amanda went on. 'By the end of it you should all have lost a minimum of four pounds.'

'Is this going to cost us anything?' Tom asked.

Amanda threw a hand in the air. 'Not a penny. Joe owes me a favour; he's doing it for nothing.'

'And where exactly is this boot camp?' Holly asked.

'Dartmoor,' Amanda replied gleefully. 'We really will be miles from anywhere.'

'There's no doubt about it, the woman's a sadist,' Holly said as she joined the others in the queue for refreshments. 'First she tortures me with an elastic band, then she announces she's packing us all off to train with the flaming SAS in some godforsaken wilderness. If she behaves like that in public, just imagine what she gets up to in the privacy of her own home.'

Kate chuckled. 'I must say Tom certainly seemed to be enjoying the role play. He was like a dog with a bone. At one point I thought he was going to jump up and lick your face.'

Holly shuddered. 'I can't believe he asked me out.'

'And the scary thing is he probably thinks he's in with a chance,' Naomi said as she poured herself a cup of tea. She winked at Holly. 'Are you sure you're not tempted?'

'Absolutely no way; for one thing, I find him physically repulsive.' Holly paused and smiled shyly. 'For another, I'm engaged to be married.'

Naomi gasped. 'You've said yes?'

Holly nodded. 'I told Rob on Friday night. He's absolutely over the moon; we both are.'

'What was the deciding factor?' Kate asked as they carried their drinks to a quiet corner of the room.

Holly shrugged. 'I don't know. All of a sudden it just seemed to make sense. I love him, he loves me; I really don't know why I just didn't say yes straight away.'

'Oh well, so long as you're sure,' Kate said, observing Holly over the top of her coffee cup. 'So when's the big day?'

'Rob doesn't want a long engagement; he reckons we should do it in the spring.' Holly turned to Naomi. 'I've already told him I know a brilliant photographer.'

Naomi smiled. 'I'd be happy to show you two my portfolio sometime and, if you need any suggestions for a venue, I've visited pretty much every licensed hotel, stately home and Grade II listed folly within a twenty-mile radius.'

'I'd love to hear your suggestions,' Holly replied. 'And in the meantime you must both come to my engagement party.' She reached into the little felt bag that was slung across her chest and produced two cream vellum envelopes. 'It's next weekend, a lunch-time do; I really hope you can come,' she said, handing them the invitations. 'Rob's managed to persuade his mum to let us have it at her place. She lives in a fabulous converted schoolhouse with a massive garden; it's where Rob grew up. Apparently, Diana fought tooth and nail to keep it as part of her divorce settlement.'

'She must be really excited about the wedding,' Naomi said.

'You know, I'm not sure that she is.'

Kate frowned. 'What do you mean?'

'When Rob and I went round at the weekend to tell her we'd got engaged, she didn't exactly seem thrilled. She made all the right noises, but underneath it all she sounded almost, I don't know, *disappointed*, which is surprising because I've always thought she liked me.'

'I expect she's just struggling to adjust to the fact she's going to have to give Rob over permanently to the new woman in his life,' Kate said. 'You did say they were very close.'

'I'm sure Kate's right,' Naomi said staunchly. 'Diana

must need her head examining if she thinks she can improve on you as a daughter-in-law.'

Holly smiled. 'Thanks for the vote of confidence, ladies – and please say you'll come to the party.'

Naomi smiled. 'Try and stop us.'

Chapter Eleven

It was a Saturday morning and Kate was giving the sitting room a long overdue spring clean. On the bookcase, a bunch of sunflowers was quietly wilting. Half their petals had dropped and now lay scattered around the vase like a rebuke. Pushing them aside, she drew a cloth across a line of books, watching as motes of dust rose up and drifted lazily through the room's muted yellow light. It was weeks since she'd done any housework. That was another benefit of living alone, she'd discovered – there was no one to bear witness to her occasional slovenliness.

As she cleaned, Kate reflected on the events of Tuesday evening. She was surprised at how much she'd enjoyed the Fat Chance meeting – an enjoyment that was due in large part to her new friends, Holly and Naomi. Normally, she didn't care for conspiratorial, female conversation – the sort where confidences were shared and relationships dissected. Its assumption of mutual preoccupations was usually unfounded in her experience, its intimacies almost always the trapdoor to some future falling out. But for some reason she couldn't quite fathom, it was different with these women.

She was reaching up on tiptoes to dust the top shelf of the bookcase when she heard the sound of the doorbell. Annoyed at the interruption, Kate went to the window and saw that there was a man standing outside. He wasn't very old – twenty-five or twenty-six at most – and standing next to him was a child – a wan little thing with stringy blonde hair. Then Kate noticed the man was carrying a suitcase, which made her think he must be selling something. She'd had people like that round to the house before – young men flogging tea towels that ran in the wash, and ill-fitting ironing-board covers. No doubt the child made a useful accessory – something to tug at housewives' heart-strings and make them spend more than they'd planned to. Kate decided she wouldn't answer the door, but just then the man turned his head and saw her peering through the window. Sighing, she threw down her duster and went to the door.

'Can I help you?' she asked the man, in a tone designed to let him know she was someone whose emotions could not be easily manipulated, especially by a child.

'Professor Kate Pendleton?' he said, sounding rather grave.

Kate felt a prickle of concern. 'Yes,' she said..

He set the suitcase down on the ground. 'My name's James Aldridge. We've never met, but we're related . . . sort of.'

'Oh?' Kate said in surprise, thinking that she and the man – who was tall and thin with pale eyes and a beaky nose – bore absolutely no physical resemblance whatsoever.

'Not by blood, by marriage,' he added, as if reading her thoughts.

Kate waited for further explication, but none was forthcoming.

'This is my niece,' the man said, turning to the little girl. 'Her mum's just passed away.'

'Oh dear, I *am* sorry,' Kate said, her creased brow registering an appropriate level of concern.

The man rubbed the end of his nose. 'She only went in to have her gallbladder removed, but something went wrong and she bled to death on the operating table.'

Kate shuddered and glanced at the little girl, who was staring fixedly at her scuffed red sandals. 'How awful,' she murmured.

The man laid a hand on the child's head. 'I've been looking after this little one ever since, but I just can't manage any more. I'm a single bloke, living in a one-bedroom flat. A girl of her age needs her own room. *And* it's the school holidays, which means I've had to take time off work to look after her.' Kate frowned, unable to see what all this had to do with her. 'I'm sorry, *how* did you say we were related?'

'It's complicated,' he replied, looking off to the side.

'But, basically, you're her next of kin. That's why I've brought her here; she's your responsibility now.'

Kate laughed. 'Next of kin? I think you must be mistaken. I don't know any Aldridges. You must have me confused with someone else.'

The man gave a half-hearted smile. 'Look, it's only a temporary thing – just for a few weeks, until Social Services can find her a foster home. If I could carry on looking after her myself, I would, but it's impossible. I need to get back to work and start earning some money.'

'Is this some kind of scam?' Kate asked caustically.

He sighed and shook his head again. 'I've brought some of her things,' he said, gesturing to the suitcase. 'Clothes and a few toys, just to tide her over. I can keep the rest of her stuff at my place for the time being.'

Kate took a step back and half closed the door. 'This is ludicrous. I can't help you, I'm sorry. Now please go away.'

He pulled a crumpled envelope from the pocket of his denim jacket. 'I don't have time to go through all the whys and wherefores – they're expecting me at work in half an hour – but this letter will explain everything.' He reached an arm through the crack in the door and set the envelope down on top of a radiator cover. 'I've given you my mobile number as well, so you can get in touch with me in case of emergency.'

Kate looked at him in disbelief. 'What do you mean, *in case of emergency*?'

Ignoring her, the man bent down and kissed the child on the cheek. 'Now you be good for the nice lady, sweetheart, and I'll see you very soon.'

The little girl blinked hard several times as if she were trying not to cry. Then, to Kate's abject horror, the man began walking away.

'Hang on, you can't just leave her here!' she cried, indignation turning to outrage. 'I don't know anything about children, and *you* don't know anything about me. How do you know I'm fit to look after a child?'

'I'm sure you'll do a better job than me,' he said gloomily, unlatching the garden gate. 'I'll call Social Services first thing on Monday morning and let them know you've agreed to look after her. I expect they'll be in touch soon.'

'I've agreed to no such thing!' Kate shrieked as she watched him unlock an old Fiat parked at the side of the road. When he didn't reply, she began marching down the path towards him, even though she wasn't wearing any shoes. 'Come back! Come back here right now!' Her voice was drowned out by the roar of the Fiat's engine.

'I don't even know her name!' she yelled as the car accelerated away at speed.

'Freya,' came a tiny, cheeping voice from behind her. 'My name's Freya.'

Kate clapped her hands to her head, scarcely able to believe what had just taken place. As the Fiat disappeared round a bend in the road, she walked back up the path. 'Well then, Freya,' she said crossly. 'I suppose you'd better come in.'

Kate's insides were churning as she led the girl into the sitting room, her emotions a bitter brew of impotent anger, disbelief and fear. She knew nothing about children. Beth, her sister, had a couple of boys, nearly teenagers now, whom she saw half a dozen times a year. She enjoyed spending time with them – they could be quite amusing at times – but that wasn't to say she *understood* them. Nor had she ever looked after them for more than a single afternoon at a stretch. This was something quite different; this was her worst nightmare brought to life.

She gestured to a battered leather pouffe that Huw had used as a footstool. 'Why don't you sit there, Freya?' The child did as she was told. 'Do you know what's going on?' Kate said, squatting down so she and the girl were at eye level.

Freya shook her head.

'That makes two of us,' Kate said, sighing. 'But don't worry. We'll soon have you back where you belong . . . wherever *that* is.'

'Okay,' Freya cheeped.

'Are you hungry? Can I get you something to eat?'

'Biscuits?' Freya enquired hopefully. 'Chocolate ones.'

'I'm afraid I haven't got any chocolate biscuits, but I think I have some Garibaldi,' Kate replied.

Freya looked confused.

'Squashed-fly biscuits,' Kate said, remembering what her nephews used to call them.

Freya made no refusal, but Kate saw the way her freckled nose wrinkled in disgust.

'No? How about a packet of crisps instead?'

Freya nodded enthusiastically.

'I've only got ready salted. Will that do you?'

Freya gave a little shrug by way of a 'yes'.

In the sanctuary of the kitchen, Kate took a few deep breaths. How on earth had she allowed this to happen? What sort of man would leave his niece with a complete stranger? Only a lunatic, surely. Never mind, she comforted herself, as soon as the child was fed and watered, she would call the police and let them deal with it. She opened a packet of crisps, shook half of them into a bowl, and poured some milk into a tall glass. She heard the sound of voices and hurried back to the sitting room, only to discover Freya had made herself at home and was watching *The Simpsons* on TV. Considering that she'd just lost her mother and then been summarily abandoned by her uncle, she seemed remarkably unruffled.

'Thank you,' she said as Kate set the crisps and milk down on the coffee table. Kate watched as she began eating the crisps, not cramming them into her mouth greedily as her nephews would have done, but eating them daintily, one by one, waiting until her mouth was empty before inserting the next crisp. There was something familiar about her, something about the determined set of her jaw, that reminded Kate of somebody. Perhaps they were related after all. Hopefully the letter would shed some light on the matter.

Kate went out into the hall and retrieved the envelope from the radiator cover. James Aldridge had written her full name and title on the front in sloping capitals. She carried it back to the sitting room, where Freya was still staring raptly at the TV.

'Right, then,' she muttered. 'Let's see what your uncle's got to say for himself, shall we?'

The envelope contained two sheets of lined paper, torn from a spiral-bound pad.

Dear Professor Pendleton, it began. *I hope you're sitting down, because what I'm about to say is probably going to come as a bit of a shock.*

Frowning, Kate pushed her glasses further up her nose.

First the basics, the letter continued. *The child in your care is called Freya Aldridge. She's seven years old and she's the daughter of my sister, Jennifer Aldridge, who died earlier this month. Before she died, my sister had been single for a long time. In fact, to the best of my knowledge, she only had one long-term relationship – and that was with Freya's dad. I never met him myself. Jenny and I weren't that close, you see. We never really confided in each other about stuff, so I'm a bit hazy on the details, but I'm pretty sure they split up before Freya was born.*

From conversations I had with my mum, I got the impression he was the one who broke it off. Afterwards, Jenny told him she didn't want him involved in Freya's life. She wouldn't even let him pay child support. That was typical Jenny — always cutting off her nose to spite her face — because she wasn't very well off and I'm sure the money would have come in handy.

As she reached the end of the page, Kate looked up to check on Freya, who had now finished her crisps and was drinking her milk, clutching the glass in both hands as she took delicate sips. Kate turned over the page and carried on reading.

After Jenny died, Freya came to live with me. There wasn't really anywhere else for her to go. My dad's dead and Mum's got Alzheimer's — she went into a council nursing home a couple of years ago. All my other relatives live up in Scotland. Freya's a great kid, but looking after her on my own has been really stressful. I try not to snap at her, but sometimes I can't help it. I realized pretty early on that I wasn't going to be able to look after her permanently. I called Social Services, but they said it was going to take them a while to sort out foster care. Then I had a thought. What about Freya's dad? I knew he and Jenny had parted on bad terms, but if he knew what had happened I reckoned he would want to do his bit. I didn't know much about him, I didn't even know his surname, but eventually I found his contact details in one of Jenny's old address books. Just out of curiosity, I googled him. That's when I found his obituary in an online architectural journal.

Something swayed and lurched in Kate's gut. She

looked up abruptly. Her heart felt like a helium balloon, rising away from her feet, which, in turn, had relinquished their relationship with the floor.

This can*not* be happening, she told herself. Reluctantly, she turned her eyes back to the page.

As you may have guessed by now, Freya's dad is Huw Pendleton. Your husband.

Kate gave a sharp intake of breath, causing Freya to glance over her shoulder. Suddenly, Kate knew why the child looked familiar. The defiant chin, the look of stoic determination – she'd seen the selfsame expression on Huw's face hundreds of times. The realization made her feel like vomiting.

'It's all right, Freya,' she said, forcing herself to smile. 'You get back to your cartoon.'

There was only one paragraph of the letter remaining.

The obituary mentioned you too. It said you'd been married to Huw for nine years. I must admit I did suspect Freya's dad was already married when he was seeing Jenny – my mum hinted at it once or twice. I don't know if you knew about your husband's affair or Freya's existence, but I'm guessing not. If this is the case, I'm sorry to be the one to have to tell you. I suppose I should explain all this to you in person, but I'm not brave enough. I'm sorry too for dumping Freya on you without any advance warning. I didn't think you'd agree to look after her otherwise. The thing is, Huw was Freya's dad and now that he's dead you're the closest thing she has to family – after me, of

course. This is only for a couple of weeks, I promise, just until
Social Services find her a permanent home. If I were you, I'd give
them a call on Monday, just to introduce yourself. Once they
know you're a professor, I'm sure they'll pull their finger out.
Anyway, I think that's everything. Freya's a good girl. I'm sure
you two will get along just fine.

  Yours sincerely,
  James Aldridge

Kate put her hand to her mouth. She felt as if she'd
swallowed drain cleaner. Everything inside her *burned*.

'What does it say?' a small voice piped up.

Kate looked up and saw that Freya was staring at
her. For a moment she couldn't speak. A fist was pushing into her windpipe, right at the base of her throat,
where the collarbones meet. Her mind was suddenly
ambushed by questions, which jostled feverishly for
position, like over-eager undergraduates in a seminar,
shooting up their hands. How did Huw meet this Jennifer Aldridge? Did their relationship last for months
– or, as James had intimated in the letter, *years*? What
had prompted their break-up? Guilt? Boredom? The
pregnancy? But the most pressing question of all was
how could a woman like Kate – a highly intelligent
woman, a woman who'd won awards and accolades –
not have realized her husband was having an affair? In
the space of a few seconds, the infinitely precious,
infinitely fragile memories Kate had of her marriage
had begun to shrink and deflate. She could almost feel

them shrivelling and collapsing around her. Realizing that Freya was still waiting for an answer, she cleared her clotted throat. 'It turns out we are related after all,' she said tightly. 'How about that?'

Freya looked at her uncertainly. 'Are you my new mummy?'

Kate felt a stab of irritation at the child's guileless-ness. What was she going to do? She couldn't very well call the police now. She couldn't bear the humiliation of having to admit her husband's indiscretion.

'No, I'm not,' she said. 'But it looks like I'm going to be looking after you until your new mummy can come and pick you up.'

Freya frowned. 'When will that be?'

'Very soon, I hope.' Kate rubbed the bridge of her nose. She could feel a pressure, a dry black puff, behind her eyes. She was supposed to be going to the theatre with some friends from the university tonight. She would have to find some excuse to cancel. All at once, she found that she couldn't see properly. The tears in her eyes were making the room wobble and shimmer. She took a shallow breath.

'I'll be back in a minute,' she told Freya. 'Be a good girl and finish your milk.'

In the downstairs cloakroom, Kate stared at her reflection in the mirror. Her face was blotchy, scared-looking, pixillated with stress. *How could he do it?* she asked herself. How could he cheat on her — and how could she not have suspected a thing? As her mind flashed back to the times Huw had claimed to be entertaining clients, away on business trips or riding his motorbike, she realized with a sickening jolt that he'd had ample opportunity to pursue other women. She'd loved the way they'd both maintained their independence and enjoyed solo activities, but now she felt foolish, remembering how she'd proudly told their friends this was what kept their marriage so vibrant.

Now, she realized she'd been deluding herself, for it was this very freedom that had allowed Huw to conduct an affair right under her nose. A ragged sob escaped from her mouth as it occurred to her that Jennifer Aldridge might not be the only one. For several minutes, she stood there, gripping the sides of the sink and staring into space. She felt as if all the blood were draining out of her, to be replaced, slowly, by an icy nausea. She splashed her face with cold water and patted it dry with a towel.

Get a grip, Kate, she ordered herself. *Don't lose control.* She went back into the hall and stuck her head round the door of the sitting room, where Freya was still engrossed in *The Simpsons*. 'I'm just popping upstairs,' she said in a thick voice. 'I won't be long.'

'Okay,' Freya said, without turning round.

The obvious place to look for evidence was Huw's home office. In the immediate aftermath of his death, Kate had spent quite a bit of time in the cosy attic room. Huw had chosen everything – the reclaimed maple floorboards, the abstract artwork, the stylish retro furniture – and Kate had fancied she could still feel his presence as she lay on the leather ottoman under the eaves, crying and remembering and crying some more. It was a while since she'd ventured up there, and now, as she pushed open the door, she experienced a physical chill on her skin, an involuntary tensing of shoulders and jaw. Everything in the room was just as it was on the day of the accident. She hadn't moved a thing, not wanting to destroy whatever vestiges of Huw's spirit still remained. The desk was littered with Post-It notes bearing scrawled phone numbers and reminders, and on the drawing board lay a half-finished sketch of Huw's final design project, a Methodist chapel conversion in the East End of London. Even his pile of motorcycle magazines lay untouched and the wall calendar was still turned to the month of his death.

In a fervour, with the urgent sense that if she wasn't occupied she would fall apart, Kate began hunting for confirmation of her husband's infidelity, pulling open drawers, flicking through his diaries, his Rolodex, his old credit-card statements. She was convinced she'd find some clue – a hotel bill, a receipt for flowers she hadn't received, a love letter even – but there was nothing.

After a fruitless half hour of searching, Kate flopped down on the Arne Jacobsen egg chair that had been

Huw's pride and joy. He'd bought a matching pair when he set up the business – one for the London office, one for home. They were originals, not reproductions, he'd informed her proudly. She'd almost choked on her cup of coffee when he told her how much they cost. As she sat there, musing on her failure as a wife *and* an amateur detective, she noticed Huw's laptop lying on the desk. She turned it on, groaning out loud as a password prompt appeared on the screen. They'd never been one of those couples that routinely accessed each other's computer files, so she had no idea what Huw's password was. After thinking for a moment, she keyed in his mother's maiden name. It was rejected. She hazarded a second guess, and then a third. Both were similarly unsuccessful. Kate chewed her thumbnail in frustration, realizing she'd hit a dead end.

By the time she returned to the sitting room *The Simpsons* had finished and Freya was flicking through the channels at great speed.

'Don't do that,' Kate said, snatching the remote from her hand and switching the TV off. She went to the Victorian drinks cabinet in the corner of the room. Huw had bought it at auction the year they got married and over the years it had been well used and well loved. In a funny sort of way, it had reminded her of him: handsome, practical, honest. She flung open one of the cabinet's glazed doors and removed a bottle of Scotch and a heavy crystal tumbler. After pouring herself a generous measure, sloshing it clumsily into the glass, so it splashed on to the pretty rug she and Huw had bought on an anniversary trip to Morocco, she sank into the leather recliner. She felt lost in it, dwarfed, as if her feet might no longer reach the floor.

For several minutes, she just sat there, staring at Freya, who had now turned her attention to the pile of magazines that were stacked under the coffee table. What was she going to do with this child . . . this *creature* . . . this cuckoo in her nest? On impulse, she picked up the phone and dialled the mobile number James Aldridge had scrawled at the bottom of the letter. It went straight to voicemail, so she left him a message, demanding he call her back right away. Why should she be the one to waste her precious time and energy liaising with Social Services when it was his wretched sister who had created this godawful mess by being so perilously fertile? Hadn't the stupid woman heard of birth control – or had she fallen pregnant deliberately, in an attempt to lure Huw away permanently? Kate wasn't going to look after her grubby offspring, not even for an evening. She *couldn't*.

The next morning, Kate woke with a numbness cauterizing her left arm from shoulder to elbow, as if an invisible body had been pressing against it all night. She rolled over to relieve the pressure, smiling as she remembered what day it was. Sunday was her favourite day of the week. It always began with a long leisurely lie-in, accompanied by Radio 4, and was followed by brunch and the newspapers at the kitchen table. Afterwards, she'd shower and dress before settling down to do a few hours' work on the papers she was writing for various academic journals. By then it would be late afternoon – time to pour herself a large glass of wine and start preparing her evening meal which, tradition decreed, was either a steak, cooked rare, or a nice piece of fish.

Kate raised her head a few inches and groped for the radio on her bedside table. That was when she noticed a small figure sitting on the high-backed wicker chair in the corner of the room, hugging a pink paisley cushion as if it were a stuffed toy. All at once, the events of yesterday came flooding back to Kate like a bad dream.

'Shit, Freya,' she said, sitting up abruptly. 'How long have you been sitting there?'

The little girl pursed her lips primly. 'It's rude to swear.'

Kate frowned. 'And it's rude to walk into other people's rooms without knocking. 'What are you doing here anyway?'

'I was scared.'

'Scared of what? Not the dark, surely. I left the landing light on for you.'

'Monsters.'

'Monsters are an entirely fictional construct.'

The little girl's forehead creased in confusion.

Kate sighed. 'It means they don't exist.'

'Oh,' Freya said, looking strangely disappointed. She gave a little shiver. 'I'm cold. Can I get in with you?'

'Get in where?'

Freya pointed to the bed. 'In there.'

Frowning, Kate drew the duvet up under her chin. 'I don't think that's a good idea.'

'Why not?'

'I just don't,' Kate snapped. She pointed to her dressing gown, which was hanging on the back of the door. 'You can put that on if you're cold.'

Still holding the cushion, Freya went over to the door and stretched her arm upwards. 'Can't reach,' she said forlornly.

Sighing, Kate flung back the duvet and got out of bed. She yanked the dressing gown off its hook, then held it out so Freya could put her arms through the sleeves. The dressing gown was knee-length on Kate, but reached past Freya's feet.

'There you go,' she said as she passed the belt twice round the child's waist, before tying it in a knot at the front. 'Warmer now?'

Freya nodded. 'What are we going to do today?' she asked.

'I don't know,' Kate replied. 'What would you like to do?'

'Feed the ducks?' Freya said, her voice going up at the end in a question.

Kate bit her lip, trying to think if there was anything she would like to do *less* than drive five miles to the nearest park in order to toss stale crusts at some mangy wildlife. She quickly came to the conclusion that there wasn't.

'Actually,' she said, thinking longingly of the *Sunday Times* lying on the doormat. 'I've got a few things to do today . . . grown-up things. I think we might have to stay indoors. I expect there'll be something on TV you can watch.'

Freya's narrow shoulders sagged. 'Okay,' she said in a voice that was barely above a whisper.

Kate felt a sudden wave of sympathy. The poor child *had* just lost her mother. She should be offering words of comfort and a maternal bosom, but it was hard to think about someone else's feelings when her heart felt as if it had been passed through a mangle. To make matters worse, James Aldridge still hadn't returned her phone call, even though she'd left several messages. Still, she reminded herself, that was hardly the child's fault.

She gave Freya's arm a little squeeze. 'I'm ever so sorry about your mum,' she said. 'And I'm sorry you're having to stay with me when we don't even know each other. But I'm going to have you on your way just as soon as I can, I promise.'

Freya blinked, her blue eyes glowing in the pale landscape of her face.

'Right then!' Kate said in the jolly tone of a children's TV presenter. 'Let's go downstairs and get some breakfast, shall we?'

Chapter Twelve

Naomi spotted Toby the minute she walked into the room. He was sitting at the bar, nibbling olives and flipping through the pages of a broadsheet. She hovered by the door for a few moments, glad of the opportunity to observe him covertly. He was wearing a pale blue suit, suede loafers and a crisp, white open-necked shirt. On his wrist she could see the glint of a gold watch. Even from a distance, he exuded confidence, wealth, charisma. Smiling, she smoothed her skirt over her hips and started walking towards him. The minute he saw her, Toby jumped down from his bar stool and opened his arms wide.

'Naomi, how wonderful to see you again,' he said, taking her in his arms and kissing her on both cheeks. 'I've been so looking forward to tonight. I haven't been able to stop thinking about you since our evening at Denholm House.' The words tripped off his tongue effortlessly. He showed no hint of insincerity or self-consciousness. Naomi could tell he was a man well versed in the art of compliment-giving. This was what had been missing from her relationship with Christopher, she realized – the sense that she was, at least for the time they were together, the most important person in the world.

She smiled, basking in his flattery. 'I've been looking forward to it too,' she said.

She wasn't lying either. In fact, she had such a good feeling about him that she hadn't bothered to respond to any of the dozens of emails that had flooded her strangersinthenight inbox.

'Would you like a drink, or shall we just go straight to dinner?' he asked her.

'Dinner, please,' Naomi replied. 'I'm starving.'

'That's what I like to hear,' Toby said, curling his hand round her waist. 'My car's just outside.'

Naomi looked at him in surprise. 'Aren't we eating at the hotel?'

'No, I've booked a Chinese restaurant a few minutes' drive away. Is that all right?'

'Absolutely,' she replied. 'I love Chinese food.'

As they exited the hotel, Naomi couldn't help feeling a twinge of disappointment. She'd assumed they'd be dining in the hotel's much-lauded Michelin-starred restaurant and had gone without lunch in anticipation. She'd even looked at the menu on the hotel's website and picked out what she was going to have: cauliflower soup with truffle oil to start, followed by a salad of seared duck breast with pomegranate. Determined not to exceed the daily calorie count set out in her Fat Chance healthy eating plan, she would allow herself one small glass of Pouilly-Fumé and absolutely, positively, no dessert. Still, she gently scolded herself, there was no point sulking – that was what wives did, not mistresses. In any case, if tonight went well, there would be plenty of opportunity for lavish dinners in the future.

She brightened as Toby led the way towards a gleaming silver Jaguar with a personalized registration. After unlocking the vehicle, he chivalrously opened the passenger door first and waited for Naomi to ease herself into the cream leather seat. As he closed the door, she gave a contented little sigh that said *I could get used to this*.

'What a beautiful car,' she said, as he slid into the driver's seat.

'Oh, this is just my little runaround,' he replied, accelerating smoothly away. 'If you and I get to know each other better, I'll take you for a ride in the Aston. It's an amazing experience, especially with the top down.'

Naomi tossed her hair back. 'I'll hold you to that.'

'I must say you're looking stunning tonight,' Toby remarked, throwing a sideways glance at her. 'The blue of that blouse really brings out the colour of your eyes.'

'Thank you,' she said, feeling herself grow pink with pleasure.

'I appreciate femininity,' he added. 'I can't bear those women who live in jeans and trainers.'

'And I like to *feel* feminine,' Naomi replied. 'I wouldn't be seen dead in trainers, outside of the gym.'

'In that case, we're a match made in heaven, although . . .' He turned as they stopped at some traffic lights and subjected her to a more lingering appraisal. 'You look as if you've lost weight since the last time I saw you.'

'I have,' Naomi said, registering the faintly accusatory tone in his voice. 'Another three pounds. I'm amazed you can tell the difference.'

'Your face looks thinner,' he said. 'To be honest, I don't think it suits you.'

Naomi frowned. None of her previous lovers had complained when she lost weight. 'But I feel so much better,' she said. 'My slimming-club leader's delighted with my progress.'

Toby made a guttural sound of disapproval. 'Those slimming clubs are a waste of time, if you ask me. People always end up putting the weight back on again.'

Naomi was about to say that, actually, she had no intention of putting the weight back on, when Toby pointed up ahead. 'This is it,' he said as he pulled into a parking bay at the side of the road.

Noami's heart sank when she saw the restaurant. Brightly lit, inside and out, it was sandwiched between a newsagent's and a launderette, and a garish poster in the window advertised an all-you-can-eat special.

'I know it doesn't look much, but the food's top-notch,' said Toby, as if he'd read her mind.

'You've been here before, then?' Naomi said.

'Oh yes, it's one of my favourite haunts,' he said, his lips twitching gently upward, towards a smile.

Naomi frowned. 'Do you bring your wife here?'

'God no, Felicity doesn't eat anything that's not macrobiotic, organic and preferably raw,' he replied witheringly.

'Ah,' said Naomi, extrapolating that this then was where he brought his mistresses.

As they walked through the restaurant's PVC door, they were greeted by a grinning waiter, who clearly recognized Toby, pumping his hand vigorously, before leading them to a table next to a large tropical-fish tank. The laminated menus were already on the table, propped up against a vase of artificial flowers, but when Naomi went to pick hers up, Toby whisked it away. 'Let's have the buffet, shall we?' he said. 'That way we get to try a bit of everything.'

Naomi shrugged. 'Sure.'

The waiter came to take their drinks order and then Toby excused himself to go to the bathroom. While he was gone, Naomi's eyes drifted to the people sitting at the next table. They were a family – a couple and their two teenage children. There was no conversing, only eating. She looked at the man, whose striped shirt was struggling to contain his flabby gut. His huge hands, like paddles, were wrapped around the cutlery and he ate in a rapid, anxious manner, as if he were expecting his plate to be snatched away from him at any moment.

The waiter arrived with their drinks. Toby was sticking to sparkling mineral water, but Naomi had ordered a large glass of wine, hoping it would help her relax. She felt slightly anxious. She couldn't work out why Toby had brought her here. In terms of ambience and clientele, it was a million miles from the dining room at Denholm House. She threw a glance anxiously towards the steaming buffet table in the centre of the room. She loved Chinese food, but generally it was packed with calories, not to mention all manner of additives. Still, she didn't have to pile her plate up to the ceiling, the way everyone else seemed to be doing.

Naomi imagined she and Toby would chat for a while before they ate, but when her date returned from the bathroom he suggested they head straight for the buffet. 'There's generally a bit of a rush, mid-evening,' he explained. 'If we go now, we'll have the best choice of dishes.'

'Fine,' Naomi said, rising to her feet. At this rate, they would be out of the restaurant within the hour – which, she reasoned, was probably no bad thing.

The food looked – and smelled – delicious and the choice was quite overwhelming. Naomi scrutinized each dish, trying to work out which were the lowest calorie options, before helping herself to a spoon each of plain bean sprouts and pak choi in oyster sauce. As she turned to go, Toby caught her arm.

'That's just your starter, right?' he said.

Naomi shook her head. 'No, that's it for me.'

A look of irritation crossed Toby's face. 'But a few minutes ago you said you were starving.'

'I am starving, but I don't want to overdo it. I'm trying to lose weight, remember?'

Toby now took on a pleading, puppy-dog expression. 'Can't you ditch the diet, just for tonight?'

Naomi hesitated, weighing up the options. If she stuck to her guns, she risked alienating Toby – a man who clearly liked his women to have a healthy appetite. If, on the other hand, she acceded to his request, she would have to starve herself tomorrow.

It didn't take her long to reach a decision. 'Oh, what the hell,' she said, picking up a pair of tongs and adding two spring rolls to her plate.

Toby smiled. 'The chow mein's excellent – the best I've ever tasted.'

Obligingly, Naomi helped herself to a small spoonful.

'You've got to try some of this too,' Toby said, grabbing a ladle and depositing a generous portion of sweet and sour chicken on to Naomi's plate before she had a chance to protest. His hand hovered over the egg-fried rice. 'And you'll need some of this to soak up all that lovely sauce.'

'No, honestly, this is plenty,' Naomi said, whisking her plate out of his reach.

A few moments later, she was back at the table, feeling slightly appalled as she surveyed the mound of food on her plate.

'Come on,' Toby said impatiently. 'Tuck in.'

Naomi picked up her fork and tentatively speared a piece of battered chicken swimming in gloopy orange sauce. As she raised it to her lips, Toby watched her with the stony-eyed intensity of a cat watching a bird. 'Don't nibble it, put the whole thing in at once,' he instructed her.

Seeing no good reason to refuse, Naomi did as she was told. As she penetrated the salty batter ball with her teeth, she moaned in pleasure. The chicken inside tasted moist and sweet and insanely good.

'How is it?' Toby asked eagerly.

'Amazing,' Naomi replied, eyes half closed.

For the next few minutes, she ate in silence – not because she had nothing to say, but, because the food was so distractingly delicious, she found herself quite unable to concentrate on two things at once. She decided therefore to eat first and talk later. Toby didn't seem to mind. In fact, the more she ate, the more he seemed to be enjoying himself. When his own plate was clean, he stood up.

'I'm going back for some more,' he said. 'How about you?'

'I'm fine, thanks,' Naomi replied through a mouth-ful of spring roll.

When Toby returned, he was carrying two plates. 'They've just brought out the Szechuan prawns, and I really wanted you to try some,' he said excitedly. 'They go perfectly with the seafood noodles, so I got you some of those too.'

He placed one of the plates in front of her. Naomi couldn't help noticing that it contained almost twice as much food as his own. She gave a little laugh. 'What's going on here? I feel like a sow being fattened up for the spit.'

Toby sat down. 'I would never describe you as a sow, Naomi,' he said. 'You're far too beautiful.'

'You're not denying it, then?'

He gave her a stare of transparently manufactured incomprehension. 'What do you mean?'

'Is that why you brought me to an all-you-can-eat restaurant . . . so I could gorge myself?'

Toby shifted in his seat. For the first time that evening, he looked vaguely uncomfortable. 'I'm not trying to make you do anything you don't want to do, Naomi. It's just that I can see you're a woman who enjoys your food and I don't see why you should deprive yourself. You like eating and I like watching you eat. It's a win-win situation.'

'Not for my waistline, it isn't,' Naomi said, frown-ing.

He leaned forward across the table. 'We're not going to fall out over this, are we?'

'Of course not,' Naomi said quickly. The last thing she wanted was to make herself less attractive to him.

'Then why don't you at least try one of those prawns? Otherwise they're going to go to waste.' His voice was gentle, almost chiding, as though he were talking to an adored but slightly wayward child.

Naomi looked down at the prawns, which were pink and juicy and heady with spice. She rubbed a hand across her stomach. It wasn't completely full; she certainly had room for a bit more. That was the trouble with Chinese food – the more you ate, the more you wanted. Sighing, she picked up her fork.

'Good girl,' Toby murmured.

Naomi ate quickly, greedily, the way she would if she were alone, lifting her hand to her mouth in a robotic rhythm, not caring if there was sauce around her mouth or pak choi between her teeth. She felt reckless, wanton, delirious almost. Toby, too, seemed to be in a heightened state of arousal. He stared at her slack-jawed as she ate, his pupils dilated as if he were drunk.

In a matter of minutes Naomi's plate was empty. 'God, those prawns were good,' she said, running her finger round the rim of the plate to collect the last remnants of sauce.

Toby's blue eyes glittered. 'What about dessert? The apple fritters are to die for.'

Naomi pressed her napkin to her mouth as a belch travelled up her oesophagus and threatened to erupt from her lips. 'Go on, then,' she said. 'In for a penny, in for a pound.'

'Excellent,' Toby said, and he clicked his fingers at a passing waiter.

The fritters, when they arrived, were huge and golden and crispy with oil. Naomi bent her head over the bowl, inhaling the scent coming from the puddle of molten caramel that surrounded them.

'Don't stand on ceremony,' Toby said, licking his lips lasciviously. 'Dig in.'

Naomi seized her spoon and began attacking the fritters, as if it weren't wine she'd been drinking, but a far more potent disinhibitor, a solvent for good manners and restraint. She couldn't remember the last time she'd eaten so much sugar in one go, and each mouthful tasted like a piece of heaven. She'd devoured one fritter and was halfway through the second when all at once she felt a rumbling in her guts. Her stomach had clearly had enough and was announcing its displeasure. The spoon fell from her hands. 'I don't think I can manage the rest.'

Toby's face fell. 'Oh, go on, Naomi, there's only a couple more mouthfuls. It seems a shame to waste it.'

'No,' she said, pushing the bowl away from her. 'I can't.'

Naomi was completely stuffed. If another morsel

of food passed through her lips tonight she would probably explode. The last time she'd felt like this was two Christmases ago. Her parents had divorced eight years ago and ever since then she'd spent Christmas Day with one or the other. That year, there'd been a misunderstanding and both her parents thought she was spending the day with them. Not wishing to disappoint either, Naomi had spent the day at her mum's and the evening at her dad's – a decision which had resulted in her eating two turkey dinners with all the trimmings, plus the usual assortment of nibbles, chocolates and booze. She'd been shocked at her gluttony that day, just as she was shocked now. Amanda would be horrified at her lack of self-control. She was going to have to starve herself for the next few days if she was to pass muster at the next weigh-in.

'Would you like another drink?' Toby said, interrupting her thoughts. 'A liqueur perhaps.'

'No, thank you,' Naomi said with an involuntary shudder. 'I wouldn't mind some water, though.'

Toby picked up the bottle of Perrier. 'I'm so glad I met you,' he said, as he filled Naomi's glass. 'You really are quite magnificent.'

Naomi smiled. The rumbling in her stomach was growing more insistent by the minute. 'Am I?' she said, taking a drink of water. She couldn't believe quite how much food she'd put away, except that the evidence was now lodged like a brick inside her. She was just wondering if she might be able to discreetly manoeuvre a couple of indigestion tablets into her mouth when Toby suddenly gripped her hand.

'Absolutely,' he said. 'In fact, you're everything I look for in a woman: attractive, intelligent, funny and, most important of all, *classy*. You should see some of the women from the website I've met up with. They look nice enough in their photos, but in the flesh . . .' He gave an imperious toss of his head. 'Common as muck.'

Naomi sat back, startled by the severity in his voice.

'You know the sort,' he continued. 'Dropped aitches, too much make-up, haven't got a clue which knife to use.' He sniffed haughtily. Then there are the limpets.'

Naomi frowned. 'Limpets?'

'The ones who think I'm going to leave my wife for them. I can usually suss them out after two or three dates. They look at you adoringly and agree with absolutely everything you say.'

'Oh,' Naomi said.

'But worst of all are the gold-diggers – the ones whose faces light up the minute they clap eyes on the Rolex.' He tweaked his shirt cuff ostentatiously. 'That's not to say I don't like to treat the ladies in my life. Speaking of which . . .' He reached into the pocket of his jacket. 'I have a gift for you.'

Naomi felt a tremor of excitement as he produced

a small, exquisitely gift-wrapped box. 'What's this?' she said.

'Just a little token of my appreciation. I know it's early days, but I wanted to show you how much I think of you.'

She took the box from his outstretched hand and peeled off the wrapping. Her heart gave a little leap when she saw the words on the box: *Tiffany & Co.* 'You shouldn't have,' she lied, lifting the lid to reveal a chunky silver bangle. It was plain, but clearly expensive – just the sort of thing she might have chosen for herself.

'Do you like it?'

She looked up at him, eyes shining. 'I love it.'

'Let's see how it looks,' Toby said, removing the bracelet from its velvet mount.

Naomi smiled as he slid it on to her arm. Yes, Toby possessed a certain arrogance; yes, he had some strange ideas about women and eating – but, given his generosity, she was prepared to overlook these minor shortcomings.

'I'm going to the Bahamas next month to check out a property investment,' he announced unexpectedly.

'I thought you were retired,' she said.

'I am, officially, but this deal looks too good to miss,' Toby said as he caressed the sensitive underside of her wrist with his fingertips. 'I was wondering if you'd like to join me. It's only five days – Monday to Friday – but we'd be flying first class and I've booked a beachfront villa. It's fully catered; you wouldn't have to lift a finger.'

Naomi was so overwhelmed that she momentarily forgot the sick feeling in her stomach. This, she told herself, was what being a mistress was all about. 'I'll have to check my work schedule,' she said, trying not to sound too eager.

'Good, let me know if you can make it asap and I'll book your flight.' His hand vanished beneath the table. A moment later, Naomi felt it squeezing her thigh. 'Have you decided whether or not you'd like to spend the night with me yet?' he said in a husky voice. 'I've booked one of the best rooms in the hotel.'

Naomi inclined her head coyly in a gesture of assent.

'In that case, let's get the bill, shall we?'

They didn't speak much on the short drive back to the hotel. Both were too busy contemplating what lay ahead. When they arrived, Toby wasted no time collecting the key card from reception and leading Naomi towards the lift. The room was, as he had suggested, utterly sumptuous: statement wallpaper, funky over-sized lamps, Egyptian-cotton bed linen with a thread count off the scale. As Naomi tossed her coat on a louche purple chaise, Toby gestured to the bottle of champagne that was chilling in an ice bucket on top of the mini-bar.

'Would you like a drink?'

Naomi's indigestion had worsened during the car journey, but it seemed churlish to refuse when Toby had obviously paid extra for the privilege.

'Lovely!' she said perkily. She walked towards the en suite. 'I'll just freshen up. Won't be a minute.'

The bathroom was equally impressive, with its monsoon shower and fibre optic lighting. As Naomi examined the designer toiletries, she couldn't help congratulating herself on bagging a man like Toby; he really was in a different league to the men she usually dated. If only she hadn't eaten quite so much at dinner, she would have really been looking forward to the sex. As it was, she felt like a big fat blubbery whale. Still, she wasn't about to back out now.

She found a couple of indigestion tablets in her handbag and popped them in her mouth. As she waited for them to take effcct, she undid the zip of her skirt and worked her hand back and forth across her tender midriff, wincing as her intestines emitted a series of angry growls in response. She caught sight of her reflection in the vast mirror above the double sinks. Her cheeks were flushed from the wine and most of her lipstick had worn off. Reaching for her make-up bag, she carried out some quick repairs. A man like Toby would expect nothing but perfection. Then she zipped up her skirt, put on her brightest smile and opened the bathroom door.

Toby was standing naked in the middle of the room, fiddling with the remote control for the music system. His chest, carpeted in whorls of grey hair, was toned. His penis was thick and long enough to bump companionably against his thigh as he strode over to her with a glass of champagne.

Naomi eyed his firm biceps as she took the glass from him. 'You know, you have a great body for a man of your—' She stopped herself, not wanting to sound rude.

Toby smiled. 'A man of my age?'

Naomi nodded.

'Does it bother you?' he asked. 'The age difference, I mean.'

'Not really – although you are a little older than the men I usually date.'

He smoothed a hand over his close-cropped hair. 'You needn't be concerned, Naomi. I have more energy than most men half my age, as I'm about to demonstrate.' He took the champagne glass out of her hand and set it down on a hand-painted blanket box. 'Let me help you out of those clothes,' he said, as he led her over to the canopied bed.

He undressed her almost ritualistically, kissing her neck over and over, and between the kisses whispering erotic words and promises; words that were the shape of his desire. Naomi found herself going through the motions, wrapping her arms wantonly around his neck; receiving his flickering tongue in her mouth, moaning softly as his hand traced the outline of her bloated stomach.

'You have a beautiful figure,' he said, working his index finger into the folds of her skin until he found her belly button. 'I don't know why you think you need to lose weight, Naomi.'

She bristled. These constant references to her size were beginning to irk her. 'I just don't feel comfortable being this big,' she countered.

'Personally, I think you'd be even sexier if you had a bit *more* meat on your bones,' Toby said.

Naomi found herself tensing as one of his hands began kneading her left buttock vigorously. She searched for some loophole in the laws of etiquette that might allow her to ask him to desist. Unable to find one, she felt she had no alternative but to let him continue.

'I'd like to buy you something nice to wear,' he murmured into her neck. 'Something long and clinging. Would you like that?'

'Yes,' she replied, her jaw clenching as his other hand cupped one of her sizeable breasts, bouncing it in his palm, as if he were trying to guess its weight.

'I have a personal shopper in London; she buys all my clothes. I'll have her give you a call.'

'Wonderful.' Keen to show her appreciation for the offer, Naomi reached down and circled Toby's testicles with her index finger, then moved her hand lower, running a fingernail across the sweet spot between his balls and his anus. He tilted his head back, so they were eye to eye. She felt the pressure of his gaze. There was something unflinching about it, a kernel of hardness.

'Are you familiar with a technique known as the Cleopatra grip?' he asked unexpectedly.

Naomi shook her head. 'I've never even heard of it.'

Toby's hand moved from her breast to her throat. 'It's the contraction of the vaginal muscles so that the penis has the sensation of being massaged,' he explained, as he stroked her collarbone in slow, sensuous movements. 'I thought that, given your wealth of experience, you might be a practitioner.'

Naomi felt vaguely insulted. What did he mean . . . *wealth of experience*? How many men did he think she'd slept with? In the next moment, she was telling herself to stop being so sensitive. A sizeable portion of being a mistress involved having sex, so it was hardly surprising Toby was keen to establish her level of expertise. 'I'm afraid not,' she said. 'But I know lots of other tricks.'

Toby laughed fruitily, while his fingertips charted a lazy yet determined course along the inside of her doughy thigh. 'I can't wait to see them,' he said. As his fingers began probing the moist cleft between her legs, Naomi closed her eyes, trying to blot out the whirlpools of nausea that were eddying beneath her ribs.

Anxious for the whole thing to be over as soon as possible, she let out a series of ersatz moans. When they failed to have the desired effect, she reached for Toby's erect penis. 'I want to feel you inside me,' she whispered seductively.

'Not yet, Naomi,' he replied, rolling away from her, so he was lying flat on his back. 'First, I want you to sit on me.'

She smiled. This was an offer she wasn't going to turn down, indigestion or not. Rising to her knees, she straddled his face in one swift movement.

'No, not like that,' Toby said, twisting his face away. 'Sit on my chest.'

'Really?' Naomi said, nonplussed.

'Yes,' he replied. 'You'll need to turn round as well, so I can see that magnificent arse of yours.'

Naomi frowned. She had accommodated some unusual requests in the past – in her experience, men generally asked their mistresses to do the things their wives wouldn't – but she'd never come across this one before. Still, if that was what Toby wanted, that was what he would get.

Wriggling backwards, she slung her leg over Toby's body, so that now she was looking at his feet. Then, gingerly, she lowered herself downwards until her buttocks were resting on his pectorals. She looked back over her shoulder. 'Am I doing this right?'

'No, you're still supporting yourself on your knees,'

he said, a note of exasperation entering his voice. 'I want to feel the whole weight of your body, as if you were sitting on a chair.'

Still, Naomi hesitated. 'I don't want to hurt you,' she said.

He sighed impatiently. 'Don't worry, Naomi. I know what I'm doing.'

'Well, okay, if you're sure.' Naomi followed his instructions, drawing her legs up so that she was now in a squatting position, with the soles of her feet flat on the bed covers.

Toby let rip a gusty moan of satisfaction. 'That's perfect.'

'Now what?' she asked him.

'Nothing,' he replied. 'Just stay exactly where you are and let me enjoy the sight and feel of you.'

Naomi was glad he couldn't see the look of apathy on her face. She failed to see what pleasure Toby could possibly be deriving from this. What's more, she had an itch on her inner thigh where his chest hair was tickling her. Just then she heard him gasp, as if he were struggling to catch his breath – and no wonder, when she was situated directly on top of his lungs. 'Is everything all right back there?' she called out.

'Fine,' he panted. 'This feels wonderful. I love being enveloped by female flesh, especially when the skin is as soft as yours.'

'Good,' Naomi said, wincing at a sudden swirl of

acid in her stomach. Her belly was drum-tight, its contents heavy and ominously compressed. What she wouldn't give for a lie down and a hot-water bottle right now.

A few more minutes went by and then Toby spoke again. 'Let's try something else now, Naomi.'

'Yes?' she said, hoping they were about to get down to business.

'I want you to do a belly flop.'

Naomi glanced over her shoulder, thinking she must have misheard him. 'I beg your pardon?'

'A belly flop,' he repeated matter-of-factly. 'It's not difficult. All you have to do is stand at the edge of the bed, then throw yourself on top of me, like a wrestler.'

Naomi looked at him askance. 'Are you serious?'

He frowned peevishly. 'Yes, and don't worry, you won't hurt me. I've done it dozens of times before – and with girls a lot bigger than you too.'

'Have you really?' Naomi remarked dryly.

'Come on, give it a go,' he urged her. 'You'll enjoy it.'

'I doubt it,' Naomi replied as she dismounted him. 'You know, Toby, I really don't feel comfortable with all this.'

'With all *what*?' he said with exaggerated innocence.

'You seem to be obsessed with my weight.'

Toby snorted. 'I thought you'd be grateful to find a man who appreciates the fuller figure, Naomi.'

She couldn't help wincing. He'd been using her

name over and over all evening. It suddenly occurred to her that he was not so much claiming the privilege of intimacy, as asserting authority over her.

'Actually, I find your behaviour a little patronizing,' she said. 'It feels as if you're treating me as an object, rather than a person.'

'None of the others seemed to mind,' he remarked, with the defiant tone of someone unaccustomed to being challenged. 'They all thought it was fun.'

Naomi could feel a vein jumping in her temple. Enough was enough; she wasn't going to be bullied into playing along with his little fat fetish. Quite apart from anything else, she would probably vomit if she acceded to his request for a belly flop. 'Well *I* don't,' she said sharply. 'In fact, I don't think we're compatible at all.'

Instantly, Toby's whole mien changed. His face looked quite different. It was as if a window had flown open, revealing a glimpse of what lay beyond the charming facade.

'Women like you make me sick,' he muttered as he rolled off the bed.

'Women like what?'

'Cock teases.'

Naomi's face stung with a blush that rose so quickly she felt almost faint. 'How dare you,' she said, jumping to her feet. 'If I'd known what sort of a pervert you were, I would never have agreed to go out with you.'

He gave a sour laugh. 'No, but you were quite happy to drink my champagne, let me pay for dinner two nights on the trot and fork out for this hotel room, weren't you?'

Almost before she knew what she was doing, Naomi had slapped him hard across the face. He didn't flinch. In that moment she realized that he was a man to whom emotions were an abstract concept. Behind his angry expression, the cogs of a cool computation continued to operate. She could almost hear the whir and click of a hidden mechanism, like the steely workings of a robot. He turned away from her and started to dress in a slow, deliberate manner.

Naomi could feel her back prickling with embarrassed sweat as she plucked her clothes from the floor and scuttled towards the en suite. She couldn't bear to spend another moment in Toby's company. With any luck, by the time she emerged he'd be gone. Her hand was on the doorknob when he spoke.

'The bracelet,' he said.

She turned over her shoulder. 'What?' she snapped.

'You don't seriously think I'm going to let you keep it after the way you've just behaved?'

She wrenched the bangle from her wrist. 'Here,' she said, flinging it across the room in his general direction. 'You're welcome to it. I didn't like it anyway.'

Once inside the bathroom, she locked the door behind her and slumped to the floor, pressing her burning cheeks against the cold limestone wall tiles. She'd had such high hopes for Toby; she couldn't believe the way things had turned out. Worst of all, she'd already dumped Christopher, so there was no substitute waiting on the bench. She was officially single, the one state she dreaded above all else. Soon, she heard footsteps and then the sound of a door opening and closing. She stood up and dressed quickly, before opening the door and peering tentatively into the room. It was empty. As she made her own escape, she noticed the crisp fifty-pound note lying on top of the dresser. Now her humiliation was complete.

Chapter Thirteen

Week 6
Holly 11st 7lb
Naomi 10st 6lb
Kate 13st

Kate looked down at Freya and gave her what she hoped was an encouraging smile. 'This is a very important day for my friend Holly, so I want you to be on your best behaviour, okay?'

'Okay,' Freya replied, wiping her nose with the back of her hand.

Frowning, Kate plucked an animal hair off Freya's sleeve. She wished the child didn't look quite so bedraggled. A search of her suitcase had failed to yield any of the hoped-for party frocks, so Kate had selected the smartest item available – a pink gingham dress with a falling-down hem that she had temporarily repaired with sticky tape. This she had teamed with Freya's least scuffed pair of shoes, a pair of white-verging-on-grey knee-high socks and a hand-knitted cardigan with mismatching buttons.

It was seven days since Freya's arrival, seven days

since Kate's calm, ordered world had been grabbed by the scruff of the neck and shaken violently. She'd called Social Services on Monday morning, only to discover James Aldridge had informed them his motherless niece was now in the care of her 'stepmother' – a title, Kate grudgingly conceded to a harried-sounding caseworker, was technically correct. When she'd emphasized the need to find alternative accommodation for Freya immediately, the caseworker had pleaded with Kate to keep the child for a week or two, until a long-term foster carer could be found. The only alternative, she explained, was to place Freya in a children's home. Kate had baulked at this. The child, she reasoned, had already suffered enough upheaval – and so, with great reluctance, she found herself agreeing to the social worker's request.

It wasn't long before she was regretting her decision. It had been easy enough to reschedule her various meetings and teaching commitments so she could stay at home. What Kate hadn't appreciated was how difficult it would be trying to work with a child in the house. Although Freya seemed content to watch TV or play on Kate's old computer, her very presence meant Kate was unable to concentrate. She was used to her own space, and doing *what* she wanted, *when* she wanted. Now the delicious sense of solitude and self-containment she'd once enjoyed seemed like a distant dream. What's more, knowing it wasn't good for children to be cooped up indoors, Kate had felt compelled to organize further interruptions to her routine, in the shape of trips to the library, walks in the park and lunches in local cafés – none of which Freya appeared to particularly enjoy.

It was Tuesday night before James Aldridge finally returned her numerous phone calls. Kate had given him a hard time at first, even threatening to report him to the police for child neglect, but he was so apologetic and so pathetically grateful that she soon softened. During the course of their conversation, he volunteered a few more tantalizing fragments of information – like the fact his sister had been a freelance artist, specializing in watercolour impressions of yet-to-be-built homes for architects and property developers. This, Kate surmised, was how she had first come into contact with Huw. James reckoned the affair had lasted around eighteen months, but he had no idea whether or not his sister planned her pregnancy. Nor did he know why Huw had ended their relationship when he did. His mother, he said, would probably know the answers to all these questions – and any more Kate might have – but given her advanced state of dementia, she was hardly a reliable source of information.

As the depth and breadth of her husband's betrayal opened like a chasm, revealing a dark abyss below, Kate realized she would never find out what had driven Huw into the arms of another woman. Now, as she watched her young charge, who had wandered off into Diana's garden to inspect a lavish begonia, Kate supposed she should count herself lucky. Freya was the one she should be feeling sorry for.

Just then, the front door swung open to reveal a slender woman in a tweedy suit and lots of chunky amber jewellery. 'Hello, are you here for the party?' she said.

Kate nodded. 'I'm Kate Pendleton, one of Holly's friends – and you must be her future mother-in-law.'

Diana smiled thinly. 'That's right.' She opened the door wider. 'Won't you come in?'

Kate looked over her shoulder. 'Come on, Freya.'

As Freya came bounding over, the smile on Diana's face froze. 'Holly didn't say anything about a child.'

'Freya's staying with me for a while,' Kate replied. 'I didn't think you'd mind if I brought her along.'

'Hmm,' Diana said, her displeasure obvious. 'Just make sure you don't let her run around the house. I have a large and rather valuable collection of Doulton. I'd be devastated if anything got broken.'

'I understand,' Kate said, feeling rather embarrassed. 'I won't let her out of my sight, I promise.' She grabbed Freya's hand and led her into the house.

'The other guests arrived some time ago,' Diana said as she set off down the hallway. 'The invitation did say two o'clock.'

'Yes, we would have got here sooner, only our taxi was late picking us up.' Kate turned her head to admire a particularly handsome bureau and saw, to her horror, that Freya had left a trail of muddy footprints on the parquet floor. 'Oh no,' she groaned.

Diana's head snapped round. When she saw the floor, she drew her breath in sharply.

'I'm so sorry,' Kate said, scowling at Freya. 'I should have checked her shoes before we came in.'

'I'd better get a mop,' Diana said, sighing heavily. She pointed to a set of double doors at the end of the hall. 'Everybody's in the drawing room; perhaps you could show yourself in.'

'Of course – and sorry again,' Kate said as Diana disappeared through another door.

The drawing room was huge, with elaborately swagged curtains and a rather noisy carpet. A couple of waitresses in black dresses moved among the forty or so guests with trays of drinks. There was no sign of Holly, but Kate spotted Naomi over by the window. She was holding a glass of champagne and talking animatedly to a good-looking man in a pink shirt.

'I'm thirsty,' Freya said.

'Me too,' Kate murmured. She pointed to a velvet wing chair beside the fireplace. 'Why don't you sit down there and I'll get us some drinks.'

'I want Coke,' Freya said.

'I would *like* Coke,' Kate corrected here. 'Please.'

Freya flung herself into the chair. '*Please.*'

Kate crossed the room and helped herself to a glass

of red wine from the waitress's tray. There was no Coke on offer, so she selected an orange juice for Freya. As she turned round she almost ran into Holly.

'Hey, Kate,' Holly said, kissing her friend warmly on the cheek. 'Diana said you'd just arrived.'

'You were right about the house – it's beautiful,' Kate said. 'The perfect setting for a party.' She smiled at Holly. 'And you look beautiful too,' she said. 'I can't believe how much weight you've lost already; I wish I had half your will power. Six weeks in and I've still only lost five pounds.' She jerked her head towards Naomi, who was laughing uproariously in response to something the man in the pink shirt had said. 'Someone looks as if she's having a good time. I was going to go over and say hello, but it looks as if she's otherwise engaged.'

Holly grinned. 'I thought Naomi would get on with Ben. He works with Rob at the estate agency. All the female clients love him.'

She caught her friend's eye and gave a little wave. The next moment, Naomi was kissing Ben on the cheek and walking over to them.

'I hope we're not interrupting anything,' Kate said as Naomi greeted her with a hug. 'It looked as if you two were getting on rather well.'

'No, it's all right, I've found out everything I need to know,' Naomi said breezily. 'He's divorced and desperate.'

'Desperate for sex?' Kate asked.

Naomi shook her head. 'Desperate for a replacement wife – which makes him an absolute no-go area for me.'

'That's a shame,' Kate said. 'He's very attractive.'

'He is, isn't he?' Naomi agreed.

'What about the man from the internet?' Holly asked. 'How was your second date?'

Naomi groaned. 'It was a total disaster. You were right about him sounding too good to be true; he turned out to be a fat fetishist.'

'Good God,' Kate said in a shocked voice. 'What happened?'

'He took me out for dinner to an all-you-can-eat-place and spent the entire evening piling my plate with food. Then, when we got back to the hotel room, he wasn't happy with straight sex. He wanted me to do all kinds of weird stuff, like sit on his chest, so it felt like he was suffocating.'

Holly covered her mouth with her hands. 'Do people really get off on that kind of stuff?'

'Apparently so. I did some research on the internet and there's even a name for it: *squashing*.'

'*Ewww!*' Holly squealed.

'I'm usually quite broad-minded when it comes to sex, but even I have my limits.' Naomi considered her champagne glass stonily. 'I'm beginning to think I should have stuck with Christopher after all.'

'Speaking of married men, where's this future hus-band of yours?' Kate asked Holly. 'I'm dying to meet him.'

'He's up in the loft,' Holly replied. 'Diana wanted him to get some old photo albums. For some reason she thinks our guests are gagging to see pictures of her darling son when he was a scabby-kneed kid.'

At the mention of the word *kid*, Kate felt a sudden wave of panic. Despite the fact she was still holding the glass of orange juice, Freya had completely slipped her mind. She craned her neck, trying to see around the clusters of guests.

'What is it?' Holly asked.

'Nothing,' Kate said, breathing a sigh of relief as she saw that Freya was still sitting on the wing chair, wearing a bored expression and swinging her feet. 'I hope you don't mind, but I've brought someone with me. She arrived rather unexpectedly; I'm going to be looking after her for a couple of weeks.' She fluttered her fingers in the air to attract Freya's attention.

'Of course I don't mind,' Holly said, smiling as Freya approached. She bent down and rested her hands on her knees. 'What's your name?' she asked the little girl.

'Freya Aldridge,' said a small voice.

Kate handed her the orange juice. 'Sorry, there wasn't any Coke.'

'Actually, I think we might have some Coke in the

fridge,' Holly said, standing upright. 'I can have a look if you like.'

'She'll be fine with juice,' Kate said, glaring at Freya to silence any protest she might be about to make.

'So, Freya, I'm guessing you must be Kate's niece,' Naomi said.

Freya shook her head.

'No? Well surely you can't be her *granny*?' Naomi exclaimed.

Freya's rosebud mouth twitched as she shook her head again.

Naomi cupped her chin in her hand. 'Well, in that case you must be her second cousin three times removed.'

At this, Freya burst into giggles. It was, Kate realized with a start, the first time she'd heard the little girl laugh. Naomi and Holly were now looking at her expectantly, waiting for her to reveal the real nature of her relationship to Freya. Kate hesitated. She hadn't told anyone about Huw's affair, not even her closest friends. But after a week of keeping her secret, the urge to confide in someone was overwhelming. She tapped Freya on the shoulder and then pointed to a glass-fronted display cabinet in the corner of the room that housed a collection of Doulton shepherdesses.

'Why don't you go and look at those pretty china ladies?' she said.

Freya stuck out her lower lip. 'Do I have to?'

'Yes,' Kate said. 'Now go on, shoo – and be careful not to touch anything.'

She waited until Freya was safely out of earshot, then turned back to the others. 'Sorry about the subterfuge, but I don't want her hearing this.' She took a deep breath. 'The thing is, Freya's not related to me at all – at least not by blood. She's Huw's.'

'Ah,' Naomi said, nodding in understanding. 'His daughter from a previous relationship.'

'No,' Kate corrected her. 'Not a previous relationship; a *simultaneous* one.'

Naomi frowned. 'What?'

'Huw had an affair. I only found out about it last weekend when Freya's uncle abandoned Freya on my doorstep.'

'Oh, Kate,' Holly said, her face crumpling in sympathy. 'I can't believe it.'

'Yes, it came as a bit of a shock to me too.' In a lowered voice, Kate quickly recounted the circumstances of Jennifer Aldridge's death and Freya's arrival.

'So you're saying this James character just turned up at your house, without any warning whatsoever, and dumped Freya on you?' Naomi said.

Kate nodded. 'It all happened so quickly I hardly had time to think.'

Holly gave a growl of disapproval. 'How could he do that to a little girl – his own niece, too?'

'Don't judge him too harshly,' Kate replied. 'He's

234

only young, and he didn't have much of a relationship with Freya before Jennifer died. I think he did pretty well to look after her as long as he did.'

'So what's going to happen to Freya long-term?' Naomi asked.

'She'll go into foster care first of all and then Social Services will probably try and have her adopted – although, given her age, I can't imagine it's going to be easy.'

Holly looked over at Freya, who was kneeling in front of the display cabinet, her breath misting up the glass. 'Poor kid, she must be feeling so confused. First, her mother dies, then she's passed from person to person like a parcel.'

'She's putting on a very brave face,' Kate replied. 'I haven't seen her cry – not once – but, inside, she must be experiencing so many conflicting emotions. I wish I could say something that would make her feel more secure.' She gave a rueful laugh. 'It's ironic really – I know everything there is to know about the human psyche, but I can't find the words to comfort a seven-year-old child.'

'And what about you, Kate?' Naomi asked. 'How are you doing?'

Kate shrugged. 'Oh, you know, bearing up.' The words tasted sour in her mouth. The truth was that Huw's betrayal had dominated her thoughts ever since she'd read James's letter. Night-times were the worst.

She'd go to bed early, reaching for sleep as if it were a blanket that she could hide underneath, but even when she did manage to nod off, she was troubled by dreams of a frighteningly voyeuristic nature. In one particularly disturbing dream, she'd watched through an open, ground-floor window as Huw and a strange woman – blonde-haired, like Freya – had made uninhibited love, grunting and groaning with gusto as their bodies contorted into improbable positions. The horror of the image had caused Kate's eyes to fly open in the dark, her heart beating so violently that it rustled her pyjamas.

'Are you sure about that?' Holly said. 'I'd be in pieces if I found out my husband had been unfaithful.'

'Well, okay, then, I'm bloody furious,' Kate admitted. 'And not just with Huw, with myself too. I can't believe I didn't realize he was having an affair.' She looked down at the gold wedding band on her left hand. Even as she spoke, she could feel the pressure of her rage growing against her ribs. 'According to Freya's uncle, it lasted well over a year. I thought I knew Huw so well; I can't believe I didn't see there was a problem in our marriage.'

'Who says there was a problem?' Naomi replied. 'Men have affairs for all sorts of reasons. Sometimes it's nothing more than a form of stress relief. You mustn't blame yourself.'

'Oh well, you *are* the expert,' Kate said, her voice

tinged with bitterness. She saw a look of hurt flash across Naomi's face. 'I'm sorry, I didn't mean –'

Naomi held up a hand. 'It's fine. To be honest, I could understand if you hated me now. 'After all, I'm a professional mistress. *I've* done what Jennifer Aldridge did to you – not just once, but over and over again. I've lost count of the number of married men I've dated; it's certainly into double figures. And, even worse than that, the whole time I was sleeping with them and stroking their egos and letting them pay for meals and nights in hotels, I never once stopped to think who I might be hurting. Wives, children . . . I didn't give a toss about any of them, just so long as I was getting what *I* wanted.' She stopped and swallowed hard. 'But now I can't help feeling rather ashamed of myself.'

'Of course I don't hate you,' Kate replied. 'It takes two to have an affair. Huw was the married one, the one who should have known better.' She paused. 'But I still can't help feeling you deserve so much more.'

Naomi took a sip of wine. 'More than what?'

'More than being another notch on a man's bedpost, someone to keep him entertained until he gets bored again.'

'Kate's right,' Holly said. 'You shouldn't be making do with another woman's leftovers. Wouldn't you prefer to have someone all to yourself – someone who's not just using you for sex and a shoulder to cry on, someone who's never going to cancel dates at short notice, someone who isn't afraid to be seen with you in public?'

Naomi gave an unconvincing shrug.

'And what about New Year's Eve and Valentine's Day and all those other important celebrations that couples are supposed to share?' Kate challenged. 'How does it feel to be on your own while your lover's spending them with his wife?'

Naomi sighed. 'Pretty shit, if I'm honest.'

'So why do you do it?' Holly asked.

'Because it's what I'm good at,' Naomi replied. 'And because it's easy; I just don't have the time or the emotional energy for a proper relationship.'

'But you're throwing your life away,' Kate said. 'These men aren't good enough for you – can't you see that?'

Naomi smiled. 'I appreciate your concern, but right now I'm more worried about *you*.' She gave Kate's shoulder a gentle squeeze. 'I can't begin to imagine how you must be feeling.'

'To be honest, I'm not sure how I'm feeling myself,' Kate said miserably. 'My mood seems to change from one minute to the next. One minute I'm seething with anger, the next I feel completely numb. In a funny sort of way, it's like being bereaved all over again – that awful sense of grief, of abandonment, of feeling utterly alone.'

'But you're not alone,' Holly said 'You've got me – and Naomi, and I'm sure there are a whole heap of other people out there who care very deeply about you.'

Naomi nodded. 'And if ever you need anything – help with Freya, or just someone to talk to – we're only ever a phone call away.'

Kate took a stiffening breath. 'You know, I'm so glad I joined Fat Chance,' she said, reaching out a hand to each of them, 'because otherwise I never would have made two such excellent friends.'

Holly smiled. 'The feeling's mutual.'

'Yeah, those meetings improved immeasurably when you two turned up,' Naomi said. 'That's what I'm most looking forward to about boot camp – the fact we'll all be able to spend a bit more time together.'

'That's the *only* thing I'm looking forward to about boot camp,' Kate remarked.

Holly pulled a face. 'Diana's offered to move in with Rob while I'm away. She's worried he won't be able to cope on his own – even for a weekend.'

Naomi drained her champagne glass and swiped another from the tray of a passing waitress. 'But he lived on his own before he met you, didn't he?'

'Yes, but Diana reckons he's so used to having a woman around he's forgotten how to work the washing machine and make the bed.' Holly frowned. 'Which, come to think of it, might be true.' Looking round, she spotted Diana on the other side of the room. Her soon-to-be mother-in-law was on her hands and knees, picking up the remains of a mini quiche that somebody had dropped on the carpet. 'Just look at her,' she murmured. 'It's so embarrassing the way she keeps fussing over everything. I thought it would be so nice to have the party here, but now I'm beginning to wish we'd just booked a room in our local pub.'

'She did seem a little tense when I arrived,' Kate said. 'And Freya traipsing mud in from the garden didn't help.'

'Is Diana more enthusiastic about the wedding now?' Naomi asked.

Holly sighed. 'Not really. It's almost as if I've done something to offend her, although I can't for the life of me think what. She used to be so friendly and sweet, but now all she does is criticize me – my hairstyle, my table manners, even the way I folded the paper napkins earlier on. I'm getting the distinct impression she doesn't think I'm good enough for her darling son. It was fine when we were just dating, but now we're actually getting married she's decided it's high time she revealed what she really thinks of me.' Holly saw that Diana had risen to her feet and was heading in their direction. 'Oh God, her ears must be burning; she's coming over.' She took a mouthful of vodka and tonic to fortify herself. 'Hi, Diana, are you having a nice time?' she asked, as the older woman approached.

Diana ignored the question. 'What's happened to Bobo?' she demanded, as if Holly were responsible for his absence.

'I assume he's still up in the loft.'

'I do hope he hasn't had an accident,' Diana said, fingering her necklace anxiously.

Holly snorted. 'It's only the loft, Diana. What's the worst that can happen – he inhales a bit of dust, or walks into a piece of low-hanging fly paper?'

'There's nothing funny about a mother's concern for her child,' Diana said in a constipated voice. 'When you have children of your own, you'll understand.'

Sensing the tension in the air, Naomi turned to Diana. 'You have a lovely home,' she said. 'And how thoughtful of you to offer to host the party.'

'Thank you. I'm glad my efforts haven't gone unnoticed,' Diana replied. 'Holly tells me you're a wedding photographer.'

Naomi smiled. 'That's right.'

'Rob and I had a look at your website last night,' Holly said. 'We love your style. We'd love you to do the pictures for our wedding – if you're available of course.'

'I'd love to,' Naomi replied. 'Have you set a date yet?'

'April twenty-second, it's a Friday. We couldn't find a Saturday in spring that wasn't already booked.'

'Personally, I don't see what the rush is,' Diana said.

Holly sighed. 'If you recall, Rob's the one who didn't want a long engagement.'

'More fool him,' Diana muttered.

Naomi began scrolling through the calendar on her iPhone. 'You're in luck,' she said after a few moments. 'The twenty-second's completely clear.'

'Brilliant,' Holly said, beaming. 'Rob will be so pleased when I tell him.'

'Where's the venue?'

'Lynton Grange – we both fell in love with it as soon as we saw it.'

'Good choice,' Naomi said, nodding. 'It's a stunning location.'

Diana gave a loud sniff. 'In my opinion they're making a big mistake. A friend of mine went to a New Year's Eve party at Lynton Grange and said there was barely room to swing a cat.'

'The banqueting hall seats a hundred,' Holly said evenly. 'And given that we're only inviting eighty guests, I'm sure there'll be more than enough room.'

'Have you chosen your dress yet?' Kate asked.

Holly shook her head. 'I've only got as far as buying a few bridal magazines. I need to find a style that really flatters my figure.'

'You definitely don't want to go for strapless, not with your shoulders,' Diana said firmly. 'What about a nice Empire-line? It'll hide a multitude of sins.'

Holly's jaw constricted. 'Thanks for the advice, Diana. I'll bear it in mind.'

'I know,' Diana said, clapping her hands together.

'Why don't I come dress shopping with you? I've got quite an eye for fashion, though I do say so myself. I'll be able to see what suits you right away.'

'That's awfully sweet of you, Diana, but I promised my mum I'd go dress shopping with her,' Holly replied.

'I see,' Diana said, her face falling. 'And how is your mother?'

'Very well, thank you. It was her birthday last week.'

'That's nice. How old was she?'

'Fifty-six.'

Diana, who had only met Holly's mother once, gasped in exaggerated horror. 'Is she really only fifty-six? She looks so much older – but then she has had a hard life, hasn't she, poor dear? Bringing up four children in a council house . . . and working in that bookmaker's can't be much fun.'

Holly gripped her elbows, so she wouldn't be tempted to slap Diana. 'Actually, Mum loves her job.'

'Yes, but it's not really a suitable environment for a woman, is it?' Diana gave a little shudder. 'I bet she gets all sorts in there . . . drunks, navvies, *criminals*.'

Holly counted silently to five. 'I think you're being a bit unreasonable,' she said. 'They're hardly dens of iniquity. All sorts of people go to the bookies; even Rob likes the occasional flutter.'

'That may be true, but it's certainly not somewhere *I'd* feel comfortable working,' Diana said. 'What about flowers for the wedding?' she went on. 'I always think yellow and cream go wonderfully well together, don't you?'

'Yes, absolutely,' Holly said.

'And a nice traditional carnation for the button-holes?'

'Fabulous idea,' Holly chirruped, even though she'd already decided on freesias.

'What about your bouquet?' Diana went on. 'Everyone seems to go for hand-tied posies these days, but a rose pomander is so much classier . . .'

As she droned on, Holly could feel an odd pressure behind her eyes, as if fingers were pushing and squeezing on the nerves, trying to dislodge the eyeballs. Suddenly, she spotted rescue on the other side of the room, in the shape of her fiancé.

'Ah, there you are, Bobo,' Diana said as her son approached. 'I was just about to send out a search party.'

Grinning, Rob held up a stack of well-thumbed photo albums. 'It took me a while to track these down. You've got tons of stuff up there, Mum. I didn't realize you'd kept my old school reports and all that stuff I did for my A-level art.'

Holly felt faintly nauseous as Diana gave Rob of the great oxygen-sucking grins she reserved for him alone. 'I'd never throw your things away, Bobo,' Diana cooed. 'They're a testament to your enormous talent and creativity.'

Rob leaned forward and kissed his mother on the cheek.' As he drew away, Diana gave a little gasp of horror and extended a trembling finger towards the display cabinet. The glass door was open and a Doulton shepherdess was lying, decapitated, at Freya's feet.

'Freya!' Kate shrieked loudly. 'I thought I told you not to touch those.'

'I only wanted to stroke her hair,' Freya said plaintively.

Rob winced. 'I'll go and get a dustpan and brush,' he said, heading towards the door.

Kate turned to Diana. 'I'm so sorry. I only took my eye off her for a minute. I'll pay for a replacement.'

Diana contorted her face into an expression of martyred agony. 'That particular model went out of production more than thirty years ago,' she snapped.

'But you'll be able to get it repaired,' Holly said.

Diana gave her a look of icy disdain. 'The join will still be visible.' As she stalked off after Rob, Kate covered her face with her hands. 'I am *so* sorry about this, Holly. I really should have been watching her.'

'Forget it,' Holly replied. 'Freya did me a big favour.'

'What?' Kate said in surprise.

Holly smiled tautly. 'She got Diana out of my face before I strangled her with my bare hands.'

Chapter Fourteen

Week 7
Holly 11st 3lb
Naomi 10st 4lb
Kate 12st 11lb

Kate turned off the car engine and looked around. According to the sat nav, she'd reached her destination, but this wasn't quite what she'd been expecting. In front of her was a long low building – a sort of glorified cowshed, with a breezeblock exterior and a roof of corrugated iron. Situated at the end of a long, muddy track, it seemed to be the only building for miles around. With a growing sense of trepidation, she reached for her jacket. The sky had been growing steadily greyer during the four-hour drive, and now a strong northerly wind was sending needles of rain across the windscreen of her car.

A few moments later, she was scuttling towards the cowshed, dragging her suitcase behind her, its wheels bouncing over the rocky terrain. Inside, a middle-aged woman with steel-coloured hair and the dark, unblinking eyes of a woodland animal was waiting with a clipboard. 'Name?' she barked, as Kate burst through the door.

'Kate Pendleton. I'm here for the –'

'Step on here,' the woman said gruffly, gesturing to a set of scales.

Kate, who'd hoped for a slightly warmer welcome, did as she was told.

The woman took a reading and jotted it down on her clipboard. 'The female dormitory is down there,' she said, pointing to a dimly lit corridor with mustard-coloured walls and pockmarked linoleum. 'Go right to the end and turn left.'

'*Dormitory?*' Kate said in dismay. 'I rather assumed I'd have my own room.'

The ghost of a smile played across the woman's lips. 'Trust me, by the end of today, you'll be so tired you could sleep in a barn.'

The women's dormitory had the look and feel of an army barracks. Along one wall was a row of bunk beds, each furnished with a thin grey blanket and a single flaccid pillow. Opposite them was a bank of metal lockers, where half a dozen Fat Chance members were busy offloading the contents of their suitcases. Kate couldn't help noticing that they all looked faintly shell-shocked.

'Well, this is certainly cosy,' she said with forced cheeriness as she went over to join them.

Adele, whose head was buried in the next-door locker, gave an unconvincing laugh. 'I suppose that's one way of putting it,' she said.

As Kate bent down to unzip her suitcase, the door to the dormitory creaked open. Looking up, she saw that it was Holly and Naomi.

'Hey, Kate,' Naomi said, smiling at her friend. 'What do you think of our luxury accommodation?'

Kate stood up and made an expressive gesture with her hands. 'Is this place for real?'

''Fraid so. Holly and I have just been recce-ing the bathroom.'

'What's it like?'

'Grim. The showers are communal.'

'*And* there's no proper loo roll,' Holly added. 'Just that horrible scratchy stuff.'

Sighing, Kate went over to the window and looked out at the bleak landscape. The rain was still coming down and a freshening wind thrashed the branches of the trees. 'What the hell have we let ourselves in for?' she murmured.

'Ah, Professor Pendleton, good of you to join us.'

Kate wheeled round and saw Amanda standing in the doorway. She was wearing full camouflage gear and black army boots. Her hair was scraped into a tight bun and her cheeks were daubed with green and brown face paint.

'Sorry, I'm late,' Kate said, trying to keep a straight

face as she took in the Fat Chance leader's bizarre appearance. 'I had to make some last-minute childcare arrangements.'

Naomi frowned. 'I thought Freya would be in her new foster home by now.'

'So did I,' Kate replied. 'Her foster mother's come down with shingles, so Freya's staying with me for another week.'

'Who's looking after her this weekend?'

'My sister, Beth. I dropped her off on my way here – that's why I'm late.' Kate shook her head. 'I feel bad about disrupting Freya's routine yet again, but I didn't want to let the side down by not coming to boot camp. In any case, Beth's deeply maternal. I know she'll take good care of Freya.'

'Does she know who Freya's dad is?' Holly asked.

Kate nodded. 'I had to tell her – and, actually, she wasn't that surprised. She said she always thought Huw had an eye for the ladies, although she never said anything to me when he was alive.'

Amanda clapped her hands together. 'Enough of the chit-chat, please. You've got precisely fifteen minutes to finish unpacking, change into your workout gear and get yourselves out into the exercise yard.'

'But it's raining,' Adele said.

'You'd better bring a waterproof jacket, then, hadn't you?' Amanda pointed to Kate's open suitcase. 'Before I go, I'd better have a look in there.' Seeing Kate's look of confusion, she added: 'A list of banned items was included in the information pack you received last week. I need to check you haven't got any contraband.'

'Ah,' Kate said, wincing. She watched as Amanda squatted down and began rummaging through her belongings with the single-minded determination of a customs official. It wasn't long before she made a discovery. 'What do we have here?' she said, triumphantly holding aloft two miniature bottles of Shiraz.

Kate flushed and bit her lip. 'Guilty as charged,' she muttered.

Amanda tucked the bottles into the capacious pocket of her camouflage jacket and continued to forage. A few moments later, a slab of Kendal Mint Cake tumbled from the folds of a towel.

'Surely you're not going to confiscate that,' Kate said indignantly. 'It's my emergency rations. What happens if we get lost on the moor during a training exercise?'

'Your instructor is ex-Special Forces,' Amanda replied. 'Believe me, he's prepared for every eventuality.'

Adele gulped loudly. 'Special Forces? He's not going to shout at us, is he?'

Amanda slid the Kendal Mint Cake into another pocket and stood up. 'He's going to do whatever it takes to knock you into shape.'

'Now hang on a minute,' Kate said. 'We didn't come here to be brutalized.'

Amanda smiled coolly. 'I suggest you refer to the disclaimer that you – and everyone else here – signed and returned. I think you'll find that clause twenty-two entitles your instructor to treat you in any way he feels appropriate.' She looked around the room. 'Are there any more questions?'

Nobody spoke.

'Good. Just one more thing . . .' Amanda held out her hand to Kate. 'Car keys, please. I don't want you doing a runner the minute my back's turned.'

By the time the members of Fat Chance had assembled outside, the rain had mercifully eased to a light drizzle, though the sky remained heavily draped with sagging clouds. The exercise yard turned out to be a tarmacked area to the rear of the accommodation block, flanked on one side by a large hill and on the other by a field of depressed-looking sheep. Waiting to greet them were Amanda and a middle-aged man with a head like a potato, wearing combat trousers and a tight T-shirt that showed off his muscular torso.

'Welcome to boot camp, everyone,' Amanda said. 'As you're all aware, the Slimmer of the Year Awards are now only three weeks away. This is our last big push. Blood, sweat, tears . . . I want all of those things and more from you this weekend. Please note, you will eat only what we give you to eat. Caffeine, carbs and alcohol are banned. Mobile phone usage will only be permitted between six thirty and seven p.m. You were all weighed when you entered camp; you will all be weighed again before you leave. If you follow our instructions to the letter, you should each have lost between three and five pounds by the end of the weekend. I wouldn't normally recommend such rapid weight loss, but desperate times call for desperate measures.' Amanda turned to the man at her side: 'They're all yours.'

The man folded his arms across his chest like a bouncer. 'My name's Joe and I was a Royal Marine commando for fifteen years. From now on, you will address me as *Staff*. You may be the boss at home, but for the next forty-eight hours *I'm* going to tell you what to do and when to do it. And let's get one thing clear right from the get-go: excuses and whingeing will not be tolerated. In the military, we don't give up when the going gets tough; we push through the pain. Remember: failure is not an option.' He turned his head and spat copiously on the ground. 'Okay, let's not waste any more time talking.' He gestured to some large tyres that were lying in a heap a few feet away. 'You're going to organize yourselves into teams of two and, between you, you're going to push one of those tyres up to the top of that hill and back down again. Anyone who fails to complete the task will be going to bed without dinner tonight.'

Naomi pointed to the vast mound that rose up beside the exercise yard. 'Surely you don't mean *that* hill.'

'Yes, I bloody well do,' Staff bellowed, with the air of someone for whom the making of friends or enemies was a matter of supreme indifference. 'Now what are you waiting for? Get off your fat, lazy arses and get up that hill.'

Two and a half hours later, Holly, Naomi and Kate found themselves in the relative sanctuary of the mess – a small, bare-walled room that contained a selection of well-worn easy chairs, and which smelled of mildew. Despite their best attempts to jolly each other along, their spirits were at rock bottom. After the horror of the tyre challenge, which everyone, miraculously, had managed to complete, they'd been looking forward to a hearty meal. What they'd received instead was a bowl of watery soup, followed by a small piece of salmon and some steamed vegetables.

'It's like being in prison,' Naomi said as she massaged her sore calf muscles.

Holly exhaled a long breath. 'Except in prison they get pudding.'

'I can't believe they're making us get up at five thirty tomorrow,' Kate said. 'I dread to think what Staff's got in store for us.'

'Thank goodness we've only got two more days of this,' Naomi said. 'I don't think I could stand much more.' She turned to Kate. 'Did you manage to speak to your sister earlier?'

'Only briefly,' Kate replied. 'My mobile lost reception after a couple of minutes.'

'How's Freya settling in?'

'Very well, apparently. Beth taught her to make fairy cakes this afternoon, and afterwards my nephews helped her build a den under the dining-room table.'

Holly smiled. 'It sounds as if she's having great fun.'

'Yes, I'm glad she's getting the chance to experience normal family life again, if only for a weekend.'

'I think you're ever so brave taking Freya in,' Holly said. 'I don't think anyone would blame you if you didn't want anything to do with her. I know I'd find it really hard in your position; it would be like having my husband's infidelity rubbed in my face every time I looked at her.'

'For the first few days it was a bit like that,' Kate admitted. 'But now I find it quite comforting to know that a part of Huw lives on – even though I'm still struggling to come to terms with the fact he had an affair in the first place.'

'Did he ever meet Freya, even when she was a baby?' Naomi asked.

'Her uncle doesn't seem to think so. From what he said, Freya's mum refused to let Huw have anything to do with her from day one. She wouldn't even take his money.'

'That must have been tough.'

'Oh, I should imagine he was quite relieved,' Kate

replied. 'Huw never wanted children; neither of us did. And if he was that bothered about having contact with Freya, he could have called in a lawyer.'

'Perhaps he was trying to protect you,' Holly said.

Kate shrugged. 'Perhaps.'

'I can't believe he didn't think about Freya from time to time over the years,' Naomi said.

'Knowing Huw, I expect he just put her in a box in his mind and filed it away somewhere at the back, under *M* for *Mistakes*.' Kate smiled sadly. 'I'm sure he'd feel differently if he could see her now. I think he'd be very proud of how well she's coping.'

'All the same, I expect it'll be a relief when she goes, won't it?' Naomi said. 'I've worked with enough sulky bridesmaids in my time to know how exhausting small children can be.'

Kate leaned back in her chair and considered the question. 'I can't deny that it'll be nice to have the house to myself again, but in some ways I'm really going to miss Freya. She's such a thoughtful little thing. Yesterday, when I was making breakfast, I cut my finger with the bread knife. It wasn't much – just a nick – but when Freya saw I was bleeding she came running over. "Does it hurt?" she asked me. "Shall I get you a plaster?"' Kate smiled. 'I find it incredible that after everything she's been through, she still has the capacity to worry about how other people are feeling. She certainly didn't inherit that from her father; Huw could be frighteningly self-absorbed.' She took her glasses off and laid them on the table. 'Freya's very observant too. The other day, she asked me why I drank so much wine.'

Naomi chuckled. 'You're hardly an alcoholic.'

'No, but I have a glass most evenings. It helps me unwind after work. When Freya said that, it made me think that I ought to consider cutting back. A woman of my age shouldn't have to rely on alcohol for relaxation. There are lots of other things I could do instead – like read a book, or take a long bath.'

'It sounds as if you two are taking care of each other pretty well,' Holly remarked.

'We are,' Kate agreed. 'And yet when Freya first arrived I was terrified I wouldn't be able to cope. I didn't know the first thing about looking after children, but it's remarkable how quickly one adapts.'

'I realize that finding out about Huw's affair must have been horrible for you, but it sounds as if Freya could turn out to be a blessing in disguise,' Naomi said.

'You know I think you might be right,' Kate said, smiling. 'It's certainly been good for me to think about someone else's needs besides my own for a change.' She looked at Holly. 'Are you and Rob planning to have children?'

Holly grimaced. 'Rob wants to start trying as soon as we get married.'

'And you're not keen on the idea?'

'I'd like to have kids one day, but not for a couple of

years at least. There's still so much I want to do before I give my life over to washing nappies and wiping snotty noses.'

'And how are the wedding plans coming along?' Naomi enquired.

'Slowly,' Holly replied. 'I still haven't found a dress, or ordered the cake, or booked the cars.'

Naomi smiled sympathetically. 'Organizing a wedding is no mean feat. I've met plenty of brides who find the whole business completely overwhelming.'

'Hmm,' Holly said. 'I'm sure I'd be making more progress if Diana didn't keep sticking her nose in.'

Kate nodded, remembering Diana's behaviour at the engagement party. 'She does seem to have some pretty strong ideas about how things should be done.'

'Tell me about it,' Holly said. 'I just wish Rob wouldn't keep kowtowing to her. He's not even inviting his dad to the wedding because of her.'

'I take it Diana and her ex don't get on,' Kate said.

Holly shook her head. 'He ran off with his secretary when Rob was a teenager. Diana was absolutely devastated. Mind you, she got her own back when it came to the divorce settlement. Her lawyer screwed Rob's dad for every penny he could get. She ended up with the family home, a quarter of a million quid and a big chunk of his pension.'

'Is his dad still with the secretary?' Naomi asked.

'Yeah, they got married as soon as the decree absolute came through. In the beginning, Rob used to see quite a lot of them – until Diana got jealous and put a stop to it.'

'How on earth did she do that?' Kate asked. 'Surely Rob had the right to see his dad whenever he wanted to.'

'Emotional blackmail,' Holly replied scathingly. 'It was a year or so after the divorce. Rob and his dad had planned this weekend fishing trip to celebrate his seventeenth birthday. Diana had been a bit offhand with him in the few days before, saying how lonely she was going to be in the house all on her own, but Rob – being a typical teenage boy – didn't think too much about it. Anyway, he went over to his dad's on the Friday night and they spent the evening getting their fishing gear together, ready for the next day. Rob went to bed around midnight, and two hours later, he was woken up by the sound of his mobile ringing.' Holly paused and looked at each of the other women in turn. 'It was Diana, ringing to inform her precious offspring that she'd taken an overdose.'

'Oh my God!' Naomi gasped. 'What did Rob do?'

'He didn't bother waking his dad up. I think he knew instinctively that Diana wouldn't want him involved. Instead, he rang 999 and told them to get an ambulance round to his mum's house. Then he took his dad's car keys and drove the six miles back home, even though he only had a provisional licence.' She shook her head. 'The poor love must've been frantic with worry. What a thing for a seventeen-year-old to cope with.'

'What happened when he got home?' Kate asked.

'Rob got there before the ambulance and when he let himself in the house he found Diana lying on her bedroom floor with an empty bottle of paracetamol lying next to her.'

'Did she have to have her stomach pumped?'

Holly gave a bitter laugh. 'There was no need. The minute the paramedics rocked up, Diana made a miraculous recovery and admitted that she'd only actually taken four tablets.'

'So you're saying she staged a suicide attempt – just to ruin Rob's weekend with his dad?' Naomi said incredulously.

Holly nodded. 'She as good as admitted it to Rob later.'

'How appalling,' Kate said. 'Rob must have been furious.'

'Well, no, actually, that's the funny thing. He said it made him realize how vulnerable Diana was and how it wasn't worth jeopardizing her happiness for anything – not even his relationship with his own father. After that, Rob cut off all contact with his dad and he hasn't spoken to him since.'

'And yet he was thinking about inviting him to the wedding?' Naomi said.

Holly nodded. 'It was my idea. I thought it would be a way of extending an olive branch. And Rob seemed up for it at first – until he mentioned it to Diana. She was absolutely horrified and declared she wouldn't go to the wedding if his dad was there.'

'Poor Rob,' Kate said. 'What an impossible situation.'

'Mmm,' Holly agreed. 'Even so, I wish Rob had stood his ground for a bit longer. Who knows, Diana might even have come round eventually. Sometimes he acts like he's still a little boy, instead of a grown man who's capable of making his own decisions.'

'I hope you've stuck to your guns about Lynton Grange,' Naomi said.

'Absolutely,' Holly said. 'I don't care what Diana says – that's where we're getting married.'

'In that case, maybe you and Rob would like to meet me at Lynton in the next couple of weeks. I've done quite a few weddings there. I could show you some of the best locations for photographs.'

Holly smiled. 'That sounds like a wonderful idea – and it would give you and Rob a chance to get to know each other better.'

'Perfect, I'll check my diary when we get back to the dormitory and we'll fix a date.' Naomi extended her arms above her head and yawned fulsomely. 'Well, ladies, if we've got to be up at the crack of dawn, I suggest we hit the sack.'

*

Seven hours later, Kate was shocked into wakefulness by a high-pitched assault on her eardrums. Groaning loudly, she swung her legs over the edge of the bottom bunk and staggered to the window. Throwing back the flimsy curtains, she saw Amanda standing just a few feet away. She was dressed in camouflage gear again and she was blowing into a long brass bugle.

Yanking the curtains shut in disgust, Kate turned back to the room. By now, all the others were sitting up in bed.

'What the hell is that?' Naomi asked.

'Our alarm call,' Kate replied.

'It can't be,' Holly said groggily. 'It feels like I only fell asleep half an hour ago.'

'Lucky you,' Adele muttered. 'I haven't been to sleep at all. This mattress is awful. I'd have been more comfortable on a bed of nails.'

Following a meagre breakfast of glutinous porridge and foul-tasting herbal tea, the members of Fat Chance assembled in the exercise yard, where Staff and Amanda were waiting for them. Almost immediately, they were plunged into an energetic warm-up routine of star jumps.

'Higher!' Amanda shrieked at Tom as he struggled to get airborne. Adele, meanwhile, was wheezing like a cow giving birth to an oversized calf.

'You lot look like a bunch of losers,' Staff roared. 'At

this rate, you're going to be a complete laughing stock at the Slimmer of the Year Awards.'

Fifteen minutes later, as the members were finally allowed to stop and catch their breath, Staff revealed what lay in store for them. 'Today, I'm going to be teaching you some survival techniques,' he announced. 'But if you think you're going to be sitting round a campfire singing "Kumbaya", think again. Your first challenge will be to build a shelter in the woods using only fir-tree branches and a machete. Then you'll be foraging for your lunch, before learning the arts of fire craft and water procurement.' He flexed his biceps menacingly. 'Any questions?'

'Erm, where exactly are the woods?' Tom asked.

Staff pointed off into the distance. 'On the other side of that valley – and guess what? We're going to be jogging all the way there.'

'I can't,' Adele said obstinately. 'My legs are still aching from yesterday. *And* I feel nauseous. I think I might be coming down with something.'

'You *can* do it and you *will* do it,' Staff growled.

At this, Adele sat down on the tarmac and crossed her legs. 'You can't make me.'

Staff went over to her, bending down so his face was only inches away from hers. 'If you're not on your feet in the next ten seconds, the rest of your team will have to *carry* you to the woods – and that's not a threat; it's a promise.'

'Jesus, Adele,' Tom says. 'Do what he says. You're the heaviest one here. I'll get a hernia if I have to carry you.'

'Shan't,' Adele said.

Staff began counting: 'One, two, three, four, five –'

'Please, Adele,' Kate said. 'Think of the team. We can do this, but only if we all pull together.'

'Six, seven, eight –'

Adele made a kind of *mmmp* noise, as if she were vomiting into her tightly closed mouth. 'Oh, all right, then,' she said crossly, heaving herself to her feet. 'But I'm going at my own pace.'

'I know you're probably going to hate me for saying this, but I actually rather enjoyed today,' Kate said, as she lowered her aching limbs into one of the mess's faded armchairs. 'I feel as if I've learned so much. I mean, who knew you could use tampons as firelighters, or carry water in a condom?'

'I know what you mean, but given the choice I'd rather have been curled up indoors with a cup of tea and a good book,' Holly replied.

Naomi glanced at Tom, who was slumped in a nearby chair, exhaling guttural snores, punctuated by the occasional whimper. 'I must say, I was really impressed with our friend over there,' she remarked. 'Who would've thought he was such a dab hand at fire lighting?'

'Yeah, but he *was* sick on the march back to camp,' Holly pointed out.

'That didn't stop him wolfing down his dinner, did it?' Kate said with a shudder. 'I don't think I've ever seen anyone demolish a plate of food so quickly.'

Holly sighed. 'The portions were tiny, though. I'm still really hungry.'

'Me too,' Naomi said. 'Even my own hand's starting to look pretty tasty.'

Kate chuckled. 'What I wouldn't give for a nice cold glass of wine with some warm ciabatta and a big hunk of cheese.'

'Stop, this is absolute torture,' Holly said, closing her eyes.

Naomi leaned forward. 'We could always perform an unauthorized reconnaissance mission.'

Holly's eyes snapped open. 'Meaning?'

'There's a pub down the road,' Naomi went on. 'We passed it earlier, en route to the woods. It's not far – less than a mile – and there's a full moon to light our way. I'm not suggesting we throw all our hard work out the window, but at least we could cheer ourselves up with a drink and a packet of crisps.'

Kate bit her lip. 'It's tempting, but what if someone sees us? Staff did say that if anyone was caught breaking the rules the whole group would have to do a midnight hike as punishment.'

Holly gestured to the deserted mess. 'Who's going

to know? Everybody's gone to bed – everybody except Tom, that is, and he's out for the count.'

Kate rubbed her hands together. 'In that case, what are we waiting for?'

Twenty minutes later, the women were standing in the lounge bar of the Pig & Whistle. To their delight, the pub was warm and welcoming and bustling with locals. There were wine bottles stuffed with candles on the tables and the walls were covered in bird prints and an ancient Lincrusta.

'Mmmm,' Kate said, as she took a sip of well-chilled Sauvignon Blanc. 'This was such a good idea.'

'It certainly beats sitting in that depressing mess,' Naomi remarked. 'Honestly, I've seen more cheerful gynaecologist's waiting rooms.' She looked around for somewhere to sit, but all the tables were taken. 'Let's try our luck through here, shall we?' she said, walking towards an etched glass door marked *Snug*.

Naomi had only taken a few steps over the threshold when she stopped abruptly. 'Oh my God,' she said in a panicky whisper. 'Look who it is.'

Peering over Naomi's shoulder, Kate was horrified to see Amanda sitting at a table in the corner, staring glassily into space. She'd changed out of her army fatigues and was now wearing jeans and a chunky sweater, and her hair was lying loose about her shoulders.

'Come on, let's get out of here,' Kate said, pulling Naomi's arm.

But it was too late; Amanda had spotted them. The next moment she was smiling and beckoning them over.

Holly hesitated. 'Why do you think she looks so pleased to see us?' she muttered out of the corner of her mouth. 'We've broken at least two camp rules – probably more.'

'I don't know,' Naomi replied, surreptitiously stuffing the packet of dry roasted peanuts she was holding into the pocket of her cagoule. 'But, if we're smart, we might just be able to talk our way out of this.'

As they drew nearer, the reason for Amanda's good humour became apparent. On the table in front of her was a single glass and, next to it, a bottle of wine that was four-fifths empty.

'Fancy seeing you ladies here,' she exclaimed, patting the banquette seat. 'Please, won't you join me?'

The three women cast nervous looks at one other.

'Are you sure?' Naomi asked. 'We don't want to intrude.'

Amanda giggled tipsily. 'Don't be silly, I'd be glad of the company.'

Naomi sat down, clutching her wine glass in both hands, as if it might be wrenched from her grip at any minute. 'Listen, Amanda, I'm really sorry about this,' she said. 'I know we shouldn't be here, but it's been such a tough day.'

Amanda frowned. 'What are you apologizing for? After what Joe put you lot through today, I reckon you've earned a drink.' She winked. 'Or even *two* drinks.'

'Oh,' Naomi said in surprise. 'Thanks, Amanda, that's very magnanimous of you.' She took a sip of wine. 'Cheers, everyone.'

Holly took her hand out from behind her back. 'What about these?' she asked, waggling a packet of pork scratchings. 'Have I done enough today to deserve them?'

'Sure,' Amanda said, her face split in a wide, deranged smile. 'They're only . . . what, two hundred calories?'

Holly studied the tiny writing on the back of the packet. 'Er, three hundred and forty, actually.'

Amanda seemed to think about it for a moment, before swiping the air with her hand. 'Oh, what the hell,' she said.

Not needing any further encouragement, Holly tore open the foil packet and offered it to Amanda. 'Want some?'

The Fat Chance leader shook her head. 'I can't.'

'But you must be starving,' Holly said. 'I was watching you at dinner; you only ate half a chicken breast and a couple of green beans.'

'No, I really can't; if I eat any more today I'll be doubled up in agony.'

'Have you got a stomach upset?' Kate asked.

Amanda sighed. 'No, actually, I've got a gastric band.'

For several moments, the three women could only gawp at her in amazement. Then Holly spoke. 'Are you having us on?'

Amanda shook her head. 'How do you think I manage to stay this thin?'

'Through the Fat Chance healthy eating programme and plenty of exercise,' Naomi spluttered. 'At least, that's what you've always told us.'

Amanda gave a burst of drunken laughter. 'So I told a little lie.'

'*Little?*' Holly said. 'I'd say it was more like a great big fat lie, with extra mayo and a side serving of French fries.'

'But I did lose weight with Fat Chance,' Amanda protested. 'Four and a half stone, to be precise. The only trouble is, within six months of being crowned Slimmer of the Year, I'd put it all back on again.'

'Just like that?' Kate asked.

Amanda tipped the dregs of the wine bottle into her glass. 'It happened right after my husband left me.'

'For another woman?' Naomi asked.

Amanda shook her head. 'Another man.'

Holly put her hand to her mouth. 'God, how awful.'

'It was – completely awful,' Amanda said. 'We'd been together for six years and married for four; I didn't have the faintest inkling Clive was gay.' Her nostrils flared briefly. 'Apparently he didn't either until one of his work colleagues made a pass at him.' She picked up her glass and took a big gulp of wine. 'For ages, I was convinced it was my fault, that I was so sexually unattractive I'd not only turned my husband off *me*, I'd turned him off the entire female race. Clive was everything to me, and when he left I felt utterly helpless. It was like walking up a familiar staircase and finding the top step missing.'

Kate, who had felt the same way when Huw died, felt a wash of sympathy for Amanda. 'Did your friends rally round?'

Amanda took another drink of wine. 'I shut myself off from everyone and everything. It was as if I couldn't summon up the energy for even the most basic interaction. I went on sick leave from my job in telesales and spent hours at home, watching TV and binge eating. Eventually, after three months, I got the sack. By that point, I knew I needed help, so I went to my GP. He diagnosed depression and wrote me a prescription. The tablets helped with my dark moods, but nothing could stop me eating.' She threw back her head and sighed. 'The weight just piled on. I was huge, two stone heavier than I'd ever been before. Every time I looked in the mirror, I felt disgusted with myself. And the more disgusted I felt, the more I ate. By this stage, I was desperate to get out of the house and back to work – except I didn't have a job to go to. Then I had a brainwave.' Her wine glass now empty, Amanda absent-mindedly reached for Kate's. 'When I won Slimmer of the Year, the managing director of Fat Chance sent me a lovely letter, congratulating me on my achievement. She also said that, if I ever wanted to train as a group leader, I'd be welcomed with open arms. I was flattered by the offer, but at the time I already had a job, so I never followed it up.'

'Ah,' Naomi said. 'So you got in touch to see if the offer was still open.'

Amanda nodded. 'Luckily for me, it was. But the last time anyone associated with Fat Chance had seen me I was a svelte size ten. Now I was a hefty twenty-two. I knew that if I wanted to work for Fat Chance I had to lose the weight – and fast. A gastric band seemed like the answer to my prayers.'

'And was it?' Holly asked.

'It's certainly not an easy option,' Amanda replied. 'I can only eat tiny quantities of food – otherwise I vomit it straight back up.'

Kate frowned. 'How tiny?'

'Breakfast is three tablespoons of cereal, lunch is the same amount of soup, and dinner is an eggcup of something mushy and easy to digest, like shepherd's pie.'

'Oh my God, is that all?' Holly said in horror.

Amanda stroked the empty wine bottle. 'Drinking

is the one pleasure I have left and of course I get drunk really quickly because there's so little food in my stomach to soak it up.'

'Does anyone else at Fat Chance know you've got a gastric band?' Naomi asked.

'No, and if my bosses found out, I'd be in big trouble.' Amanda's head lolled to the side, so that it was resting on Kate's shoulder. 'You won't tell anyone, will you?'

The three women looked at each other.

'No,' Kate said firmly. 'Of course we won't.'

Amanda sighed and a line of drool began leaking from the corner of her mouth. 'I'm sorry if you feel I've let you down. I'd never advise anyone to follow in my footsteps. At the end of the day, a balanced diet and plenty of exercise is the best – and safest – way to lose weight.' She hiccupped loudly. 'It would mean so much to me if we could win Biggest Loser at the Slimmer of the Year Awards. I'd love to have that wonderful feeling again . . . that sense of being better than everybody else.'

'Judging by how everyone's pulled together this weekend, I think we've really got a chance,' Holly said. She tipped the remaining pork scratchings straight from the packet into her mouth. 'Just out of interest, how do you know Staff? This course must cost a packet. I can't believe he's agreed to do it for nothing.'

Amanda grinned. 'Joe's my brother. When he left the army, he set up his own company, running survival courses for bored businessmen. He agreed to forego his usual fees as a special favour for his big sister.'

'Ah, so the sadistic streak runs in the family, then,' Naomi said.

Amanda's face crumpled. 'Do you really think I'm a sadist?'

'*Noooo*, of course we don't,' Kate replied in an exaggerated tone. 'Naomi's just teasing you.' She licked her lips. 'But you can be quite scary.'

'Oh,' Amanda said in a wounded voice.

'I mean it's good that you're so strict with us, but a little pat on the head every now and then wouldn't go amiss,' Kate went on. 'In psychological terms it's known as positive reinforcement; it's a highly effective way of encouraging good behaviour.'

Amanda nodded slowly, but she was so drunk Kate wasn't sure she was taking it all in. '*Positive reinforcement*, eh?' she slurred. 'I'll try to remember that.' She groped for her empty wine glass.

Kate stood up. 'I'll get another bottle in, shall I?'

Less than twenty-four hours later, the members of Fat Chance gathered in the exercise yard for the final time. It was the moment of truth, time to find out if all their hard work had been worth it. First in line was Adele. She climbed aboard the scales and stared straight ahead, exhaling noisily as if pressing air out of her lungs would make her lighter.

Amanda squinted at the digital display. 'Oh, *Adele*,' she murmured.

Adele groaned. 'I haven't done very well, have I?'

'That's right, Adele, you haven't done very well at all,' Amanda replied in a stern voice. Suddenly a smile broke out across her face. 'You've done *exceptionally* well!' she shrieked, jumping up and down. 'Six pounds, Adele. *Six* whole pounds!' As a stunned-looking Adele stepped off the scales, Amanda threw her arms round her. 'You clever, *clever* girl – see what you can achieve when you put your mind to it!'

Adele's eyes were shining. 'I can't believe it,' she kept saying. 'I can't believe this boot camp lark actually works.'

'You'd better believe it,' Staff said, holding up a warning finger.

Adele lifted her hand and blew him a kiss. 'Thank you,' she said. 'Thank you from the bottom of my heart.'

One by one, the members of Fat Chance mounted the scales. All of them had lost weight – some only two pounds, others more – but everyone felt the same shared sense of achievement. When the final weigh-in was complete, Amanda went over to her brother and linked her arm through his.

'Joe and I would like to thank you for all the hard work you've put in this weekend,' she said. 'I know it's been tough, but everybody's given it a hundred and ten per cent and I want you to know that I'm very proud of all of you.'

Kate leaned towards Naomi. 'Now *that's* positive reinforcement,' she said under her breath.

Instantly, the Fat Chance leader's eyes swivelled towards her, like an animal following the motions of its prey. 'Kate, is there something you want to say?'

'Yes, actually, there is, Amanda,' Kate said. 'I wanted to thank you – and Joe – for giving us the opportunity to come to boot camp. It's been a very memorable weekend and a terrific bonding experience.'

'That's so true,' Holly said, nodding her head. 'It feels as if we're a real team now.'

Naomi started clapping. 'Hear, hear.'

One by one, the other members of Fat Chance started clapping and stamping their feet on the tarmac, until the whole yard reverberated.

Chapter Fifteen

Week 8
Holly 10st 13lb
Naomi 10st 1lb
Kate 12st 6lb

Holly's nostrils flared in annoyance as the Mini screeched to a halt, propelling her forward and causing the seatbelt to dig painfully into her breasts.

'Sorry, folks,' Diana called out. 'I didn't realize that was a junction up ahead.'

What – even though there's a great big 'Give Way' sign right in front of you? Holly was tempted to ask. Sighing, she rested her head against the window and wished for the fiftieth time that she hadn't let Rob talk her into letting Diana come. They were going to Lynton Grange to meet Naomi, who was well acquainted with the venue and keen to show them some of the best locations for photos. It wasn't until late last night, as she was doing the ironing, that Rob casually mentioned Diana had volunteered to drive them there.

'It's sweet of her to offer, but we've got a perfectly good car sitting outside. We can drive ourselves,' Holly replied.

Rob came over to her, then. 'The thing is,' he said, absently-mindedly smoothing a hand over the freshly ironed pillowcase that was lying over the back of the sofa. 'I think Mum's feeling a bit neglected.'

'*Neglected*?' Holly said. 'How can she possibly feel neglected when she treats this place like a second home?'

Rob chuckled. 'Don't exaggerate.'

'I'm not exaggerating – she's always here,' Holly said, angrily driving a wonky crease down the sleeve of one of Rob's work shirts. And, to be perfectly honest, I'd rather we saw a bit less of her.'

Rob frowned. 'That's my mother you're talking about.'

'Yes,' Holly said. 'And I know she must get lonely sometimes, what with living on her own and everything, but you're not her little boy any more and, as a soon-to-be-married couple, we need our space. Perhaps you could find a tactful way of putting that to her.'

'Okay, if that's what you want,' Rob said, in such a flat tone that Holly knew he'd do no such thing. 'So, anyway, is it okay if Mum comes tomorrow? She hasn't got much on this weekend; I know she'd really enjoy a run out.'

Holly sighed. 'I suppose she could drop us off and have a wander around the gardens while we talk to Naomi.'

'We can't let Mum drive us all the way there and

then leave her on her own,' Rob said. 'And I know she'd love to have a look inside the place. Where's the harm in that?'

Holly sprayed starch furiously on to the shirt's collar. 'You know how obsessed she is with this wedding,' she told him. 'If we let her set one foot inside Lynton, she's going to start interfering with our plans, the way she always does.'

Rob shrugged. 'She just wants to feel she's a part of our big day, that's all.'

'And she will be a part of it,' Holly replied. 'She can sit on the top table in her big hat and have a lovely time. But, like you said, it's *our* big day, not hers, and we're going to do things exactly the way *we* want to.'

'Of course we are,' Rob said with an appeasing smile. 'What time are we meeting Naomi again?'

'Four thirty.'

He began walking towards the kitchen. 'In that case I'll tell Mum to pick us up at four.'

Now, as they left the suburbs behind them and entered open countryside, Holly was beginning to regret giving in so easily – not least because anyone who got into a car with Diana was taking their life in their hands. Her future mother-in-law was a terrible driver, speeding along the roads with the misplaced confidence of a boy-racer, occasionally braking abruptly in response to perceived threats in her peripheral vision.

'I do hope this place is going to have enough of a wow factor,' Diana said as she swerved to avoid an oncoming lorry. 'We don't want the guests thinking we've scrimped.'

What do you mean – 'we'? Holly thought to herself. She and Rob were paying for this entire wedding themselves.

'Honestly, Mum, it's gorgeous,' Rob said. 'Just wait till you see it.'

In the back seat, Holly cringed as Diana took her eyes off the road to throw her son a look of maternal indulgence. 'I can't wait, Bobo – and if it's not up to scratch, we can always cancel the booking.'

'I'm afraid that's not an option, Diana. We're getting married at Lynton Grange and that's all there is to it,' Holly replied. She kicked the back of Rob's seat. 'Isn't that right, Rob?'

'Well . . . erm . . . yes, I suppose so,' Rob replied, throwing an anxious look in his mother's direction. 'But don't forget we have only visited the place once. We might feel differently about it second time round.'

It wasn't the response Holly had hoped for. '*You* might, but I won't,' she said sulkily.

There were a few moments of awkward silence. Holly caught Diana's eye in the rear-view mirror. A thin smile was playing about her lips. Holly got the sense her mother-in-law was pleased she'd caused a rift between them.

After a few minutes Holly pointed to a patch of woodland up ahead. 'The house is just behind those trees. 'You'd better slow down or you'll miss the turning.'

Diana slammed on the brakes, causing the motorist behind her to beep his horn in annoyance.

'Where's this turning, then?' she demanded, craning her neck to the left.

'We're not quite there yet,' Holly explained. 'It's just round the next bend.'

'Then why didn't you say so in the first place?'

A few minutes later, they were turning into a long gravel drive. Ahead of them lay an elegant Georgian pile with two sweeping side elevations, capped by a handsome sloping roof. A flight of stone steps at the front of the house led down to a flagstone terrace, laid out with low clipped box hedges arranged in geometric patterns – and, beyond that, a well-kept lawn, fringed by graceful weeping willows.

'Is that enough of a wow factor for you?' Holly said, fighting to keep the sarcasm out of her voice.

'It looks very nice,' Diana conceded. 'But, if you don't mind, I shall reserve judgement until I've seen the inside.'

'I thought you might,' Holly murmured.

Diana cocked her head like a bird. 'What was that, dear? I can't hear you when you mumble. I do hope you're going to speak more clearly than that when you say your vows.'

'Nothing,' Holly said, sinking back into the seat.

Naomi was waiting at the front door. 'Hi, guys,' she said. 'Come on in.'

As Diana stepped into the entrance hall with its flag-stone floor and tapestry lined walls, she shuddered ostentatiously. 'It's awfully cold in here,' she said, cross-ing her hands over her chest and rubbing her arms vigorously. 'Don't they have central heating?'

'Yes, but it costs a huge amount to heat a house of this size. They only put it on when there's a function,' Naomi explained. 'Let's go through to the orangery where it's warmer.'

Rob pointed to the black leather case Naomi was carrying. 'Is that your portfolio?'

'Yes, I know you've had a look at the website, but I've brought some more pictures to show you. And, afterwards, if you've got any questions—'

'Oh, I have plenty of those,' Diana interposed. She flashed Naomi a narrow-eyed smile.

As she stalked into the house, leaving the others to follow in her perfumed wake, a mortified Holly mouthed the word *sorry* at Naomi.

Inside, tea and cake was waiting for them in Lyn-ton's elegant orangery. Built in a classical style, it had a high ceiling and a floor of worn black and white hex-agonal flags. 'I love this room,' Holly said, as they made themselves comfortable on a set of wingback chairs. 'I'd definitely like to have some pictures in here.'

Naomi turned towards the arched windows that ran the full length of the orangery. They offered a spectacular view across the rear lawn, which lay in a shimmering patchwork of sun and shadow. 'Yes, it's very atmospheric, isn't it?' she said. 'That's the great thing about this house – the light's fantastic.'

Diana gave a loud sniff. 'Those windows could do with a good clean. They're covered in finger marks.'

'I'll mention it to Louise, the wedding coordinator,' Naomi said. 'She's normally a stickler about cleanliness.'

Diana looked around with an exaggerated display of concern. 'Where is the wedding coordinator anyway? I thought she would at least deign to say hello.'

'Don't worry, she's left you in my capable hands,' Naomi replied. 'I've done several weddings at Lynton. I'll be able to give you a guided tour.'

'Oh,' Diana said. 'I rather hoped we could wander around the place at our leisure.'

'Actually, that's not a bad idea,' Holly said. 'Why don't you take yourself off for an hour or so while we talk to Naomi?'

Diana knitted her eyebrows together. 'Are you trying to get rid of me?'

Holly opened her eyes wide in a mock show of surprise. 'No, Diana, why on earth would I want to do that?'

'You tell me, dear.'

There was a long, embarrassing silence. Then Naomi spoke. 'As I said, there aren't any functions here today, so we can go where we please. We won't bother with upstairs, though – because, as I'm sure Louise has already explained to you, that'll be out of bounds on the big day.'

On hearing this, Diana's lips stretched open in a rigid cry, like the lips of a corpse to which death had come too suddenly. 'What, you mean we won't even have free run of the place?'

'It's fine, Mum,' Rob said. 'The banqueting hall's a decent size – and there's a separate room for dancing, as well as the orangery *and* the gardens. We really don't need any more space.'

'No, but it would've been nice,' Diana protested. 'That way, the guests would have felt they were at a lovely country-house wedding, instead of being shoe-horned into some glorified golf-club function suite.'

A tremor of anger flashed through Holly. She waited for Rob to say something and when he didn't she turned to Diana. 'That's rather unfair.'

Diana's hand flew to her throat. 'Don't be so sensitive, Holly. I'm only trying to be helpful. Your wedding day is a once-in-a-lifetime experience; it's important that you think of every last detail.'

Naomi cleared her throat. 'Would you like to see some of my pictures?'

'Yes, of course,' Rob replied. 'Mum hasn't seen the website – this is a good chance for her to get an idea of your style.'

Naomi pushed the teapot aside to make way for her portfolio. 'As you can see, I take a reportage approach,' she said, turning to the first page of her portfolio, which showed a bride and groom enjoying a private moment in a vine-covered pergola.

'*Reportage?*' Diana said contemptuously.

'Naturalistic,' Naomi elucidated. 'I treat the wedding almost as if it were a documentary.'

Diana took a noisy slurp of tea. 'How very novel.' She reached for the portfolio and began flipping the pages in quick succession, holding the pages gingerly between finger and thumb as if it were a pornographic magazine. She paused at a shot of two young bridesmaids standing beside a chocolate fountain, both smiling guiltily.

Diana pointed to the smaller bridesmaid. 'She's got chocolate round her mouth. That's not very attractive, is it?'

'Maybe not,' Naomi replied. 'But that's the whole point of reportage: it's honest – it captures the spirit of the moment, rather than some airbrushed fantasy.'

Diana pursed her lips. 'But you must have some sort of plan of action – otherwise how can you be sure you've got photos of all the key family members?'

Naomi shook her head. 'I try to approach each

wedding without any pre-conceived ideas and just go with the flow.'

Diana raised her eyes to heaven, but, finding no help there, she turned instead to her son. 'What do you think, Bobo?'

Holly glared at her fiancé. He'd loved the images he'd seen on Naomi's website. If he didn't stand his ground now, she would never forgive him. 'Honestly, I think it'll be fine, Mum,' he said, sounding rather hesitant.

'But don't you want some nice formal portraits of the family?' Diana threw a quick glance at Holly. 'Of *our* side, at least.'

'I'm more than happy to do a small number of posed family shots,' Naomi interjected.

'That's good of you,' Diana said sarcastically. She reached out and slammed the portfolio shut. 'I think I've seen enough, thank you. Let's take a look at the dining room, shall we?'

A few minutes later, they were standing in Lynton Grange's grand banqueting hall. The room boasted many original features, including gilded wall panelling and a high stuccoed ceiling covered in sheaves of painted roses. The circular dining tables were dressed as if for a wedding, with cream linen tablecloths, napkins tied with organza bows and antique silver candelabra. Above them, glass chandeliers twinkled in the light that flooded through the large windows. Holly glanced at Diana, who was looking around the room with stagy diffidence, not saying anything. She seemed to be enjoying the awkwardness her silence was causing. After a few moments, she gestured to the vast fireplace that yawned from the far wall. In its jaws was a glass urn containing a towering arrangement of lilies.

'Those flowers are rather funereal,' she said archly.

'Lilies are a very popular choice at weddings these days,' Naomi replied smartly. 'And they smell gorgeous.'

Diana didn't reply. She was too busy running her fingertips over a wall sconce to check for dust.

Rob went over to one of the tables and picked up a piece of silverware. 'The tables look great, don't they?' he said. 'Are we having this colour scheme for our wedding?'

'Yes,' Holly replied. 'Except the bows will be pink to match my flowers.'

'I still think yellow would be less saccharine,' Diana said as she examined one of the gold-painted dining chairs with a grimace of disapproval.

'The room's stunning, though, isn't it, Mum?' Rob said.

'It's pleasant enough,' Diana conceded.

'Louise was telling me that Duncan Stone's daughter had her wedding here a couple of months ago,' Naomi remarked.

Diana's hand flew to her breast. 'Duncan Stone, the MP?'

Naomi nodded. 'Yep. The guest list sounds amazing – there were a couple of lords, a Radio 4 presenter, even a member of European royalty.'

'*Really?*' Diana said. 'Oh well, if it's good enough for royalty . . .'

'Quite,' Naomi said with a small smile. 'And, as far as the photos go, you really are spoilt for choice at Lynton. The wall panelling makes a wonderful backdrop; so does the fireplace. But remember we don't want the pictures to look contrived, so don't worry about being in the right place at the right time – that's my job.' She turned to look at Diana, who appeared to have lost interest in the conversation and was now walking round the room like a sergeant major inspecting the barracks. Every now and then, she'd stop to look at something: the heavy brocade drapes, the solid oak floor, the over-sized Venetian glass mirror above the fireplace.

'Are you okay, Mum?' Rob called out.

'Hmm,' she replied as she paused beside a row of oil paintings which, as Louise had explained on Holly and Rob's earlier visit, depicted Lynton Grange's illustrious former owners. Suddenly, Diana clapped her hands together delightedly. 'Look, Bobo,' she cried. 'A dachshund!'

Holly frowned. *A dachshund?* The image seemed to detach itself and float into the air like an absurd little hologram. She went over to Diana and saw that she was standing in front of a painting of a man in military uniform – head aloft, medals gleaming, moustache freshly waxed. Sitting at his feet, rather improbably, was a small, tan-coloured dachshund.

'Oh yeah,' Rob said, coming up behind her. 'Handsome little fella, isn't he?'

'Bobo had a pet dachshund when he was a boy,' Diana said. 'Mr Tickles, his name was.'

Holly gave a little chuckle. 'How come you never told me about Mr Tickles?'

Rob put his arm round her shoulders. 'I guess I just forgot.'

'They were absolutely inseparable,' Diana said, cocking her head in sentimental recollection. 'Bobo was devastated when Mr Tickles died. He insisted we give him a proper Christian burial in the garden – we had candles and prayers and everything.' She gave her son's fiancée a superior look, as if to indicate that she had a whole treasure trove of heart-warming memories dating from Rob's childhood that Holly could never hope to rival, not even if she and Rob spent the next hundred years together.

'Poor Mr Tickles,' Holly said, leaning her head on Rob's shoulder. 'But don't worry, darling – you've got me to keep you warm now.'

Rob smiled. 'I'd have you over a dachshund any day.'

Diana gave a loud sniff. 'I think I'd like to see the garden before the light goes,' she announced.

'Good idea,' Naomi said. 'Are you planning to have pre-dinner drinks outside?'

Holly nodded. 'In the rose garden. We fell in love with it as soon as we saw it.'

'Great choice,' Naomi said. 'I'll be able to get some wonderful shots there. Let's head on over there now, shall we?'

As the small group made its way across the gently undulating rear lawn, Holly touched Naomi's arm, indicating that she should hang back.

'I'm sorry about Diana,' Holly said as soon as the others were out of earshot. 'If I'd known she was going to be this difficult, I would have never let her come.'

Naomi waved her hand in front of her face. 'Honestly, it's fine. I'm used to dealing with finicky parents.'

'Yeah, I can tell,' Holly replied. 'Mentioning Duncan Stone was a stroke of genius. Diana definitely perked up after that. Oh, and I'm intrigued . . . which member of European royalty was at his daughter's wedding?'

'None of them,' Naomi said, looking faintly sheepish. 'I made it up to impress Diana.'

Holly grinned. 'I like your style.'

Just then, a loud shriek rent the air as one of Diana's high heels got stuck in a mound of loose earth. Moments later, arms flailing wildly, she fell to her knees.

Holly bit her lip and tried hard to keep a straight face. 'Are you all right?' she called out.

'Does it look as if I'm all right?' Diana snapped as she wrenched her shoe – now separated from her foot – out of the ground.

Rob knelt down beside her and hooked a hand under her armpit. 'Here, let me help you up.'

'I don't know if I can stand,' Diana said weakly.

Rob gestured to Holly. 'Give us a hand, will you?'

'Drama queen,' Holly said under her breath as she walked over to them.

With Rob holding one arm and Holly holding the other, Diana was quickly on her feet. 'Look at that,' she said, kicking a small pile of earth with her good foot.

Holly frowned. 'It's a molehill.'

'Yes, and that molehill might've done me a serious injury. I could sue.'

Holly sniggered. 'Sue who? The mole?'

Diana glared at her. 'You wouldn't be laughing if one of your wedding guests tripped over and broke their neck.' She bent down and rubbed her lower leg. 'I think I've sprained my ankle. It's probably going to swell up like a balloon later. There's no way I'll be able to drive home.'

'Oh dear,' Naomi said, spotting an opportunity to get Diana out of the way. 'In that case, why don't you go back to the house and rest up? We won't be very long.'

Diana put on a pained, stoical face. 'No, it's all right. I shall soldier on. I need to make sure this rose garden is up to scratch.' She took hold of her son's arm. 'Come on, Bobo, lead the way.'

With Diana's injured ankle hindering their progress, it took them several minutes to reach the rose garden, which occupied a sunny, south-facing plot in a secluded part of the estate. Springing from the fertile soil was every imaginable species of bush and tree: loose-limbed ramblers bowed under blooms the size of saucers; hybrid tea roses, bushy and soft-scented; vigorous damasks with their loose flowers and dense grey-green foliage; low-growing floribundas, shimmering in a perfumed haze.

'Isn't this beautiful?' Holly said as they reached the ornate sundial in the centre of the garden. 'It's even more romantic than I remembered.'

Stepping back, Naomi made a square with her fingers and framed Holly inside. 'If I can get you two next to the sundial with the sun behind you, it will make the most amazing picture,' she said.

Diana raised her eyebrows sceptically. 'That's all very well and good, but what are they going to do if it rains?'

Holly could feel a pulse jumping at her temple. Her reserves of patience were rapidly draining away. 'We'll just have to move the reception into the orangery,' she said wearily. 'It's no big deal.'

'What about a nice marquee – then you're covered for every eventuality?' Diana said. 'My niece had a lovely marquee at her wedding. It was ever so luxurious. It had a sprung floor *and* real glass at the windows.'

'We can't *afford* a marquee,' Holly said through gritted teeth.

'All right, it was only a suggestion,' Diana replied. Just then, she spotted a stone wall some twenty or so feet away. It stood at approximately eye level and marked the western boundary of the estate. 'What's on the other side of that wall?' she demanded.

'Farmland,' Naomi said.

Apparently unwilling to take Naomi's word for it, Diana began limping towards the wall.

'What are you doing, Mum?' Rob asked.

'Just checking the view,' she replied. When she reached the wall, she stood on tiptoes and peered over the edge. On the other side lay a thuggish clump of cow parsley and beyond it a field, bounded by a scraggy hedge of hawthorn. 'Oh dear,' she said in an aggrieved tone. 'How very disappointing.'

Holly's heart sank. 'What are you talking about?'

'Come and see for yourself, dear.'

Holly, who didn't have the advantage of high heels, had to climb on to a nearby love seat to see over the wall.

'What is it?' Rob asked her. 'What's the problem?'

Holly shrugged. 'Search me. As far as I can see, it's just a field.'

'It's a complete eyesore,' Diana corrected her. 'You'll have to speak to the wedding coordinator about tidying it up before the wedding. We can't have our guests seeing it like that.'

'Honestly, Diana, I really don't think that's necessary,' Holly said. 'None of our guests are stilt-walkers; they won't even be able to see over the wall.'

'There's no need to be facetious,' Diana snapped.

'And there's no need to nit-pick.' At this point, Holly noticed that Rob was trying to semaphore caution with his eyebrows over the top of Diana's head. She gave a small shake of her head in response.

Diana drew herself up to her full height. 'I want Bobo's wedding to be absolutely perfect. He is my only son, after all – and if you're not prepared to speak to the wedding coordinator, then I will.'

'Erm, do you mind if I butt in here?' Naomi asked.

'If you must,' came Diana's withering reply.

'I'm afraid Louise doesn't have any jurisdiction over that land; it belongs to a neighbouring farmer,' Naomi explained. 'In any case, I have to agree with Holly. It's really not that bad. None of my previous clients have mentioned it.'

Diana gave her a glacial smile. 'Your previous clients obviously weren't as exacting as I am.'

Naomi opened her mouth to fire off a retort, then closed it again, not wanting to appear unprofessional.

'Look, Mum, there's nothing we can do about the field, so let's just forget it, okay,' Rob said.

'I'm sorry, Bobo, but I can't forget it. I shall have nightmares about this wedding until I know that field's been spruced up. I shall have to speak to the land-owner, that's all.' She glared at her son's fiancée. 'You may be prepared to settle for second best – but I, my dear, am not.'

Suddenly, all the anger that had been welling up inside Holly for weeks came bubbling to the surface. She was sick of playing the dutiful daughter-in-law, sick of trying to be nice to Diana, sick of biting her lip whenever she criticized her wedding plans. In that moment, Holly realized Diana was jealous of Holly for stealing her only son away. She felt she under-stood Rob better, loved him more ardently, had the superior claim on his affections – and Holly knew that if she married Rob, she and Diana would go on jostling with one another like groupies at a stage door till the bitter end.

'Shut up, Diana!' she hissed. 'Just shut up, okay? I don't care if you want that field looking like something out of the Chelsea Flower Show, and the Archbishop of Canterbury conducting the service. This is my wed-ding not yours, so from now on I'd appreciate it if you'd keep your opinions to yourself.' She paused, breathing heavily. The relief of finally getting it out was like a morphine rush; her body felt flooded with its opiates.

Diana, meanwhile, was rearing away from her as if from a wild animal. 'My God!' she shrieked. 'The girl's taken leave of her senses.'

Rob stepped between the two women. His face was ashen. 'That's my mother you're talking to,' he told Holly. 'I think you should say sorry.'

'And I'm your future wife,' she retorted. 'You're always making excuses for Diana. Why can't you be on my side for once?'

Rob took a sharp intake of breath, but before he had a chance to speak Diana was pushing him aside and jabbing her finger in Holly's face.

'I've always had concerns about your mental stability,' she told the other woman. 'And now I've got the proof.'

'Huh?' Holly said, gawping at her nemesis in disbelief. 'If anyone around here is ready for the men in white coats, it's you.' She took a step forward, so that her face was just inches away from Diana's. 'It makes my flesh crawl the way you treat Rob, as if he belongs to you – dropping in to ours every five minutes to check up on him, telling him what he should and shouldn't be doing, getting him to ferry you here, there and everywhere. Why can't you just cut the flipping apron strings and let him get on with his life?'

Diana shot Holly a low-lidded look of contempt.

'How dare you!' she screeched. 'How dare you speak to me like that?'

'Now come on, you two,' Rob said, raising a hand out to each of them. 'I think we all need to calm down.'

'Don't tell me to calm down,' Diana flashed back. 'Your future wife has just insulted me and now she's refusing to apologize.'

'You're the one who should be apologizing,' Holly said, her heart lifting with the unfamiliar freedom of being honest. 'Ever since you found out we were getting married, all you've done is pour cold water on our plans. You've made my life a misery with your unasked-for advice and sarcastic asides.'

Rob gave a turbulent sigh. It was obvious from his expression that he would rather be anywhere else. 'That's not very fair,' he said. 'Mum's only trying to help.'

'No, she isn't. She's trying to take over,' Holly replied. 'She thinks she can do a better job of planning our wedding than me.'

Diana put her hand on her chest, as if she were having palpitations. 'What a ridiculous suggestion,' she said.

'Oh, come on, Diana, why don't you just admit the truth? You don't think I'm good enough for your precious Bobo, do you?'

Diana's mouth opened and closed as if she were a fish on the riverbank, but no denial issued from her lips.

'See!' Holly said triumphantly, turning to Rob. 'I was right.'

'Why are you doing this?' Rob asked, covering his face with his hand.

Holly uttered a low growl of exasperation. 'Because I'm sick of taking orders from that interfering old crone!'

'You little—' Diana said, raising her hand as if she were about to strike Holly.

'Mother!' Rob cried.

Diana's hand fell to her side. Then, without another word, she turned and began limping away in the direction of the car park.

'Where are you going?' Rob called after her.

'Home!' she said over her shoulder.

'What about your ankle? I thought you said you wouldn't be able to drive.'

There was no reply.

Rob stared at Holly reproachfully. 'Now look what you've done. She's going to be sulking about this for days.'

'I don't care,' Holly replied. 'I'm glad she's gone. This was supposed to be a special day for us and she's ruined it.'

Rob's jaw tightened. 'No, Holly, you did that all by yourself.' His gaze returned to Diana. 'I'm going to have to go after her.'

As he spoke, Holly felt a flash of anger, succeeded

by a slow wave of tired resignation. What did it matter? 'Fine,' she said. 'You take Diana home. I'll grab a lift with Naomi once we've finished up here.' She glanced at her friend, who had been watching the fireworks from the sidelines in embarrassed silence. 'If that's okay with you?'

Naomi nodded. 'Sure, no problem.'

'Right, then. I guess I'll see you at home,' Rob said.

'Yes,' Holly replied. 'And when I get back, your mother had better not be there.'

'But she's hurt herself,' Rob protested. 'What if her ankle turns out to be broken?'

'If it was broken, she wouldn't be able to walk.'

'Yes, but, even so, I don't think she should be left on her own.'

'So why don't you go to hers?' Holly said. 'Stay the night if you want. In fact, I think it would do us both good to spend a night apart. It'll give us time to think.'

Rob frowned. 'Think about what?'

Holly bit her lip and stared into the distance. 'Diana's nearly at the car now. You'd better get a move on.'

'Okay, I'll see you tomorrow, then.'

'Yeah,' Holly said, not meeting Rob's eye. She watched him as he began jogging across the lawn. Inside, she felt empty, but otherwise calm, with a blank, suspended sensation, as if at any moment now real life would resume. She turned to Naomi. 'I'm so sorry you had to see all that. You must think I'm such a bitch.'

'Not at all,' Naomi replied. 'Diana's the bitch. I'm surprised you managed to bite your tongue as long as you did.'

'Hmm, I could've been a bit more tactful, though, couldn't I?'

'Nonsense, tact would never have worked with a rhinoceros-skinned creature like Diana,' Naomi said. 'You needed to give her a short, sharp shock and that's exactly what you did. And, now she knows you're not some frightened little mouse she can walk all over, she should let you get on with having the kind of wedding you want.'

Holly sighed. 'There's not going to be a wedding.'

Naomi made a clucking noise. 'Come on now. Don't let this ruck with Diana upset you. It'll all blow over in a few days.'

'No, I'm being serious,' Holly said. 'I don't think Rob is the man I want to spend the rest of my life with.'

Naomi stopped and stared at Holly. 'But you can't let one little row put you off. It's Rob you're marrying remember, not Diana.'

Holly's cheeks grew warm. 'Actually, it's got nothing to do with Diana. I've been having doubts about marrying Rob for ages.'

'*How* long?' Naomi asked.

Holly looked at the ground. 'Since the day he proposed. I didn't mean to string Rob along; I really thought I was doing the right thing by agreeing to marry him. And it's not as if I don't love him – I do. It's just that I'm not *in love* with him.'

'And are you absolutely sure about this?' Naomi asked. 'Don't rush into anything you might regret.'

Holly nodded. 'I can't marry him; I don't *want* to marry him.'

'Oh, Holly,' Naomi murmured.

Holly blew out a puff of air through pursed lips. 'I'm going to tell him tomorrow, when he gets back from Diana's, and then I guess I'll have to start looking for somewhere to live.'

'But finding a new place is going to take time, isn't it?' Naomi said.

Holly shrugged. 'I've got a couple of friends who won't mind me crashing on their sofa.'

'You know what? I've got a spare room. Why don't you come and stay with me for a couple of weeks while you sort yourself out?'

'Oh, I couldn't do that,' Holly said. 'I've imposed enough on you already – dragging you all the way out here, only to tell you I won't be needing your services as a wedding photographer after all.'

'Seriously, Holly, it's no trouble – and I'd be glad of the company.'

Holly smiled. 'Well, okay, then, if you're sure. Thanks, Naomi, you're a good friend.' She turned and looked back at the house. The sun was just beginning its long descent; mackerel clouds, rose and silver, lay behind the tall chimney pots. She felt strangely elated. It was as if someone had lifted a great stone off her body and now she might be about to rise up into the air, like a balloon.

Rob was in a foul mood when he returned from Diana's early the following morning. He stomped into the kitchen, where Holly was sitting at the breakfast bar, eating a bowl of raw porridge oats with rice milk. There was no kiss, no greeting, not even a smile. He was wearing a nasty, hand-knitted sweater that Diana had made for him years ago, and a lank diagonal of hair plastered across his forehead gave him a guileness look.

'You really hurt Mum's feelings yesterday,' he said as he flicked the switch on the kettle.

'She hurt my feelings too,' Holly replied.

'Yeah, well, you were the one who started it.' He took a mug from the cupboard and slammed it down on the worktop. 'Mum's ankle's much better, thanks for asking.'

'So it's not broken after all,' Holly said wryly.

'There's no need to be sarcastic.' Rob shook his head. 'I can't believe you refused to say sorry for your behaviour. Mum was still fuming about it this morning. If you've got any sense, you'll send her some flowers in lieu of an apology.'

Holly set down her spoon. 'Like I said yesterday,

Diana's the one who should be apologizing to me,' she said calmly.

Rob turned to look at her. His expression was mulish, defensive. 'Don't be so bloody stubborn, Holly. Just do it, okay?'

'No,' Holly said flatly. 'I won't.' Splaying the fingers of her left hand, she eased off Rob's engagement ring. The gesture felt good, like a belt loosened by a notch, or the removal of an uncomfortable pair of shoes.

Rob gave her a strange, almost threatening look. 'What do you think you're doing?'

She held the ring out to him. 'I'm sorry, Rob. I can't go through with it.'

'What are you on about?' he asked irritably.

Holly's innards recoiled at the thought of what she was about to do. 'I can't marry you,' she said.

He laughed, a taut atonal laugh. 'Is this your way of getting back at me because I took Mum's side instead of yours yesterday?'

'No, this has got nothing to do with yesterday.' Holly put the ring down on the breakfast bar. 'I care about you, Rob, I really do, and I've enjoyed living with you. But *marriage*? It would never work; I know it wouldn't. We'd end up making each other miserable.'

His mouth twisted in a hard, dry grin of contempt. 'Fuck me, you're serious, aren't you? What is it . . . have you met someone else?'

Holly shook her head emphatically. 'No, it's not

that. I just don't think we're right for each other.' She reached a hand out towards him. 'I really am sorry, Rob. I feel awful about changing my mind like this. I should never have let things go this far.'

He glared at her, his face congested with rage. 'So why *did* you?'

She shrugged. 'I don't know . . . I was confused.'

'Confused? *Demented*, more like,' he snarled. 'Mum was right . . . you *are* mad.'

Holly stood up abruptly, her hot face flaring. She felt awful, choked with guilt. Rob probably felt sick just looking at her. 'I've packed a suitcase. I'm going to stay with a friend,' she said, unable to meet his eye. 'I'll come back tomorrow for the rest of my stuff.'

He leaned towards her, his mouth so close that his spittle peppered her face with bitter shrapnel as he spoke. 'Yeah, you do that. And don't forget to leave your door key before you go.'

Chapter Sixteen

Kate put a hand to her temple. They'd only been here half an hour, but already she could feel a headache coming on. The activity centre's advert in the local paper had made it all sound so appealing – the word 'soft-play' suggesting a gentle, non-threatening environment that would provide mental and physical stimulation for the under-12s. In fact, as Kate now knew, it was a euphemism for a grubby, windowless dungeon where any sound was amplified tenfold and where bad behaviour was actively encouraged. Sighing, she reached for her paper cup of tepid, greyish coffee. If she could only block out the noise, the smell of chips and the rank airlessness, she could almost imagine she were enjoying relaxing me-time in a fashionable city-centre café.

It was a week since Kate had returned from boot camp, feeling lighter, brighter and more energized than she had done in years. On the way back, she'd stopped at her sister's house to pick up Freya. Even though it had only been two days, the little girl seemed plumper and more talkative than Kate remembered – a side effect, no doubt, of Beth's tender loving care.

'She knows you're here. She's just in the back garden saying goodbye to the cat,' Beth explained as she handed over Freya's things.

'I hope she behaved herself,' Kate said.

'She's been no trouble at all. In fact, it's been an absolute pleasure having her. The boys adore her too; they keep asking when she's going to come and stay again.' A shadow passed over Beth's broad face. 'I do hope this new foster mother's going to give her lots of love and attention. After everything she's been through, she'll need it.'

'Don't you worry, I'm going to be keeping in very close contact with Social Services *and* Freya's uncle,' Kate replied. 'And if there's any indication she's not thriving in her new home I'm going to kick up one almighty fuss.'

Now, at last, the day of Freya's departure was almost upon them. On Monday morning a caseworker would arrive and take her to her foster parents' home, just a few miles away. Kate had been pleased to learn that, as well as raising two girls of their own, the couple in question had successfully fostered several other children and, if everything worked out, they were keen for Freya to stay with them long-term.

As a special farewell treat, Kate had organized an outing to the activity centre. After a cursory exploration of the play area, where hyperactive children thrashed around in the ball pond and slid down snot-smeared plastic slopes while emitting ear-splitting shrieks, Freya had sensibly retreated to the relative calm of the coffee lounge, where Kate was waiting.

'Are you excited about tomorrow?' Kate asked as Freya foraged for chocolate chunks in a vast ice cream sundae.

The little girl shrugged.

'You'll have your own room.'

No reaction.

'And two older sisters – that'll be nice, won't it?'

When Freya still didn't respond, Kate pushed her coffee cup to one side and leaned across the sticky table top. 'I expect you're feeling a bit nervous,' she said. 'I would be too if I were in your shoes – but you'll soon settle in.'

Freya gave a little sniff. 'Why can't I stay with you?'

Kate had to swallow hard to dislodge the pebble of guilt that seemed to be stuck in her throat. 'Oh, sweet-heart, it just wouldn't work,' she said.

'Why not?' Freya asked.

Kate looked off to the side, wondering if she should make something up. She decided it would be better to tell the truth. 'The thing is, Freya, I'm just not cut out to be a mum.'

'Why not?' Freya repeated

'I'm too grumpy and too selfish and too fond of peace and quiet.'

'*I* can be quiet,' Freya said in a stage whisper.

Kate smiled. 'I know you can, but I don't want you tiptoeing around me like a little shadow. I want you to make lots of noise and have fun and be around other children.'

Freya frowned and prodded her ice cream.

'I'll come and visit you, though.'

Freya looked up. 'Promise?'

'I promise,' Kate replied in a solemn voice. 'You can come and stay with me too, if you like. I'll redecorate your bedroom any way you want. You can choose the colour on the walls, the carpet, the duvet cover, everything. Would you like that?'

Freya nodded energetically.

Kate smiled, remembering how she'd crept into Freya's room the night before to turn off the light and found her sprawled across the double bed, one arm flung wide, head turned at an awkward but absurdly touching angle. Her face was so serene, so trustful, that Kate had had a sudden urge to hug her there in the dark. She didn't, not wanting to wake the little girl. Instead, she pulled the duvet cover up over her shoulders and whispered, 'Sleep tight, Freya,' before silently retreating.

'So,' she said, reaching across the table to wipe away a smear of chocolate sauce on the end of Freya's nose, 'would you like to go and play when you've finished your ice cream?'

Freya gave a little shiver and shook her head.

'I don't blame you,' Kate said, glaring at a small boy who was bashing his sister over the head with a plastic hammer a few feet away. 'It is pretty grim in here. Let's go somewhere else, shall we? You can choose. There's a zoo not far from here, or we could go to the pictures, or have a walk in the park.'

Freya looked at Kate shyly from under her eye-lashes. 'Can we go to the supermarket?'

'The supermarket,' Kate said in surprise. 'What for?'

'I used to go the supermarket every week with my mum.' Freya lifted her head as she spoke. The pain in her eyes was raw. Kate could almost hear the little girl's heart giving a little ping of distress, like a signal from a sonar at the bottom of the ocean. She knew that Freya had no desire to buy anything; she simply wanted to do something that reminded her of her mother.

'Well, if that's what you want, that's what we'll do,' Kate said. 'There's a Waitrose at the end of the road – and while we're there we can pick up something nice for your tea.'

'Mum always went to Barney's,' Freya said wistfully.

Kate tried not to show her distaste at the mention of the budget supermarket chain. She raised her coffee cup to her mouth to mask the lie she was about to tell. 'You know, I'm not sure we've got one of those.'

Freya pushed her half-eaten ice cream away. ''S okay,' she said in a suffocated mumble.

Kate sighed. 'No, hang on a minute, I've just remembered . . . there *is* a Barney's near here. I think I know the way.'

It took Kate ages to find the supermarket, which was hidden in the middle of a rundown trading estate on the other side of town. After she and Freya had picked their way across the litter-strewn car park, they collected a trolley and made their way towards the entrance, where a young woman in jogging bottoms was screaming expletives into a mobile phone, oblivious to the sobs of the small child clinging to her legs.

On entering the dimly lit store, Kate was greeted by a powerful aroma – not the smell of freshly baked bread or chickens roasting on a spit, but an unappetizing combination of school dinners and cleaning fluid. Once her eyes had grown accustomed to the gloom, she found herself in what looked like an aircraft hangar. The laminate floor was badly scuffed and the signage was basic, consisting largely of fluorescent cardboard signs, listing goods and prices. Kate headed for the fruit and veg section, where she was amused to see the humble Desiree elevated to the status of 'speciality potato'. Kate's heart sank. Her regular supermarket understood her needs and aspirations. It knew she was the sort of person who liked to cook in harmony with the seasons, joyfully debating the merits of sunblush tomatoes over pomodorino and never deigning to slice her own pineapple. Here, they didn't even know the meaning of organic.

'Right then,' she said. 'What shall we have for dinner?'

'Crispy pancakes!' Freya said, with the same level of enthusiasm with which other people might request fillet steak.

Kate suppressed a smile. 'Anything else?'

'Baked beans and mash.'

'Okeydoke,' Kate said. 'I think I can manage that.'

'Not that sort of mash,' Freya said, tugging at Kate's sleeves as she reached for a bag of potatoes.

Kate frowned. 'What other sort is there?'

'The sort that comes in a packet.'

'Ah,' Kate said, suppressing a shudder.

As they rounded the corner into the next aisle, Kate was faintly alarmed to discover that, instead of being neatly stacked on shelves, goods were displayed in packing boxes piled on the floor. After some considerable time she found a teenage assistant and asked him where she might find the instant mashed potato. He explained that it was several aisles away, next to the washing powder.

'Where's the logic in that?' Kate muttered, pushing her wonky-wheeled trolley away.

Moments later, as she helped herself to a brand of baked beans she'd never heard of, she noticed a man in chinos and a Barbour jacket stocking up on dog food.

They exchanged embarrassed looks, before the man scurried away, head down.

The next aisle contained a haphazard selection of confectionery and baked goods, where Freya was instantly captivated by a box of cakes with lurid pink icing.

'Can we have some of these?' she asked.

'Of course,' Kate replied. 'Get two boxes if you like.' Her gaze drifted to a packet of long-life croissants shaped like dog turds. It was hours since she'd last eaten – a modest lunch of pitta bread and hummus from the Fat Chance list of low-calorie lunches. She picked up the packet and frowned at the box of nutritional information on the back. Mercifully, it was in a foreign language, allowing her to remain ignorant of the contents' calorific value. With a blissful sense of recklessness, she tossed them into her trolley.

After stopping in one of the numerous freezer aisles for the crispy pancakes and an insipid-looking chocolate mousse for Freya's dessert, they made their way to the tills, where a lone, gum-chewing operative was scanning items with more speed and less care than Kate would have thought humanly possible. After queuing for what seemed like an eternity, it was finally her turn. Not only was there no one to help her pack, there weren't even any free carrier bags. Thus, Kate found herself throwing things straight into her trolley in a vain attempt to keep up with the assistant's manic swiping.

By the time they left the store, mobile-phone mum had disappeared, but in her place a man on a mobility scooter wearing what looked very much like pyjama bottoms was shouting abuse at passing shoppers.

'Well,' Kate said, as she pushed her trolley briskly towards the car. 'I really enjoyed that.'

Freya reached up and put her hand in the crook of Kate's arm. For some inexplicable reason, it made Kate feel like crying.

By the time they got home, it was almost six o'clock. 'Dinner will be ready in half an hour,' Kate told Freya as she started unpacking the shopping. 'Why don't you go upstairs and wash your hands – and while you're up there, you can see the present I've bought you?'

Freya gave a soft intake of breath. 'You've bought me a *present*?'

Kate nodded. 'It's in my bedroom, hanging up on the wardrobe door.'

Freya ran out of the room and bounded up the stairs. A few seconds later, Kate heard a series of loud squeals. Smiling, she went up after her.

When she reached the bedroom, Kate found Freya stripped to her vest and knickers. 'Goodness, someone's keen to try her new dress on,' she said, smiling.

'Will you help me?' Freya said, hopping from one foot to the other in excitement.

'Of course,' Kate replied, going over to the wardrobe

and pulling the dress off its satin hanger. She hadn't intended to buy anything quite so girlie, but when she saw the pink ballerina dress, with its full net skirt and intricately beaded bodice, she knew Freya would love it.

'Every little girl needs a proper party dress,' she said as she slid it over Freya's raised arms. 'And nobody deserves one more than you.'

Kate dropped to her knees to do up the row of fabric-covered buttons at the back. 'There you are,' she said, making a final adjustment to one of the shoulder straps. 'You look beautiful, just like a princess.'

She watched as Freya went over to the cheval mirror, reaching out a hand to touch the glass, as if she couldn't quite believe she was the girl in the reflection.

'What do you think?' Kate asked.

Freya ran back across the room and flung herself against Kate's hip. 'I love it,' she said, throwing her arms round Kate. 'It's the best present ever.'

Kate swallowed, caught unawares by a giddy gust of affection. It was a long time since she'd felt such powerful emotion – not since Huw's death, in fact. Now, as she bent down and kissed the top of Freya's head, something tight and compressed began unfurling within her, like the tendrils of a vine reaching for the light.

Chapter Seventeen

Week 9
Holly 10st 11lb
Naomi 9st 13lb
Kate 12st 5lb

Amanda surveyed the members of Fat Chance like a Roman emperor presiding over a gladiatorial arena. 'I need a volunteer,' she said.

Instantly, Tom was on his feet.

'I'm sorry, Tom,' Amanda said, indicating that he should sit back down. 'I meant a *female* volunteer.'

Tom's monobrow undulated like a monstrous caterpillar. 'That's sexual discrimination, that is,' he muttered.

'So sue me.' Amanda folded her arms tightly under her bosom. 'Come on, ladies, don't be shy. This is a really fun challenge; it's all about fashion.'

Kate raised a hand in the air. 'In that case, I'm game.'

'No, you're not quite what I had in mind either,' Amanda said, her eyes flickering over Kate's tailored tuxedo trousers and soft cashmere sweater. I'm looking for someone with no fashion sense whatsoever, someone who regards shopping as a chore, someone who never buys anything that can't be washed at forty degrees.' She slid her eyes towards Adele, who was sitting in the second row, hands clasped in the generous valley of pleated polyester skirt between her knees. 'Someone like *you*, Adele.'

'Oh no,' Adele said in a quavering voice. 'Not me . . . please.'

'Come on,' Amanda said, beckoning to her victim. 'Let's have you up at the front.'

With a sigh of weary resignation, Adele stood and began edging her way along the row of chairs. By the time she took up position beside the flip chart, she was flushed all over – a mottled, dark-red flush that began at her clavicle and rose all the way to her scalp.

Amanda clasped her hands together. 'Right, Adele, I'd like you to start by telling us what thoughts went through your mind as you purchased each and every item of clothing you're wearing today.'

Adele gave a little shake of her shoulders, like a shiver. 'Do I have to? It's really not that interesting.'

'I'll be the judge of that, thank you,' Amanda said briskly. She pointed to Adele's feet. 'Let's start at the bottom and work our way up, shall we?'

Obligingly, Adele lifted her right foot a few inches off the floor and gave it a little wiggle. 'I bought these mainly because they were the only ones in the shop that would fit me.'

Amanda frowned at the chunky, Velcro-fastened

sandal. 'Correct me if I'm wrong, but aren't those men's shoes?'

Adele nodded. 'My feet are so wide that the women's ones always pinch.'

'Hmm, they're not very elegant, are they?'

'No, but they're nice and comfy.'

'And they make your calves look enormous.'

Adele sniffed. 'That's because my calves *are* enormous.'

Amanda moved closer and plucked at the pink, floral fabric of Adele's voluminous skirt. 'What about this thing? Do you honestly think it's doing you any favours?'

'It's a pretty colour,' Adele said defensively. 'And I like the way it swishes when I move.'

'It looks like a tent, and all that gathering round the waistband only draws attention to your tummy.' Amanda shook her head disparagingly. 'It's a mistake plus-sized women often make – they think that wearing baggy clothes will hide the rolls of fat that are lying underneath, when all it really does is emphasize how big they are.'

Adele chewed on her dry bottom lip, but offered no response.

'And what's with this top?' Amanda asked, touching Adele's arm and making her jump. 'That neckline's far too high; it makes your boobs look as if they start under your chin. The colour's all wrong too.'

'I thought black was supposed to be slimming,' Adele countered.

'It is – for most people – but unfortunately not for someone like you, with sallow skin. It just makes you look washed out.' Her eyes moved downwards. 'Are you wearing a bra?'

Adele looked mortified. 'Of course I am.'

'Well, it's obviously not the right size because you've got shocking cup spillage.' Amanda giggled. 'I mean, seriously, Adele, you could have someone's eye out with one of those.'

Adele blushed an even deeper shade of crimson and crossed her arms protectively over her breasts.

Amanda's unapologetic probing continued. 'You're single, aren't you?' she went on.

Adele nodded morosely.

'Would you *like* to be in a relationship?'

Another nod.

'Looking for love is difficult enough when you're overweight, but you're *never* going to find a man if you're fat *and* badly dressed,' Amanda continued remorselessly. 'The way you look right now, most men would be more inclined to feed you a sugar lump than ask you out on a date.' She gave a little wink to take the sting out of her comment, but it wasn't enough for Kate.

'I'm sorry, Amanda, but I think that's a bit unnecessary,' she said in a loud, clear voice. 'It's one thing to offer constructive criticism; it's quite another to belittle someone.'

'Believe me, Kate, I've been trying to be-*little* Adele for the past six months, but so far she's only managed to lose a stone.' Amanda threw back her head and gave a great honking laugh.

'Well, I think a stone's very commendable,' Naomi said stoutly. 'This isn't easy for us, Amanda, you know.'

'I know it isn't,' Amanda said. 'And that's why I've decided to give you a helping hand.' She took Adele's arm. 'Us two girls are going to disappear for ten minutes or so,' she announced. 'Why don't the rest of you take a break and we'll see you very shortly?' With that, she turned and began frogmarching Adele towards a door at the back of the room, which led to the ladies' loos.

'I wonder what Amanda's doing to her,' Naomi said as she joined the others at their usual spot by the window, coffee cup in hand.

'God knows,' Kate replied. 'Did you see the look on her face? Like a deer staring down the barrel of a gun . . .'

'I know the feeling,' Holly murmured. 'I felt the same way when I had to tell Rob the wedding was off.'

Kate looked at her, confused. 'Don't say you've had to change the date.'

Holly shook her head. 'There's not going to be a wedding. Rob and I have split up.'

Kate gave a little gasp. 'Oh, Holly, I'm so sorry.'

'Don't be,' Holly replied. 'It was my decision.'

'What happened?'

'I just realized Rob wasn't the right man for me. I care about him, I really do, but I know we could never make each other happy in the long-term.' Holly gave a long sigh. 'Rob's a great guy and I thought he'd make a great husband, but then, last week, when we met Naomi at Lynton Grange, the wedding suddenly felt real for the first time – you know, like it was actually going to happen. It suddenly dawned on me what a monumental mistake I'd be making if I married him.'

'How did he take the news?'

Holly shuddered. 'It was horrible – although I have to say he seemed more angry than upset.'

'And there's no chance you two might get back together?' Kate asked.

'Absolutely none. I've already moved my stuff out of his flat.' Holly's face drooped. 'I was right about Diana as well. She was thrilled to hear we were splitting up. She came round to the flat while I was packing my stuff and insisted on standing over me to make sure I didn't take anything that belonged to Rob. Then, when I was leaving, she told me she was glad the wedding was off and that she never thought I was suitable wife material.'

Kate looked at her askance. 'Those were her exact words?'

'Yes, and, to be honest, I don't blame her for having

a go at me. I've not only broken her son's heart – I've ripped it out and trampled all over it in five-inch, spike-heeled stilettos.'

'Don't be too hard on yourself,' Kate said. 'At least you had the guts to break it off with him before it was too late.'

Naomi nodded in agreement. 'That's what I said.'

'I still feel shitty,' Holly replied. 'I should never have accepted his proposal in the first place. It was an awful thing to do – leading him on like that. I'd be furious too if the boot was on the other foot. I'm not surprised Rob never wants to see me or speak to me again.'

'Is that what he said?' Kate asked.

'Yes – although I'm hoping he'll feel differently once he's had a chance to calm down. I really would like us to be friends again one day.' Holly put a fist to her temple. 'What a horrible mess, huh?'

Naomi rested her hand on Holly's arm in a gesture of comfort. 'He'll get over it, you'll see.'

'So where are you living now?' Kate asked.

'In my spare room,' replied Naomi.

'It's only till I find a place of my own,' Holly added. 'I don't want to outstay my welcome.'

'Nonsense, you can stay as long as you like,' Naomi said. 'It's nice having you around.' She turned to Kate. 'Speaking of house guests, what's the latest with Freya?'

'She went to her new foster home yesterday,' Kate said. 'I couldn't stop thinking about her, I was so worried.'

'Worried about what?' Holly asked.

'I thought she might find it hard living with other kids, after seven years as an only child. Or that her foster parents would force her to eat carrots, which she absolutely loathes, or that they'd forget to leave the landing light on at night – the poor little thing's terrified of the dark, you see.' Kate sighed into her teacup. 'And a hundred and one other things. I can't tell you what a relief it was when her caseworker rang this morning to let me know she was doing really well. She's getting on with her foster sisters like a house on fire and she loves the fact they've got lots of animals. Her foster mum's even promised to buy her a guinea pig.'

'That's great news,' Naomi said. 'I'm really glad things have worked out for her; she's such a sweet little thing.'

'You know, I thought I'd be so pleased to have the house back to myself again, but the place seems awfully quiet without her.' Kate drew in a breath and let it out again slowly. 'Kids are devious little things, aren't they? They creep up on you and steal into your heart when you're not looking.'

'You can still keep in touch with her, though, can't you?' Holly asked.

'Of course, Freya's part of my life now and she

always will be,' Kate replied. She jumped as a series of loud claps rang out. Then Amanda's voice came booming across the room. 'Can I have bums back on seats now, folks?'

Knowing how much Amanda hated to be kept waiting, the members abandoned their drinks and hurried back to their chairs. As soon as everyone was in position, Amanda threw an arm towards the door. 'Ladies and gentlemen,' she said in an operatic voice. 'I give you Miss Adele Allsop!'

Two dozen heads turned expectantly, but the door remained firmly shut.

'Adele!' Amanda said again, rather more irritably this time. 'You can come out now.'

When Adele still failed to appear, Amanda gave a little growl and marched over to the door, reaching for the handle at precisely the same time Adele pulled it open from the other side. Amanda lurched forward and banged her shin on the doorframe, prompting a loud cry to issue from her pink-frosted lips.

'What are you playing at?' she snapped. 'Why didn't you come out when I called?'

'Sorry, Amanda, I had to spend a penny,' replied Adele, who was hovering out of sight. 'I'm a bit nervous.'

'It's a pity you couldn't just cross your legs,' Amanda said. 'Your weak bladder has cost you your grand entrance.' She looked over her shoulder and fluttered her eyelashes theatrically at the members. 'Honestly, I don't know why I bother sometimes.'

'Come on, let the dog see the rabbit,' Tom called out impatiently.

'Do you have to be so uncouth?' Amanda snapped at him. She grabbed Adele by the wrist and propelled her into the room.

'Oh my God,' Naomi gasped. 'That's not Adele! It can't be.'

Kate broke into a smile. 'It bloody well is, you know.'

Adele's transformation was remarkable. The lank hair that usually hung limply on either side of her loaf-shaped face was now sculpted into an elegant chignon, softening her features and accentuating her long and surprisingly slender neck. What's more, for the first time anyone in Fat Chance could remember, Adele was wearing make-up. Her ruddy complexion was concealed with a dewy foundation, and skilfully applied blusher revealed that she was, after all, in possession of cheekbones – and a rather good pair at that. Gone were the billowing skirt and nondescript black T-shirt. In their place were navy wide-legged trousers and a soft jersey wraparound top in baby blue. The sensible sandals, meanwhile, had been swapped for super-chic satin slingbacks with a two-inch kitten heel. The overall effect was nothing short of stunning: Adele looked taller, classier and at least three stones lighter.

As the members continued to gawp in disbelief,

Amanda nudged Adele into position in front of the flip chart. 'Go on,' she said. 'Give us a pose.'

Adele flinched as if she'd been slapped.

'Like this,' Amanda said impatiently, thrusting one leg out and shaking back her hair, as if she were a celebrity on the red carpet.

With an embarrassed sigh, Adele did as she was told.

'Don't forget to smile,' Amanda hissed.

Adele's mouth grudgingly went up at one corner.

Amanda turned smugly towards her audience. 'So,' she said. 'What do you think?'

Instantly, Tom was on his feet. 'You look beautiful, Adele,' he said in a quavering voice. 'A veritable goddess of a woman.'

Adele's face grew pink with pleasure. Amanda, meanwhile, was grinning from ear to ear. 'Anyone else?' she asked.

Kate waved her hand in the air. 'Tom's right, you look amazing,' she told Adele. 'I can't believe the difference. You're an inspiration to us all.'

'Thank you,' Adele replied. 'I couldn't believe it myself when I looked in the mirror.'

'Do you *feel* different too?' Kate asked.

Adele thought for a moment. 'Yes, actually, I do. More feminine, and just . . . I don't know . . . more normal, I suppose. I don't feel like hiding myself away any more.' She gave a little grimace. 'I don't go out much, you see – not of an evening, anyway. My friends are always inviting me for drinks and meals, but I nearly always say no, or else I persuade them to come round to mine instead. Whenever I'm in public, I feel so self-conscious about my size, especially if I'm eating or drinking. I always think people are looking at me and thinking – *Ugh, that woman's revolting. Why can't she stop stuffing her face?*'

'Oh, Adele,' Kate said kindly. 'I'm sure they're not thinking that at all.'

Amanda gave a whinnying laugh. 'I'm sure they *are*, dear. After all, you don't see ladies as big as Adele every day of the week.'

Kate fired a quick, steely-eyed glare in Amanda's direction. 'But now that you look so gorgeous, you'll be able to go out all the time, won't you?' she told Adele.

'I'd like to,' Adele replied. 'Only . . .'

'Only *what*?' Amanda snapped.

'Well, I'd never be able to recreate this look on my own, not in a million years,' Adele said. 'It's easy for you, Amanda. You've got a natural sense of style; you know about clothes and make-up and stuff. I, on the other hand, haven't got a bloody clue.'

'She's absolutely right, ' Amanda said, addressing the room. 'I do have good taste; I always have done. Even as a teenager, I was always immaculately turned out. The boys used to flock round me, like moths to a flame.'

She smiled and hugged herself, as if recalling some pubescent romantic encounter. 'But, you know, dressing to impress can become second nature to Adele too – for every single one of you in this room, no matter how overweight you are. You just have to know the tricks of the trade.' She turned back to Adele. 'Let's break this outfit down, item by item, and you'll see what I mean.' She gestured to Adele's bottom half. 'The first thing to remember is that big girls should always wear trousers that are at least as wide at the foot as they are at the hip. It's no good going for a tapered or a straight leg – you'll end up looking like an ice cream cone.' She prodded Adele's fleshy hip with a manicured forefinger. 'And if you've got a backside as big as a bin wagon, like Adele here, always choose a flared leg; it tricks the eye and makes your bum look much smaller. Also, note how these trousers fall right to the bottom of the heel of Adele's shoes, giving the illusion of height.'

Amanda brushed the palms of her hands against one other in a businesslike fashion as she turned her attention to Adele's upper half.

'Okay, if you've got a short body, wearing long tops that extend below the hip is an absolute no-no; they'll only make you look even more stunted. Tops that end right at your hipbone, like this one, on the other hand, elongate the body, making you appear taller and slimmer. Oh, and if you have a round tummy, it's best to wear textured fabrics and wraparound tops that create folds across the stomach area.' She grimaced. 'This has the effect of detracting from any *other* rippling in the area. Okay, now I'd like you all to take a good look at Adele's bust.'

Tom chuckled suggestively. 'I don't mind if I do.'

'Before *I* worked my magic, Adele's boobs looked like a couple of ferrets in a duffel bag,' Amanda continued, to Adele's obvious mortification. 'But now, as you can see, they're firm and pert.'

'They are, aren't they,' Tom said, craning his neck for a better view.

'It's all down to a good, supportive bra,' Amanda said. 'I've kitted Adele out with a pretty-yet-practical minimizing bra with a smooth, double-moulded cup – and, best of all, it only costs nineteen pounds ninety-nine.'

Kate leaned towards Kate. 'I sense a sales pitch coming on . . .' she murmured.

'Made from a unique, breathable microfibre, the Jessica Shape and Lift Bra is specifically designed with the fuller-figured woman in mind and will help reduce your bust by up to five centimetres,' Amanda declared excitedly. 'Yes, that's right, ladies – five whole centimetres!' Reaching behind the flip chart, she produced a large bra box, slightly crushed at both ends. 'You'll be pleased to hear I've managed to acquire a limited stock of Jessicas on your behalf, which I'll be selling at a twenty per cent discount on a first-come, first-served basis. I've a full range of sizes and they're available in black, white and nude.'

Naomi snorted softly. 'Never mind Slimmer of the Year, it looks as if Amanda's going for *Saleswoman* of the Year,' she said to Kate.

'So you see, Adele,' Amanda went on. 'Dressing to flatter one's body shape is easy when you know how. Now you'll be able to take yourself off on a shopping trip and buy yourself lots of lovely new things.'

'Thanks, Amanda, I really appreciate your help,' Adele said. 'I just hope I can remember everything you've told me.'

'You don't need to,' Amanda said crisply. 'I'll write you a crib sheet. Remind me to give it to you before you leave tonight.'

'Brilliant,' Adele said, beaming.

'And, while I'm at it, I'd better give you the number of my beautician. That moustache really isn't doing you any favours.'

'Ouch,' Naomi said, cringing with embarrassment.

'You'd better take my number too,' Tom said, smiling broadly at Adele.

'What?' Adele said, eyeing him warily.

'My phone number – so we can arrange to go out for dinner,' Tom said, smoothing back the hair at the side of his head with a stubby hand. 'That's if you'd like to, of course.'

Adele blinked several times in quick succession. She

looked from Tom to Amanda and back to Tom. 'I don't know what to say.'

'Say *yes*, you idiot,' Amanda said, smiling broadly. 'I reckon it's the best offer you're going to get this year.'

'Well, okay, then,' Adele said. 'Yes.'

'I think you make a lovely couple, don't you?' Amanda said, giving Adele a gentle shove. 'Okay, dear, back to your seat now, you can return those clothes at the end of the evening.' She pushed her hair behind her ears. 'Right, now that the fun bit's out of the way, let's get down to business. I'd like to start by reiterating how I impressed I was with your efforts at boot camp. I just hope you're managing to keep up the good work as we're now just days away from the Slimmer of the Year Awards. The coach will be picking us up from the pub car park at four p.m. sharp, so please make sure you're here on time. Remember, if just one person fails to show up, we'll automatically be disqualified from the competition. Is that understood?'

Her question was greeted by a series of emphatic nods.

Amanda's eyes narrowed. 'My spies tell me the Guildford crew are booked in for high colonics on Friday.'

Tom gave a loud snigger. 'Sounds like a bum deal, if you ask me.'

'Thank you for that asinine contribution, Tom,' Amanda said tersely. 'Strictly speaking it's not against the rules, but in my opinion they're sailing pretty close to the wind.' She thrust her chin out. 'If we win Big-gest Loser, I want us to do it with honour and integrity, through good old-fashioned hard work. Remember, when it comes to weight loss, there is no such thing as a quick fix.'

Naomi bowed her head towards Kate and Holly. 'Has she forgotten about her little confession at boot camp?' she whispered furiously.

Amanda's head snapped round. 'Did somebody in the back row wish to speak?'

Naomi smiled sardonically. 'Believe me, Amanda, you wouldn't want me to repeat it in public.'

Chapter Eighteen

Holly couldn't stop smiling as she studied her reflection. Her long hair, which she usually wore in a ponytail, was backcombed into a soft, Bardot-style bouffant. Her make-up too had a retro feel. Liquid eyeliner, flicked at the corners of her eyes, gave her a sexy, feline look, and her pink glossed lips were full and sensual. Her eyes drifted downwards to her dress – a silver satin sheath that, thanks to Amanda's Miracle Slimming Panty and a built-in boned corset, hid her soft stomach, while accentuating her full bust.

'That dress looks amazing on you,' came Naomi's voice from behind her.

'Thanks,' Holly replied. 'I never thought a dress this figure-hugging would flatter a figure like mine.'

'Trust me, Nick's eyes are going to be out on stalks when he sees you,' Naomi said. 'It's nice of him to offer to pick you up when it's not even on his way.'

Holly went over to the dressing table and picked up a silver clutch trimmed with marabou. 'I know. I said I was happy to meet him at the hotel, but he wouldn't hear of it. He said I was doing him a huge favour, so the least he could do was give me a lift. But really he's the one doing *me* a favour. This do is a big deal for the agency — it's usually only the top brass and their other halves who get to go.'

'It sounds like fun. I just wish I was coming with you; I really don't feel like working tonight,' Naomi said with a sigh. 'I suppose I'd better get going soon. The wedding's in some godforsaken field in the middle of nowhere. It's going to take me ages to get there.' She went over to her friend. 'There, that's better,' she said, smoothing a stray strand of Holly's hair into place. 'Now, is there anything else I can help you with before I go?'

Holly shook her head. 'You've been amazing. I owe you big time. Oh, and I promise not to spill anything down this dress.'

Naomi patted her shoulder. 'Don't worry about that. Just concentrate on having a good time.'

Ten minutes later, Holly was standing in Naomi's living room, pacing up and down in front of the large bay window. She couldn't believe how nervous she was feeling. Nick's phone call, which had come just a few hours earlier, had taken her by surprise. His girlfriend had come down with food poisoning. Would Holly like to take her place as Nick's plus-one at the British Advertising Awards that evening? It had taken Holly all of five seconds to say yes. Who, after all, would turn down the chance of a free dinner and as much champagne as they could drink, all amid the plush surrounds of a five-star hotel in the heart of London's West End? It was only when she put the phone down that Holly began to panic. Straight away she went to find Naomi, who was sitting at the dining-room table with her laptop, editing photos for a wedding album. In the short time the two women had been living together, they'd grown close, and Holly knew her friend wouldn't mind the interruption.

'What on earth am I going to wear?' Holly wailed, after telling Naomi about the invitation. 'This is a seriously smart do; I can't show Nick up.'

'You must have *something* in your wardrobe we can work with,' Naomi replied. 'What about a little black dress we can jazz up with a corsage and some fabulous heels?'

Holly shook her head. 'Now that I've lost weight, nothing fits any more – and I haven't got time to buy something new; Nick's picking me up in less than three hours.' She folded her arms across her chest. 'I'm half tempted to call him and tell him I can't come after all.'

'You'll do no such thing,' Naomi said. She looked

Holly up and down. 'What size are you – a fourteen?'

Holly shrugged. 'On a good day.'

'Well, let's see if you're having a good day today, shall we?' Naomi stood up and began walking towards the door. 'Come on.'

'Where are we going?'

'Upstairs, to find you something gorgeous to wear. I've got tons of party dresses. I'm bound to have something that'll fit you.'

'I thought you had to finish that wedding album,' Holly called out as Naomi set off up the stairs.

'Sod the album,' Naomi replied. 'This is much more important.'

Half an hour later, and Holly had temporary custody of a beautiful dress, as well as a matching clutch bag, some Swarovski crystal earrings and a pair of black patent shoes with a four-inch heel.

'What about your hair?' Naomi had asked a little later, when Holly emerged from the shower with a towel wrapped round her head.

'Oh, I'll just tie it back,' Holly replied. 'This isn't the time to be experimenting.'

At this, Naomi had taken her friend's elbow and marched her to the spare bedroom.

'Sit down,' she said, pointing at the dressing table. 'You're going on a date. You can't go out looking the same way you do at work.'

'But it's not a date,' Holly protested as the towel was pulled from her head.

Naomi picked up a bottle of styling product and began spraying it liberally over Holly's hair. 'How do you know it's not?'

Now, as she awaited her escort's arrival, Holly felt like an exotic butterfly that had gnawed its way out of its fat, drab little chrysalis. She *felt* different too: more grown up and more interesting somehow. All she had to do was remember not to drink too much champagne and end up saying something stupid to one of the bigwigs at Danson & Jolley who would be sharing their table.

Just then, a sleek black convertible pulled up outside the house. Holly's stomach constricted. Was there time to go to the toilet? Probably not. She would just have to cross her legs until they got to the hotel. She went to the front door, feeling ridiculously dry-mouthed as she opened it and saw Nick standing there. He was wearing a black tuxedo and his usual three-day growth of stubble was nowhere to be seen. He gave off a faint scent of vanilla and Holly had an urge to step closer in order to get a deeper breath.

'Wow,' he said, taking a step backwards. 'You look amazing.'

'Do I?' she said, touching her earrings self-consciously.

'Damn right you do,' he replied. 'That dress is incredible.'

She smiled. 'You scrub up pretty well yourself.'

'Why, thank you, madam.' He gave a sweeping bow and gestured to the car. 'Your chariot awaits.'

'I'm really glad you could make it, especially at such short notice,' Nick said as they left the suburbs behind. 'The MD paid a fortune for this table. He wouldn't be happy at the sight of an empty seat.'

'I'm looking forward to it,' Holly replied. 'It's not often I get the chance to go to a black-tie event.'

'I hope your fiancé doesn't mind me borrowing you for the evening.'

Holly frowned. 'Who told you I was engaged?'

'Cara.' Nick paused to negotiate a roundabout. 'Actually, I'm a little hurt you didn't tell me the good news yourself.'

'Sorry,' Holly said. 'I was going to mention it, but you've been up to your eyes in it at work. I didn't think you'd be particularly interested in hearing me blather on about my wedding.'

'On the contrary,' Nick said. 'I'm *very* interested.'

Holly glanced across to see if Nick's tongue was in his cheek. It didn't seem to be. 'Anyway, it's all academic now,' she said. 'Rob and I have split up.'

He threw a quick look at her. 'Are you serious?'

'Deadly,' Holly replied. 'I've even moved out of his flat. I'm staying with a friend at the moment.'

'And was it a mutual decision?'

Holly stared at her lap. 'Actually, no, I was the one who instigated it.'

'It all seems very sudden,' Nick said. 'What happened?'

'I just realized Rob wasn't the one for me. I think deep down I always knew, but for some reason I just couldn't admit it to myself until now.' Holly cleared her throat, reluctant to go on. 'So how was Melissa feeling when you left? Does she know what gave her the food poisoning?'

'Ah,' Nick said, licking his top lip. 'I'm afraid I told you a little white lie; there's actually nothing wrong with Mel.'

Holly frowned. 'So why isn't she coming tonight?'

'We had another row a couple of days ago. She went mental because I had to work late again. When I got home, I discovered she'd cut the sleeves off my best suit.'

Holly put her hand to her mouth. 'Oh, Nick, what did you do?'

'I quietly and calmly told her I'd had enough of her irrational behaviour, that I would be spending the night at a hotel and that when I came back the next day after work, I'd appreciate it if she wasn't there any more.'

'How did she react?'

'She suddenly went all meek and started apologizing, but I think she could tell from the look on my face that my mind was made up. When I came back to the flat the next day she'd gone, and so had all her things.'

A current of excitement cut a valley from Holly's throat into her belly. 'So that's it, then – you two are finished?'

Nick nodded. 'Frankly I'm surprised it lasted as long as it did. Mel and I were incompatible in so many ways. She's a vegetarian; I eat red meat three times a week. Her favourite pastime is shopping; I'd rather read a good book. She loves reality shows; I'd rather gargle with nettles.' Nick sighed. 'I should never have asked her to move in with me. It was far too soon – we barely knew each other. Anyway, she's gone now and it feels like a weight off my shoulders. And, listen, I'm sorry for lying to you about her being ill; it's not something I'm in the habit of doing. It's just that I didn't want to go into all the grisly details on the phone.' He pulled on the handbrake as the traffic lights turned to red. 'So,' he said, turning to Holly. 'It looks as if we're both single.'

A dimple appeared in Holly's left cheek. 'It does, doesn't it?'

Inside the Dorchester Hotel, there was a palpable air of drama as the great and the good of the advertising world gathered for one of the biggest nights in the industry's calendar. The pre-dinner champagne reception was in full swing by the time they arrived.

Holly felt a delicious sense of anticipation as they entered one of the hotel's luxuriously appointed function rooms and were instantly absorbed in the throng.

'Here you go,' Nick said, swiping a couple of glasses of champagne from a passing waiter's tray and handing one to Holly.

'Isn't this amazing?' Holly said, casting an admiring glance at the statuesque woman beside her, who was wearing a stunning gold goddess dress and lots of expensive-looking jewellery. 'I'm glad I dressed up.'

Nick took a sip of champagne. 'There's something I've been meaning to ask you. I hope you won't be offended.'

'Go on,' Holly replied, wondering what he was about to say.

'Have you lost weight?'

'You noticed, huh?' Holly said, feeling herself blushing. 'I joined a slimming club a couple of months ago. I've lost a stone and a half already.'

'It suits you,' Nick said. 'Not that you didn't look good before, because you absolutely did.' He smiled. 'Shall we go and find our table?'

'That's a great idea,' Holly said. 'I could do with sitting down. I've borrowed my friend's shoes and they're half a size too small.'

Nick extended his arm to her. 'In that case, you'd

better take hold of this. We don't want you falling over. Not this early in the evening anyway.'

'Why, thank you, kind sir,' Holly said, smiling, as she linked her arm through his.

A few minutes later and Holly was in the hotel's grand ballroom, taking her place at a large circular table, filled with Danson & Jolley's most senior executives. Angela Abraham, the agency's famously hard-nosed director of communications, physically recoiled as Holly sat down next to her.

'What the fuck are you doing here?' she said in her nasal voice that always reminded Holly of a mosquito's whine. 'I didn't think the below-stairs mob were invited to this sort of thing.'

'She's my guest, Angela,' said Nick, who was sitting to Holly's left. 'And less of the "below stairs", if you don't mind. Holly's my right-hand woman and she happens to be very talented.'

Angela's plum-coloured lips peeled back in a sneer. 'Very talented at taking phone messages, you mean? Or booking meeting rooms, or making cups of coffee. That is what PAs do, isn't it?'

'Partly, yes,' Nick said evenly. 'But Holly also happens to be hugely creative. She's had a couple of wonderful ideas for ad campaigns – one of which has already been approved by the client.'

'My, my, appearances *can* be deceptive,' Angela said

witheringly. She downed half a glass of champagne in a single gulp, before rising to her feet. 'Excuse me . . . must go and powder my nose.'

As soon as she was out of earshot, Holly turned to Nick. 'That woman scares the living daylights out of me,' she said softly.

Nick leaned in closer. 'Me too. She's got all the warmth of a part-submerged crocodile.'

Holly grinned. 'Now that you come to mention it, there is something vaguely reptilian about her.'

'It's the hooded eyes,' Nick said. 'Or possibly the flickering tongue. Rumour has it she's caught quite a few of Danson & Jolley's finest on the end of it.'

'You mean . . .' Holly's wide eyes said what she couldn't bring herself to articulate.

Nick nodded. 'Yep, apparently that sofa in her office has seen quite a bit of action. It's already had to be reupholstered twice.'

'You're kidding!' Holly whispered.

Nick winked. 'Well, okay, so I made that last bit up.'

'You are awful,' Holly said giggling. 'And, hey, thanks for sticking up for me, even if you were using a large dollop of artistic licence.'

He looked at her solemnly. 'I meant every word of it. You've been absolutely brilliant, Holly. I don't know how I would have managed without you.'

Holly gave a little shrug. 'It's nothing. I'm just doing my job.'

'You're too self-deprecating by half.'

'Sorry. Is it really irritating?'

'No,' Nick replied. 'Actually, it's rather endearing.' He turned towards the stage area, where a technician was making last-minute adjustments to a microphone stand. 'It looks as if the show's about to start.'

'Mmm,' Holly said. But she wasn't looking at the stage. She was looking at the constellation of russet freckles that was situated just behind Nick's left ear. She took a sip of champagne and sighed contentedly. Something told her it was going to be a good night.

It was certainly one of the more unusual marriage ceremonies Naomi had attended. As a long, slow summer dusk fell, the bride and groom had exchanged their vows at the foot of a three-hundred-year-old beech tree, while a white-robed humanist minister muttered a string of incantations before strewing herbs at their feet. Afterwards, the bridal party had repaired to the reception venue – a vast Mongolian yurt pitched nearby.

Carl had caught Naomi's eye as he gave his best man's speech. He wasn't conventionally handsome – his features were too uneven for that – but she still found him extremely attractive. There was something wild and elemental about him, as if he might glow with the force of his own coiled energy if the lights were turned off.

Afterwards, as she snapped away on the fringes of the dance floor, she'd accidentally-on-purpose trodden on his foot. Her apologies having been smoothly brushed away, they'd talked for a while and Carl had displayed all the signs of sexual interest – the puffed-out chest, the prolonged eye contact, the seemingly absent-minded running of his hand through his hair.

Then, an hour or so later, as Naomi was packing up her cameras, she noticed Carl heading outside. This, she recognized, would be her opportunity for a discreet exchange of phone numbers. She found him staring up at the night sky, a glass of brandy in one hand, a cigar in the other.

'Leaving so soon?' he said, as she walked slowly past him.

She smiled and nodded.

'That's a shame,' he said, exhaling a ring of smoke. 'The party's just beginning.'

She let her eyes wander very deliberately from his face to his crotch. 'If you like, we could have a private party of our own,' she said, tossing her hair flirtatiously to one side. 'That's if you've got the nerve.'

'Oh, I've got the nerve all right,' he murmured, staring at the valley between her breasts. 'The question is, do you have the stamina?'

She raised her eyebrows. She hadn't expected him to be quite so forward. 'What about your wife?' she said, referring to the waiflike redhead she'd seen him dancing with earlier.

'She's just left; our babysitter's only booked till eleven,' he said. 'I told her I'd grab a lift with a friend.'

Naomi gave a purr of pleasure. 'So what are we waiting for?'

A few minutes later, she found herself pinned against the very same beech tree where, a few hours earlier, the happy couple had said 'I do'. Except this time, she wasn't working out how she was going to capture the dusty shafts of light that fell through the branches; she was thinking about the enormous bulge in Carl's loose linen trousers and how good it would feel when it was inside her. She shuddered with pleasure as he freed her right breast from its balconette bra cup and began gently flicking his tongue across her nipple.

'That feels amazing,' she said, closing her eyes and abandoning herself to his expert ministrations. As he turned his attention to her left breast, she reached for the waistband of his trousers, releasing the drawstring tie with one well-timed tug. To her surprise, he wasn't wearing any underwear. 'That makes two of us,' she murmured.

He pulled her down on to the grass. 'I don't have any protection,' he said huskily, as he pushed his trousers down.

'No problem,' she said, groping for her camera bag. A few moments later, he was inside her. Naomi didn't know if it was the power of the ancient beech that loomed above them, or the half a glass of champagne she'd drunk for Dutch courage before following Carl outside – but, as he began thrusting, she felt almost as if she were part of the landscape. She could feel the springy earth beneath her back, smell the wild garlic lifting off the breeze, see the stars in the sky above her that were so many and so white they looked like chips of ice, hammered through the fabric of the sky. Then, all at once, an ugly voice brought her crashing back down to earth.

'You bastard!' the voice said – or rather shrieked. 'You dirty, cheating bastard!'

Looking up, Naomi saw Carl's wife standing a few feet away, her mouth contorted in disgust.

In one swift moment, Carl had rolled off Naomi and was on his feet. 'It's not how it looks, Helen,' he said, frantically pulling up his trousers. 'I can explain.'

His wife staggered backwards, as if she were in shock. 'I couldn't find the car keys in my bag,' she said. 'Then I remembered they were in your jacket pocket, so I came to find you.' She drove her fist into her temple. 'How *could* you?' she screamed. 'How could you do this to me?'

'Come on now, darling, don't make a scene,' Carl said, throwing an anxious look towards the yurt, where a few people had now gathered at the entrance. 'We can talk about this at home.'

'Don't darling *me*,' she said furiously. She glared at Naomi. The pain in her eyes was raw. 'What sort of person are you?'

Naomi stood up. She searched for the right words, but they had been sucked away into a subterranean cave of shame. 'I-I'm sorry,' she managed to stammer.

'Is that all you can say?' Helen screeched. 'You have the gall to seduce my husband at a *wedding*, and all you can say is *sorry*. You revolting woman, you . . . you . . . filthy *parasite*!' She started crying, her staccato sobs ringing out like a car alarm.

Naomi grabbed her camera bag and began running towards the car park. She didn't look back.

Back at Naomi's house, a black convertible was drawing up to the kerb. Holly sighed softly as Nick pulled on the handbrake. She'd had a wonderful evening. Nick had been so charming and witty – and very attentive too. He'd barely spoken to anyone else all evening.

'Thanks for taking me home,' she said.

'Thanks for coming,' he replied. 'I really enjoyed it.'

'So did I. Cara's going to be green with envy when I tell her all about it on Monday.' Holly glanced at the house. 'I'd invite you in for coffee, but Naomi will be back any minute.'

Nick smiled. 'No problem. I ought to be getting home anyway. I've got an early start tomorrow.'

'Don't tell me you're working on a Sunday.'

'God, no, I'm playing football; it's about the only exercise I get these days.' He patted his stomach. 'And it's starting to show. I used to have a six-pack, would you believe?'

'I keep thinking I should join a gym,' Holly said. 'I need to burn off some more calories if I'm going to reach my target weight by Christmas.'

Nick gave her a look of such unexpected tenderness she felt a lump rise in her throat. 'I think you're beautiful just the way you are,' he said.

'No, I'm not,' she replied. 'At least not compared to most of the girls at Danson & Jolley.'

'I can't say I've noticed any of the other girls.' Nick lifted his hand and ran his finger along the curve of her cheekbone. 'You will stop me if I'm being unprofessional, won't you?'

Holly smiled, wondering if he could sense the dampness of her palms and hear the cantering of her heart. 'Do you see me offering any resistance?' she asked him.

The next moment Nick was drawing her towards him. His weight wasn't heavy against her, just warm and solid, and his lips when they touched hers weren't hard or forceful; they were gentle, tender. Holly found herself surrendering to his embrace and as she felt his tongue, hypnotically warm in her mouth, and his fingers cradling her head in his hands, she felt a flood of pure passion surge through her, then lost all sense of herself in the utter, uncomplicated bliss of the moment.

As Naomi set off on the long drive home, she felt drained of energy, her body limp, as if it were about to accordion inwards. Helen's words had burrowed deeper than she cared to admit. What was it she had called Naomi . . . a *parasite*? Was it the truth? Was Naomi a vile predator who sucked the lifeblood out of other people's marriages? The more Naomi thought about it, the more it seemed that her carefully constructed fantasy of sexual freedom was like the sandcastles she used to build on the beach as a child, waiting for a high tide. Even if the sea didn't claim them, the sun did, eroding them so that by morning they were almost gone. All at once, Naomi felt something stinging in her eyes. She wiped her cheek angrily with the sleeve of her cardigan. The pleasure she usually took in being footloose and fancy-free had evaporated, vanished, as if it had never been anything but a shabby delusion. Sadness and loneliness engulfed her like a physical pain.

There was a light on in the living room when she pulled up outside the house. She found Holly curled up on the sofa in her dressing gown, nursing a mug of low-calorie hot chocolate.

'I thought you'd be in bed by now,' Naomi said, flopping on to the sofa.

'I couldn't sleep,' Holly replied. 'I'm too excited.'

'I take it you had a good night, then.'

'I had a *wonderful* night,' Holly said. 'The awards ceremony was brilliant fun, even though we didn't win anything.' She paused and bit her lip. 'But what really made it a night to remember was when Nick kissed me in the car, just before he dropped me off.'

'I knew it!' Naomi exclaimed in delight. 'I bet you two have been flirting over the photocopier for ages.'

'Honestly, we haven't,' Holly said, smiling shyly. 'The kiss came out of the blue. I had no idea Nick saw me as anything other than his fat, dowdy PA.'

'Stop that,' Naomi said sternly, holding up a warning finger. 'Repeat after me: I, Holly Wood, am a gorgeous, sexy woman that any man would be lucky to go out with.'

Holly rolled her eyes. 'I, Holly Wood, am a gorgeous, sexy woman that . . .' She giggled and shook her head. 'I'm too embarrassed to say the rest.'

'Didn't you say Nick had a girlfriend?' Naomi said, kicking off her shoes and drawing her feet under her body.

'Not any more,' Holly replied. 'She didn't really have food poisoning; they've split up.'

Naomi grinned. 'Excellent. Does that mean you two are an item?'

'It's a bit early for that,' Holly said. 'We've both just come out of relationships, so neither one of us wants to rush into anything, especially when we've got to work together. But we've arranged to go out for dinner next week – it won't be a date exactly, just a night out where we can relax together and see if there might be any potential for a relationship.'

'That sounds very grown up,' Naomi remarked.

'Yeah, well, I want to be sure I'm doing the right thing. I don't want to make the same mistake I made with Rob.'

'You really like this guy, though, don't you? I can tell by the look in your eyes.'

Holly nodded. 'I've always liked him, right from the day he started at Danson & Jolley. Whenever he comes near me, I feel breathless, giddy almost, like I might be about to pass out.' She sighed. 'I can't believe this is happening to me.'

'Well, it is, so you'd better make the most of it.'

Holly set her mug of hot chocolate down on the table. 'So how was your night?'

Naomi smiled weakly. 'In a word: shit.'

'Didn't you get the pictures you wanted?'

'No, it's not that.' Naomi felt her insides shrink as she recalled the night's events. 'I had sex with someone at the wedding.' She paused and rubbed her eye with the back of her hand. 'His wife caught us.'

Holly gave a little gasp.

'It was awful,' Naomi went on. 'You should have

seen the look on her face – like she wanted to drive a stake through my heart.'

'Can you blame her?' Holly said gently.

'Not really. I'm sure I'd have felt exactly the same way if I were in her shoes.' Naomi sighed. 'I don't know if I can do this any more.'

'Sleep with married men, you mean?'

Naomi nodded. 'I used to tell myself it was just a bit of harmless fun, that I wasn't hurting anybody, but I can't use that as an excuse any more. Look at Kate – I know she's putting on a brave face, but I'm sure that underneath it all she's devastated about Huw's affair. Then there was this woman tonight . . .' She picked up a cushion and hugged it to her chest. 'I think I should stick to single guys from now on.'

'For what it's worth, I think you're making the right decision,' Holly said. 'And, who knows, you might even meet someone you actually want to settle down with.'

'Yeah,' Naomi said, smiling. 'I think I might finally be ready for that.'

Holly yawned into her hand. 'Right, I'm going to go to bed. It's a big day tomorrow and I need my beauty sleep.' She smiled. 'Two awards ceremonies in the space of two nights – aren't I a lucky girl?'

'I just hope we go home from Slimmer of the Year with a trophy, otherwise Amanda's going to be in a foul mood,' Naomi said.

'What time shall we leave here tomorrow?'

'I'll have to meet you at the pub,' Naomi replied. 'I had a phone call earlier on from a guy who wants me to do his wedding in a couple of weeks' time. It's a bit of a rush job – apparently the photographer he'd originally booked has let him down. I said I'd meet him at the reception venue tomorrow at two thirty.'

'Where is it – anywhere nice?'

Naomi shrugged. 'I've never even heard of the place, but he's given me directions. I'll spend about an hour with him, then go straight to the pub. The coach isn't leaving till four, so I should have plenty of time.'

'Okay,' Holly said, rising to her feet. 'I guess I'll see you tomorrow, then.'

Naomi smiled. 'Night, Holly. See you tomorrow.'

Chapter Nineteen

'You're looking very pleased with yourself,' Amanda said as Holly boarded the coach.

'Am I?' Holly asked.

'Yes, I watched you walk across the car park and you had a huge grin on your face.' Amanda lowered her voice. 'You're not pregnant, are you?'

'God, no,' Holly said in horror. 'Whatever gave you that idea?'

'There's a glow about you I haven't seen before.'

'Can't think why,' Holly replied, growing hot as she remembered the feel of Nick's lips on hers and the text message he'd sent that morning, telling her how much he was looking forward to their dinner date. She smiled at Amanda. 'Listen, good luck for today. I really think we can do it.'

Amanda sighed. 'We're going to need more than luck.' She jerked her head towards Tom and Adele, who were sitting a few rows away, hand in hand. 'I'm sure those two have put on weight since boot camp. It must be all those romantic dinners they've been having.'

Holly waved at Kate, who was sitting across the

aisle from the lovebirds. 'Ah well, at the end of the day, it's the taking part that counts.'

'I can't say that's ever been my philosophy,' Amanda said with a disparaging sniff. 'What have you had to eat today, if you don't mind me asking?'

'Hardly anything,' Holly replied proudly. 'A small bowl of muesli for breakfast, and three low-fat crackers with cottage cheese for lunch.'

Amanda tutted. 'I want you to eat healthily, not starve yourself.' She reached into her handbag and produced two cereal bars. 'If we do make it on to the winners' podium, I don't want you fainting in all the excitement. This should keep you going for a while – and give one to your friend over there.'

'Thanks,' Holly replied. She began walking down the coach towards Kate. 'A present from Amanda,' she said, dropping the cereal bar into Kate's lap as she slid into the seat beside her.

'How thoughtful of her,' Kate said. 'Although I must admit, I have come prepared.' She opened her tote bag to reveal a cheese and pickle roll, wrapped in clingfilm, a four-finger KitKat and a can of full-fat Coke. 'The minute that weigh-in's over, I'm getting stuck in. Sod the calories. I've been eating like a rodent for the last week in preparation for this competition and this is my reward.'

'Make sure the camera crew don't catch you at it,' came Adele's voice from across the aisle. 'That could be *very* embarrassing.'

'What camera crew?' Kate asked, frowning.

'The one from *Loose Talk*, that daytime chat show. They're dedicating a whole programme to the weight-loss industry and they want to get some footage from the awards.'

'I can't imagine it's going to make for riveting viewing,' Holly remarked. 'Who wants to watch a load of nobodies walk up and down the steps to a podium?'

'I dunno,' Tom interjected. 'I could watch Adele walk up and down stairs all day.' He reached across and squeezed Adele's ample thigh. 'Especially if I was lying at the bottom of the stairs and she wasn't wearing any undies.'

'Cheeky!' Adele said, giving the side of his face a playful tap.

Holly sighed. 'I'd have made more of an effort with my appearance if I'd known we were going to be on TV.'

'You look lovely,' Kate said, patting her friend's arm. 'Absolutely radiant, in fact. Single life is clearly agreeing with you.'

'Actually . . .' Holly began. Before she could finish the sentence, a piercing shriek of feedback filled the coach. Then Amanda's voice came booming over the PA system.

'We're all here now, except for Naomi. Does anybody know where she is?'

Holly stuck her head into the aisle. 'She had an

appointment earlier, a work thing,' she called out. 'She was supposed to be coming straight here afterwards.'

Amanda released an exasperated breath. 'Well, she's cutting it very fine. If she doesn't get here soon, we're going to have to leave without her.'

'I'll give her a ring,' Holly said, reaching for her mobile. 'I expect she's just got held up in traffic.'

Amanda waited while Holly made the call, all the while throwing anxious looks across the car park.

'She's not answering,' Holly said, frowning. 'It's going to voicemail.'

Amanda looked at her watch. 'Five more minutes and then we really will have to go.'

When five minutes came and went, Amanda came stalking down the coach. 'Do me a favour and leave a message on Naomi's voicemail, will you?' she asked Holly, thrusting a piece of paper into her hands. 'Tell her she'll have to make her own way to the venue; I've written down the address for you.'

'What if she doesn't make it on time?' Adele said in a panicky voice. 'If everyone's not there, we'll be disqualified. Then all our hard work will have been for nothing.'

'She'll be there,' Holly said firmly.

'Of course she will,' Kate echoed. 'She'd never let us down.'

'She'd better bloody not,' Amanda said darkly. 'Because if she costs us that trophy I'll tell you one thing for nothing: she won't be welcome at Fat Chance any more.'

Naomi stared at the tray that had just been placed in front of her. It held two plates. The first contained the biggest roast dinner she'd ever seen. There was a huge slab of medium-rare beef, encircled with a thick rind of fat and smothered in an oily gravy. Nestling beside it was a monstrous sausage, so fat it seemed to be bursting out of its skin, as well as a dozen roast potatoes, crispy with goose fat, and a Yorkshire pudding the size of a frisbee. Two sprouts and a solitary baby carrot formed a token vegetable accompaniment. On the other plate was a pudding – a steaming Vesuvius of sponge, topped with an inch of golden syrup and floating in a swimming pool of custard.

'I can't,' Naomi said, turning her head away. 'I'm not hungry.'

'Oh, come on, Naomi,' her captor said in a mellifluous tone. 'I spent ages preparing this. Won't you at least try some?'

Naomi pushed the tray away. 'I can't believe you're doing this,' she said. 'Please, can't you just let me go? I won't say a word to anyone, I promise.'

He stroked his chin thoughtfully, as if he were considering her offer.

'I was supposed to be meeting a friend over an hour ago,' Naomi went on. 'She'll be worried about me.

Why don't you give me back my phone, so I can send her a text to let her know I'm okay?'

He shook his head. 'No, Naomi, I'm sorry. You seem to be forgetting that we're operating under my rules now.'

'And your rules include force-feeding me, do they?' she snapped. 'How utterly charming of you.'

'Don't exaggerate,' he replied. 'I'm only doing what's in your best interests. The simple truth is you've gone too far with this silly diet of yours. I'm just helping you get back up to a healthy weight, that's all.'

'But I *am* a healthy weight,' Naomi protested.

He clicked his tongue on the roof of his mouth. 'I don't know why you insist on arguing with me. Most women would be thrilled to be in your position. I mean just look at this place. Isn't it wonderful?'

Naomi had to admit he had a point. The room that formed her prison was a large, light-filled space of graceful proportions. The walls were filled with amazing artwork – bold, abstract canvases jostling for position alongside more traditional portraits and still lives. There were colourful ethnic rugs on the floor, and the furniture was a mixture of contemporary and antique – all of it solid and clearly expensive. Her captor's eclectic style could also be seen in the finer details – in the heap of shiny, sea-burnished pebbles on the windowsill, the old cigar box, découpaged with pictures of fifties pin-up girls, the Aztec statues cast in bronze.

'You have a beautiful home,' she said in a measured tone. 'However, I don't appreciate being kept here against my will.'

'But you could be mistress of this house, free to roam wherever you wanted, if only you'd agree to my terms,' he replied.

Naomi could feel her irritation growing. 'How many times do I have to tell you, I have no desire to be your mistress?' she snapped. 'Why don't you find someone else to play your twisted games?'

He looked at her with such ravenous admiration it made her full-to-bursting stomach turn. 'Because I love you,' he said.

Naomi gave a grunt of disbelief. 'I didn't get that impression the last time we met.'

Naomi's ordeal had begun several hours earlier, as she set off for her appointment with Roger Foster, the groom-to-be she'd spoken to on the phone the previous day. The journey took longer than she'd anticipated and led her to the outskirts of an unfamiliar village, some twenty miles or so from her home. After following the directions she'd been given, she found herself outside a striking, modernist house. All smoked glass and steel, it looked like a cross between a 1950s spaceship and a state-of-the-art submarine. It would, Naomi knew instantly, be a fabulous backdrop for photos. She was tempted to take some test shots there and then while the light was good, but she was already ten minutes late so, with her camera bag in one hand and her portfolio in the other, she made her way towards the front door. The intercom crackled into life even before she'd had a chance to press the buzzer.

'Hi, Naomi, come on up to the first floor,' a disembodied voice told her.

On entering the house, Naomi found herself in a large entrance hall with a dramatic vaulted ceiling. Everywhere she looked, some interesting architectural feature caught her eye – a triangular window, a dividing wall made of glass, a staircase that seemed to float in mid-air. She made her way across the room, her heels echoing on the slate floor. As she climbed the stairs, her mind was buzzing with the photographic possibilities; she couldn't wait to have a proper look around the place.

She'd assumed there would be someone waiting upstairs to greet her – the wedding coordinator, perhaps, or even Roger Foster himself – but when she reached the top of the staircase there was no one. She looked from left to right, wondering which way to turn.

'Hello?' she said.

'Make your way down the right-hand hallway,' a distant voice announced. 'It's the door at the end.'

Feeling somewhat bemused, Naomi followed the instructions, arriving at what appeared to be an empty room. As she set down her portfolio and camera bag on a stylish modular sofa, she heard the door bang shut behind her. Turning, she was stunned to see a familiar face standing with his back to the door – a face she hadn't seen since a rather embarrassing evening several weeks earlier.

'Toby!' she gasped. 'What are you doing here?'

'I invited you over to discuss my wedding photos,' he said with a wink. 'Not that I'm actually *getting* married, of course.'

Naomi blanched. '*You're* Roger Foster?'

'Yes, sorry about the subterfuge,' Toby said. 'After what happened the last time we met, I figured it was the only way I was going to persuade you to come to my home.'

'You *live* here?' Naomi said in surprise.

'I do, although I must admit it is a little large for one person.'

Naomi frowned. 'What happened to your wife?'

'Felicity left me last week. Buggered off with her yoga instructor. Good riddance, I say.'

A spider of anxiety crawled up Naomi's spine. There was something about Toby's basilisk stare that put her on edge – that and the deep frown line in the middle of his forehead, which didn't dissolve when he smiled. 'Why have you brought me here?' she asked him.

'We're meant to be together, Naomi: *you* know it, and I know it,' he replied. 'I want to look after you; I want to give you everything you've ever dreamed of.'

Naomi laughed nervously. 'This is some kind of joke, right?'

'I can assure you it's nothing of the kind.' Toby threw his arm wide. 'Please, make yourself comfortable. I think you'll find everything you need here – TV, DVDs, a selection of books.'

'Do you know what? I think I'll pass,' Naomi said, reaching for her camera bag. 'Could you move away from the door, please?'

Toby didn't flinch. 'I'm sorry, I can't do that,' he said. 'It really would make things a whole lot easier if you'd just agree to cooperate.'

Naomi put her hands on her hips. 'Are you threatening me?'

He smirked, as if he found her reaction amusing. 'I tell you what I'm going to do,' he said. 'I'm going to prepare a delicious meal for you. I'm sure you'll be able to think much more rationally on a full stomach.'

'I don't want food; I want to leave,' Naomi replied. 'Now, please, get out of my way.' As she moved towards him, Toby raised his right hand. She saw with a start that he was holding a short black baton, attached to his wrist by a strap.

'I don't want to use this,' he said. 'But come any closer and I might have to.'

Naomi squinted at the thing. 'What is it?'

'A stun gun. It administers an electric shock, causing intense pain and temporary paralysis.'

Naomi took a step backwards.

'Good girl,' he said. 'Now, I'd like you to put your camera bag on the floor, go back to the sofa and sit down.'

Naomi decided that the most sensible course of action was to do as he said. When she was seated, Toby leaned forward and picked up the camera bag.

'What are you doing?' she asked him.

'Just making sure you don't call in the cavalry,' he said, tearing open the Velcro on the bag's front pocket and removing her mobile phone.

Naomi groaned inwardly. 'How did you know that was in there?' she asked him.

'The house is covered by CCTV, inside and out,' Toby replied coolly. 'I was watching you as you got out of your car and I saw you put your phone in the bag.'

He set the bag back down on the floor and slipped through the door. A moment later, Naomi heard the sound of a key turning in the lock. As soon as he'd gone, she went to the window, looking for a possible means of escape. To her dismay, it was covered by a metal grille – newly fitted, judging by the shininess of the screws. She pressed her face to it and peered through the glass. The nearest house was several hundred yards away; there was no possibility of attracting its occupants' attention. The only person who knew she was meeting with a client was Holly, and she would be halfway to Margate by now. She hadn't even had the good sense to give her friend the client's name or the address of the reception venue. A dark flower of dread started to bloom inside her. She felt a rising helplessness, a mounting urge to cry. Toby had clearly planned this little escapade with military precision. She wondered what he had in mind for her. Another round of squashing, perhaps, or possibly something even more depraved.

As she walked back across the room, she heard a gentle whirring noise coming from above. Looking up, she saw an electronic eye, discreetly mounted in the centre of a ceiling fan.

'Fuck you,' she said, holding a finger up to the camera. 'Fuck you with knobs on.'

By the time Toby delivered her meal, Naomi was feeling more scared than angry. As she listened to her captor's declaration of love, she realized he was delusional – in which case, there was no telling what lengths he would go to in order to keep her here. If she were to emerge physically unscathed, and with her dignity intact, she would have to come up with a plan. In the meantime, there was no point antagonizing him any further. Sighing, she drew the tray towards her. 'I'll eat as much as I can,' she told him.

Toby's features glowed with a dark victory. 'Splendid!' he said. 'I shall enjoy watching you.'

For several minutes after he'd gone, Naomi just

stared at the plates of food in front of her. Although she'd hardly eaten a thing all day, she had no appetite. Then, slowly, she felt the fog start to lift – the one that descended over her in times of stress or high emotion, the one that inhibited logical thought. She picked up the plastic cutlery Toby had provided and speared a fat roast potato. Half a dozen chews, followed by a hefty swallow, and it was gone. She turned her attention to the sausage, performing a vicious circumcision on it, wincing as a globe of fat cracked under her molar. When she went to attack the roast beef, the plastic knife snapped in half. Tossing it aside, Naomi picked up a slice of meat with her fingers. Gravy dripped down her chin as she bit into it. Ignoring it, she took another bite, and then another. Naomi smiled to herself. She would give Toby what he wanted. She would eat and eat until it was all gone.

If you reached out a hand, you could almost touch the excitement inside the Margate Winter Gardens. Fat Chance members of all shapes and sizes had descended on the venue from across the country, each desperately hoping their group would be going home with one of the coveted crystal trophies.

'Okay, people,' Amanda said, shepherding her team into a corner of the crowded bar. 'For those of you who haven't been to the awards before, we've got an hour or so to mingle before the official weigh-in.'

She turned to Holly. 'Have you heard from Naomi yet?'

Holly shook her head. 'I just called her again – it's still going to voicemail.'

Amanda looked at her watch and sighed. 'She really is taking it to the wire.'

Just then, Tom spotted the buffet table. 'Oh my God, would you look at that,' he gulped. 'I can't believe they're offering us food *before* the weigh-in. What is this, some kind of endurance test?'

'Have something to eat if you're hungry,' Amanda told him. 'One fruit kebab's not going to hurt you.'

'You know what I'm like,' Tom replied. 'I can't eat just one of anything. Once I start, I have to keep going.' He made a jutting, chicken-like movement with his neck as he loosened his tie. 'I can hear voices in my head. Those sausage rolls . . . they want me to ravish them.'

'They want you to *what*?' Adele said as Tom began walking towards the table, as if in a trance.

Kate smiled. 'I think he means *ravage*.'

'You've got to stop him,' Adele said to Amanda. 'He won't listen to me.'

'Tom,' Amanda said in a stentorian voice. 'Step away from the buffet.'

Tom stopped in his tracks.

'Now turn around and come back here.'

Tom did as he was told. His eyes had a glazed

expression and his Adam's apple was bobbing up and down hungrily. Amanda held out a small plastic box and pumped two sugar-free mints into his palm. 'Suck on these,' she told him. 'They'll help control your cravings.'

Suddenly, Adele gave a yelp of excitement. 'Oh my God, I've just seen Kirsty Montague!' she squealed.

'Who?' Kate said, looking round. Following Adele's pointing finger, she saw a stunning young woman in a red dress and lots of lipstick standing over by the window. She looked like a gorgeously plumed exotic bird who had inadvertently strayed into a flock of starlings.

'Kirsty Montague,' Adele repeated. 'She's my favourite *Loose Talk* presenter; she always seems so warm and genuine when she's interviewing people.'

'I wonder if she's looking for interview subjects now,' Amanda said, dusting the lapel of her peplum jacket. 'I might just go over and volunteer my services. I'm sure *Loose Talk* viewers would be interested in hearing from a past Slimmer of the Year.'

All at once, her smile was replaced by a sneer that trembled like an electrical current across her top lip. 'I see the Guildford crew have arrived,' she said, glaring at a group of newcomers. All of them – even the men – were wearing identical baby pink tracksuits and silver trainers.

'Who's that woman at the front?' Holly asked. 'The one with the enormous breasts.'

'Lorna Hardacre, the group leader.' Amanda's jaw tightened. 'She and I do *not* get along.'

'Why not?' Kate asked.

'Lorna was runner up when I won Slimmer of the Year. She's never forgiven me for beating her.'

Kate frowned. 'But that was years ago, wasn't it?'

'Mmm, but Lorna's the sort of woman who can hold a grudge forever,' Amanda replied. 'By a horrible coincidence, we did our leader training together. She didn't waste a single opportunity to put me down. I still get angry when I think about it.'

'She sounds very competitive,' Holly said.

'That woman would cut out one of her kidneys with a blunt steak knife if she thought it would help her win Biggest Loser for the third year in a row.' Amanda fluffed her hair with a hand. 'Right, I'm going over to introduce myself to Kirsty. Wish me luck, everyone.'

'You'd better be quick,' Kate said. 'I think your nemesis has just had the same idea.'

Amanda turned and saw that Lorna was now plotting a determined course across the packed room, her eyes firmly fixed on Kirsty Montague. 'Oh no, you don't, lady,' she hissed as she began striding towards the camera crew, arms pumping at her sides, as if she were in a power-walking race. The two women reached their destination at precisely the same time, almost cannoning into each other like a couple of cartoon characters.

'Hello, Kirsty,' Amanda trilled breathlessly. 'It's lovely to meet you in the flesh. You look much smaller than you do on TV.'

Kirsty smiled, showing off a row of orthodontically perfect teeth. 'It's the cameras; they add at least a stone.'

'I'm Amanda Evans, Fat Chance group leader and former Slimmer of the Year,' Amanda said, accidentally-on-purpose driving the heel of her shoe into Lorna's foot. 'I was wondering if you'd like to interview me for your report.'

'Oh.' Kirsty turned to a man standing next to her wearing a headset. 'What do you think, Bob?'

The man nodded. 'Sounds like a great idea.'

Lorna elbowed Amanda aside roughly. 'Actually, I was just about to suggest the same thing.' She thrust her large hand into Kirsty's dainty one. 'Lorna Harda-cre, leader of the Guildford branch of Fat Chance, two-time winners of the Biggest Loser category.'

'Wow, that's impressive,' Kirsty replied. She looked at Bob again.

He shrugged. 'Why not interview them both together?'

'Would that be okay with you ladies?' Kirsty asked.

'Absolutely,' Amanda replied crisply.

Lorna intertwined her fingers, crushing the knuckles of each hand in a rhythmic alternating squeeze. 'Bring it on.'

'Perfect,' Kirsty said. 'I'm not going to ask you anything too challenging, so just relax and imagine you're chatting with a friend.'

'How's my make-up?' Amanda asked, turning her face to the light. 'Do I need touching up?'

'You're fine as you are,' Bob said.

Lorna leaned towards Amanda. 'That gold eye shadow doesn't do you any favours,' she said in a pugnacious whisper. 'Talk about mutton dressed as lamb.'

'You're a fine one to talk,' Amanda retorted. 'Who do you think you are in that tracksuit – the oldest WAG in town?'

'At least I fill my clothes,' Lorna said, thrusting out her bosom. 'Have you ever thought about having a boob job, Amanda? It might help you look more feminine.'

'No thanks, Lorna,' Amanda replied. 'If I had boobs as big as yours, they'd need their own postcode – and I get quite enough junk mail as it is.'

Kirsty cleared her throat. 'Er, is it okay if I interrupt you there? It's just that we're on a very tight schedule and it's going to take a while for Bob to get you both mic-ed up.'

'Sorry, I'm all yours,' Amanda said, smiling flirtatiously at the man with the headset. 'I do hope you've got warm hands.'

By the time the camera started rolling, a sizeable crowd

had gathered to watch the interview. Kirsty's first question was innocuous enough.

'So, is Fat Chance the same as all the other slimming clubs out there?' she asked. 'A weekly meeting, followed by a weigh-in?'

Lorna clasped her hands together and assumed the earnest expression of a vicar delivering his sermon. 'That's the basic format, yes, but Fat Chance leaders are encouraged to use their initiative. I can't speak for my colleague' – she turned and gave Amanda a filthy look – 'but I, for one, have always been an innovator, which is probably why my group have done so well at the awards in recent years.'

Amanda sniffed. 'Yes, but there's a fine line between being an innovator and being a bully.'

'What are talking about?' Lorna snapped.

'I'm talking about your colonic irrigation directive.'

'Colonic irrigation?' Kirsty said. 'Is that a recommended technique for weight loss?'

'It can help reduce bloating and speed up the process of digestion,' Lorna said authoritatively.

'In actual fact, Kirsty, there's not a shred of medical or scientific evidence to support *any* of the alleged benefits of colonic irrigation,' Amanda said. 'And, even if there were, I don't believe any member of Fat Chance should be *forced* to undergo the procedure.'

Lorna gave a nervous laugh. 'I don't know where you've got your information from, Amanda, but I'm not in the habit of forcing my members to do anything.'

'Ah, so you're telling me you *didn't* threaten them with expulsion from the group if they refused to have a colonic in the run-up to the awards? Only that's what I heard from a *very* reliable source.' Amanda looked around the room. 'Perhaps one of your members would care to confirm or deny this on camera.'

The colour rose on Lorna's neck and cheeks. 'The colonic was merely a suggestion,' she replied. 'Although perhaps I should have made it clearer that the treatment *was* optional.'

There was a brief silence, before Kirsty spoke. 'Let's move on, shall we?' she said brightly. 'Lorna, perhaps you could tell us what some of the most common misconceptions are about slimming clubs.'

'Well, for starters, an awful lot of people think they're just for women,' Lorna replied. 'They've got this image in their head of a bunch of stay-at-home mums sitting in a circle gossiping. But twenty per cent of Fat Chance members are men – and, you know, the people who join the club come from all backgrounds and walks of life. In my group, for example, I have a nurse, a restaurant manager, a trainee accountant . . .'

Amanda shot her rival a superior look. 'I have a *professor* in my group. She's an expert in body language.'

'She sounds fascinating,' Kirsty said.

'Oh, she is, and she's super intelligent of course. She and I have lot in common.'

Lorna made a spluttering noise. 'Do me a favour,' she muttered.

'I beg your pardon,' Amanda said.

'What on earth would you have in common with a professor?' Lorna replied. 'Let's face it, you're not the brightest bulb on the chandelier. Do you remember that quiz they gave us on our first day of Fat Chance leader training?'

'That was years ago,' Amanda said, her voice rapidly ascending in pitch.

Lorna smiled cruelly. 'If memory serves me right, you thought a glycaemic index was some sort of encyclopedia.'

'So what? In this business, brains aren't everything,' Amanda hit back. 'When it comes to helping people lose weight, qualities like team spirit and empathy are far more important.'

'So why is it I've won Biggest Loser two years running, and you've won sweet eff-all?'

'Oooooh,' Amanda said, clenching her fists. 'You, you, you . . .' In the absence of a suitable insult, she reached out and gave Lorna a hefty shove in the ribs, sending her teetering backwards into a group of onlookers.

'How dare you!' Lorna shrieked as she lurched forward and shoved Amanda back.

At this juncture, Bob began frantically panto-miming his throat being slashed. 'Cut!' he yelled at the cameraman. And then when the camera kept rolling, 'For Christ's sake, *cuuuut*!'

Naomi gave a loud belch. 'Pardon me,' she said to the empty room. She ran a hand over her stomach. She looked as if she were six months pregnant – which, given the quantity of food she'd consumed, was hardly surprising. She stood up and meandered over to a funky Perspex storage unit, which took up almost the entire width of the room. Careful to keep her back to the CCTV, she squatted down and pretended to be perusing a row of DVDs. Then, as discreetly as possible, she stuck her fingers down her throat. It made her cough, but nothing more. She took a deep breath and repeated the action, pushing her fingers down further. A moment later, she tasted bile in the back of her throat and then her guts contracted violently.

Clamping her hand over her mouth, Naomi hurried to the centre of the room, where Toby would have the best view of her. Then, with a voluptuous sense of gratification, she opened her mouth and vomited copiously all over a rather beautiful Afghan kilim. Even when her stomach had stopped spasming, she remained bent double, one hand on the back of the sofa for support. Above her, she could hear the CCTV revolving. She wiped her mouth with the back of her hand and waited.

Soon, Naomi heard the sound of footsteps on the wooden floor outside. In an instant, she had torn open her camera bag, grabbed her trusty Nikon and taken up position. As the door opened, she lifted the camera and pressed the shutter release, sending a blinding flash of light directly into Toby's eyes. Her captor gave a yelp of surprise and stumbled backwards, straight into the bucket of soapy water he'd left there.

Naomi's heart was in her mouth as she ran out of the room and down the hallway, still holding her precious camera. She could hear Toby yelling at her, but she couldn't catch what he was saying. As she reached the top of the stairs, she glanced over her shoulder, just in time to see him losing his balance on the wet floorboards and landing squarely on his coccyx.

Serves you bloody well right, she thought as she made her escape.

'Oh, big fat hairy dangly bollocks,' Adele said crossly.

Amanda frowned. 'Must you use such filthy language?'

'I'm sorry,' Adele said, not sounding remotely apologetic. 'But it's the best way of expressing how I feel.' She turned to Holly. 'She's not coming, is she?'

Holly glanced at her mobile for the millionth time. 'There's still a chance.'

'No, there isn't,' said Tom. 'Our group's up next; Naomi's shafted us, good and proper.'

They were standing against the wall in a long corridor overlooking the car park. In a room a few feet away, a Fat Chance official was carrying out the final weigh-in for the Biggest Loser category. After a considerable amount of pleading, Amanda had arranged for her group to be weighed last, but time was fast running out.

'I'm sure Naomi hasn't let us down deliberately,' Kate said. 'Something must've happened to delay her, something really important.'

'What could be more important than this?' asked Adele.

Kate could think of at least a dozen things off the top of her head, but thought it best not to make Adele any more upset than she already was.

'I do hope nothing's happened to her,' Holly murmured.

Just then the door to the weigh-in room opened and a soft, tubby, blond boy of a man emerged. 'You're next up,' he told Tom, who was standing at the head of the queue. 'Good luck, mate.'

Tom turned to Amanda. 'What do we do?'

Amanda looked crushed, like a child who'd just been shown a film of Santa's execution. 'What *can* we do?' she said, holding up her hands in a gesture of defeat. 'The rules say all the weigh-ins must be completed by 7 p.m. I'm sorry, folks. It looks like it's all over.'

'Shit,' Holly said, slumping against the wall. 'I'm sorry, everyone. I really thought she'd make it.'

'I don't know if I've got the stomach to sit through the awards now,' Adele said. 'We're not nominated in any other category.'

'Me neither,' Tom replied. 'Can't we just go home?'

Amanda sighed. 'If that's what you all want.' She smiled sadly as one by one the other members voiced their agreement. 'Fair enough,' she said, pulling her mobile out of her shoulder bag. 'I'll give the coach driver a ring and tell him to meet us out front in ten minutes.'

As Amanda began punching in numbers, Holly wandered over to the window and stared out at the stretch of golden sand that lay beyond the car park. The sun was just setting, a fat fierce ball that spilled gold on to the surface of the sea and made her squint and lift a hand over her eyes. She was surprised at how disappointed she felt – hollow and rather tender inside, as if she'd been exposed to a mild toxin. She was just about to turn away when she saw a distinctive yellow Beetle pulling into the car park. Squinting harder, she could just make out the face behind the wheel. 'Looks like we won't be needing the coach driver after all,' she said, breaking into a smile.

'*Where the hell have you been?*' Amanda cried, as Naomi came tearing along the corridor towards them. 'We've all been on pins, wondering whether or not you were going to make it.'

Naomi skidded to a halt and tried to catch her breath. 'It's a long story,' she gasped. 'Suffice to say I've just broken the speed limit in three counties to get here.'

'Is everything okay?' asked Holly, frowning.

'It's a long story,' said Naomi, who was still struggling to make sense of the afternoon's events herself. 'The bad news is I've just eaten *the* most enormous meal. Seriously, you've never seen anything like it. It must have been three thousand calories at least.'

Amanda looked at her aghast. 'Please tell me you're joking.'

'I'm sorry, I had no choice,' Naomi replied. 'I'll explain everything after the weigh-in.'

'So what's the good news?' Kate asked.

'I've vomited half of it back up.'

Adele raised an eyebrow. 'Only *half*? Is that the best you could do?'

Three hours later, the members of Fat Chance were sitting in the bar, sharing a commiserative drink before the long journey home.

'Two pounds. Two measly pounds,' Amanda said as she joined Holly, Naomi and Kate at their table. 'That's all there was in it.'

'Sickening, isn't it?' Holly said, taking a sip of vodka

and tonic. 'I think I'd have preferred it if Guildford had completely thrashed us, rather than just pipping us at the post.'

'Lorna Hardacre's going to be unbearable after this,' Amanda said. 'I just hope *Loose Talk* airs our interview in its entirety, so people can see what a nasty piece of work she is.'

Naomi sighed. 'I can't help thinking I'm to blame.'

'What are you talking about?' Holly asked.

'If I hadn't eaten that meal earlier on today, I might have been two pounds lighter.'

'Oh, Naomi, you mustn't think like that,' Amanda said. 'What you did today was nothing short of heroic.'

'She's right,' Holly said. 'I can't believe you managed to stay so calm. I'd have been hysterical if some nutter had kidnapped me and force-fed me roast beef. You played an absolute blinder by making yourself sick like that.'

Naomi smiled. 'I know how important the competition was to all of you. There was no way I was going to let you down.'

'I dread to think what would have happened if you hadn't managed to escape,' Kate said. 'That man's dangerous. I do hope you're going to report him to the police.'

Naomi nodded. 'First thing tomorrow: abduction, unlawful imprisonment, crimes against weight loss – I hope they throw the book at him.'

Kate patted the star-shaped trophy that sat in the middle of the table. 'Personally, I think we should all be very proud of ourselves for coming second. And I for one would like to thank Amanda for all her hard work in getting us to this point. I know it hasn't been very long since I joined Fat Chance, but I feel like a whole new woman.'

Amanda smiled. 'Thank you, Kate. It's nice to know my efforts are appreciated.'

'I wonder if we'll all be sat here this time next year,' Naomi said.

'Surely *you* won't be with us for much longer,' Amanda replied. 'You're only four pounds off your target weight.'

'Oh, I don't know,' Naomi said. 'Call me a masochist, but I kind of look forward to those weekly meetings. Tuesday evenings wouldn't be the same without them.'

Holly nodded. 'I know what you mean. Fat Chance feels like my second family. It funny looking back and remembering how nervous I was when I turned up for my first meeting. What about you, Kate? What will you be doing in a year's time?'

Kate tapped her chin thoughtfully. 'I don't know if I'll still be coming to Fat Chance, but I'll definitely keep in touch with everyone. Hopefully, I'll be spending lots of time with Freya too. Social Services have already said she can come and stay with me at half term. I can't wait.' She smiled. 'Oh, and I've got this holiday home in the south of France – it's nothing fancy, just a little stone cottage overlooking a vineyard. I haven't been there since Huw died – I felt like it had too many memories – but I think I might spend the whole of next summer there. Provence is beautiful at that time of year.'

'It sounds gorgeous,' Naomi said. 'I love that part of France.'

'In that case, you must come and visit.' Kate looked at Holly and Amanda. 'You two as well.'

'*Me?*' Amanda said, pressing her hand to her chest in surprise. 'You'd want me to come.'

'Absolutely, the more the merrier,' Kate said. 'Unless of course you get a better offer.'

Amanda made a snorting expostulation with her lips. 'Fat chance.'

LEONIE FOX

PRIVATE MEMBERS

Welcome to St Benedict's Country Club and Spa. As a home away from home for the A-list, naturally membership comes at a premium – only the over-sexed, the over-rich and the over-beautiful need apply.

Take a tour of the sauna and work up a sweat before indulging in an intimate Swedish massage. Should your mood need enhancing further, this chic retreat comes with its own drugs baron and you simply must sample the foie gras in the Michelin-starred restaurant. Do watch out for the fiery-tempered chef, though, more prone to filleting his light-fingered staff than the freshly caught sea bass …

WAGs and racing drivers rub shoulders on the famous golf course, site of many a hole in one, and you'll be able to join your celebrity companions for a glass of Cristal in the luxuriously appointed terrace bar after a hard day's posturing for the paparazzi.

But beware. The St Benedict's experience involves more sex, bad behaviour, blackmail and deviance than most women can handle. Are you ready to join the Club?

'Blissfully trashy' *Elle*

LEONIE FOX

MEMBERS ONLY

Remember the sexy shenanigans at St Benedict's? The exclusive country club and spa with more millionaires per square foot than the Hamptons in midsummer? Well, the four gorgeous golfers' girls are back … let Cindy, Laura, Keeley and Marianne suck you into their naughty world where intrigue, blackmail and depravity bubble beneath the steamy waters of the Jacuzzi.

The girls go gossip crazy when fading soap actress Amber Solomon catches her billionnaire hotelier husband in flagrante with the housekeeper and messy divorce proceedings ensue. He won't part with a penny and she's damned if she's going to join the next series of Hell's Kitchen to keep herself in Krug.

Meanwhile, an oversexed American teenager is prowling the spa and Swinging is having a revival among the WAGs and their footballers. But will the Solomons' battle royal disrupt the delicious decadence of Delchester's favourite Spa resort and end in disaster? Of course it will!

'A decadent blast of fun' *Heat*

'A romp of naughtiness to be devoured and delighted in' *The Sun*

LEONIE FOX

UP CLOSE AND PERSONAL

Juliet, Nicole and Yasmin.

Best friends for ever. Stunning, sexy and anything but sensible.

Yasmin is a straight-talking game player who's got no-strings sex down to a T. So why is she suddenly craving commitment from the one man she can't have?

Nicole is trapped in a passionless marriage but tangled up in a passionate affair. Should she risk the safety of her happy-ever-after for something that's oh-so-sexy but oh-so-risky?

They both envy **Juliet**, who seems to have it all. She's bagged a gorgeous toy boy of a husband, but is she still entertaining naughty thoughts about a dangerous old flame?

These girls will go to the ends of the earth for one another … and any lengths to get their men. But when everything starts to unravel, will they choose friendship – or sex?

'A romp of naughtiness to be devoured and delighted in' *Sun*

'Blissfully trashy' *Elle*

Psst

want the latest
gossip on all your
favourite writers?

Then come and join us in . . .

THE
BOOK BOUTIQUE

. . . the **exclusive club** for anyone who loves to curl
up with the latest reads in women's fiction.

- All the latest news on the best authors.
- Early copies of the latest reads months before they're out.
- Chat with like-minded readers as well as bestselling writers.
- Excellent recommendations for new books to read.
- Exclusive competitions to get your hands on stylish prizes.

SIGN UP for our regular newsletter by emailing
thebookboutique@uk.penguingroup.com
or if you really can't wait, get over to
www.facebook.com/TheBookBoutique

He just wanted a decent book to read ...

Not too much to ask, is it? It was in 1935 when Allen Lane, Managing Director of Bodley Head Publishers, stood on a platform at Exeter railway station looking for something good to read on his journey back to London. His choice was limited to popular magazines and poor-quality paperbacks – the same choice faced every day by the vast majority of readers, few of whom could afford hardbacks. Lane's disappointment and subsequent anger at the range of books generally available led him to found a company – and change the world.

'We believed in the existence in this country of a vast reading public for intelligent books at a low price, and staked everything on it'
Sir Allen Lane, 1902–1970, founder of Penguin Books

The quality paperback had arrived – and not just in bookshops. Lane was adamant that his Penguins should appear in chain stores and tobacconists, and should cost no more than a packet of cigarettes.

Reading habits (and cigarette prices) have changed since 1935, but Penguin still believes in publishing the best books for everybody to enjoy. We still believe that good design costs no more than bad design, and we still believe that quality books published passionately and responsibly make the world a better place.

So wherever you see the little bird – whether it's on a piece of prize-winning literary fiction or a celebrity autobiography, political tour de force or historical masterpiece, a serial-killer thriller, reference book, world classic or a piece of pure escapism – you can bet that it represents the very best that the genre has to offer.

Whatever you like to read – trust Penguin.